RULES OF WAR

Iain Gale has always had a life-long passion for military history. He is the editor of the *National Trust for Scotland* magazine and art critic for *Scotland on Sunday*. He lives outside Edinburgh with his wife and children.

IAIN GALE

Rules of War

HARPER

Harper
An imprint of HarperCollins*Publishers*
77–85 Fulham Palace Road, Hammersmith, London W6 8JB

www.harpercollins.co.uk

This paperback edition (2009)
1

First published in Great Britain by HarperCollins*Publishers* 2008

A catalogue record for this book is available from the British Library

ISBN: 978 0 00 725356 2

Set in Sabon by Rowland Phototypesetting Ltd, Bury St Edmunds, Suffolk

Printed and bound in Great Britain by Clays Ltd, St Ives plc

For Alexander, Ruaridh and India

The Low Countries, 1706

N
W E
S

NORTH
SEA

R. Rhine
R. Leck
Rotterdam
R. Waal
R. Meuse

Breda

Bergen-op-Zoom

Ostend • Bruges •

• Antwerp

FLANDERS   Ghent   R. Scheldt   BRABANT

R. Lys

Diest •

R. Senne

Menin • Courtrai • Oudenarde •   Brussels •

R. Scheldt

• Lille   • Ath   • Merdorp
• Ramillies

FRANCE   • Mons   • Namur

• Charleroi

0   10   20   30 miles
0 10 20 30 40 50 kilometres

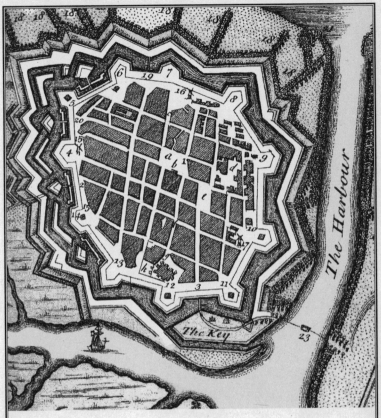

OSTEND

RULES OF WAR

ONE

Captain Jack Steel, his right hand clenched tightly around the grip of his sword, stared into the morning mist. He paused, listening closely to the emptiness. Then, relaxing his hold on the sword hilt yet keeping it, still sheathed, close by his side, he took up the pace and walked on and waited for death. If it came to him it would be from the front. But the only noises Steel could hear as yet were close behind him. He could sense the presence of his men there although he could not see them, knew that they carried their muskets primed and their bayonets fixed. His men; a company of the finest infantry in all of Queen Anne's army. The finest infantry in all the world: British Grenadiers.

Yet at this moment, not even the knowledge of their presence was of any real comfort to Steel. Such mists as this he knew could often be the soldier's friend, shrouding whole armies from unwanted eyes as they advanced to spring a surprise attack. But, he knew too, from bitter experience, that this watery grey haze could also be a deadly foe. With every step now he felt the growing presence of the enemy; imagined the tall horsemen who would appear like ghosts

1

from the enfolding shroud of grey, heard in his imagination the cruel hiss of their sabres as they slashed down towards him. Steel hoped to God that his mind was only chasing phantoms. His commanders had assured him that the French were still far away to their front and he was realistic enough to know that, whether or not this proved to be the case, at this precise moment the only people in whom he could place his faith were those very commanders, and the men who followed him to battle. Ignoring the knot of fear that gnawed at his stomach, Steel brushed away the horrors in his mind and pressed on.

It was approaching six-thirty on a cool May morning – Whitsunday – on a barren patch of high ground which straddled the border between the Spanish Netherlands and Dutch Brabant. This should have been by tradition a day of rest and godliness, but Jack Steel knew that this day would not see God's work. They were moving west in the vanguard of the army and his orders left him in no doubt as to their purpose. 'Halt before the village to your front and and take positions for assault.'

The trouble was that Steel had no earthly idea of where that village might be. Nor, for that matter, where he might find the enemy. And now he was starting to wish that the spectres in the mist would prove real. As far as Steel was concerned, battle could not come soon enough. He cussed to himself and spat out the wad of tobacco on which he had been chewing and eased the worn leather strap of the short-barrelled fusil which it was his unique privilege as an officer of Grenadiers to carry on his shoulder. The soft ground was caking his boots with mud and particularly to someone of Steel's tall frame and muscular build, every step seemed heavier than the last.

The sound of raised voices made him look to his left.

Instinctively, his right hand went across to the sword hilt and began to ease the newly greased blade from its scabbard. The red-coated figures of two of his men appeared through the swirling mist, apparently oblivious to their officer, one goading the other in some private joke. Steel relaxed and let the sword slide back. He was about to address them when from behind him another voice, its thick Geordie accent reassuringly familiar, muttered an order whose anger and purpose, though muted, were bitingly clear.

'Quiet there, you two men. You're both on sarn't's orders now. And don't go thinking that I don't know who you are.'

Steel turned to the rear and saw the large frame of his sergeant, the Geordie, Jacob Slaughter, his face boiling with rage. 'God's blood, Jacob! Wasn't this meant to be a surprise attack? Advance to contact with the enemy were my orders, without a word spoken. What price now surprise? The French'll have us for breakfast. Who the hell were those men? Are they ours? Do I know them?'

Slaughter shook his head. 'New intake, sir. But they'll give you no more trouble. On my word.'

'I'm sure they won't, Jacob. Not once you've finished with them. But it's too late now for all that. They'll learn soon enough from the French. Keep talking like that and they won't see another dawn. It's no fault of yours. This army's not what it was.'

Steel knew himself to be right. This was not the same army that had carried its colours at bayonet-point deep into the French lines at Blenheim two years ago and sent the combined armies of France and Bavaria limping back to Alsace. The casualties it had incurred in that bloody campaign had been high and Steel's unit, Colonel Sir James Farquharson's Regiment of Foot, had been no exception. There had been other battles too since then and now, of the men with whom he had started this war four years ago, barely half remained, their fallen comrades replaced with green recruits, some of them fresh from Britain. The two garrulous soldiers were only too typical of that lack of experience. Steel shook his head as he paused for a moment and more men advanced past them. He watched one slip on the boggy ground and grope to retrieve his musket and the tall embroidered mitre cap which marked out the Grenadiers, however inexperienced, as a class of their own. And he knew that, for all the losses, the men he had about him now in the company, those who had managed to stay alive these past two years, were as good as he would ever find. Marlborough might have made the army, but this company belonged, heart and soul, to Jack Steel.

Steel wiped a weary hand over his eyes: 'I tell you, Jacob. What this army needs is another victory. Another Blenheim. And Marlborough knows that as well as we do. That's why we're here, in this bloody fog.'

Two tall shapes approached them out of the mist. Two of Steel's fellow officers, clad in the distinctive blue-trimmed scarlet coats of Farquharson's regiment, one a lieutenant in his late twenties, the other an ensign of no more than nineteen. Unlike Steel, who chose to tie back his long brown hair with a black silk ribbon, both wore fashionable, full-bottomed brown wigs, falling to their shoulders.

The older of them spoke, breathlessly: 'Jack, thank God! Impossible to make out a thing in this damned soup. Have you any idea at all where we are?'

'Henry, for once I will admit that I'm almost as confounded as you. Although, I presume, as we have been travelling due west, that we must by now be approaching our allotted positions in the line.'

Lieutenant Henry Hansam reached into his coat pocket and producing an engraved silver snuff box, took a pinch before continuing. 'Pray remind me, Jack, what exactly it is we are supposed to be doing in this infernal bog.'

Steel, raising an eyebrow, turned to Slaughter and winked. 'Would you oblige the lieutenant, Sarn't?'

Sergeant Slaughter smiled. He knew what Steel intended. They had survived together through the horrors of four years of war and enjoyed a friendship unique between an officer and his sergeant. Though frowned upon by the more ortho-dox elements among the officers, it was this which had earned their company its enviable reputation within the rank and file of the army and which ensured that fighting on the field of battle, Steel and his sergeant were the equal of anything the enemy might send against them. Slaughter knew that Steel enjoyed teasing the good-natured Hansam and relishing this chance to help him, he adopted the persona of a respectful corporal.

'Well, if you remember, Mister Hansam, sir, the order came from the duke hisself. And we had it direct from Lord Orkney. Press the right flank, says he. You may as likely find the ground just a bit soft there. That's what he says, sir.'

'A bit soft? Soft? Christ almighty, Jack. We're advancing through a damned marsh. The men are coated in mud. Heaven knows how many have lost their weapons. It's madness.'

Steel smiled. He turned to the younger officer. 'Williams, you heard Lieutenant Hansam. Run along and tell My Lord Orkney that he has committed us to, um ... to madness. There's a good fellow.'

The ensign smiled, but did not move.

Hansam frowned: 'Damn it Jack. You know what I mean by it. No general in his right mind would have an army advance across a bog like this.'

Steel laughed, and patted his friend on the back. 'Of course, Henry, you're quite right. You and I know that our commander-in-chief, His Grace the Duke of Marlborough, is the most brilliant general of our age. Tell me truly that you would not follow him to the death. Tell me that there's not a man of this army who would not do the same. Of course it is not logical to send infantry into battle through a marsh. But since when did Marlborough ever fight by the rules? Was that how we won at Blenheim? Or on the Schellenberg? Now where the devil is our company?'

Looking about him he tried to make out more men of their company of Grenadiers through the mist. They were the tallest men in the regiment and it was not hard to spot them. He was aware of two men to his right and left, their scarlet coats discernible even in this gloom. But beyond them there were only shapes and voices. Somewhere off to the left lay the remaining nine companies of the regiment, and beyond them the bulk of the allied army under Marlborough. As was the custom, it was the honour of the Grenadiers to advance on the extreme right of the battalion, and as Farquharson's was posted on the far right of the line Steel's company now found themselves at the outer limit of the army. But at this moment Steel felt as if they might as well be on another continent.

As the snuff began to irritate his nasal passages, Hansam sneezed and spoke through his handkerchief. 'You're right of course, Jack. But we've been advancing now for close on two hours through this damned fog. For all we know the entire French army could be no more than a few yards directly in front of us.'

Slaughter coughed, respectfully: 'Oh no, sir. We had his lordship's word that the French was well to our front. Other side of that village, sir.'

'Village?' Steel replied.

'Aye, a village. Which, were it not for this fog, you would see plain as day directly over there.' Guessing, he pointed.

'The village of Autre-Eglise. Our objective.'

Hansam strained to peer through the fog: 'Damned strange name.'

The younger officer, Tom Williams, the company's ensign, who until now had remained silent, spoke up eagerly: 'It means "other church" in French, sir.'

Hansam smiled at him: 'Thank you, Lieutenant. I was aware of that. But thank you all the same.'

Steel spoke: 'So where d'you suppose the first church might be, Tom?'

Hansam smiled, and seized the opportunity: 'Why, Jack, in another village, to be sure. Autre, Autre-Eglise, perhaps.'

'Very droll, Henry. Now I think we had better follow the men, d'you not. It wouldn't do for them to find the French before we do, eh?'

As the officers moved away obliquely to their left and front to find their platoon and they all began to advance as fast as the ground permitted, Steel contemplated how life seemed constantly to bring one full circle. He had come through the slaughter of Blenheim two years ago and last year's bloody adventure in Spain only to find himself back here again on Flanders soil, where his soldiering had begun and where the British army always seemed to be. Flanders – where, at a godforsaken place called Steenkirk, he had first tasted battle, as a seventeen-year-old ensign.

He had been fourteen years with the colours since then and naturally he knew why they were really here now. Of course, Marlborough needed a victory. Blenheim seemed an age ago and their Dutch allies were becoming restless. Last year had seen no northern triumphs, just an endless succession

7

of marches and counter-marches. True, they had broken the massive French lines of fortification which traversed occupied Belgium. But there had been no opportunity then to exploit that success with a victory in the field. Now, Steel knew, here and in London, Marlborough's enemies were again intriguing against him. The only answer was a victory. So, they were here to beat the French and if that meant crossing this filthy bog, then that was what they would do. Snapping back to the matter in hand, he grew aware now that, with every step forward they took, their line of battle was becoming increasingly ragged.

He turned to Slaughter: 'Try to dress the line, Sarn't – wherever it is. We can't afford to lose any men before we've even found the enemy.'

'Right you are, Mister Steel.'

Steel sighed: 'And Jacob, do try to just address me as "sir". At least allow me the appearance of being a captain.'

Steel, although promoted to captain after Blenheim by Marlborough himself, had not yet had the field promotion ratified by the high command at the Horse Guards. That had been two years ago and now he had almost given up hope. He could only presume that he was out of favour at court and he did not need to guess at the reason. He had a lover in London – if that were the right term for someone with whom you had fallen so surely out of love. Arabella Moore was a jealous mistress, ten years his senior and so dangerously close to the queen as to be able to deny him his captaincy. Doubtless Arabella had heard of the romance that Steel had forged in the days before Blenheim, a liaison with a pretty Bavarian girl who he had hoped might bring him lasting happiness. But now Louisa Weber was beyond his reach. On his return from Spain he had found her married to an officer in the Royals. Well, in truth, he too had not been over-faithful to her and so it was for the best. But it had not prevented Arabella's jealousy, nor her continuing spite. Clearly, if she could not have him, then she was determined at least to block his advancement in the army.

What, Steel wondered, would he have to do to achieve on paper the promotion he had earned and now so urgently needed? The bounty from Blenheim and most of that he had gleaned in such danger in the previous year's campaign had dwindled all too fast. Very soon he would again be in serious debt. Pursued yet again, no doubt for the endless round of an officer's expenses and mess bills by their assiduous regimental adjutant, Major Frampton. He prayed that this coming fight might yield an opportunity for fortune and glory for, in his experience, one seldom came without the other. And neither could be achieved without that danger to which Steel was now so helplessly addicted. For, despite all his horrors of phantoms in the mist, he knew that it was the thrill of beating fate which made him a soldier; the knowledge that at any moment he could be killed or horribly mutilated and the unparalleled exhilaration which came after a battle, that delirious moment when you knew that you had cheated death, once again. There must now be an opportunity for him to impress again, to bring himself to the attention of Marlborough and even the queen herself. He would be gazetted captain.

A voice brought him back to the present. Slaughter cocked his musket: 'Rider, sir. Coming from our left.'

Again, instinctively, Steel's hand closed around the grip of his sword and he made to draw the blade.

The cavalryman rode straight at them through the mist. Steel saw a scarlet coat, but knowing that the French too dressed many of their finest cavalry in red, did not relax his hold on the sword but drew it further from its sheath. Slaughter took aim. It was only at ten yards that they realized that the man had not yet drawn his sword and seconds later they saw the green cockade that he wore in his tricorne hat: the allied field recognition symbol for the campaign. Steel recognized him as a young cornet of English cavalry.

The man reined up, doffed his hat and spoke in clipped and haughty tones which marked his position as an aide-de-camp. 'Cornet Hamilton, sir. Attached to the general staff. I carry orders from Lord Orkney for Colonel Farquharson. Can you direct me to him? Where is he?'

Steel smiled at him and indicated the mist: 'You're guess is as good as mine, Cornet. I think you'd be just as well to give them to me. Captain Steel – I command Farquharson's Grenadier company.'

Hamilton frowned and weighed up his options. 'Very well. Your regiment is to halt at once, Captain. You have advanced too far. The French are standing just beyond this ground. Ten battalions of them at least, as far as we can tell. You will halt and form your lines, here. No further.'

Steel nodded; 'Thank you.' He turned towards Williams who had appeared from the mist. 'Mister Williams, go and find the colonel. Tell him to halt at once. Form lines here.'

As Williams hurried over to the left of the regiment, Hamilton replaced his hat and pulled round his horse. Steel watched him gallop away into the mist and losing sight of him, returned to the business in hand.

A hundred yards away to the left, Cornet Hamilton picked his way with care through the redcoated ranks who now stood at ease in their regiments scattered across the hillside. As he approached the rear formations the mist gradually became thinner until he eventually emerged on the crest of a ridge. From here, even through the clouds of grey, the entire allied army was laid out before him. He rode slowly along the front of a regiment of Dutch infantry and found a knot of mounted officers, some of whom were attempting through their telescopes to get a better view of the situation unfolding below them. Looking quickly and unobtrusively at their faces he found the man he was seeking and trotting up, reined in, saluted and whispered towards him.

Close by, but out of earshot, to the front and centre of the group, an upright figure in a red coat emblazoned with a garter star, his gold-trimmed hat crowning an expensive, full-bottomed wig, darted piercing emerald green eyes across the field. John Churchill, Duke of Marlborough, captain-general of the allied army, turned to speak to the man at his side, William Cadogan, his trusted quartermaster-general: 'You know, William, I would that we had gone into Italy, as I had originally planned. But I do believe that we shall beat the French today. So I really must not protest at that prospect. All things told, you must agree that this is good ground. What say you, Field-Marshal Overkirk? Will it suit your Dutch?'

'We will fight the French wherever we may, Your Grace. This is as good a position as I have seen to cross swords with them. My men will not let you down.'

'I am certain of it, Field-Marshal. I have every faith in them.' He turned back to Cadogan: 'Is that not so, William? We rank our Dutch allies quite as highly as our own boys.' Cadogan opened his mouth to reply but was interrupted by a small, dark-haired man with a prominent nose who wore a modest, blue civilian-style coat and sat on a bay horse alongside the duke.

Mijnheer Sicco van Goslinga, the newly arrived Dutch field deputy to the general staff, had been deep in thought for some minutes. Now he was frowning. He shook his head:

11

'I am sorry Your Grace, but I must protest at your opinion. It will not do to deploy on our right. You see the ground there is no more than marsh. With such hedges, ditches and marshes it would be madness to move infantry over such ground. You must agree, sir.'

Marlborough smiled back at him: 'Thank you for your advice, Mijnheer. And I shall take note of it and if it should indeed be madness then I give you my word that should it fail I shall summon a physician.'

Cadogan suppressed the beginnings of a smile.

Marlborough quickly turned back to his left: 'Hawkins? Have we intelligence from the right flank? Are Lord Orkney's men in place?'

Colonel James Hawkins broke off from his conversation with Cornet Hamilton and nodded to Marlborough. 'Aye, sir. I have it from the cornet here. They are this moment halted above the village. The right of your line is secure, Your Grace. Although Hamilton here tells me that we just stopped the infantry in time, or our lads would have been on the French already by now.'

Marlborough laughed. 'They shall be at them soon enough, James. That will do for the moment.'

Half a mile away, to Marlborough's right, another knot of officers stood before their men. Steel peered across the valley. At last the mist was lifting and the countryside was revealed to them. In the course of reforming the line, they had fallen back some fifty yards and found a small area of less boggy ground. Steel gazed now across acres of fields green with young corn, a rolling plateau of open country, quite without hedges or walls of any sort.

Hansam spoke: 'This is good cavalry country, Jack. The horse'll have a field day.'

'I daresay they will, Henry, but it looks rotten bad for us. We're to take that village and as far as I can see as soon as we step off you can bet that the French artillery will open up. And not so much as a ditch for cover. Nothing to stop a ball from carrying away four, six . . . ten files of infantry. I wonder that our guns will not do the same, ere long.'

Beyond the marshes which flanked the stream running below their position on a gentle hill beyond the waving corn, the entire Franco-Bavarian army stood before them, strung out on a front four miles long. White and blue uniforms as far as the eye could see, punctuated only by the red of the Irish mercenary regiments in French pay – the Wild Geese – and that of the cavalry of King Louis' own bodyguard, the Gens d' Armes. It was the whole might of France. Well, he thought, they had broken them at Blenheim and they could damn well do it again today.

Williams spoke: 'Seems to me there's more of them here than there were at Blenheim, sir.'

'You may be right, Tom. King Louis has half a million men under arms, they say.'

'But we shall best them again, sir. Of that I'm certain.'

Steel smiled and clapped the ensign on the back. 'Aye. I'm as sure as you. Now, look to the men. Don't have them standing-to for too long at a time. Stand them at ease a while.'

As Williams looked to his order, Steel gazed down at the ground. For the last few minutes he had been aware that his right leg was slowly sinking into the boggy field. He cursed and began to doubt Williams' certainty. Not here too? The whole area was sodden. How did Marlborough intend them to advance on this? Struggling to keep his balance and desperate not to reveal his plight to the men, he reached down with both hands to ease his leg free from the mud into which it was disappearing and swore gently into the cool morning. He gave one last pull and with a squelch the tall black boot emerged from the boggy ground. Steel shook his leg, tried to remove some of the mud and looked over his right shoulder.

Slaughter was grinning, shaking his head. 'You're like me, sir. Must 'ave ate too big a breakfast. Don't know when to stop. Always like that before a fight. Nerves, it is.'

'Jacob, if I wanted your homespun wisdom on the subject of my diet I would ask for it. It's the ground, man. D'you see? Too soft. Even here.'

Slaughter stamped his foot which came down hard on the earth. 'Ground seems fine and firm here to me.'

Steel was in no mood to be teased. 'Shut up, Jacob and dress the damned line.' He paused, regaining his better humour. 'We must make ourselves pretty for the enemy gunners.'

Steel turned back to the front and stared at the army before him. In the centre he saw a puff of smoke and an instant later a single cannon shot broke the silence. He watched as the ball arced from the French lines towards the allied centre. Hansam reached into his pocket and brought out the gold half-hunter that he had taken from the body of a dead Bavarian at Blenheim. One of the few timepieces among the officers of the regiment, while it could hardly be called accurate, it was now his most prized possession. He flicked it open.

'One o'clock, precisely. You would not suppose that your Frenchman would be quite so exact. Do you not think, Jack? Sloppy fellow as a rule, you'd say. And you'd be damned right.' Hansam replaced the watch in his pocket.

Steel smiled and shook his head. 'Never underestimate your enemy, Henry. The French may seem to care more about their food and their women than their fighting, but you

14

should remember. In the thick of it and at their best, they're just as good as you or I.'

Hardly had the echo of the single French cannon died away than a battery of six English twelve-pounders in the centre of the allied line opened up in reply, sending a hail of round-shot into the enemy infantry. It seemed to Steel that the instant that they fired the French guns too opened up and he watched mesmerized as the balls criss-crossed in a mid-air ballet. There was a curious beauty to it. But all too fleeting, for the reality soon came upon them. He reckoned the range at around a thousand yards. Long, but not quite long enough to spare them from harm.

To his right Slaughter growled a command: 'Steady.'

Steel watched the black dots of the six cannonballs grow larger as they drew ever closer. As always their progress seemed to be slowed down, until in the last fifty yards he lost them as their true speed became evident.

Slaughter growled again: 'Steady now.'

The French gunners, aware of the boggy ground, had fired high for impact rather than attempting to bounce their cannonballs before the enemy for greater effect. Two of the roundshot flew over the heads of the company but four found their mark, crashing into the line of redcoats and cutting bloody paths through the ranks. One of them took the head off a grenadier and carried it open-mouthed into the rear ranks, mitre cap and all, gouting blood, before smashing into the front two ranks of a regiment to their rear. Just behind Steel a young private, one of the new intake, threw up his meagre breakfast. He heard Slaughter calling to the leading men of the files: 'Close up. Close the ranks. Someone get rid of that body. You, Jenkins. Move that bloody mess.'

This was how it always began. Standing in line, bearing the cannon fire until they were at last given the command to attack. It was the proving ground; what transformed a man into a soldier. And Steel knew that there were no better soldiers at standing under fire than the British and no better men among them than the Grenadiers. This was how you learned your trade.

Steel looked to his left along the line of the entire regiment. In the centre he could see the two colours of shining silk waving in the breeze, one the blue and white saltire of Scotland, the other the colonel's own colour with the Farquharson arms in the centre of a red ground, crowned with the motto *Nemo Me Impune Lacessit*: 'No one provokes me unpunished'. They would prove those words again today, he thought. Before the colours, mounted on a black charger and flanked by the adjutant, Colonel Sir James Farquharson raised his sword high above his head.

His colonel had grown up in the past two years, thought Steel. Blooded on the field of Blenheim he had earned the respect of his battalion, including that of Steel. The arrogant, vain colonel had given way to a new man, a man hardened to the reality of battle, alive to the responsibilities of raising a regiment. Farquharson was aware at last that this regiment he had paid for, clothed, equipped and trained was no plaything, but a finely honed tool of war, an instrument to be cherished; nurtured. Yes, thought Steel, you deserve to be our colonel now old man, and we deserve you. As he watched, Sir James brought down the sword, its point levelled towards the enemy. Even above the gunfire, Steel caught the words of command. ' 'Tallion will advance . . . Advance.'

As Sir James finished the six drummers positioned directly behind the Grenadier company along with those on the left flank began to beat the regiment into the attack.

'*Rat tat dum, rat dum tidi dum. Rat ta dum, rat tum tidi dum.*' The unmistakable tattoo of the 'British Grenadiers'.

Behind him, Steel sensed the men growing restless, swelling with pride and adrenalin. Now they would move on his command.

'Grenadiers, with me. Let's be at them, boys.'

Slaughter, his sergeant's halberd with its gleaming axe-head poised at the diagonal above the end of file man, offered his own words of gentle encouragement. 'Come on you lazy buggers! Get on. They won't bloody wait. This is what we're here for, 'ain't it? Let's get into them.'

As one the battalion stepped off. The slow march to attack, at a pace calculated to be just sufficient to preserve order in the ranks, yet as fast as possible on a field of battle. Hardly fast enough, thought Steel, and he waited for the French cannon to adjust their range for maximum effectiveness. There was the dreadful lull as they did so and then seconds later the balls came screaming in again. The drums were hammering harder now, urging the men on, their rhythm insistent even under the bombardment. Looking briefly to his left he saw the entire line of Orkney's brigade swinging across the plain and down the hill towards the stream. We must cross that, thought Steel. Just get through those marshes and we will be fine. Just have to make it that far. Was that so much to ask? Dear God, he prayed, to no being in particular. Whatever you might be, grant me just that one wish. Get us across the stream and let us be at the French. And do not let me die. But if I must be hit then do for heaven's sake please let me die. Do not let me be crippled. Let me live, for God's sake, let me live to carry the battle to my enemies. Your enemies for all I know. The Queen's enemies. Marlborough's enemies. Let me live to kill the French. As he repeated the gruesome litany in his head, Steel realized that they had made it to the foot of the slope and were now on the edge of the marsh, close to the stream.

He turned to Williams: 'Tom, for God's sake, keep the men close together. Don't let them become bogged down. You must keep formation.'

Slaughter's voice too growled out the familiar words above the din of battle: 'Close up. Right shoulders forward. Close your ranks, you buggers.'

Steel looked back to the front, into the rain of shot and mouthed his useless prayer. Although in his heart he knew that if this miserable Whitsunday were to be the moment he would die, it was ordained already and there was nothing any words could change about that. But he knew that he could fight and that if the fates let him reach the French lines he would do his damnedest to make sure that this day would surely not be his last.

TWO

There was a trick in battle to keep your body engaged in the
matter in hand, while your mind became detached from the
grim possibilities of every passing minute. It was a ploy that
Steel knew well, and had used many times. But this morning,
for some inexplicable reason, it had as yet eluded him. He
was sweating hard now. His thick coat felt ever heavier about
him and the gun slung over his back seemed to drag him
down and slow his pace. While he was relieved that their
own guns were laying down a heavy bombardment, there
had been no respite from the French cannon fire and with
almost every step that they took towards the enemy it seemed
to Steel that another redcoated figure tumbled from their
ranks in a ragged heap. Ahead of him and to the left, he
could see, through the thick white smoke, the tall frame of
George Hamilton, Earl of Orkney, conspicuous in the plate
armour which covered the upper half of his body, advancing
on foot at the head of the brigade. Here, thought Steel, was
a soldier to reckon with. A man towards whose station any
officer would aspire. Not only was Orkney a sound tactician,
he was brave. And for Steel the latter counted just as much

19

in battle as any technical or military skills. They had moved with surprising ease at first over the boggy ground and Steel wondered why he had doubted Marlborough's judgement in choosing this terrain. Certainly their pace had slowed, and the stream had at one point seemed to be impassable. But they had come through that and managed to cut their way through the vicious hedge of *chevaux de frise*, a barrier of bayonets stuck into treetrunks, which the French defenders had laid across the path of their assault.

Now they were trampling on bramble thickets as they bridged the valley of the Petite Gheete, the stream which flowed directly in front of the village of Autre-Eglise and as they advanced French and Walloon sharpshooters took their toll on the redcoated ranks before dropping back towards the enemy lines. Most of them, he reckoned, were Walloons – French-speaking Netherlanders, and their loyalty and stead-fastness he knew to rank as nothing compared to any French regulars, unquestioningly loyal to the Sun King. Even as he looked, an entire company of Walloon infantry turned and streamed back towards the French lines.

As they ran a cheer went up from the British line. One of the Grenadiers, Dan Cussiter, shouted after them: 'Go on. Bugger off back to Paris before we kick your arses.'

The men, desperate in their terror to laugh at anything, cheered his bravado and Steel heard Slaughter's booming voice. 'That's enough, there. You'll be in Paris yourselves as soon as likely. But not if you don't dress your ranks. There'll be time for cheering soon enough, my lads.'

It was vital to preserve discipline now, lest the men, fired by the sight of the retreating infantry, should break ranks and give chase only to find themselves faced by what Steel knew to lie head up the slight hill: the full might of the French battle lines. As the Grenadiers began to find themselves on firm ground, Steel, gradually regaining his composure, shook his limbs and tried to settle his nerves. And as he did so he heard a command from the left: the unmistakable tones of Major Charles Frampton, the adjutant: ''Tallion halt. Form your ranks. Prepare to attack.'

The command was taken up by the other field officers and as one the men came to a stop. They were still a good hundred yards out from the French but Steel knew that this was only a temporary halt.

He looked back and found Slaughter. 'We advance on the command, Sarn't!'

A roundshot came crashing past his head and smashed into the ranks behind, disembowelling one of the Grenadiers, Donaldson, a bluff, pleasant lad from Edinburgh, and taking the leg off another, Ned Tite. As the man lay writhing on the ground, his screams unsettling his comrades, Steel motioned to Slaughter to have him hauled away. They could not stand here long, he thought, would not endure much of this pasting. As if in answer to his concern another command came from the centre of the line.

''Tallion will prepare to advance. Charge your bayonets.' The steel-tipped muskets which till now had been carried either at the high port or snugly in the shoulder, were brought down until they were level with the ground.

''Tallion – Advance!'

Again the drums struck up, this time a less noisome rattle. More of a tap, but a sound which when recognized, Steel knew, would bring a chill to the hearts of any enemy of Queen Anne. Grimly, the battalion moved up the hill and still the shot crashed down among them like a scythe reaping the corn. As they came up against the first houses of the little village of Autre-Eglise, it became obvious that the French had not been idle. Every street, every alleyway had been fortified

21

with anything that had come to hand. Domestic furniture mainly, taken from the abandoned houses; prized possessions pressed into more practical service. But though hastily erected, Steel could see that the barricades had been made with experienced hands. Chairs and tables had been lashed together and stuck through with swords and bayonets – anything which would make their passage more hazardous.

Behind the fortifications stood the French and as the Grenadiers broke like a wave upon the wooden wall, the white-coated ranks let go with a devastating volley. But it was not enough to stop the red tide. Steel, seeing an opportunity, placed his foot on a table leg and leapt on top of a barricade. Below him a dark-skinned French infantryman looked up and attempted to stick him with his bayonet, but Steel was too quick and, parrying aside the weapon with his sword, brought its razor-sharp blade humming down into the man's head, cleaving in half his black tricorne and with it the head within.

Exultant, Steel turned back momentarily towards the red-coats: 'With me, Grenadiers. We're in, lads. Death to the French.'

Followed by a half-dozen of his men, Steel threw himself over the wall and landed in a knot of white-coated soldiers. Such was their surprise that two of them dropped their muskets and ran back into the village. Of the others three were engaged by Steel's men. Matt Taylor, a corporal and the company apothecary, used the butt of his musket like a club and hammered it hard into a Frenchman's jaw. Steel winced at the crack. He found himself face to face with the tallest of the group, a huge mustachioed hulk of a man, a sergeant who wielded his spontoon like a farmer's scythe and stood grinning just beyond the reach of Steel's blade. Steel began to fence with him, cutting at the wooden staff and carefully sidestepping the stabs and swings of the evil pointed head. Treating the man's weapon as if it were a sword, Steel cut to the left and parried it away and then with one swift movement lunged in fencing-salle style and skewered the big Frenchman squarely through the heart. The man stopped in mid-swing, stared wildly at the tall British officer and then, blood spouting from his mouth, fell backwards, stone dead.

Retrieving his sword from the corpse, Steel looked around. To his left more Grenadiers had succeeded in storming the village and were steadily pushing back the French and Walloon lines. He turned to his men: 'The village is ours. Well done, lads.' He looked to Slaughter: 'Stand the men easy for a moment, Sarn't; and post a guard. They'll be back. We can be sure of that.'

Slaughter threw him a grin. 'That was a fine fight, sir. Did you see 'em run?'

'They ran all right. But we must have suffered in the assault. What's our strength?'

'Hard to say, sir. I know that a score of the lads went down on the hill and I dare say we may have lost half as much again in the fight.'

'Yes. I thought as much.'

Still, he thought, thirty per cent casualties was what you might expect in a frontal attack and of them perhaps a third again would have been fatal. Ten good men dead then from his company and the day still young. Who, he wondered, had gone down? Was Williams hit? Or Hansam? Steel wiped the sweat from his forehead with his sleeve and looked about. His fears were quelled as from a neighbouring street the young ensign approached him. There was a cut on his right arm, his sleeve was drenched in blood and his face was quite white.

'Tom. Are you hit?'

'It's nothing, sir. A scratch. French officer. I sent him off, sir. Pity. Damned fine swordsman.'

He winced as the pain in his arm cut in and managed a weak smile which told Steel that his wound, though serious, was not life-threatening.

'I'm sending you to the rear. Best get that wound dressed before an infection sets in. Don't want you to lose that arm, eh?'

Williams nodded and began to walk towards the lines.

'He'll do well, sir, that one. General, likely as not.'

'If he manages to stay alive long enough, Jacob.'

From their left a tall figure approached – a senior officer. There was no mistaking the chiselled features of Lord Orkney. There was blood on his breeches and he had lost his sash. Otherwise, thought Steel, the youthful, forty-year-old general appeared miraculously unhurt.

'Sarn't, stand the men to attention. Officer approaching.'

'Officer approaching. Stand to there.'

The Grenadiers straightened up and shuffled into three lines.

Orkney nodded to Steel. 'You did well, Captain.'

'Thank you, My Lord. But it was my men's doing. The Grenadiers, sir.'

Orkney peered into Steel's face. 'Captain Steel is it not? The hero of Blenheim? Well, whoever claims the glory, it was as well done today as then. We have the village and I do not intend to give it up lightly. I have left your colonel in the centre of the position. Take your Grenadiers and join with those of the First Guards and General Fergusson's regiment. Place yourselves on the side of the village closest to the French lines. Have your men construct defences. When they come on again, as they are sure to do, we'll give them a taste of their own style, eh?'

'Indeed, My Lord. You may rely upon us.'

Orkney was about to compliment Steel further when both men noticed five horsemen approaching from the allied lines. All were dressed in the elaborate uniform of the general staff and all appeared to be aides. It was as unlikely a sight as either of them had ever seen on any battlefield.

'What d'you make of this, Captain Steel? A group of young gentlemen about town and dressed for the court? By God! Do I see red heels? What the devil shall we make of it?'

'I do not know, My Lord. But I hazard that we are about to discover.'

The horsemen reined in before Orkney and the two leading riders dismounted. Steel recognized one of them as Benjamin Harley, an aide-de-camp to Marlborough himself. The young man made an exaggeratedly low bow to Orkney and began to speak. His accent was disarmingly soft and quite out of character with the battle raging around them.

'My Lord. You are to disengage the enemy forthwith and retire two hundred yards.'

Orkney's bushy eyebrows arched high above widening eyes and his face took on the hue of his coat. For an instant he was speechless. Then, as the aide waited in silence, he found his voice. 'Disengage? Retire? Are you quite mad, sir? We have the village. This ground is ours. And, God please you, so too will be the day. I shall not disengage, sir. No, sir. I shall not retire.' He spat the words in contempt. 'On whose authority have you this order?'

The aide smiled, smugly. 'It comes direct on the Lord Marlborough's authority My Lord. It is his express wish that you should disengage the enemy with all speed and return to your starting line.'

Orkney stared at him in disbelief. For an instant Steel wondered whether the general was about to strike the young aide. And in truth he too felt rising indignation. This was too much to take. The duke he trusted implicitly, would follow to the ends of the earth. But to take this order from a young aide, without proper explanation for what seemed utter folly? Orkney took a pace towards the aide.

Steel saw that the boy's hand had fallen to his sword hilt. This was getting dangerous. Now was not the time for such an argument. He intervened: 'Sir – if the order has come from the duke himself, d'you not think that it might be prudent to obey? No matter how galling.'

Orkney, his eyes ablaze with rage, turned on him: 'Captain Steel, I do not need your advice. I . . . and you, Steel, have left good men lying dead and dying back there. Men who died to take this place. Will you betray them now? We do not retreat. How can you agree with this madness? We are the victors, dammit. We have taken our objective. We have this ground. I shall not surrender it, not even for My Lord Marlborough.'

'Indeed I too will never betray any of my men, sir, dead or alive. But it is an order, My Lord.'

Orkney regained his composure and, turned again to the white-faced ensign. 'What is its purpose then? According to the rules of engagement the duty of a commander is to win battles, not to yield at a whim whatever ground he gains. For what possible reason could My Lord Marlborough desire me to retreat?'

Steel noticed that the other aides had now dismounted. One of them, slightly older than Harley, moved forward to speak. 'Excuse me. Lieutenant the Honourable Greville Bennett, My Lord. It is not a retreat, Lord Orkney. Merely a tactical withdrawal.'

Orkney smashed his fist into the palm of his left hand: 'Tactical withdrawal?' He spat the words. 'Marlborough sends me five of his liverish boys to tell me this. To tell me to retreat. For it is a retreat, dammit, man. No less. Why, I should . . .'

Again Harley's hand darted nervously to his sidearm. Steel was about to stand between them when from the mouth of a sidestreet two further horsemen appeared. One was unmistakable as William Cadogan, the Duke of Marlborough's right-hand man and quartermaster-general. At his side rode another officer, slightly more portly than Cadogan and older. Steel recognized him at once; Colonel James Hawkins, attached to Marlborough's staff and one of the duke's oldest friends, had been instrumental in Steel's advancement to date. He was as good a mentor as he had ever had, but one whom he had not seen these past few weeks.

Hawkins and Cadogan rode up to Orkney and both men dismounted. Cadogan greeted the seething general with a smile. 'What ho, George. You look as if you may have gone beyond yourself for once. Hold up. Have you not had the duke's instructions? You are to retire and regroup, My Lord.'

Orkney seemed to stagger. He shook his head. 'Do not tell me, William, that what this . . . boy has said is truly the case. That I am indeed ordered to abandon this place. It is my victory, Cadogan. We have the ground. Look for yourself.'

'I am afraid, George that it is quite so. You see, fact is, you are simply too good for us, and for the French. Fact is, your attack was never more than a diversion intended to draw away the marshal's reserves from his centre.'

Orkney's face became an even deeper shade of pink: 'Diversion? My attack a diversion? I'll give His Grace diversion, by God. Tell that to those men lying dead upon that plain and at the barricades. Tell them why they died, by God.'

Cadogan shook his head. He nodded and made to grasp Orkney's shoulder, but the general recoiled. 'I know, George,

I know. But fact is the duke did not think it prudent to inform you, or any of his commanders . . .'

Orkney laughed: 'Not prudent? God's blood, William! When is it prudent then to attack at all?'

A French battery on the high ground behind the village, observing the group of officers standing in the square, had ranged them and now shot began to fall perilously close, crashing into the cobbles and sending up splinters of stone.

Cadogan spoke again, in a more official tone: 'Lord Orkney, the clear truth of the matter is, you have no cavalry in support of you. Look beyond the village. His Grace has commanded all the horse to move to the centre there to engage the enemy and to rout him. And that will happen. Look for yourself. You are isolated – stay here and you will without doubt be outflanked. You must retire, my friend, and you must do so at once. I am truly sorry.'

Orkney rubbed at his wig with his hands and then at his rheumy eyes. Finally, staring at the aide he nodded. 'Very well. I shall do as you ask. But only as you come direct from His Grace and at the personal request of Lord Cadogan here. Inform the duke that I intend to ride to him forthwith and if I find you to be at fault then I shall not hesitate to make you pay, so help me.'

As Cadogan smiled and clapped the general on the back, Hawkins, who had remained silent, walked up to Steel, smiling. 'They're old friends, Jack. I grant you it goes against everything we should do. But there is sense in it, brilliance even. No doubt they will settle it amicably over a glass of wine, once we have beaten Marshal Villeroi.'

'Are we winning then, sir?'

'Now, Jack, I would be a foolish man to say that, wouldn't I? While you were up here taking this village, down there on the plain there has been a great cavalry battle. General

Overkirk has turned the French horse. Now though comes the real crisis. If this next manoeuvre goes according to the duke's plan then I do believe that very soon we might well be the victors. It's as well that I found you, Jack, although you'd have got it by hand of an orderly just as well. The Guards are to remain here in the village until the last, to cover the withdrawal. You and the other companies of all the brigade's Grenadiers under Lord Orkney's command are needed forthwith in the centre where we intend to make a grand assault. Take your company and report to the Dutch. I'll see Colonel Farquharson. You will be seconded to a Major van Cutzem of the Dutch infantry.'

'You come here merely to deliver orders? Colonel Hawkins, I know you better than that.'

'Indeed you do, Jack, and you are quite right. I have you in mind for a particular purpose. I can say no more of it as yet. I had not seen you for a fortnight and simply wanted to make sure that you still lived. Keep yourself safe this day, Jack, I shall have need of you ere long.'

Orkney had left to rejoin his staff and as Cadogan mounted up and Hawkins went to join him, he cast a glance back over his shoulder. 'Oh, and Jack, I forgot to wish you good luck. Though it always seems to run with you.'

Steel smiled and nodded. Even as the French battery continued to fire, the shot coming in just above their heads and crashing into the walls of the surrounding houses, he strode across to where Slaughter and the men still stood at attention.

'Stand down, Sarn't.'

Hansam approached him, eager-eyed: 'So, do we attack?'

Steel stared at the ground, and drew with his sword in the dirt. 'No. We're moving out.'

Slaughter spoke up: 'After the French already, sir. Is the battle won then?'

'Not exactly, Jacob. We're to move backwards and to the left – not forward. We are to withdraw and proceed to the centre.'

Hansam shook his head, laughed and reached for his snuff box.

The sergeant spoke in disbelief: 'What, after taking the village and climbing up that bloody hill? And with all those men dead?'

'Those are our orders. We are seconded to a Dutch battalion. I'd take it as an honour if I were you, Sarn't.'

Steel could see the logic in Marlborough's strategy, although he could not condone the decision not to vouchsafe the plan to Orkney, and he sympathized with the general's indignation. If you were to mount a convincing feint upon the enemy's flank intended to draw out his reserves, what better way to do it than persuade your own men that it was in earnest? It was not fair – but then, thought Steel, what was fair in this new warfare in which every fight brought some new surprise. As much had been plain to him in Bavaria before Blenheim, and since then he had seen time and again evidence of a changing attitude which directed their actions in every theatre of the present conflict, from Flanders down to Spain and Portugal.

He stopped drawing maps in the dirt and looked up: 'Move the men out, Sarn't. Column of threes. And try to keep the files at a little distance. We don't want to present too good a target to the French gunners.'

Slaughter, still seething at the inexplicable order to move back, took out his fury on the Grenadiers. 'You heard the officer. Marching formation in threes. And look sharp about it. You there, Sullivan. Get in step, damn your eyes! I said move.' To emphasize the need for haste he prodded another particularly slow Grenadier, whose stature made up for his lack of wit, with the haft of his halberd. 'Come on Milligan, you lump of lard. We don't want you to be late for the next dance, do we? Let's give the Frenchies back their village now. Quick as you can, lads. Mustn't keep 'em waiting.'

They marched off to the left and down a narrow street and out of the village, slightly to the south and west of the way they had come up, but still close enough to see the limp red mounds which were the bodies of their fallen comrades. Slaughter noticed the nervous glances cast towards the dead: 'Eyes front now. Pick up the pace there, Tarling. The Frenchies won't wait all day for us. You don't want a bayonet up your arse, do you?'

As they made their way down the slope and towards the centre of the allied line Steel realized that they were marching in a dip in the ground and thus quite invisible to the enemy, even positioned as they were on the higher ground. There was no way in fact that the French could possibly know that Marlborough was moving the right wing into the centre or what he intended. Casting a glance to his left, up to the British lines, Steel saw that the regimental colours of every battalion in Orkney's brigade were still in place with their escort on the ridge-line. On Marlborough's instruction a token force had been left there quite deliberately so that to the untutored eye what remained on the crest would present the appearance of several battalions in close order. He realized too that it was quite brilliant. Steel knew in that moment that his confidence in the duke had not been misplaced and he knew too that soon Orkney would understand. Within minutes the duke would have a huge advantage of numbers in the centre of the battlefield. And then they would see what happened.

Ahead of them now Steel could see the flank of a Dutch battalion, blue-coated and poker-straight, standing quite still, despite the withering fire from the French cannon on the rising ground to their left. Steel spotted the officer and waved the men on.

Major Henk van Cutzem was very nearly Steel's equal in height, with a shock of long blond hair which he wore tied back like Steel, although in his case such was its volume that most of those who did not know him took it for a full wig. He wore a slim, fair moustache and beneath it for an instant, Steel fancied that he caught the faintest shadow of a smile. He nodded in greeting.

'Captain Steel?' The Dutchman's English was impeccable.

'Major.'

'Welcome. You may fall your men in on the right of our line.'

Steel bowed: 'You do me an honour, Major. My thanks. But I should not like to unsettle your own Grenadiers.'

'On the contrary, Captain Steel. The honour is ours. You come with a reputation. You are a hero, a veritable Achilles. They say that at Blenheim you led your company to rescue your regiment's standard – from the French cavalry, no less. King Louis' own bodyguard?'

Steel nodded.

'You led infantry against cavalry to save the colour?'

'I led Grenadiers, Major.'

'Quite so, Captain. But this is not within the rules of war. It goes against all logic. Why did you do it?'

'A question of honour. Couldn't allow the French to get away with our colour.'

'Quite so. Honour.' He paused. 'Do you believe in honour, Mister Steel?'

Steel winced at being called 'Mister', a lieutenant's title. He felt sure that the Dutchman had not intended it callously, but nevertheless it reminded him sharply that his captaincy, won so hard at Blenheim, still remained merely a brevet rank.

'I believe in it with all my heart, Major. Why else do we fight save for honour? The honour of our regiment. The honour of our country and that of our monarchy. The honour, surely, of ourselves?'

Van Cutzem nodded and smiled. 'Of course, Captain. We fight for honour. Although I of course fight also to save my homeland from the French. Speaking of whom, I believe we are about to witness an example of honour at work.'

Opposite them, before the solid rank of motionless, white-coated French infantry, stood two officers. From such a distance Steel could not tell their rank. As he and the Dutchman watched both of the Frenchmen drew their swords. With a flourish they brought up the blades in the salute before lowering them alternately to the left and to the right. Then they replaced the swords in their scabbards and gave a formal bow towards Steel and the Major in turn. Steel nodded in return and smiled and was about to say something droll to van Cutzem when to his surprise the Dutchman took a pace forward and removed his hat. Bending over in an exaggerated bow which brought his fair hair almost in contact with the ground, van Cutzem swept his hand and hat before him with a flourish and straightened up.

Steel watched him closely, smiling at the polite salute. Van Cutzem turned and rejoined Steel. He noticed the smile: 'You find something amusing, Captain?'

'D'you really, honestly think it helps? All that? Surely we're here to fight them? To kill the French. Of course we give them fair quarter. But why bother with the dramatics?'

'You don't ever make the formal salute? Never? I am surprised, Mister Steel. If you hold honour as dear as you say, then surely this must be part of your code also?'

'I don't believe in bowing to the enemy, Major. I'd sooner lick their boots.'

'Then it is pride which you hold dear, not honour.'

Steel laughed. 'Pride. Honour. Don't play word games with me, Major. I know what I'm fighting for and so do you. But if you want to continue your little charade, then don't mind me. It's amusing to watch, a game, if you like. But it's not war.'

Van Cutzem stared at him and his cheeks coloured. After a few moments he spoke, staring at the ground. 'War? Do you know what war is, Steel? I'll tell you what war is. War is three decades of misery and terror. War is a tale of horror told at a fireside by a maimed father, to his young son. A tale punctuated by sobbing and silence. It is a tale sometimes so painful that it can never be told.' Van Cutzem, his rage now visible in his ice-blue eyes, stared hard into Steel's face. 'My grandfather was killed in cold blood, in front of his children. He was stripped and tied to a cross and roasted alive while his wife was raped and then had her throat slit. The children, my own father among them, were cast out into the fields to live like animals. Happily for me my father survived, although he lost a hand in the process. His sisters did not survive. We do not know their fate. That, Captain, is what war means in these parts.' The Dutchman spoke quietly now: 'That, Mister Steel, is why we use these "absurd" conventions and rules. That is why it is so important to obey such rules of war. We never want to descend into that hell again. We will do anything to avoid it. Anything. And so we fight the French. But it must never again come to that.' His bitterness subsiding, van Cutzem lowered his eyes. 'Please God that we shall never have to witness such things again. That is why, Captain Steel.'

Steel nodded: 'I'm sorry, Major, truly. I should have thought. Forgive me if I have offended you. It was not intended.'

Of course, he longed to tell the major that he did understand only too well what he was talking about, that he had seen such atrocities. Committed not a hundred years ago, but ten. In Sweden and Russia and again, most hauntingly in his mind, only two years ago in Bavaria. The sights which informed his dreams and woke him, sweating hard, in many a cold night. Whole populations massacred, regardless of their age and sex. A village put to the sword. Women raped, children spitted like rabbits. This was not the stuff of history or folk myth, this was happening in their time. Even, for all he knew, as they spoke. They lived in an age of war and terror. He was tempted to tell van Cutzem, but half of him realized that the man would not, did not want to believe him. Why dispel his illusions of this courtly warfare? Steel knew that world to be coming to an end, just as Marlborough had forged a new army and was rewriting the rules of engagement. So as they participated in these great events they were making a modern era. And whenever it finally happened, tomorrow or five years hence, sometime within their own life span – if they were yet spared a French bullet – the old world would soon be gone for ever. Steel would allow the major his dream of chivalry. He knew the reality. Then his gaze settled on something over to the left. For an instant Steel doubted his own vision and his reason and wondered whether van Cutzem was not after all right and perhaps the age of chivalry had returned.

THREE

Looking across to his left, past the Dutch infantry in their serried dark-blue ranks, Steel beheld a sight which left him open-mouthed. On the plain below their position, formed up in a line which stretched between the villages of Taviers and Ramillies and the huge grass-covered mass of what Hansam had lately and with some authority informed him was an ancient Celtic burial mound, lay a hundred squadrons of allied cavalry: perhaps fifteen thousand men. The sunlight glinted off their drawn sabres and flashed on polished cuirasses and harnesses. Not even as a young ensign, while serving in the northern wars between Sweden and Russia, did Steel remember having witnessed such an awesome spectacle of military might.

Van Cutzem too was staring at the cavalry: 'Now we shall see a fight. This is why Marlborough has brought the French to battle here. This must mean victory.'

Steel watched as the horsemen began to trot into position and felt the ground start to tremble. 'I do believe you may be right, Major. But what are we to do? Do we attack Ramillies itself? Certainly our cavalry may defeat the French, but they cannot take a position which has been so heavily fortified by the enemy. We will have won the open ground but in all truth the field will not be ours.'

Van Cutzem shook his head: 'That may be so, Captain. But our orders are to stand. We are to wait until the cavalry have attacked. My generals believe that the day will be resolved by a cavalry battle, not by the infantry. I'm sorry. My orders and yours too, are to stand here.'

Steel put a hand to his head: 'And be shot to shreds by the French guns?'

'If that is what it takes. Those are my orders, Mister Steel. And I am very much afraid that at the present time, as you find yourself under my command, you must obey them also.' A horseman cantered up to the major and the rider, a Dutch dragoon, muttered a few words of Flemish. 'And now excuse me, please. I am summoned by my brigadier. Perhaps we shall advance after all.'

Van Cutzem took his horse from the orderly who had been holding her, mounted and rode towards the rear of his regiment. Steel bit his lip and shook his head. First they had been pulled out of a hard-won foothold and now seemed destined to be left to the mercies of the French artillery. The first decision he had understood. But the second? Sometimes he wondered whether his own commanders were fully aware of any of the many wasted opportunities offered by a battle-field. His musings were interrupted by activity to the front as a body of men approached them.

Slaughter had seen them too: 'Grenadiers. Stand to. Charge your muskets.'

Forty weapons were levelled towards the horsemen, bayonets fixed. Steel looked at the advancing troops and as they grew closer saw with relief from the green cockade in their hats that they were of the allied side.

'At ease, men. They're ours.'

As the ragged column neared them he began to hear snatches of broad Scots dialect. He also saw that, whoever they were, these men had been badly mauled. This bloody mess was, it seemed, what had once been a battalion or more of redcoats. And Scottish troops at that. But under whose command were they, he wondered.

Slaughter came to his side: 'That's not a sight I ever like to see, sir. Unsettles the men too. Poor buggers.'

A man passed them, a junior officer, perched on a make-shift seat made from a musket carried by two of his men, one of whom was sobbing. The officer's left leg had been sheared clean away from the bone and his calf was hanging by the thinnest of tendons. To judge from the colour of his face he had lost a great deal of blood. He said nothing but stared with glazed eyes to his front, still in deep shock. Steel wondered how he would fare when the pain finally cut in. The longer the shock, they said, the worse the agony when it came. Slaughter cursed. Evidently they had been repulsed with some force. It impressed Steel that they were not in rout, but retreating in a controlled manner, their sergeants keeping them in line despite their evident exhaustion and distress. As Steel stood watching, one man – a big fellow with an almost bald head, walking at a fast pace – pushed past him, knocking against his arm with some force. The man did not apologize but carried on.

Steel, regaining his composure, shouted after him: 'Mind your step, sir. Have a care. Even on a field of battle we yet have manners.'

The man turned and Steel saw, even through the mud and blood which had spattered across his once-white breeches, that he was an officer. He turned and walked back towards Steel and as he did so wiped a hand across his face, removing some of the dirt which cloaked his features. 'And who might you be, sir?'

His accent was not unlike Steel's own; soft and with a slight Scottish burr.

'Captain Steel. Sir James Farquharson's Regiment of Foot. I command the Grenadiers. Who, may I ask, might want to know?'

Again the man wiped his face and stared hard at Steel: 'D'you not know me?'

'I was not aware that I should, sir.'

The man smiled and Steel registered his confidence: 'Well, you certainly are aware now, Captain Steel. Argyll is my name. I command those Scots regiments in Dutch service which for the last hour have been engaged with the enemy.' He pointed towards the village which lay in the centre of the battlefield: 'Over there. Against Ramillies. And now, I have had enough of playing with the French. The pleasantries are finished. I intend to take it.' He paused, then looked at Steel again: 'You recognize me now, I'll wager.'

Steel blustered through his embarrassment. John Campbell, Duke of Argyll. Not only was the man a general. He was a general of Scottish troops and a close friend of Sir James Farquharson, his own colonel. In fact Steel had seen Argyll several times in the past campaign in conversation with Sir James. But on those occasions he had not been dressed in quite this manner. Now he looked to all the world like the meanest junior officer.

Steel stiffened to attention: 'I am most dreadfully sorry, My Lord. I really did not know you. Your . . . your appearance. Your dress. I . . .'

Argyll laughed: 'I am disappointed. But in truth I suspect that were I now to look in a glass I should not know myself. I imagine that I can hardly present a noble appearance. For the present however, such things are not important. What I am concerned with is prising the village of Ramillies away from the French. And I very much fear that we must go again.' Steel saw a thought pass over his mind. 'Steel, yes. Jack Steel, is it not? You are the officer, are you not, who saved Sir James's colour at Blenheim?'

For the second time in two hours Steel had to admit that the honour was indeed his.

Argyll smiled broadly and clapped him on the shoulder. 'Then you are a brave man, Steel, and at this most pressing moment I need every brave man that I can find. Your command is where at present?'

Steel gesticulated to the Grenadiers who stood twenty paces to his rear. 'We are detached to a Dutch command, My Lord, and await our orders to attack.' He added: 'Should they ever come. For the present I am commanded to stand here.'

'Well, Captain Steel, your waiting just came to an end.'

A French cannonball, fired at an unseen target, flew past them. Steel watched as the younger Grenadiers flinched and those few remaining veterans pretended to ignore the ever-present danger. Slaughter stood leaning upon his halberd, keeping a careful watch over his charges.

Steel spoke: 'I have my orders, sir.'

Campbell smiled at him. 'I am your orders now, Steel. Come on, man. I'm not waiting here to die and I believe that you and I are cast in the same mould. The fight is over there, Captain Steel. You are a Scot, I perceive and Sir James Farquharson's man, an officer of whom he speaks most highly. It's men such as you and I that are fighting to build a new world. We are Britons, Steel, but do not forget that we are also Scots. We above all others protect the faith of our homeland. I take it, Steel, that like myself, you have never any greater wish than to see these French Papists and their Jacobite allies sent to hell?'

Steel was surprised at the passion of Argyll's impromptu political rant. Although he did not share his bigotry, he did certainly believe in the concept of Union. Uncertain quite how to respond, he settled on diplomacy and merely nodded.

Argyll smiled: 'I knew it. Now bring your men. We've a village to take.'

As the duke loped off towards his brigade, Steel turned grim-faced to Slaughter. 'Sarn't, it seems that we're to attack the village. Form the men up. Battle order.'

'You had an order then, sir? I thought that Major Cutzem wanted us to stay put.'

'Firstly, it is my place to think, Sarn't, not yours. Secondly, I think that we can assume that Major van Cutzem's order simply did not reach us. Wouldn't you say?'

Slaughter laughed: 'Order, sir? I can't mind any order from the major.'

'You see. Let me do the thinking.' Steel turned to the company: 'Grenadiers. With me.'

Hansam walked towards him: 'Is this wise, Jack? To disobey an order so blatantly? It is a court-martial offence.'

'I accept full responsibility. I am the senior officer, Henry. Do not worry. You are exonerated. We must take the village. We cannot rely upon our masters to notice every ebb and flow of the situation on the ground. It seems that the duke is engaged in a great cavalry battle to our left wing. It's up to men like you and I, Henry. You know that at the crisis it is ever not the generals but the men and the officers in the field – the captains, lieutenants and ensigns and not least the common soldier – who change the course of a battle.'

Hansam nodded: 'Very well, Jack. But should we fail they will throw us to the dogs, for certain.'

Steel laughed and grasped his friend by both shoulders: 'But we shall not fail, Henry, you and I. Poor Tom – that he should miss this for naught but a scratch.'

Slaughter had formed the company into the assault formation, doubling the ranks to extend the line and ensure that every man would be able to find a target when the moment came. 'You heard the officer. Sling your fusils. Make ready your grenades.'

Instantly, sixty pairs of hands draped the thick leather slings of their weapons over right shoulders and fumbled with the straps of the big black leather bags which hung at their right hips. Each of them contained four hollow three-inch-diameter iron balls weighing some two pounds filled with gunpowder, stopped with a wooden plug and topped with a fuse of hemp dipped in saltpetre: grenades. Slaughter barked another command and the company moved to the left with Steel and Hansam at their front.

They had gone hardly twenty yards when from Steel's left came a shout. 'Hello! I say, wait there, Captain Steel. What are you doing? I have orders here to advance. Do not leave. You attack with us.'

Steel raised his hand and Slaughter barked the command to halt.

Major van Cutzem rode up to the head of the assault column. 'Captain Steel. Where are you going? Have you new orders. From whom?'

'I have, Major. Directly from Lord Argyll who commands a brigade in Dutch service. I am ordered to attack Ramillies.'

'But Lord Argyll does not command you. I do. And I have orders to attack Ramillies – with you.'

'I take my orders from Lord Argyll, Major.'

Van Cutzem narrowed his eyes: 'This is an outrage. I shall complain to the highest authority. I shall have you court-martialled.'

'Perhaps so, major. But before that I shall have taken Ramillies. And then I really don't think that it will matter. Do you?'

The Major scowled at Steel. 'You may assist your Lord Argyll to take the village, Captain Steel. But you will see that it will be a Dutchman to whom Ramillies falls. I shall take the village, sir. And without your assistance.'

Without a further word, van Cutzem reined his horse around and galloped back to his regiment.

As Sergeant Slaughter goaded the redcoats into action, Hansam looked at Steel and shook his head. 'Really Jack. You go too far. He is Dutch, Jack. You know the Dutch. They do exactly what they say they will do. He will have you cashiered for this.'

Steel laughed: 'Not if we take Ramillies and all become heroes, Henry.'

Emerging from the slight dip in the ground in which they had been sheltering, they saw before them the village of Ramillies. Around a high-spired church were clustered a few dozen houses of nondescript, vernacular design. It was clear that between these the French had constructed sturdy barriers from anything that had come to hand. If anything, thought Steel, they looked more impenetrable than those around Autre-Eglise. Argyll was right. The only way to take this place short of reducing it by bombardment, would be with a frontal assault led by Grenadiers.

Behind the barricades the village appeared to be teeming with white-coated French infantry, among whom Steel thought he could discern flashes of light blue, which must mean they were reinforced by Bavarians.

Hansam was at his side: 'How many d'you think, Jack? Five battalions? Ten?'

'Hard to say. God knows, they're so packed in there. It seems that King Louis' marshals haven't learnt anything from Blenheim, eh?'

It was impossible to say how many French and Bavarian infantry battalions there might be in the village, so densely were they packed. It reminded Steel with chilling closeness of that bloody Bavarian plain, and the little village which had given its name to the battle. There, down by the stream whose waters by the end of the day had flowed red with French blood, the enemy had filled Blenheim so full of men that when the allied assault had come they had not been able to manoeuvre or to fight. Perhaps, he wondered, the same fate might befall them today? Either that or they would hold the village and it would be the attackers, including Steel and his Grenadiers, who would be the ones to suffer and die on the barricades.

Marching on, towards the village, they soon found that they were walking past and often, from necessity, on top of the bodies of the redcoats who had fallen earlier in the day attempting to take Ramillies. It was not a sight calculated to raise the spirit of an assault force. Particularly when any of those who were not actually dead reached out and grasped with desperate hands at the ankles and calves of those who now went in to the attack. Twice Steel watched as one of his company stamped upon the face of a wounded man in an attempt to shake him off and saw Slaughter move to help by using the wooden shaft of his halberd.

Now the French artillery had got their distance and the roundshot began to fall a short way to the front. Within seconds though the red-hot metal was tearing its way into the ranks. They must advance as the book commanded: 'As slow as foot can fall'. He knew that his men could deliver their assault at a run, but this way they would keep the equilibrium of the other battalions. To his left he saw Argyll, on foot at the head of the brigade, turning occasionally to shout encouragement and urging his officers to keep pace with him. At thirty yards out a puff of white smoke rippled along the line of the village defences and seconds later the musketballs ripped into the bodies of Steel's men, tossing them back like puppets in a dance of death. Instinctively they lowered their heads against the storm and pressed on. At the same time the French artillery on the ridge overlooking Ramillies opened up with canister shot, each projectile spraying out a deadly hail of tight-packed iron balls into the face of the oncoming infantry.

It seemed to Steel as if his whole world were collapsing; his command ebbing away in a sea of blood. He looked around and saw to his front the distant figure of the Duke of Argyll. The general was almost at the barricades now and the Grenadiers of his leading battalion, Borthwick's, Steel thought, were up with him. Close by to his left Henry Hansam was screaming obscenities towards the French lines as he pushed on towards the village. Ten yards out now and closing.

Steel cast a glance to his rear and gave the command which he hoped would be heard: 'Uncap your fuses.'

He saw Slaughter, his halberd pointing at an angle towards the enemy, yelling at the men, repeating his order and pushing them on. Looking back to his front, feet moving automatically one after another, he saw the village grow closer. The French line spat out another deadly volley but Steel remained unscathed. He heard Hansam cry out and saw him grasp his arm. He smiled at Steel, mouthed that it was only a scratch and walked on. Five yards out. Three.

This was it. Steel half-turned his head to the rear and shouted at the top of his voice: 'Halt! Blow your matches!'

The company came to a stop as the Frenchmen, seeing with horror what was about to happen, rushed through the motions of ramming home their musketballs. It was too late.

Steel smiled and shouted the final command: 'Throw . . . grenades.'

With an easy motion the company hurled their bombs in an overhead action, full-toss directly into the French line. The fuses had been cut to perfection and no sooner had the grenades landed among the tightly-packed enemy than they began to explode. Steel watched awestruck as the shards of metal casing ploughed through the French, mangling flesh and bone and sending men and parts of what had been men in all directions. Looking to the left he could see that the Grenadiers in the centre of the brigade had met with similar success. As the smoke began to clear he saw Argyll climb atop one of the barricades, sword in hand. Steel watched as the duke was struck first by one musketball, then another, but miraculously did not seem to be harmed.

'Grenadiers. With me.'

There was no time for the bayonet now and Steel's men knew it. Forgetting the slung fusils across their backs, each of them reached to his side for the short infantry sword carried for just such an assault as this. Then, baying for blood, they climbed the parapet and crashed down upon what was left of the decimated French defenders. Directly in front of him a dark-skinned French infantryman, his off-white coat covered with blood, sank to his knees and begged for his life. Steel walked past him but hardly had he passed than he heard the familiar hiss as behind him a Grenadier drew his sword up into the man's chin and through the teeth. This was no time for mercy. In his immediate vicinity most of the defenders appeared to be in flight. Ahead and slightly to the right, up a narrow street Steel could see the church and before it a mass of redcoated infantry, standing in two lines, facing him: it looked like the best part of two companies. Their coats were trimmed with yellow and above their heads floated a silken colour. A red cross on a white ground – English. As he watched, from a street to the left of the redcoats there emerged another body of men. They wore dark blue coats and Steel recognized them as Dutch. At their head he could see quite plainly now the figure of Major van Cutzem. How the devil the man had managed to reach the centre of the village before Argyll and Steel, God only knew, but there he was, code of chivalry and all. But Steel's annoyance turned to amusement as he realized that the Dutch officer's moment of glory was about to be stolen by the fact that the village had already been occupied by a regiment of English foot.

He called to Slaughter: 'Best watch this, Jacob. It would seem that our friend Major van Cutzem is a little late. He hasn't taken the village. He's been beaten to it. Now we'll see some sport.'

The sergeant peered down the street towards where the two units were standing opposite one another beside the church. His laugh turned to a gasp of horror. 'Christ almighty. It's not a bloody argument he's in for, sir. Look at that standard. They're not Englishmen, Mister Steel. Those men are Irish.'

Steel looked again at the device on the colour. He had missed something. But there was no mistaking it now. A red cross on a white ground, and there, in its centre, a gold harp. This was no St George's Cross, but the flag of an Irish regiment.

'We've got to warn him, Jacob.'

But his words were lost. It was over in an instant.

As they watched the densely-packed Irish infantry opened up against the bemused Dutch with a well-timed and precise volley. For a moment the street was obscured in white smoke. When it cleared Steel felt sick to the stomach. The Irish volley had ripped into the uncertain Dutch at such close range that hardly a musketball had not found its mark. Fully three score of the Dutch infantry lay dead and dying on the cobbles and there at their head Steel could see the unmistakable, blond-haired figure of Major van Cutzem.

Slaughter spat on the cobbles: 'Poor bugger. He can't have realized.'

'So much for bloody chivalry.'

The Irish gave out a cheer, but they did not pursue the retreating Dutch survivors. This was impressive stuff. They looked as if they meant to stand and if the allies were to secure this place, Steel knew he would have to take the fight to them.

'Tarling, Hancock, Mackay. Each of you find ten men and follow me. Sarn't Slaughter, find the others, and Mister Hansam. Tell them we have business at the church.'

With the thirty men following close behind, Steel moved quickly up the street towards the red-clad infantry, who held their fire. He could see the colour more clearly. A white ground bearing a red cross; yellow facings and a red cross – Irish Jacobites. He knew these men now: Clare's regiment. Dragoons originally, now converted to a regiment of foot. Their commander was the exiled Viscount Clare, Charles O'Brien. Steel had known O'Brien once, in what seemed now a previous life, before the Jacobites had charmed the young Irishman across to their ranks with talk of the right of kings and divine monarchy. Then they had both been younger. Two impressionable ensigns of foot, fighting the French in a place called Neerwinden where the river fed down to the sea and where King William's British army had run from the French with its tail between its legs and left six thousand men dead on the field. How far they had come since then, he thought. And what quirk of fate, he wondered, had brought Clare to face him here.

At forty yards out from the Irishmen, Steel halted the Grenadiers. There were around thirty up with him now. It was hardly a fair fight. Thirty against nigh on a hundred men. Perhaps it might be more prudent to wait for assistance. But then, Steel was not noted for his caution.

'Grenadiers, uncap your fuses.' They would do it the hard way.

Slaughter looked at him quizzically. 'Do we attack, sir?'

'What else can we do? Have the men light their bombs.'

Slaughter had barely opened his mouth to deliver the command when with a great shout, from a small street to the right, Argyll and the best part of two companies of his vengeful Scots infantry burst out and crashed into the flank of the Irishmen.

'Bugger the grenades, Sarn't.' He raised his voice. 'Unsling your fusils. Company, fix bayonets.'

The Grenadiers carefully replaced their bombs in the leather pouches and with a swift motion twisted the new-fangled socket bayonets on to the muzzles of their fusils.

'With me. Charge!'

With his own gun still slung across his back and his great sword raised high above his head, Steel began to run towards the mêlée at the end of the street. Argyll's men had come round the side and front of the Irish line and partly blocked their view of Steel, who seized the chance. Reaching the line he threw himself into the crush and connected with an ensign of Irish dragoons who extended his sword-arm and lunged

49

at Steel's chest. He parried away the cut with ease and dealt the boy a blow with the hilt of his sword which knocked him out cold and sent him to the ground.

Steel hissed at Slaughter: 'By God, Jacob. I wouldn't like to be one of Clare's men. You know Argyll believes them to be the devil's soldiers.'

He saw the duke wielding a Highland broadsword almost as heavy as his own. His face was frozen in a rictus of fury and he was chopping his way through a forest of Irishmen, severing limbs and heads as he went.

Argyll caught sight of Steel: 'Steel, by God. What luck this? A whole regiment of heathens. Papists. Heretics!' Possessed by his fervour, he ran headlong into a group of three Irish dragoons spitting one on his sword and punching another full in the face with his gloved fist before slitting his throat.

Steel looked at Slaughter and knew what was required. Both men ran to help Argyll who was now locked in a duel with the remaining dragoon and had not seen a fourth come round behind him. Steel fell upon the man and with a savage uppercut of his blade, sliced the back of his head. To his left four more dragoons appeared, intent apparently on saving their comrade engaged with Argyll. Steel could see now that the man was an officer and then recognized him as O'Brien himself. He had been a noted swordsman when they had fought under the same colours and Steel could see that he had not lost his touch. Every blow that Argyll aimed towards him, O'Brien met with an expert parry. As the dragoons hurried to rescue their commander, Steel and Slaughter turned to face them and he noticed that they had been joined by a half-dozen of the Grenadiers.

Slaughter hissed at them. 'You took your bloody time. Corporal Taylor, Mulligan, you others there, with me. The rest of you, with Captain Steel.'

Steel squared up to one of the dragoons and feinting to the left with a blow of his sword dealt him a tremendous kick in the groin which felled him to the ground. As each Grenadier found a man in turn, Steel noticed that Argyll had been joined by more of his own men, including one of his sergeants, a huge, barrel-chested brute armed with what looked like a captured cavalry sabre. He and the duke were fighting O'Brien together now yet still it seemed as if the Irishman was more than capable of beating them off. Steel cut to the right to parry a thrust from a dragoon's bayonet and on the return stroke pierced the man through the stomach. Slaughter had dispatched another of the enemy and for an instant the two men stood uncertain of who to take on next. At that moment a clatter of hooves on cobbles announced the arrival of a party of redcoated English dragoons.

At their head rode a young cornet of horse wearing a broad grin. He was shouting like an excited schoolboy. 'The field is ours. The field is ours. The French are retreating, the day is ours, my boys.'

A single shot broke against the noise of steel on steel as Slaughter, who had unslung his fusil from his back, fired into the air. With the cornet's words, it was enough. Grenadiers and Irishmen alike broke apart in their individual combats and stood at the *en-garde*, uncertain of what to do.

O'Brien disengaged from Argyll who, along with the big redcoat sergeant slowly backed away. Taking care still not to quite drop his guard, the Irishman gently raised the tip of his sword until it was pointing skywards and as the general stood motionless, his own blade still held out before him, the young Jacobite reversed his hand so that the blade now pointed directly towards the ground. Argyll watched for a moment and then, as Steel looked on, gave a barely perceptible nod towards the sergeant who, with a great lunge of the sort one might execute in a fencing salle, sprang towards O'Brien and buried his blade deep in his heart. The Irishman's soft, green eyes expressed his utter surprise, then as they glazed over, he dropped his sword, grasped at the blade in his chest and fell to the ground. Steel was lost for words. The sergeant straightened up, withdrew the long blade and turned to Argyll.

'Good work, McKellar. That's a sovereign for you.' He turned to address his regiment: 'Each one of you men shall have a sovereign for every Papist officer slain today.'

The sergeant saluted his commander with his bloody blade and walked away to discuss the good news with the men and tally their scores.

Steel turned on Argyll: 'You murdered him. Your Grace, Clare was surrendering. He was offering you his sword.'

'That man was a Papist and a traitor and he suffered for it. I told you, Steel. I fight not only for my queen and my country. I fight for a greater Britain, for a nation free from such perverse unbelievers. I fight for truth, Steel. For truth. For freedom and against superstition. If you would care to discuss the matter further, I await your pleasure.'

Turning, Argyll walked away from Steel and the others, pausing only to clean his sword blade on the white coat of a dead French soldier.

Steel watched him go in silence and looked down at the body of the Irishman. Around him the Grenadiers were taking the surrender of Clare's dragoons and he realized that the cannon seemed to have stopped firing. From beyond the town came the rolling noise of musketry and a confused cacophony which he recognized as the sound of one army in full flight and another in pursuit. It seemed that the cornet had been right. The battle was won. He shook his head, and said to no one in particular, 'If that's freedom and truth, then I want no part of it.'

He thought of his younger brother, Alexander, a Jacobite who had left the family five years back. His whereabouts were currently unknown although Steel presumed that his allegiance, like that of poor, dead Clare, lay still with the old king and the old monarchy. He thought how easily it might have been Alexander rather than O'Brien who had met his end on the sergeant's blade. He shivered and realized that one day he might meet him himself on a field of battle. He prayed that it would not be and called down a silent blessing on his brother, wherever he now was. Was it too much to hope that perhaps one day they would be reunited in a Scotland where all might be treated equally and where principle and religious bigotry did not divide families?

Slaughter was at his side. 'You're right there, sir. Though I know there's some among our own lads that'd agree with the duke.'

'I dare say there are. We're all fighting for different things, Jacob; praying to different gods. But from what I can see, sometimes there's no difference between Argyll's idea of a new world and the blind bloody hatred I thought we might have left behind when Her Majesty came to the throne.' He looked across to where the body of van Cutzem lay, among those of his men, face down in the bloody dirt. 'I met a man on this field today who believed that war could be civilized with artificial rules and politeness. I told him that he was wrong and now he's dead. And he was wrong, Jacob. The only way that we're going to make a world worth living in, apart from kicking fat King Louis off his throne, is to start realizing that all war is brutal and nasty. It's kill or be killed. The only winner is the man who gets in the first volley. Clare knew that.' He pointed after Argyll. 'And that man knows it too. But we shouldn't hate like he does. That's not war. We all have principles, our own codes of war. And we're all after glory, Jacob. All of us, you, me, Mister Hansam, Mister Williams. Glory and honour. Those are the only two things that matter in this life. Those and life itself. But we're soldiers, we're paid to take life. So they're all that we have left. Rob us of them and you make us no better than common murderers.'

Night came. As far as the eye could see around them dead bodies littered the ground. And most of them wore the white coat of France. They shone pale and motionless in the moonlight. Occasionally a heavy groan would reveal some still with a trace of life. But within minutes the scavenging peasants who roamed the battlefield had found the man and all was silent again.

The heat of the day had gradually given way to night and following orders from Lord Orkney, the regiment, with the Grenadiers in the vanguard, had pressed on in the pursuit. Their passage had been marked by a constant drumming – specific instructions from the high command to drive the enemy before them in fear. The noise had begun to irritate Steel, who was chewing on a large cud of tobacco as he rode, in a vain attempt to salve a headache. Tom Williams, his wound dressed and his arm in a sling, had rejoined them and was fired by the victory.

For miles in the wake of the retreating French army the dead and wounded lay along the road. Steel's men watched impassively as the French cried out for succour. Occasionally a kindly Grenadier would stop to give them some water. But for the most part they chose to ignore the cries. Hadn't they suffered enough themselves at the hands of the French in Ramillies? They had left too many good men back on that field to admit thoughts of compassion. Not quite yet. Besides, they had been ordered to advance immediately by their commander. Such was the haste of the enemy's flight that many had left their possessions back on the field and knew that they would not see them again.

The French army being dispersed, many regiments had separated and drifted into leaderless groups. At times, as Steel's men advanced through the darkness they would see isolated figures running ahead of them on the road, who at the sound of their approach would dart away into the open country. The French were everywhere, and yet nowhere. They were merely individual fugitives and deserters from an army that had effectively ceased to exist. The pursuit was bloody and relentless and if the British did not quite wear the countenances of murderers, then neither were they all gentlemen.

Hansam rode up to join Steel: 'It was a great victory, Jack. You may be certain that the bells will be rung in London and Lord Marlborough's health drunk throughout the land.'

Steel said nothing.

They had halted for a moment in their hurried march towards the west on a rise in the ground above the village of Meldert, near on fifteen miles from the battlefield. Now the day was breaking about them. But this morning the dawn mingled with another glow which the company watched with interest and curiosity. It came from the northwest from the direction of the town of Louvain, a key crossing-place on the defence line of the River Dyle, which lay some seven miles off. While most of the men were puzzled at its source, offering a variety of opinions, Steel was in no doubt. He had seen similar sights too many times before.

Hansam too saw the glow: 'Fires, Jack? Have the French reformed, d'you think?'

Williams was standing beside them now: 'What d'you suppose it is, sir? Another battle? Have our cavalry caught up with the French rearguard?'

Steel shook his head. 'No, Tom. The French haven't the stomach for another fight just yet. And our cavalry as I hear, are too far to the south. No, that is the sign of an army that has given up the fight. The French are burning their supplies lest they should fall into our hands. That's the funeral pyre of Villeroi's army.'

Slaughter and two of the men, Mackay and Cussiter were standing watching the glow as they shared a piece of dried sausage one of them had found in a Frenchman's haversack. Cussiter spoke as he chewed: 'Did you see them surrendering? They just laid down their arms like so many fat poltroons and gave themselves up to us. Call themselves soldiers, indeed.'

Mackay nodded: 'Did you see 'em, Sarge? I couldn't see nothing but the seats of their breeches.'

Slaughter shook his head: 'You'd best make what you can of it for now. You can be sure you'll see more of them just as soon as King Louis can send them back. The French ain't finished yet.'

Cussiter spat into the fire: 'It was the cavalry that decided it, weren't it, Sarge. Never seen such horses. Crashed into the French like a blade goin' through the corn.' He gesticulated with his hand, as if to sever Mackay's head.

Mackay backed away and laughed: 'Cavalry or whoever it might 'a been, it was the general as won that battle an' that's the truth. It was Marlborough. Our own good Corporal John.'

Now Slaughter spat at the fire, making it hiss as the fatty gristle hit the flames. ''Tweren't cavalry. 'Tweren't even Marlborough, though he's as good a general as ever I served under. What won that battle was the men. Plain and simple, lads. 'Twere you and me won that battle and don't you ever bloody forget it.'

*   *   *

Steel, dismounted now, wandered among the men, nodding greetings to those he recognized in the gloom. He scratched at the filthy rag wrapped around his neck and dreamed of a bath. At least as the victors there were such pleasures to look forward to. They would advance, he presumed, to Brussels. It seemed the clear objective. Where after that though, he wondered?

He found Slaughter standing on his own, staring into the embers. 'So, Jacob, tell me where you think we're bound after this great day?'

'Well, sir. If I were the great duke his self, I would want to catch the rest of the Frenchies. So I would make for Brussels and by that cut them off.'

'By God Jacob, we'll make a general of you yet.' He saw Williams: 'D'you hear that Tom? General His Grace the Duke of Slaughter here would have us march on Brussels and catch the enemy running for home.'

Williams laughed. 'That would be a fine thing, sir.'

Slaughter grinned: 'Thank you indeed, sir. But I think I'll stick to being a sergeant and let His Grace make the decisions.

'Nevertheless, I think you may be right, Sarn't. But I also believe that Marlborough intends us to push the French from the Netherlands once and for all and to do that he will have to take the remaining forts. Everything from Malines and Ghent to Bruges, Oudenarde and Antwerp. They will be our next objectives.'

'Not more 'sieging, sir?'

'I believe so. And I know how you enjoy it, Jacob.'

Slaughter spat into the flames. The Grenadiers that could hear him laughed. Brave as he was in battle, the sergeant was known for his enjoyment of home comforts and in particular, on the right occasion and with due propriety, of pretty women. And if there was one thing he was unlikely to find in the siege lines around a fortress it was a willing harlot. And then there was the question of his extreme dislike of enclosed, dark spaces, and there were always enough of those in a siege. It was the reason he had joined up in the first place, to be away from what life he might have had in the new coal mines around his native Durham. Slaughter cursed and spat again.

Steel, gazing into the fire, could not help but recall the words of Colonel Hawkins in Ramillies: 'I shall have need of you ere long.' But how long, he wondered, would that be?

Had he only known it he could have had that answer quicker than he thought. For barely four hours later, less than half a mile away from Steel, close to the village of Meldert, a man was waking up with a mind filled with such thoughts. Having spent the night wrapped in his cloak by the roadside, James Hawkins was attempting to drink a cup of coffee. Attempting, because his servant, Jagger, had sworn to him that it was real coffee and he did not wish to hurt his feelings. But to Hawkins it smelt more like the swillings of a Flemish alehouse. Still, it was something, more than was to be had by most. Orkney, he knew, had not eaten for a day and perhaps Marlborough too. He had not woken in the brightest of spirits. But with the recollection of how complete their victory had been his aches and tiredness had gone. Now, as he drank, his mind raced with the prospect in hand. They must surely exploit this initiative over the French, but subtly and with no little care. Looking about him through the dawn, he saw a few yards off the distinctive figure of Marlborough, together with a few servants and several of the general staff. Hawkins handed the half-empty cup to Jagger and then, seeing how crestfallen the poor wretch looked, decided to keep the brew and went to join them.

Adam Cardonnel, Marlborough's personal secretary, was speaking animatedly and waving a piece of paper. 'Everything is yours, Your Grace. We have taken eighty standards; fifty cannon, tents, baggage, the food still hot together with muskets without number and prisoners by the score. Lord Hay's dragoons alone have captured two entire battalions of French foot. The Walloons are coming over to us by the hour. We are hard pressed to keep them safe, My Lord. The Danes would have revenge upon them for their treatment in Italy last month.'

From the duke's left Cadogan spoke up, quietly: 'By my reckoning, sir, the French have lost near on thirteen thousand men, but some put it at near double that number, if we include the deserters and turncoats.'

Cardonnel spoke again: 'My Lord, we have even taken their famous negro kettle drummer of the Bavarian Horse Guards. Have I your permission to dispatch the man to the queen in London, sir? He would make her an elegant servant and a true prize.'

Marlborough smiled and nodded: 'Indeed, Adam. Send the blackamoor to the queen. That was a fine thought. Though in truth, I'd have liked to keep him as one of my own servants.'

The company laughed, glad of the lightness at last in the duke's voice. Like Hawkins, Marlborough had passed a restless night, having had only his cloak for a cover. He had slept badly and for company in his rustic bed had had only the tiresomely enthusiastic and over-opinionated van Goslinga who punctuated the night with anecdotes of the battle. Happily though, one of the footmen had found some chocolate in the French generals' supplies and Marlborough now cradled the hot, richly aromatic liquid in the silver-mounted cup made from a coconut which he always carried in his personal baggage. As the laughter subsided, Cadogan spoke again.

'Our own losses are light, Your Grace. Two colonels only killed and two score other officers and but a thousand men dead in all. It is a triumph. They will praise you throughout the realm, Your Grace. Your enemies in London had thought that the only news they would hear these few months would be from My Lord Peterborough in Spain. But now you have proved them wrong once again.'

Marlborough smiled and took a sip of chocolate, which he had not offered to any of his generals. They did not expect it, such was his reputation for parsimony. For, if Marlborough was renowned for his care in his treatment of the soldiery he took equal pains to keep certain things purely to himself.

Hawkins sipped again at his own acrid brew and winced and looked with envy at the steaming cup in the commander-in-chief's hands.

Marlborough put it down and spoke: 'My Lord Peterborough may indeed prosper in his Spanish campaign, for it is there that his friends the Tories believe this war is to be won. But we know better, gentlemen. We know that if we beat the French here, in Flanders, then we shall send a shock through that misguided nation deeper than anything Peterborough may achieve. Perhaps now those in London will do as I ask and replace him with Lord Galway.' He picked up the cup, took another sip and continued: 'Their losses are not as great as they were after Blenheim, gentlemen. But I fancy that the effect is ten times as tumultuous.'

He looked at each of them in turn. 'But what now? Eh? What will the Sun King send against me now I wonder? We have the summer ahead of us and a campaign to conduct, at our leisure. We must make best use of that which God has provided.'

A grunt from behind the duke made him turn. Lord Orkney

stood with his arms folded. He was shaking his head. 'The French are fools, Marlborough. What have they done? They have retreated behind the Dyle and then abandoned that position where they might have held us at bay.'

Marlborough looked at him, blank-faced. 'The French, My Lord Orkney, are no longer an army. They do have a line of defence, but they have nothing with which to defend it. Marshal Villeroi is beaten. We have but one objective. Now we must drive deep into the area of fortresses still held by the French and keep what army they may assemble from out-marching our flank and making the sea. God save us if they should, even in their parlous state, see our weakness there and flank us. We should be cut off from our only supply route with England. It is absolutely imperative that we isolate and if necessary besiege the port of Antwerp. But first we must take Ghent and Oudenarde.'

Cadogan interjected: 'And Ostend and Dunkirk also, Your Grace, d'you not think? Do not forget those ports. They harbour privateers in French employ. Neglect them and whatever port we use for our supplies will be harried and taken. Believe me sir. I have direct experience.'

Marlborough laughed: 'Yes, William. I am aware of your run-in with the privateers. But at least they let you away with your life. We shall have to see how it goes before we begin to besiege a port.' The company laughed. All save van Goslinga who, not understanding the good-natured jibe, stared blankly.

Marlborough too was staring now, into the middle-distance. He set his chin in his hand and after a while spoke again. 'William, I do believe that you are right.'

Orkney spoke up: 'We'll need the best of the army for that, Your Grace. Lord Argyll and his finest. And Lord Mordaunt too.'

At last Hawkins spoke his mind: 'We'll need more than good tactical officers, sir. If we are to take Ostend and Dunkirk against privateers we will need guile and stealth by the measure. Might I suggest one more officer whom we might find most useful?'

Marlborough looked intrigued: 'Hmm? Yes, James?'

'Captain Steel, Your Grace. That is, acting Captain Steel. Of Sir James Farquharson's regiment. You will remember him from Blenheim, sir. He carried out a . . . most delicate task for us. You promoted him brevet rank. His elevation is not yet ratified.'

'Indeed, Hawkins? Not yet? Of course, Captain Steel. By all means. Why did not I think of him sooner? Yes. He has wit as well as bravery, as I recollect. We shall as you say need every bit of guile we can muster. I hazard that in the taking of these places we shall not be dealing with your ordinary enemy. Privateers, mercenaries, and who will the French leave to command them, d'you think? You can be sure that Marshal Villeroi will have taken the cream of his own officers hobbling back to Versailles to plead their case to King Louis. No, we shall be dealing with the dregs. Passed-over officers left in charge of seemingly impregnable fortresses. Well, we shall show them that they are not so impregnable, eh, gentlemen? And now, if you would, allow me a moment. My head aches and I must write the news of our victory to the queen. William, take yourself off after the cavalry and ensure that the pursuit continues. My Lord Orkney, pray do the same with the foot. Force the march if you will. We must press them hard and take the Dyle by tonight. We cannot afford to rest. You know that the fate of all Europe hangs in the balance.'

FOUR

Steel stood quite still in the middle of the street and gazed at the windows of the houses up ahead. The single shot had come from somewhere in there, ringing out clear and long against this cool May morning, shocking the company to an abrupt halt. Behind him the men crouched apprehensively, eyes darting around. They were entering Wippendries, a small village a few miles north of Brussels.

'See where it came from, Sarn't?'

'Couldn't say for certain, sir. Third house on the left at a guess.'

There was an uproar at the rear of the column: 'Shit!'

'Quiet, that man there!'

'But Sarge. The bullet went through my bloody hat. Ruined it. Look.'

It was Tarling. The musketball had indeed hit his tall Grenadier's mitre cap, obliterating the white embroidered thistle in the centre and leaving a scorched hole trimmed with filigree fragments of gold wire.

Slaughter stared at the punctured hat: 'Well, you're bloody lucky it didn't go through your brain then, Tarling, aren't you.'

Steel spoke: 'Sarn't, you and four men, come with me. The rest of you stay with Lieutenant Hansam. And keep your bloody heads down.' As he spoke another shot cracked out, the ball whizzing past Steel's ear. 'Christ. That was a bit close. Taylor, Cussiter, Mackay, come on. With me. Fix bayonets, and leave your hats behind.'

Moving fast and keeping low the four men moved along the left side of the street. Another shot rang out, ricocheting off the cobbles and glancing up at one of the houses. They paused. Slaughter tucked in close beside Steel: 'They're lousy shots, sir. Don't you think?'

'Probably conscripts. Though if that's the case then why the hell are they bothering to shoot at us and not legging it back to Paris?'

'Perhaps they don't really want to hit us. Just scare us off.'

'Don't be ridiculous. Why would they do that? What have they got to gain? This bloody village? The French army's gone home. We're chasing them back to Paris.'

It was two days now since the battle and in all that time Steel and his men, like the rest of the army, had hardly been allowed to rest. Marlborough intended to push the French back as far as they would go and their orders were to advance in forced marches to the northwest until otherwise instructed. Slaughter ducked instinctively as another musketball sang high over their heads.

'Perhaps that's it, sir. Perhaps they're not even soldiers at all, just civilians. Scared, like.'

The ball that had missed Slaughter and Steel hit the cobbles behind them and sent shards of stone up into the calf of Private Mackay who screamed and clutched at his bleeding leg.

Steel raised his eyes: 'There now. Are you satisfied? You and your damned theories. What does it matter who they are? They're bloody shooting at us, Jacob.' He unslung the fusil from his back and, knowing it to be loaded already, cocked the hammer. 'Mackay, stay there. The rest of you come with me. Second house along. Through the door. Charge!'

As the musket discharged again above their heads the Grenadiers kicked at the door of the house and it gave way. Inside the darkness took them by surprise. The shutters were closed and there was no other light source.

Steel shouted: 'Open a window!'

Tarling obliged and they moved through the interior quickly as Steel had taught them, one man moving to every opening, waiting and listening before getting into the rooms. One by one they called out:

'Nothing, sir.'

'No one here, sir.'

'Upstairs then. Look out.'

From the top of the wooden stairs there was a crack of musketry and a flash of flame as the gun fired again. Aimed at Steel, the bullet flew hopelessly wide of the mark and embedded itself in the far wall of the hall.

He called out: 'Now!'

Together Steel and Slaughter rushed the stairs and threw themselves on the figure at the top. It was hard to see anything in the shuttered house.

'Get him downstairs, Sarn't. I want this one alive.'

They half-pushed, half-dragged the sniper down the wooden staircase and threw him to the floor, where he lay motionless and whimpering, covered by the bayonets of Cussiter and Tarling. He was slightly built and dressed in pale buff-coloured breeches and a nondescript waistcoat.

Slaughter smiled: 'What did I say, sir? Civilians.'

Steel yelled: 'On your feet!'

The figure did not move. But they could hear his soft sobbing now. Steel bent down and turned him over. 'It's a boy. No more than a lad. Can't be more than ten. No wonder he couldn't hit us.' Pulling the boy to his feet he waved away the bayonets and turned to the would-be assassin. 'You idiot. What did you think you were doing? We could have killed you.' The boy looked at him, not understanding the foreign tongue. Steel gave up. 'Bloody hell, Jacob. We're looking after children now.'

With Slaughter carrying the boy's antiquated and inaccurate fowling piece, they moved to the door and pulled it open to the blinding brightness of the day.

But it was not the light that stopped them in their tracks. Steel found himself staring down the barrel of a gun. It was never a pleasant experience, in particular when as now the man with his finger on the trigger was clearly very angry. He was some inches shorter than Steel and was dressed in a brown woollen coat and a tattered round-brimmed hat. Behind him stood another two dozen men, similarly armed and all in civilian dress. The man addressed Steel in a guttural Flemish that he did not understand.

'I'm sorry. I don't speak your language.'

The man tried again and pressed the musket unpleasantly close to Steel's face. Steel, unable to take his eyes off the weapon, whispered to Slaughter, 'Any sign of the rest of the company?'

'End of the street, sir. Formed in two lines. Facing this way.'

Steel tried the man again: 'I don't know who you are but I am a British officer and those are my men at the end of the street. If you shoot me forty muskets will bring you down.' The man looked puzzled and spoke again, this time in French. This was better.

'They think we're French, sir.'

66

'Yes Sarn't. I can see that.'

'Mijnheer, we are British, not French. We mean you no harm. We have beaten the French in a big battle.'

The man looked suspicious. 'English?'

'Yes, English. Friends. Please . . .'

The man smiled and backed off, but still did not lower the gun. Without moving his eyes from Steel's, he spoke again and pointed at his chest: 'Jan.'

From the rear of the group another man pushed forward. 'You are Englishmen?'

'Yes. We are British. Scots. Ecossais. Thank God, you speak English.'

'Yes, I speak good English. You will not harm us?'

'No. We have beaten the French in a great battle. We are pushing them out of your country.'

The man thought about Steel's reply, then smiled and nodded. 'Then you are welcome, sir. I am sorry. My people are nervous. We have seen so much horror here. Too many soldiers. French soldiers. Yesterday they came again. Many were injured. Some died. And some of them took our food. They killed two men who tried to stop them.'

French deserters. Steel knew what would happen now. He'd seen enough of this before. In Russia, Bavaria, Spain, and here in Flanders. Break an army, rob it of cohesion and officers and what were you left with? Nothing more than a rabble, and a murderous, rapacious rabble at that, devoid of any principles or morals. There was nothing more dangerous in this world than a leaderless army.

The taller villager spoke to the man with the gun and at last it was lowered. Steel smiled and nodded in thanks.

'You have beaten the French? Yes, we heard. The French are beaten. But you see we still cannot believe it. Any men with guns. I'm sorry. We are very happy. For many years we have had French soldiers here. We are ruled by the Spanish and their French friends. Your battle will bring us freedom. We thank you for that, sir.'

As the man spoke, another villager had been translating and Steel saw that the entire group of men was smiling now.

'Sarn't. Have the company stand down. I don't think we need worry.'

'You are welcome, Captain. Please excuse us. We are peasants and to us many soldiers look the same. We have to be careful. But look, we have armed ourselves. And,' he added proudly, 'I am an officer. Like you.'

He smiled, his face full of hope, and Steel, humouring him, responded with a respectful nod. 'Well your men have no need to worry about the French any more. They are beaten. They won't be back quickly. Where are we exactly?'

'You are in Wippendries. We are only a small village, but you are welcome to share what we have.'

Steel surveyed the militia, took in their assortment of weapons and their ages. A single platoon of French regulars would have accounted for the lot of them in five minutes. But clearly, they had spirit and Steel knew that sometimes, on the battlefield, that could mean the difference between life and death for any troops – farmhands and guardsmen included.

The man spoke again: 'You are welcome to stay in our village, Captain. We would be honoured. Perhaps we can make up for shooting at you.'

Steel laughed. 'Perhaps. Don't give it another thought.'

You silly bugger, he thought. You don't know how close you and your bunch of brave, stupid yokels came to death. If that shot had hit Tarling instead of his cap, we'd have had you quicker than any French bastards.

'We'll stay the night if we may. It will be a good chance

for a rest. We've been forcing the march to catch the French.'

'That is good to hear, Captain. We hate the French. For too long they have been our masters here. Like you, if we see any French, we kill them.'

While ordinarily Steel would have agreed, he found himself thinking again of Argyll's outburst in Ramillies and couldn't help but wonder that there was so much hatred in this campaign, of a sort he had not seen these past seven years. Not since the bloody carnage in the north when he had watched with horribly detached interest as the Swedes and Russians had bled each other dry. This was a new and unexpected twist to the war. He knew that the French had been an occupying power here in the Netherlands, but till now he had not been aware of just how much they had been resented. He should have been cheered, he knew, by the news that the Belgians were his allies, but instinctively, something told him that this was going to complicate the conduct of the campaign. And Steel did not like complications – especially when they involved civilians.

Some six miles to the southwest, similar local hospitality was being extended to another allied soldier, albeit on a grander scale. The Duke of Marlborough stood, surrounded by his immediate military family and a small bodyguard of dragoons in the great hall of the ancient Château de Beaulieu, five miles north of Brussels. Despite the lavish reception which had been laid on in his honour, the commander-in-chief was not happy.

'I should not be here, William. This is not a general's work and I am no politician. My place is out in the field, chasing the French, following up our victory. We cannot be complacent.'

William Cadogan, quartermaster-general, laid a friendly hand upon the duke's shoulder. 'Your Grace, you must be patient. The French this day have quit the capital. We shall enter Brussels tomorrow. We should rejoice. But before we can possess the city we have pressing business here. It is an affair of state and you are the de facto representative of Her Majesty. It is your duty.'

Marlborough sighed and rubbed at his temples. 'Yes, yes. I know. How my head does ache so. I have written to the duchess about it. I hope for a cure – the queen too. They suggest . . .'

Hawkins interjected: 'I am sorry, Your Grace, but Cadogan is right. You must attend. You are rightly perceived as the victor and these men would laud you as a conqueror, as the liberator of their country. It falls to you, like it or not, to meet with these politicians. All are gathered here. The magistrates have come from Brussels together with the Estates of Brabant. Not only this, My Lord, but the entire Spanish government here in the Netherlands have declared against Louis and pledged themselves to Charles III, our candidate for the throne of Spain. The fate of Europe is in your hands. You must now treat with them. Now, your Grace.'

Marlborough glared at him with steely green eyes. 'Oh, James. I do so wish you were not always so very right.'

Van Goslinga had re-entered the great hall now and smiled insipidly at the duke. Marlborough hissed, under his breath: 'That man again. That odious little man.'

Not hearing the comment, the Dutch liaison officer smiled ingratiatingly. 'Your Grace, the deputies and magistrates would meet with you now, if you please.'

Together, Hawkins, Marlborough and Cadogan were shown through into the grand salon of the castle. The painted and gilded walls were hung with vividly coloured Brussels tapestries depicting scenes of courtly life in the Middle Ages and portraits of the Dukes of Brabant. In the centre of the room stood a long table and around it sat some twenty middle-aged and elderly men in full wigs. Hawkins noticed that, while those on the right had the pale complexion of northerners, those seated to the left were more swarthy and sported moustaches. All were dressed in sombre black coats. It looked to the duke and Hawkins something like a meeting of physicians, but where in the centre of the table there should have been a cadaver ready for dissection there lay sheaves of paper and charters sealed with red wax and on top of them the swords of the deputies and the Spanish officials, their hilts pointing deliberately in the direction of the victorious British general.

As Marlborough entered the men rose as one and made low bows over the table. The duke returned their greeting. The man nearest to him, a short, pale Dutchman with a small white goatee beard, spoke in mannered English.

'We are a proud people, Your Grace. For four hundred years we have resisted French tyranny. For two hundred years we have been ruled by the Hapsburgs. Since 1515 by the Spanish. Under Spain our people were massacred for their refusal to accept the Catholic doctrine. We fought them for eighty years, until 1648. For the last thirty years we have been fighting against the French King Louis. The French bombarded our city of Brussels for three days in 1695. They reduced it to nothing – only the town hall survived. But from the ashes we have built the city you see today. We are survivors, My Lord Duke, and with your help we have thrown off the yoke of French rule. We pledge allegiance now to Charles III and ask you to acknowledge a new united Belgian state.'

Marlborough bowed. 'Thank you, mijnheer. I am a general, not a statesman. But I will accept your declaration and communicate it to my queen in England. I am aware of your country's long agony under King Louis. I believe that our late victory has truly brought that to an end. I assure you that there will not be the least change in regard to religion. I intend to recall the ancient charter well known as the "Joyous Entry of Brabant". I assure you that my men will be kept in firm control. They will not plunder or devastate your land or take your goods and they will pay due respect to your people. If they do not then they shall suffer for it. Any man – be he common soldier or officer – found stealing so much as a cherry from one of your orchards shall pay with his life. It will be death without mercy, gentlemen. Although I trust that I know my men well enough to say that I shall not need to implement such a penalty.'

As one the deputies, magistrates and Spaniards rose to their feet and applauded Marlborough.

The Duke smiled and as he did so inclined his head to the side in a whisper: 'I pray to God, Hawkins, that we can stay true to our word.'

'Oh, you need have no fear of that, sir. The men'll do whatever you desire them to. The punishment is only for show. They wouldn't dare.'

Steel leaned against the wall of the house and, gazing into the farmyard, watched the man, Baynes, a wily country boy from the Scottish borders, near the town of Jedburgh. He was wrestling with two wiry yellow legs, attempting to avoid the claws as he manoeuvred them into his haversack.

Unaware that he was being observed, Baynes was muttering half to himself and half to the chicken which, still alive, he was determined to conceal. 'C'mon you little bugger. One more push. Just one wee heave and in you go. Get your bloody head in there.' The bird, its head covered by cloth, panicked and nipped the Grenadier on the forefinger.

'Ow! Ye little bugger, I'll give you something to nip about. I was only going to eat yer legs but now I'll boil the lot of you. Get in there will you.'

'Having trouble, Baynes?'

The man froze and slowly turned towards Steel: 'Ah. Yes. I can explain, sir. It was fair game, sir. I just found her walking about. And you yourself, sir, heard the good man telling us that we were to share anything in the village.'

Steel raised his eyebrows. 'So you, Baynes, being a kindly sort of a man, thought, "Now wouldn't that be a fine mascot for the regiment? I'll just take her to Colonel Farquharson and the adjutant and save her from the pot." Am I right?'

'How you do it sir, I don't know. Quite right, Captain Steel, sir. Right you are again.'

'By rights, I should have you hanged, Baynes. In Bavaria you would most certainly have been hanged. There the duke decreed that anyone found stealing anything would be subject to punishment by death.'

Baynes was shaking now. 'Stealing? me, sir? No sir. Not stealing. Not me.'

'Yes, Baynes. Stealing . . . Now put the bloody chicken back where you found it and we'll say no more. Now get back to the company and wait. And don't worry – I'll find you some rations.'

Three hours later, his belly full of roast chicken, Steel was awoken by a cry and then another. No light pierced the pitch-black of the night, but he did not need to see to know that something was not right. Reaching for his sword, he leapt to his feet and not bothering with his coat, despite the cold of the night, buckled the belt around his shirt.

'Sarn't?' He sensed, rather than saw in the darkness, Slaughter's large frame at his side.

'Came from over there, sir. Edge of the village.'

Another cry. Higher in tone now and unmistakable as that of a man in agony.

'Come on. Alarm. Company to arms!'

Around him in the darkness the Grenadiers began to rise and fumbled for their weapons. Quickly, as another cry rent the air, Steel and Slaughter, followed by the night-watch picquet, made their way through the silent streets towards it.

They turned down a narrow alley and emerged in a small square on the edge of the village. In the centre stood a cherry tree and around it were gathered some twenty of the village militia. All were armed, some with captured French-pattern muskets, but most with swords or knives. For a moment they seemed not to have noticed Steel and his men. And when they did, they smiled and nodded. Jan, their self-appointed officer walked forward. In his hand he held a short knife.

'Ah, Captain Steel. Welcome. I am sorry that we did not invite you to our evening entertainment. I thought that your men were too tired. And we did not know we would have such sport tonight.'

Steel felt no offence at their lack of hospitality. This was not the sort of sport he cared for. Tied to the tree was a man in the uniform of a French officer. Another man was standing behind him, held fast by two villagers. The faces of both men were frozen in terror and Steel could see why. Beneath the flickering torchlight he counted six dead bodies lying sprawled on the cobbles. They too wore white uniforms and were covered in blood. None of the dead seemed to have had any weapons and the two officers had long since lost their swords. Clearly this was a party of lost and desperate Frenchmen who, looking for food, had had the misfortune to stumble into Wippendries. It had been a fatal mistake. From the positions of the bodies, the cuts they bore and the agonized expressions etched deep into the visible faces, he could see that this had been no struggle, but a careful massacre.

Jan jerked his thumb back to the French officer who, Steel now saw, bore bloody cuts on his arms and legs. 'He makes too much noise,' he laughed. 'So now we are going to cut out his tongue. Then perhaps we will take his sight. Who knows?'

He moved towards the French officer, who stared at Steel with terrified eyes and muttered protests. Jan grabbed the back of the Frenchman's head with his left hand to hold it still, while his right came up with the gleaming butcher's blade.

Steel moved. He switched his sword from the right hand to the left and, taking a step forward, pulled Jan round to face him and landed a punch squarely on his jaw, knocking him to the ground. Another of the militia turned to attack him but Slaughter was there first. He jabbed the butt of his musket into the second man's stomach, winding him and knocking him to his knees before following up with a swift swipe to the head which laid him senseless. One of the villagers raised a musket and fired. The ball struck one of the Grenadiers on the coat, passing harmlessly through the tail. Two more of the Dutchmen rushed towards the redcoats and overpowered Tarling who was thrown to the ground. One of the villagers raised his hand to strike with a shining cleaver but Cussiter had seen it and felled him with a shot that hit him in the temple. The other man sprang away and as Tarling struggled to his feet, Steel waved his men forward.

'Grenadiers. To me.'

From behind him Slaughter and fifteen redcoats moved across the square and in one movement levelled their muskets, bayonets fixed, directly at the mob.

'Drop your weapons! Oh Christ, you don't bloody understand.'

He signed to them and one by one the men let their swords and muskets clatter to the ground. Jan was getting to his feet now, rubbing his jaw. He turned on Steel.

'My God! What are you doing? Don't you hate the French?'

'What was I doing? You ask me? You're no officer. You're a bunch of barbarians.'

'No, it is they who are the barbarians. They steal from us and rape our women. Well now its our turn.'

Steel shook his head and turned to Williams who had arrived with another ten men. 'And there I was, Tom, threatening to hang Baynes for stealing a chicken – from these vermin. I don't care how hard their lives have been under the French, they can't do this. These men are French soldiers, officers too. They have nothing to do with the government. They're a retreating army. And they're hungry. There are rules, articles of war. Cut him loose, poor bugger.' He turned back to Jan. 'If you wore a uniform I'd bloody well put you on trial. Or better still hang you right here for what you've done.'

The villager, still holding his jaw, shook his head. 'You do not know what it is like. Your people have not suffered like mine. Believe me, Captain, I am not alone. All over Brabant this is happening. Right now. And you cannot stop us.'

Steel looked at Slaughter: 'Take their weapons, Sarn't, and lock them up for the night.' He looked about and spotted a grain store at the entrance to the village. 'There. That'll do. And post sentries. I don't want my throat cut. We'll bury these poor bastards in the morning.' He motioned to Jan: 'And don't forget this one. Tom, you escort your fellow officer. Keep an eye on him.'

As the Grenadiers began to herd the villagers to their makeshift jail, Steel walked over to the wounded French officer, who had been cut free and was inspecting his wounds. 'Are you badly hurt?'

'They're not deep. They were only playing with me. The real stuff hadn't begun.' He shuddered. 'I don't know how to thank you, Captain.' He bowed to Steel: 'Chef de Bataillon Jean D'Alembord at your service. I am in your debt, sir.'

'You fought at Ramillies?'

'Indeed. I have the honour to command in the Regiment du Roi.'

'You were routed by our dragoons.'

D'Alembord shrugged. 'And now, to our disgrace, our great army is no more. I do not even know where the rest of my regiment may be.'

'I am sure that you will find them in time. In France perhaps. For the present though, you are my prisoner, Commandant. I trust that we can agree on your parole?'

There was a noise from behind them, hooves and a clatter of hobnailed shoes ringing on the cobbles. Steel called across the square: 'Alarm. Grenadiers. To me.'

A score of his men came running from the prisoners and reached him while the newcomers were still hidden in the shadows of the street. Steel heard them before he saw their faces or their coats.

'Hold, there!'

The voice was English and he recognized it instantly. Into the square rode the Duke of Argyll, followed on foot by his sergeant, a young captain and a half-company of Scots infantry. Argyll galloped hard across the square, his sword drawn, straight for Steel. 'Hold hard, sir. Who are you?' He checked his impetus and pulled hard on the horse's reins. 'Why, it's Captain Steel.'

His surprise turned to astonishment as he surveyed the scene. Saw the dead French infantry, the ground awash with their blood. He grinned at Steel. 'By God, sir. You have done well. Six dead and two more to go? You surprise me, Steel. I had taken you for a weaker man.'

He turned to the sergeant who had followed up with the rest of the redcoats. 'You see, McKellar. You must not judge a man by first appearances. Well done, sir.'

Steel shook his head: 'You mistake me, My Lord. I am not the author of this murder. This is the work of the village militia. It is torture, sir. No more than torture and murder, done in cold blood. If we had not come upon them when we did the commandant here and his lieutenant would have also suffered horribly.'

Argyll's grin fell away. 'Torture? Murder? By God, sir. I was not mistaken then. You are a friend of the French.'

Slaughter had arrived back from the barn and, seeing Argyll, snapped to attention next to Steel. 'That's all the men locked away, sir. Under guard. Their officer too, sir.'

Argyll squinted: 'What? Who's locked away? What officer?'

Slaughter turned directly to the question: 'Why the village militia, Your Honour. Them that did this. We have them under guard, sir.'

'Then you will damn well remove your guard, sergeant. Forthwith.'

Slaughter smiled: 'Now that, Your Honour, I cannot do as Captain Steel himself has ordered me to place them under guard.'

Argyll, his face puce, turned to Steel: 'Captain Steel, I will not have this rank insubordination in my brigade. Place this man on a charge and then see to the release of your prisoners. My God man, they're on our side!'

Steel coughed: 'I don't think that either course of action would be wise, sir.'

'Wise? Not wise? I gave you an order. What are you saying?'

'Not wise, sir, firstly because my sergeant has done nothing wrong. Secondly because we are no longer brigaded under your command. And thirdly because the men I have under guard do not make war as it should be made, but as barbarians.'

Argyll clenched the reins in his fists: 'Then it is you, sir, who should be on a charge. I'll have you court-martialled, sir, damn you.' He paused, and attempted to regain his composure. 'Captain Steel, I must confess, I do not know you. I do not know you at all. I am given to understand that you are a hero. You gained promotion at Blenheim. You fought alongside me at Ramillies. So how can you grant parole to these men? You must know that we cannot trust them.'

Hansam, having arrived with the remainder of the company, had been watching the proceedings and now spoke. 'Do you not consider, My Lord that perhaps my Lord Marlborough will extend them parole?'

Argyll turned on him: 'It is not my place or yours lieutenant to conjecture what Marlborough would or would not do. Parole? What good is parole if they should come in again and fight against us next month or next week? I have no time for parole. Any Frenchman, officer or 'listed man, taken in the field will die. He will die. I offer no quarter. Nor do I expect to receive it.'

Steel spoke up: 'Nevertheless, My Lord. We must obey the articles of war. These men have asked me for quarter and I intend to grant it. To do otherwise would be bloody murder.'

Argyll surveyed the situation. Steel, his sergeant and another officer now stood between him and the two Frenchmen. Beyond them stood more than thirty Grenadiers, the finest soldiers in the army. For his part he had his sergeant, a junior officer and an unreliable half-company of dubious ability or inclination. A sound tactician, he sensed that it was time to retreat. But not without a final, verbal salvo.

'Mark me, Mister Steel. For I shall certainly mark you, should I ever have the chance. This is the second occasion on which you have dared to challenge my judgement and I am not a man to be challenged. Nor am I a man to be bettered, by God.' He turned to the column. 'Sergeant McKellar, we march on Brussels.'

They watched him go. Hansam sighed: 'Jack. I swear I do not know how you manage it. You make more enemies of your own side than you do of the French. He is a brigade commander.'

Slaughter scratched at his stubble and spoke, quietly. 'And there was me thinking that once we'd beat the French, we'd have a nice, quiet summer.'

Steel clapped him on the back. 'Really, Jacob? You know me better than that. And I know that you were never a man for the quiet life. I think that we might move the billets over here. And you had better post a full guard. I intend to get some rest, and both of you should try to do so too. Remember, we've a people to liberate tomorrow.'

FIVE

Steel rode at the head of the company, keeping the little bay mare at a steady pace up the wide cobbled street. While being careful to keep his face firmly to the front, he was aware that on either side of him, from the open windows of their red brick or half-timbered houses, the people of the Upper Town of Brussels, men and women of all ranks and ages, craned their necks to catch a glimpse of the great army that it seemed had so transformed their country. Fathers balanced babies on their shoulders and women blew kisses at the unshaven, dirt-spattered redcoats who tramped the stones and the lace-bedecked officers who rode at their head. It was Friday 28 May. A mere five days after the battle which had so swiftly propelled the French from the Netherlands, and Steel's Grenadiers marched proudly at the head of Farquharson's regiment, in the centre of one of the longest processions of soldiers which the population of this great city had ever seen. Flowers rained down upon the heads of the troops, some of whom stooped down mid-pace to pick them from the ground and tucked them into their coats until the army began to look as if it were part of some great pagan festival.

In a sense it was. Marlborough had been given the freedom of the city by the Estates of Brabant and, having for four days pushed his men on in pursuit of the French, was now of the opinion that they needed and deserved a rest. The news had spread quickly and the taverns and bordellos of the city lay open for business. Their proprietors knew what the soldiers wanted, for in this part of Europe, this ill-fated avenue of blood, every major town had long ago become used to the needs of a conquering army. One look at the men who now entered its streets was enough to tell every publican and madam that just as soon as the pomp and formality were ended, they were, all of them, going to do a roaring trade.

Steel looked from side to side, acknowledging the shouts and salutes. They passed out of the street, turning right past a towering Gothic church. They were moving steadily downhill and ahead of them the street opened out into a wide, elegant square. Passing a tavern, Steel saw that its door was guarded by one of the biggest men he had ever seen, a civilian, but a man who would certainly not have looked out of place in the ranks of the Grenadiers. He noticed that the same was true of every one of the inns which lay around the square and knew that, for all their weariness of battle, few of the soldiers in this army would pass a peaceful night. If there was any sight uglier than an army without leaders, there was nothing as unruly as a victorious army given up to the temptations of the flesh. He was not one to deny his men their pleasures. But he knew too what the morning would bring. Heavy heads, absences from the ranks, broken jaws and punishment parades. And then in the coming weeks the cases of the pox, harlots claiming injury and new women – camp followers – bearing their screaming bundles of humanity and claiming fathers for their bastards.

Steel knew. He had seen it time and time again. But he

would do nothing to prevent it. Could not – debauchery was in their blood. As much a part of soldiering as was standing in line under fire and doing for your enemy before he put an end to you. It was just another part of the world he loved and he would have it no other way. Sometimes though he wished that his men could exercise a little more discretion.

He turned to Hansam, who was riding at his side, waving a white lace handkerchief at one of the prettiest of the girls. 'You will notice, Henry, how quickly a people can always come to love us. But you will also recall that it is not generally so.'

'The army is always unpopular, Jack. Especially at home. We take the blame for all ills. To the government this war is a drain. Our men are a burden on society, and ever drunk and debauched.' He took a pinch of snuff from a silver box and dabbed at his nose: 'We are little loved.'

'All the more important then for us to relish such adulation when we can, eh?' Steel waved his hand at a group of pretty girls who were leaning out from a first-floor window so that their lowcut dresses showed a good deal more than usual décolletage.

Hansam saw his gaze: 'I believe that you may have a mind for dalliance this evening, Jack. I swear, since your German girl went off with that man in the cavalry, I have scarce seen you in the company of women.'

Steel smiled and thought about his 'German girl'. Conjured her face in his mind; Louisa Weber. He had not thought of her for some days. But when he did it was never without a twinge of heartache. At one point, after Blenheim, he had thought that they might settle. But Spain had called him away and now she was lost to him.

'Don't worry, Henry, I am not melancholy. Besides, you did not see me in Spain, this past year.' He thought for a moment, then shrugged. 'Although you know that Louisa's betrayal was a deep hurt to me.'

He smiled again as one of the girls took a favour, a piece of pink lace, from within the scoop of her bosom and threw it towards him. He caught it. 'Yes. Perhaps tonight I shall allow myself a little female company. I seem to have been in that of men for so long I have forgot what it is like to see a face that does not need a hot razor taken to it.'

Hansam laughed above the clatter of their horses' hooves on the cobbles. 'Well, you had better not form any too lasting a relationship. I cannot think that the duke intends us to delay here for long.'

'Calm yourself, Henry. I do not intend to fall in love. Merely to find a little amusement.' He turned in the saddle to speak to Williams, who, as a junior officer, was marching on foot at the head of the men directly behind him. 'What say you, Tom? Shall we find an alehouse this evening or should it be more of an amorous soirée among the ladies of the town?'

The ensign blushed and Slaughter, who was walking alongside him, his sergeant's halberd resting on his shoulder, raised his eyebrows. Williams replied, 'I . . . I think that we should be pleased to . . . to please the ladies, sir.'

Steel laughed, but not cruelly. 'You wish to please the ladies, do you? Aye, Tom. I'm sure that they will be mightily pleased with you too.' He made sure that his voice would be heard at least by the front few ranks of the Grenadiers and continued: 'In fact if we should find us some ladies then we shall all be sure to please them all right.'

As he had hoped, the men in the front few files cheered and muttered ribald remarks. It was good for morale. Tease the ensign, make him blush and let the men see that although you were an officer and a gentleman you were on their level in some things at least. An officer must have a human edge. That was one of the tricks of leadership.

Hansam spoke: 'I do not know where you will find your concubines, Jack. Although I do hear that here in the Upper Town the people speak mostly French and are of . . . refined persuasions.'

'In that case, Henry, d'you not think that it's down there in the Lower Town that we ought to look.'

The comment, again in a deliberately raised voice, brought another loud cheer from the men which turned to laughter as, turning sharply to the right, as directed by one of the English dragoons who had been posted as marshals throughout the town, they passed a small bronze statue of a naked boy. It was a fountain, fashioned in such a way that its spouting water made it appear that the boy was relieving himself into the street. Soon the entire regiment was convulsed.

Steel turned to Hansam: 'If that work of art is indicative of the coarseness of the native humour then I do believe that we might all be in for a stimulating evening's sport, Henry. I don't think that long-term attachments will be on tonight's menu, do you?'

The streets had become narrower now as they entered the Lower Town and as they continued, the men's laughter, loud as it was, was drowned by the roars of the civilian crowd, who mobbed the redcoats, pressing forward even further than before.

Williams shouted up to Steel, 'Do you hear how they're cheering for the British, sir?'

Steel shook his head: 'They're not cheering for us because we're British soldiers, Tom. They're cheering because we beat the bloody French. D'you hear their accent, Tom? They're not speaking French any more. That's Flemish. They're cheering because we're not French and we're not Spaniards, nor even

85

Dutch. They're cheering because at long last they believe that they might have a chance to be bloody Belgians. They don't give a tuppenny toss who we are as long as they're free.'

Hansam agreed: 'The captain's right, Tom. Our illustrious commander has brought this people liberty from the French if they want it and that's not something they'll give up lightly again. How does it feel, to have given a nation back its freedom?'

Williams smiled: 'I think I might develop a liking for it, sir.'

Steel saw that the young ensign had caught sight of a pretty girl at the side of the street who was throwing flowers to the soldiers and that she appeared to have returned his gaze. He shouted down to him above the din. 'And so you should, Tom. I do believe that even Sarn't Slaughter might enjoy a little of the victor's spoils.'

Steel looked to his rear and saw that Slaughter too was smiling broadly and waving his hand in acknowledgement of the rapturous cries. In his arms he cradled a huge bouquet of tulips and his face had been kissed so many times that rouge had rubbed off on to his stubble.

Steel guffawed. 'You've got a public, Jacob. They love you. If I didn't know better I would take you for one of the actresses at the Queen's Theatre in the Haymarket. One of the prettier ones, of course. Why Sergeant, you're the image of pretty Mrs Oldfield herself.'

The men took the rare chance to laugh at their sergeant and as Slaughter smiled and cursed, Steel turned back to Williams: 'Make the most of it, lad. Tomorrow they might be chasing us from the town.'

The boy was just wondering how he might go about finding the girl later in the day when a raven-haired woman old enough to be his mother rushed forward from the crowd and flinging her arm around his slender waist kissed him full on the lips. Around him the Grenadiers cheered and whistled. When Williams eventually contrived his release his face was bright red.

Steel laughed. 'That's it, Tom. Please the ladies. Show them what a British officer's made of.' The front of the column was pouring out of the end of the street now and Steel, seeing a gaggle of senior mounted officers up ahead, called back to his men, 'Face front. In your own time, Sarn't. Restore the men to order, if you will.'

Ahead of them the Grand Place opened out from the street and the Grenadiers filed into position alongside the other regiments formed up in its square. Directly opposite them stood the town hall which along with half a score of semi-derelict buildings still bore evidence of the terrible French bombardment of over a decade ago. It was clear though that the city's burghers had spared no expense on rebuilding. With crow-stepped and curved gables and ornate marble façades, these buildings were as much a statement of political intent and independent spirit, thought Steel, as they were works of architecture.

Brought to order by their sergeants, the men were marching proudly now, trying as best they could to keep in step in the way the new training manual required. Steel saw that the wide square was filled with troops of all the nations which made up this polyglot allied army. English, Scots and Danes in their bright red, the Dutch and Prussians in blue and the units of other smaller states. Above their heads the brightly-coloured silks of the colours and standards snapped and fluttered in the summer breeze. The drums had been assembled en masse along the west side of the square and were beating out an almost unbearably loud, cacophonous tattoo, which all but drowned the cheers of the crowd which pushed and jostled for room against the houses around the Grand Place to find a better view of the great and the good.

They marched deeper into the square, past a mounted aide who, just as he might have done at Horse Guards, was signalling them where to take position. As swiftly and deftly as any regiment in the army, they moved from column into line and formed up slightly to the left of the Guards. Steel calmed his nervous mount with a gentle pat to the shoulder and surveyed the scene.

To the left of the drummers, before the town hall, a high grandstand had been erected on wooden poles and there, under a red velvet canopy, sat a group of soberly dressed men in black, evidently government dignitaries. To their left and at a short distance sat the commander himself with his entourage. Steel gazed for a moment at Marlborough's placid, weather-beaten face and wondered how one man had achieved so much in a few years. The French were on the run and Flanders almost taken. But Steel knew that this war was far from over. Louis was not yet beaten. What great plan, he wondered was even now forming in that agile mind?

Up on the dais, Marlborough raised his hand to the crowd and another great cheer went up. Hawkins turned to him and said, in a whisper, 'You are their saviour, Your Grace.'

'So, Hawkins, it would seem.'

'I suggest that you savour the moment, sir. I fear that it may not be a lasting sentiment.'

Marlborough frowned. 'Yes, I am quite aware of that. This ceremonial is all very well. But it is not war.'

'Most certainly, Your Grace. But I suspect that it is far from over.'

Hawkins pointed across the square, where from a side-street there now issued a long procession of men in a bizarre assortment of dress.

Marlborough rubbed his eyes and spoke in a whisper. 'What the devil? What now? James, what on earth is that?'

'As I understand it, Your Grace, it is the customary way of honouring a visiting head of state. The men of the guilds and the *parlement* will parade in medieval dress in a re-enactment of a rite of feudal allegiance.'

Hawkins was right. Both men saw now that the members of the procession were dressed in full suits of armour while boys walking alongside them wore the uniforms of squires and heralds.

Marlborough smiled and waved and hissed under his breath: 'How long now, d'you suppose?'

'One hour. Maybe two.'

Marlborough brightened: 'And then we may leave?'

'Until we dine, Your Grace.'

'And then?'

'I am very much afraid, My Lord, that they intend us to enjoy more of the same.'

The food had been cleared although the glasses, half-filled with wine and brandy, still remained. Within the small, striped campaign tent, which had been hastily erected by his footmen at the rear of the grandstand on the Grand Place, Marlborough stood over a map-covered table, surrounded by his aides and senior officers.

He shook his head: 'What bliss, to gain but a moment's peace from those prattling merchants.'

Hawkins spoke: 'They mean well, sir. They do you honour.'

Marlborough glared at him: 'Honour? What do they know of honour? They know nothing more of honour than they have read in a book. The honour that I know is that found on a field of battle. This is politics, James. Politics and damned provincial, continental politics at that. This is not my way.'

'They have declared support for the true king, sir. For Charles III, the true King of Spain.'

'Which is, I grant you, our purpose in this war. But what am I to do. I must act, but how? Am I to become Governor of Belgium myself? That was never a part of my plan. Do I declare the country independent? The Austrians are our allies and we should support their claim to government. But I am persuaded that there is deep intrigue here which I do not as yet understand. There is a movement that would have independence from all foreign crowns, Spanish, French and Austrian, a body of opinion that would have a free Belgian state. But gentlemen, surely that way anarchy lies. If we grant such powers to a state over which sovereignty has been held by ancient dynasties then who is to say what other states will take notice? What of Ireland? And how do we match such an action with the talk of union with Scotland now current at home and so sorely desired by the queen? We must argue against separation, not in its favour.' He lowered his voice: 'Moreover, our spies tell me that there are men out there willing to fight and to die for such a principle. Either we are with them or we are against them. And if we are against them then they will surely harry us.'

He looked at Hawkins. 'What am I to do, James? What would you do? London is too distant to ask for help and even The Hague has not answered me. I know that these people now see me as their saviour. But mark me – there will soon come a time when we move on and they will be left to the mercies of the Dutch. And what shall they call me then? This great victory is no more than Pyrrhic, this vaunted liberty only temporary. Yes, we may have saved the Belgians from French dominion, but only to sell them off to the Dutch. Now we are camped in the very heart of their country and our war will lay waste their land. I tell you that the same

Dutchmen who now welcome me here will soon again be battling with the French who already offer them a line of forts which will isolate our trade.' He slammed his fist down on the table and held his other hand to his head. 'These damned headaches. It is too much for one man to bear.'

Cadogan placed a hand on his shoulder. 'Perhaps, sir, It would be prudent to return to the festivities. We have been away overlong.'

Marlborough rounded on his friend: 'Dammit, William. Will they not let me be? I am a soldier. Must I keep reminding you of all people of that? I have had my fill of these dour politicians and worthies. We must continue our pursuit of the French. My God, we may chase them back to Paris now if we have a mind to and capture the old king himself, on his gilded throne at Versailles. We must above all cut Marshal Villeroi's lines of communication and to this purpose it is my intention to pass the Scheldt at Gavre.'

Cadogan spoke: 'Your Grace, you must appreciate that we find ourselves in the most delicate of situations. We are assured both by our agents and those gentlemen through there, that a handful of the most sizeable of Belgian towns still remain in French hands. That is to say that their towns-people still support the French. All that it would take to have them rise in arms would be one incident. One spark put to the powder-keg and it might become a civil war. Perhaps a three-way struggle if you count in the independent Belgians. And then what, Your Grace? Should we then be in pursuit of the French, no matter how great our success, with foes to our rear and indeed all about us, we shall be in grave danger of losing our means of supply. Before anything of the sort is allowed to happen, we must secure a port. It is my duty to you, My Lord, as quartermaster-general to insist on no less.'

He paused, made sure that Marlborough's fury had abated

and continued: 'For the sake of our national integrity and to prevent the Dutch from taking our trade, we must have Ostend. Dunkirk and Ostend must be taken and once they are in our hands they must not be lost again. My Lord, you are as aware as I that there is a flotilla of the Royal Navy currently riding in the Channel awaiting just such an eventuality. Their captain himself is with us this day in Brussels. George Forbes, the Earl of Granard. He awaits your word. He has gunboats and bombships expressly designed for just such an assault. We can lay waste the port of Ostend or at least support an attack by land to force its surrender. It is the obvious direction in which to focus our labours.'

Marlborough spoke, calmly now: 'Yes, James. I do know that and I have indeed made the acquaintance of My Lord Granard. An amiable fellow, if somewhat over-eager to prove the ballistic capabilities of his vessels.' He smiled at Cadogan: 'It was most propitious of you, William to have procured the assistance of the navy. And I agree with you fully that Ostend is a prime objective.' He flashed another knowing smile at the quartermaster-general. 'And so, you will in the end have the better of your French privateers.'

The other officers grinned. Cadogan coloured and raised his voice. 'Sir, they took all my possessions. Every single last item. The money. Fifty thousand crowns destined for the army. And a parcel of jewels belonging to My Lady. Even my private correspondence.'

Hawkins interjected, grinning. 'Some of which, I understand, Cadogan, was then published in Paris. A most amusing read. Something about a . . .'

Marlborough pretended to glare at him: 'Really, Hawkins. I hardly think . . .'

'I am sorry, Your Grace.'

Cadogan recovered his temper: 'As I was saying, Your

Grace, we must take Ostend. We must avail ourselves of a port of supply ... and curtail the activities of the privateers once and for all.'

Hawkins interjected: 'It does occur to me that there may be but one problem.'

'James?'

'Well, Your Grace. Far be it from me to doubt my own commander and I sincerely mean you no disrespect in this matter.' He scratched his head: 'But have you thought carefully enough as to exactly how we are to take Ostend? Oh yes, you know as I do that it was fortified by Vauban some ten years back. It has forts, gabions, ramparts crammed with cannon. It is in fact a classic example of Vauban's great art with application to the coast, using the sea as natural defence on one side and manmade entrenchments on the other. That is one thing. We can besiege such a town. You are the master of such siegecraft. And we have the cannon. But have you thought of its garrison?' Marlborough narrowed his eyes as Hawkins went on. 'Oh yes, you may bombard it with gunships and assault it from land. But believe me, I know that town. Ostend is a nest of wasps. It is a northern St Malo from which the French privateers creep out to take our shipping and whose streets and alleyways will make you pay a high price in men. Higher even than at the Schellenberg. And I know that you can never forget the slaughter there nor the effect of taking that bloody hill upon your popularity at home.'

It was Cadogan now who raised his voice: 'Yet we must take it.'

Lord Orkney, who up till now had remained silent, spoke up: 'As I recall, I did, when we spoke of this matter before, name Lord Argyll as a man who might lead such an attack. But now I am given to understand that the majority of the

93

enemy in Ostend will be pirates. Have I grasped this correctly, Lord Cadogan? You would fight French privateers, pirates, on their home territory? Fight them in the streets of Ostend, with formed infantry?'

'If that is what it takes.'

'You would engage bandits with regular troops?'

'If it be so.'

Orkney shook his head and laughed: 'My dear Cadogan, you are as aware as I am that such a thing cannot be done. Your regular infantryman is a simple creature. A pressed-into-service, drink and whoreing driven dimwit. He is trained by rote and kept to it by the lash. Your redcoat is simply not capable of fighting in the way that such men fight. They're privateers, My Lord. Ruddy pirates, man. Each of them carries his own arsenal, has his own dirty tricks. They're skilled in the art of one-to-one combat in a way that our boys simply are not. They fight to the death and offer no quarter.'

The last words made Cadogan turn away. Hawkins began again, turning slowly to Marlborough: 'What we might do though Your Grace, if you and Lord Orkney will allow me, and begging Lord Cadogan's pardon, is to use a certain amount of guile to enter the port. Contrive to place a man or men inside the port and storm it from within and without at the same time. And use in the first instance a specially chosen forlorn hope. A hope that, if you pardon my expression, would really have some hope in such a situation. A unit trained to fight as individuals. To use their own initiative. Not even the wiliest of privateers would outwit such a deception in league with such a body of men.'

Marlborough thought and then nodded. 'You're right, James. And you mentioned before the officer who might effect just such a plan.' Marlborough smiled. 'Yes, James. I think that perhaps if anyone could manage it then it will be that man. He has always seemed to me to display a level head and sound judgement.'

'I would call him a trifle headstrong, Your Grace.'

'Indeed, sir. Nothing was ever achieved in battle, James, without officers taking initiative. He is also of admirably sober character, I believe.'

Hawkins nodded. 'Oh yes, sir. He is admirably sober. You're right there. Jack Steel is our man. You could not do any better.'

Clutching the bottle of heavy, Rhenish wine in one hand and holding his glass in the other by its stem, Steel leaned back in the wooden dining chair and took care to pour himself another generous measure before taking in the scene. The little panelled room stank of wine, sweat and sex. In that degree. It was not perhaps the most debauched gathering of which he had ever been a part, but it was certainly worthy of record. Tom Williams sat next to him, his right leg propped on the tabletop, his left on a drum. His coat lay open and his shirt front had been undone by a pretty girl with doll-like features and rather too many beauty spots for comfort, who was running her fingers over his chest as she whispered into his ear. Whatever it was she said, in French presumably, the ensign was too inebriated to be affected. Steel, although he knew that he himself was none too sober, was keeping a close eye on the boy. It was all too easy to have your pocket picked in such a place as this and even though the girls seemed genuine enough, there was no sure way of knowing their true purpose.

Across the round oak table another of the young women was lying in a drunken stupor while beside her Lieutenant Laurent, the regiment's French Huguenot officer, was well advanced in his own amorous adventure, his hand tucked inside her companion's dress and his lips clamped firmly over her mouth. Next to him Lieutenant McInnery appeared to be winning a game of backgammon, which was fortunate, thought Steel. For when he was beaten the lieutenant generally had a mind to kill his opponent.

In the far corner of the room an ancient man and an ugly, toothless hag plucked away at a harp and a guitar to serenade the company and from time to time the innkeeper or his rotund wife would arrive through the open door bearing wine and plates of food which none of the officers had ordered but which they would find in the morning had all been diligently charged to their accounts. The wall behind them, whose drab, olive-coloured paint, touched by the flickering shadows, had become faded and yellow with pipe smoke, was dominated by a large painting in the Dutch style of the young god Bacchus being seduced by a pair of half-naked dryads. It was a fitting parallel for their own scene, he thought, if a little more wanton.

As he gazed at the painting, the girl seated beside him, who for the past five minutes had been toying with the buttons of Steel's breeches, to no avail, leaned over and pressed her ample bosom closer to his face.

'*Je vous désire, mon capitaine.* Now. Yes?'

Steel stared at her. She smiled and pushed at the lace-trimmed top of her dress so that it fell further down her cleavage, and whispered to him: 'You see, Jack, how the lace of my dress just covers the tips of my breasts? Or . . . perhaps it does not, quite. Yes? Is that better? It is the latest fashion. *Le tout Paris* is wearing such gowns.'

She pressed closer to him until Steel could smell her breath. It reeked of wine and as she moved to kiss him he caught her musky odour mixed with the lavender oil which she had applied a little over-liberally. Steel avoided her kiss and as he did so, Laurent, who was sitting directly opposite grinned and spoke: 'From where I sit madam, there is not very much of your gown to wear at all.' The girl giggled, muttered a French expletive and pretended to slap his face.

They had taken accommodation and two private dining rooms on the upper floor of the Roi d'Espagne, an inn on the Grand Place and for the last three hours had been enjoying the local cuisine washed down by a generous amount of wine and in the company of several ladies to whom they had been introduced at an assembly that afternoon in the city's Guild Hall. Steel's attentions had gradually devolved upon this pretty, French-speaking blonde from the Upper Town. Her name as he recalled was Mathilde Remy. Her father she had said was a grain merchant, a man of some importance. Mathilde was all of seventeen, but with her comely figure she might have been anything from fifteen to thirty. She was pretty enough and on some nights there was nothing better than a pretty girl to take you away from the horrors of the battlefield.

He raised the half-full glass to his lips, took a sip and realized that he had drunk his fill of wine. He rose unsteadily to his feet: 'Ladies, gentlemen, I bid you goodnight.'

Williams looked up at him, glassy-eyed. His face was covered in rouge marks in the shape of lips and both his shirt and breeches were undone.

Steel groaned and shook his head: 'Oh God, Tom. Please, I beg you. Do not go too far. Although I guess you are now too drunk to cause any serious damage. Or even to comprehend what I am saying to you. Remember, I expect you at six. No later.' He turned to Hansam: 'Henry. This young man is in your care now. Look after him.'

Hansam smiled, waved good-naturedly, mouthed goodnight and returned to his own business in hand which was with a mature and experienced-looking brunette who claimed that she was descended from Charles the Bold and seemed determined to prove it. Williams attempted to salute and not realizing that he had a half-full glass in his hand merely succeeded in drenching himself in the overpriced wine. His companion called for another bottle.

Mathilde gazed up at Steel. He met her eyes, nodded and gave her his hand to help her to her feet. Leaving the room, they climbed the few uneven wooden stairs to the level above and found his modest bedroom. He lit the candle on the dressing chest and closed the door, before removing his boots, stockings, breeches, waistcoat and shirt. Then he turned and saw the Paris gown draped over a chair and Mathilde lying naked on the bed. He felt not only desire, but an intense sense of relief, washing over him. In one rare moment it banished from his troubled mind all thoughts of soldiering and responsibility and promotion and prestige and reminded him that this, like any night, might be his last.

Later, drowsing in the shadows thrown by the thin, pale light that crept beneath the door, Steel was roused by muffled voices which seemed to come from the fireplace. In the room below them someone was talking loudly and the noise was carrying up the chimney. It was an English voice, one that he did not recognize but from its tone he knew it must be an officer.

'And I tell you, sir, that he is misguided. I am aware that you know that full well yourself. And you know too that should we continue to pursue this campaign in the Low Countries rather than in Spain where as we speak young Mordaunt's father My Lord Peterborough directs his own campaign with half the army, then we are lost.' Steel could place the voice now. It belonged to Major Charles Frampton, adjutant of his own regiment, Farquharson's. Extracting himself from Mathilde's arms, Steel rose from the bed and, naked and shivering, crouched down in the darkness and pressed his ear to the chimney to listen more closely. From his slurred delivery, Frampton appeared to be even more drunk than Williams. There was no denying though that his words sounded like dissent and Steel strained to hear more against the din of the dreadful musicians and the general hubbub from below. Such views were not of course, unusual among Marlborough's officers. Everyone had his own opinion on how a campaign should be conducted. It was the same in all armies, although at present Steel was only too aware that there was a considerable movement which held the view that the war should be fought not here in Flanders, but in Spain. Hadn't one such attempt to discredit the duke and do just that almost cost him his own life only two years ago? But Frampton? Surely the man could do no real harm. It still irked him that such men, whom in battle he would trust with his life, could be so openly disloyal to their commander. Particularly now, after such a glorious victory. Marlborough was hailed as a victor and Frampton's addled wishes must be no more than the daydreams of a lost cause.

Frampton again raised his voice: 'I tell you, a civil war in the Netherlands could mean the end for all Marlborough's grand intentions. The war would move in its entirety to Spain at last. You and I would gain by it and be with old friends. My Lord Peterborough is the commander we need. Not this damned Churchill.'

Steel smiled at Frampton's derogatory use of Marlborough's family name.

A second voice spoke now and told Frampton to shut up. Steel did not recognize the man, although he was certainly another officer, with a slight lisp, it seemed.

'Frampton, you'd do best to keep a level tongue in your head. Even here.'

'But I know that Mordaunt is with us. Stands to reason, he's Peterborough's son. And we might count on the support of Argyll. He has no great love for the captain-general and he'd rather be in Spain. More Catholics to kill.'

Both men laughed. Steel wondered about Mordaunt. He knew that he had been forbidden by Marlborough from marrying his daughter. Surely though, the man was too brave a soldier to be swayed by personal bitterness. Argyll though seemed a more probable prospect.

The second man was speaking again now. 'In truth, I am convinced that civil war would spell our commander's downfall. It falls to us to strike the spark. A few pamphlets ought to do it. It will need no more. This country is as volatile as a powder keg.'

'But what shall it say, this pamphlet? How are we to damn Marlborough's virtue? After such a victory?'

'We have no need to worry about that. He may have routed the French from this land, but he has filled it with more soldiers. Our coats may be of a different colour, but we are soldiers all the same, and the people here, for all their smiles and thank yous, do not trust the military. Our pamphlet requires merely the information that during the campaign in Bavaria, before Blenheim, the duke made it his personal business to lay waste the entire country. Whole populations were driven out, their homes and farms burned to the ground. You need only draw on your worst imaginings and amplify them. Such things did happen, for all we know. But for our purposes who is to know that Marlborough himself did not plan them in detail? It is certain that once a thing is committed to print it is nigh on impossible to undo its truth in people's minds. We do not sign the sheet, but say that it is from "a friend". Marlborough and his generals and, I dare say the British as a whole, are not to be trusted. Believe me, Frampton, such a scheme will undermine the bold commander quicker than any army sent by King Louis. It will set Flamand against Walloon afresh and provoke a general revolt too against the British army. The Dutch may secede from the army and who knows what the Danes and Hessians will do? And we must not forget to play to their religion. Remember that the people of the southern Netherlands are Catholic. They abhor Calvinism and will thus resent any Dutch attempt to unify their country into the state that it was before the Reformation. Our task will be made doubly simple.'

Steel listened more closely. While Frampton might be nothing more than a garrulous drunk his companion seemed in deadly earnest, and now he was into his stride.

'All that we need is a man to print and publish the sheets. But we must act fast. Marlborough will not want to stay here sitting on his arse for longer than he must. You and I will write the stuff. Money is no object, our friends in London have seen to that. Trust once broken is hard to repair, and what Marlborough needs now is the trust of these people. Without that his great ambitions have no whit of a chance. For all its glory, his great victory will be as naught. And when the time comes, there will be willing officers ready to take command under Peterborough. You and I, Frampton. Argyll, Mordaunt and whoever else has the soundness of mind to join us. And there will be many. By the time we're done with him Churchill will wish the French were still masters here.'

The voices faded; Steel returned to bed, turning over in his mind the implications of what he had overheard. He did not sleep.

SIX

The fortifications of Ostend could not be described as one of Marshal Vauban's greatest triumphs, but they were enough. It was eight years now since the great French military engineer had come to the port with his teams of masons and scores of convicts pressed into service as labourers. He had built on top of the town's existing defences, which between 1601 and 1604 had withstood more than three years of siege as the Dutch had held at bay the Spanish forces of Archduke Albert of Austria in one of the most infamous and gruesome engagements of close on eighty years of bloody wars.

Steel stood on the gentle incline in the ground that rose to the west of the port, looking across the flats and prayed to himself that their current endeavour would neither take quite so long or be quite so sanguine an affair. Vauban himself, in his treatise, had prescribed forty-eight days for a successful siege, from the digging of the first trench line to the surrender of the garrison. Perhaps that would be long enough for them to break this fort of his.

Ostend lay under a vast expanse of the clearest of blue skies and a wind was blowing inland across the Channel, tossing up white horses of spray in the blue-green sea and sending the sands drifting into the marram grass. It blew from England. And in a thought that crept unbidden into his idle mind, Steel realized that it was four years since he had touched that shore and he wondered now when, if ever, he might do so again. They had marched here a week ago, smelling the sea before they saw it; cresting the dunes and finding themselves on the coast at a place where the breezes whipped at their hair with a pleasant, cleansing saltiness.

Out in the Channel Steel could make out the masts of more than a dozen ships, a British fleet under Admiral Fairborne, and behind them the greater bulk of other vessels including gunships which must soon bombard the port. And after that had been done, when in theory at least the place was reduced to a smouldering, corpse-strewn wreck, when the British navy had once again ruined its reputation by massacring civilians, then they would go in. He squinted in the sunlight and took in what he could of the defences that would have to be breached.

Ostend had been designed specifically as a fortified naval base, surrounding the valuable port at the wide mouth of the harbour and as such was very different to the great string of Vauban's inland forts which had occupied so much of Marlborough's energies in the last year of campaigning in Flanders.

The defences divided in two. To his right stood a single small star fort, the Fort of St Philip consisting of a single line of earthworks and within them a four-pointed stone wall, inclined gently in to allow the defenders maximum visibility and to expose the attackers to the greatest possible fire. Steel knew that the fort's purpose was to guard the mouth of the river against seaborne invasion, covering the water with the dozen guns which protruded from its crenellations. He knew too that this little star fort would not be their objective, although it might prove a costly source of flanking fire during their assault. No – they were bound for the town itself. It rose to his left, a forbidding three levels of grass-covered slopes of compacted earth glacis, crowned with a solid masonry wall from which on this side alone he could see the great pentagonal towers of five bastions, each with interlocking fields of fire.

Between Steel and the town lay a vast expanse of marshland, the Marais St Michel, across which there was, according to even the most sympathetic of local guides, no safe causeway. The only way in and out of Ostend, save by sea or the river, was via a single narrow road which ran along the coast, just behind the dunes of the broad, sandy beach. It entered the town by a solitary fortified gate, directly under one of the defensive bastions, and it was this at which he now stared directly. Since their arrival here a week ago it had not opened and he knew that it would not be opened again until they either took the town or abandoned the siege. It was the only way in and Steel realized that any man approaching along it would be the target for a hundred pairs of eyes and as many muskets. He looked up from the gate to where in the walls the cannon poked their wicked black muzzles from the embrasures and tried to imagine the terrible carnage which would ensue the moment that a formed unit of infantry attempted to advance along the road, let alone storm the walls.

'Pretty-looking place, ain't it. Don't you think, Jack?'

He had not noticed Hansam, standing at his side. 'Hmm? Oh, yes. Pretty. Very pretty, Henry. Marshal Vauban's inventiveness never ceases to surprise me. He is quite brilliant.'

'Brilliant perhaps, but he is quite out of favour at the French court, they say. Virtually in exile.'

'The French don't know a genius when they have one. That

man has done more for the French military than all King Louis' swagger. Look, Henry. You notice how, with a simple geometrical design he is able to direct never less than eight cannon at the one place, sometimes as many as fourteen and at the same time ensure that no part of the defences is weakened or exposed. He creates areas into which no man can advance.' He pointed to the right of the town. 'Look. What d'you see there?'

'I see three layers of defence. A glacis lined with infantrymen, more muskets behind on a tenaille and behind that the cannon at the parapet.'

'Yes, but do you see how there are three distinct fields of fire? The man is a wonder, Henry. No less.'

'Well, 'twill be up to us to undo the wonder. For we have to take this place.'

Steel looked on and imagined again the blood and the smoke and the screams. Behind the parapets he could make out two buildings higher than the rest. The sloping roofs of powder magazines, filled with enough gunpowder and shot to keep Marlborough at bay for God knew how long. And there were sure to be more elsewhere in the town. He knew too, from having toured captured forts, that within those walls there would be tunnels and secret passages that would allow the garrison to move freely from wall to wall shielded from enemy fire. Knew about the freshwater wells which prevented an attacking force from poisoning the water and about the ingenious way in which the windows of the powder magazines allowed the air to circulate freely yet prevented the slightest spark from entering. He knew the thickness of the walls – five feet in some cases – and knew that at every corner a cylindrical masonry sentry box with a single gun slit would allow chosen marksmen to fire down on the enemy to pick off officers among the attackers.

He spoke, without looking at Hansam: 'Yes. It will be quite a task, Henry. Even with the help of our friends on the sea. I wonder whether the duke has anything else up his sleeve?'

'I sincerely hope that he has. For I cannot see how we can take it by the usual means. For seven days our engineers have been digging and look what we have.'

He pointed to where, directly in front of them, at the edge of the marshes, a long ditch, the Steene trench, snaked its way from the dunes on the left up to the little town to their right, from which the engineers had coined its name. Normally by this stage in the siege other, similar trenches would be edging towards the besieged town with further parallel works to the Steene trench. Into fortified bays cut at intervals into these trenches the allies would customarily drag their guns and thus bring the town or fort under fire. But here that had proved impossible, so wet was the ground. It was clear that, quite apart from Vauban's skill, Ostend had its own natural defences.

Looking down they could see hundreds of men, British and allied infantry, hacking away at the ground, extending the great trench. Others used shovels to fill large four-foot-high wicker gabions with the earth dug from the ditch.

'I can't help feeling, Henry, that all this might be in vain. There is simply no means by which we can conduct this siege by any normal procedure.'

A respectful cough from behind was followed by the sound of Sergeant Slaughter's voice:

'Beggin' your pardon, sir. But the men have been asking me if you know when we might be going to attack and, erm, how we are supposed to do so, seeing as the whole place is a stinking, sodden marsh.' As if to prove his point, the sergeant swatted a large mosquito which had settled on his face.

Steel nodded and spoke with uncharacteristic terseness:

'Yes, Jacob. I am quite aware of the men's impatience. And believe me, I share it. But in truth I simply do not know the answer to either question.' He pointed out to sea where the fleet bobbed just outside the range of the French guns. 'See out there. Out there lie our bombships. Great vessels crammed with mortars which when we do attack or shortly before, will fire everything they have into that poor town. Perhaps that's how we'll do it, Sarn't.' He smiled, cynically: 'Or perhaps we could just do as the Turks like to do and fire some French heads into the town. Perhaps that would do the trick.'

Slaughter had scarcely seen his officer more animated and realized that the men's frustration at this lack of action was nothing as compared to Steel's. He was not surprised at this restlessness. There was nothing worse for a soldier than boredom. It gave you time to think. And for most of the men that was something to be avoided. After Brussels, rather than pushing west, the brigade had camped at a small village called Aarsele, some fifteen miles west of Ghent, and had waited for Marlborough and the remainder of the army for ten days. The men had grown restless and impatient. The locals had been pleasant enough, and less ready he thought to murder the French than previously. They were merely content, it seemed, to be alive.

Steel, as he allowed himself a rare few days' rest, could not help but agree with them. As they had waited, other units had arrived bringing with them news that all Brabant seemed to be falling to Marlborough. After Brussels other towns, garrisoned mainly by native Belgians formerly loyal to France had opened their gates. Aalst, Gavere, Ghent and Bruges had surrendered, along with Malines and Oudenarde which they had thought they would have to invest. At last Antwerp's governor had opened the great city to the triumphant allies.

Finally, as they reached the middle days of June and the weather had grown noticeably warmer, they had struck camp and marched north, led once again by the duke, through Lichterwelde and Torhout, up to the sea. Now the men were hungry for action. But again they did little more than sit and wait.

Since then too, other, more curious things had started to go wrong. Throughout their march, Marlborough's ruthless policy of ensuring the death penalty for looters within the army had been respected for the most part and the farmers had been paid for their produce. Watching them arrive at the camp in the morning and set out their stalls before leaving satisfied with their takings had been a pleasant way to pass the time. In the last two weeks though that had changed. To the west of their present camp the rotting bodies of two redcoats, neither thankfully from Farquharson's, left hanging from the gallows for the three days since their execution, testified to the breakdown of the system and the punishment which would be meted out to others who did not obey.

As yet, within Steel's brigade at least, no one else had chanced their life for so much as a scrawny chicken. Yet even so, there had been a distinct change in recent days in the demeanour of the local farmers. In fact for the past two days none of them had come to the camp and there were no fresh rations. Last night and again this evening the company would be forced to rely upon stale rations and what beef and pork had been salted down in barrels. They had sent out a party under Hansam and another under Williams, furnished with heavy purses, in search of supplies, but both had returned empty-handed, Hansam with the news that as they had entered the village the peasants had run into their houses and closed the doors, Williams saying that they had been jeered at on the road by farm labourers and that the village appeared to be shuttered and barred. Steel wondered what to make of it. How very different it was, he thought, from the reception they had enjoyed in Brussels. And that could not be explained by urban sophistication. Something had happened to unsettle the local populace, to turn them so roundly against the redcoats. It was not good for morale. Neither of course was the lack of fresh food. He hoped to God they would fight soon. He had scarcely ever seen the men so preoccupied.

Slaughter broke his reverie. 'I'm sorry, sir. I didn't mean to step out of line. Won't do it again.'

Steel smiled at him: 'No, Jacob. It's I who should apologize. I am aware that the men are unhappy and if it were in my power I would have them attack. But to do so now would be suicide. We must wait until we can make a breach in the walls. It won't be long, I'm sure.'

He turned and walked back down the hill, following Hansam towards where the Grenadiers had made their bivouac on the right flank of the regiment's other companies. As usual Steel's men had been ordered to provide the picquet and it had fallen to them again to send out yet another foraging patrol. He wondered that it had not yet returned, and called back up the hill to Slaughter, who was close behind him. 'Sarn't, any sign of Mr Williams' patrol yet?'

'Still out, sir.'

'How long have they been gone now?'

'Best part of two hours, sir. Shall I send out another to find them?'

'We'll give them another half-hour. Mister Williams has probably got himself lost. Or found some local girl.' But he thought it unlikely.

Steel turned towards his tent but as he did so a glint of steel on the edge of the wood caught his eye. He reached for his sword, but saw quickly that it was only Williams at the head of the missing patrol. A second glance though revealed that all was not well. The young ensign looked pale and was nursing a wound to his arm. Behind him the men hobbled into the camp, some leaning on each other for support. One of them, Steel noticed, Mulligan, had taken a bad cut to the head and was holding his white cotton stock to his left eye. Several others had lost their caps and one was without a gun. Steel dashed across to Williams, followed by Slaughter and a handful of the men.

'Tom! What on earth happened?'

'Strangest thing, sir. We were attacked.'

'Attacked? Not by the French, surely?'

'No, sir. By local peasants. We entered the village again and, just like yesterday it was all shuttered and locked. But then a great crowd of people came at us from behind one of the houses. Men, women and children, all waving pitchforks and clubs they were, sir.'

Steel raised his eyebrows: 'You're not telling me that you were beaten off by women and children, Tom. That they did this?'

Williams nodded, puce with shame. 'I instructed the men not to open fire on them, sir. I did the right thing, didn't I?'

Steel patted him on the shoulder. 'Yes, you did quite the right thing, Tom. We can't kill women and children, even if they do attack you. But have you any notion as to why on earth they might do it?'

'They were cursing, sir. And calling us names. In French.'

Steel shook his head. Why, he wondered, had the population turned so suddenly and so violently hostile? What could possibly have driven them to this? His men – indeed as he knew, all the army – had instructions to take particular care to win over the population to their cause. They were there to liberate the country from French tyranny. To bring peace. Why then should they have become the object of such hatred?

Frampton approached him, saw the blood on Williams' coat and the wounded men: 'Spot of bother, Captain Steel?'

'Nothing really, sir. A few of my men were attacked by local villagers. Seems curious, sir. Don't you think?'

Frampton flashed his most unctuous smile. 'No, not really. Doesn't surprise me at all in fact. I guessed that something like this would happen eventually. They don't trust us, you see, Steel. Hate all soldiers. In their blood, d'you see? It was only a matter of time before they turned on us.'

Steel did not see – did not agree. He had met some of these people and they were not the illogical yokels that Frampton painted them. Could it be that something or someone had deliberately turned them against the British army? There was something about Frampton's smug assuredness that triggered a thought in his mind, a memory of overheard conversation. As Frampton walked off, Steel turned back to the exhausted forage party.

'Tom, take Mulligan and get yourselves looked at by a doctor. Or by Matt Taylor at least. Then report back to me. I want a full account of what happened.'

Taylor, Steel knew, was as good as any apothecary or quack practitioner. Skilled with herbal remedies he had learned at Chelsea Physick Garden, he was able to cure everything from a dose of fever to a hit from a musketball.

As the men walked into the camp, Williams approached Steel: 'There is one thing, sir. We found these in the village. I thought they might be of interest.' Williams reached into his coat and brought out a bundle of torn printed broadsheets and handed them to Steel. Steel looked at them and began to read the French text. He understood just the gist of it. 'Marlborough's rape of Bavaria ... women and children

111

massacred . . . this will be the fate of Belgium . . . English no better than the French oppressors . . .'

'Might they be of some use, sir?'

Steel clapped Williams on the shoulder. 'Yes, Tom. Great use. You did well to find these. Now take yourself off to Taylor.'

Steel looked again at the papers, thumbing through them. So this was Frampton's work – it had not been idle chatter. This he realized could do everything the major and his co-conspirator had planned: raise the population, bring down Marlborough, move the war to Spain.

Slaughter found him reading: 'Seems to me, sir, we've got ourselves in a right pickle now.'

Steel looked up: 'Sarn't?'

'Well, sir. We've got the Frenchies to our front in that bloody great fort, ha'n't we? Plus, we're sitting in a ruddy bog beside the sea, getting eaten alive by these bloody creatures' – he swafted at another fly – 'and now we find we've got the bloody locals at our backs. They won't sell us any food and they've damn near tried to fillet poor Mr Williams.'

'Yes, Jacob. It is a bit of a pickle. I pity the duke in getting us out of this one. Although I think that I may just have found a way to help him.'

Standing on the top of a sand dune, just beyond the six-hundred-yard range of Ostend's cannon, Marlborough was mulling over much the same thought. He folded the slim, brass-bound field telescope with which his wife had presented him after Blenheim and handed it to Cadogan, who with Hawkins had walked forward from the rest of the general staff to take a closer look at their objective. Marlborough brushed a marsh mosquito away from its feasting on his cheek and spoke quietly to Cadogan.

'Can we do it, William? Can we take this place?'

'Oh, we'll do it, Your Grace, God willing. We'll do it. That is to say, you shall do it.'

Marlborough smiled. 'And how long d'you suppose it will take us. Twenty days? Thirty? Marshal Vauban's magic forty-eight? Do tell me.'

'You know, Your Grace, of the last great siege here. That of 1604?'

Marlborough frowned. 'How could I not know it? Have I not been reminded of it more times than I can remember in these last few days? Do I not know how General Spinola sat here with Prince Albert's army, precisely where we now stand, for no less than three years before he was enabled to take this place? Do I not know that it cost him more than eighty thousand men? Very nearly twice the size of this army. Thirty thousand Dutchmen too perished within the walls, from wounds, pestilence and disease.' He turned to Hawkins: 'What is it about this place, James? Is it cursed?'

The colonel shrugged. 'Perhaps it is, sir. But it could be that it's also just damned hard to take. It was a natural defensive position even before *Monsieur* Vauban worked his genius here.'

Marlborough balked at the name. 'Vauban. Damn the man and damn his genius. He haunts me like the flux and will do so till the day I die. Vauban and his damned forts. D'you know he has published his writings in another book. *Oisivetes* he calls it. His "idle thoughts". I wish to God that the man could have been more idle. Seems to me all his life he's never had one damned idle minute.'

Hawkins spoke: 'It is said that he has constructed more than eight score of forts and defended citadels.'

'And it seems to me, James that I must have besieged every one. But this one, this is a singular place. Look at it. Water

113

on the one side. Well, that might not be too much of a trouble. But it's these damned marshes to our front. How are we to construct even a second parallel trench if all we can dig is marsh water?'

Cadogan smiled hopefully: 'Well, we can be certain that it will not fall as did so many other towns of late, by the will of the people. The men who defend this place are very different. A few French regulars, a few Walloons to be sure, but for the most part, apart from the garrison who serve the guns, privateers in French pay. They will not throw open their gates. They know that they can expect no quarter and so they will extend none to us.'

Marlborough nodded in agreement. 'Yes. This will be a very different affair. At Ghent, as at Antwerp and Oudenarde, I know that it was my personal assurances that there would be religious toleration and general liberty which made the people so willing to welcome us in.'

'That may be so, Your Grace. Personally I do not believe that these people prize their independence greatly. But to own their liberty is quite another thing.'

Marlborough looked up and gazed at a seagull, which hovered on the warm air current over the dunes before swooping down towards the town. 'So how then are we to take it. What intelligence do we have?'

Hawkins spoke: 'Our spies are posted, as you know, in the sea ports along the Channel coast. *Monsieur* Chandos is most particular. He sends his fondest best wishes by the way.'

Marlborough laughed. 'Old Chandos is a charming man. He masquerades as Governor of Ath for the French, encourages their complete trust and yet in reality he is the very best of my agents.'

Hawkins went on: 'Ostend is precisely as Lord Cadogan would have it. The place is a nest of privateers and pirates.

Chief among them is a Frenchman, name of René Duguay-Trouin, who, enjoys a certain celebrity, if our sources are to be believed.' He smiled. 'Very popular with the ladies, I'm informed.'

Cadogan snorted. 'That blaggard. Calls himself a privateer. Nothing more than a common thief.'

Hawkins grinned. 'Was it not he who took your own frigate in the Channel, My Lord? You will have met the gentleman then?'

Cadogan grunted. 'Gentleman, indeed.'

Hawkins continued: 'Of course, Duglay-Trouin aside, the town does have a de facto governor, name of the Comte de la Motte. Reasonable sort of chap apparently, as Frenchies go. The garrison might prove to be unreliable if tried. Mostly Walloons in French pay. They have some ninety cannon and a quantity of powder stored in five magazines. This map shows the locations as best we can tell them. A single shot might do untold damage, although at present we cannot drag the cannon into range. Our best hope it would seem lies with the guns on our own ships, out to sea.' Together, they looked towards the flotilla. 'Oh, and there are ships of the French navy in the port. Two men o' war anchored in the harbour and of course Duglay-Trouin's own vessels.'

Marlborough sighed. 'Are you certain that is all?'

'There is one further matter of which you should be aware, sir.'

Hawkins beckoned to a footman who came running with a saddlebag. The colonel reached inside and producing a thick sheaf of papers, placed them on the folding field-table.

Marlborough eyed them with distaste. 'More of those damn broadsheets?'

'I am very much afraid so, sir.'

'By God, I am scandalized and defamed enough at home

by Defoe and Tutchin in their rags. The *Observator* is the scourge of my life. Do not tell me, James that this damnable gutter press is to follow me even here.' He began to read and the rage spread visibly across his face. 'But this is treasonable, man. Who d'you suppose is behind them? If such liberties can be taken of writing abominable lies without being detected, then where shall we be? It cannot be the French who are behind it – they are too much in disarray – and so its author must needs be closer to *home*.' He continued in a quieter voice: 'I am aware that certain officers in this army are in the habit of writing home anonymous letters according to their own political affections. Would that I knew though who they might be. I am aware too that certain gentlemen even now are voicing their opinion that my use of Lord Orkney's men at Ramillies was not wise. That I should not have first sent him into such an attack and then when he had all but carried the place, pulled him back.'

Hawkins spoke: 'They do tend to accord the blame to Lord Cadogan, sir.'

Cadogan bristled and glared at Hawkins. 'You know, Hawkins, that I was merely carrying out orders.' He realized what he had said: 'Orders, of course with which I whole-heartedly agreed, Your Grace.'

Hawkins continued: 'But in effect, Your Grace, the crisis produced by the writing in this new publication is somewhat more serious and immediate than a slur on your character.'

Marlborough grasped the paper and began to read. Hawkins went on: 'It is more dangerous than before, sir, you will appreciate. They talk of religious matters, assert that we intend to place a Dutch regime in power over them when these people as we know are naturally Catholic and thus in effect more inclined towards the French, or even their own countrymen.'

Marlborough raised his voice: 'But you both know that we do not intend anything of the sort. Certainly our Dutch allies may have a say in the government of their Belgian cousins. But to have any part in governing this country is not our intention. Never was. The Dutch carry everything with such a high hand that they are not beloved anywhere. God save us from them.'

Cadogan attempted to calm him. 'Of course that is not our plan, Your Grace. Although I do suspect that it will indeed be the eventual solution to the government of this ill-figured land.'

'It will bring only ill. The people must be governed by Charles II alone. Have I not myself refused his offer of the governorship for that very reason. Perhaps if he were to come here himself; show himself to the people.'

They knew he was grasping at straws. Hawkins pointed to the paper: 'It is too late for that, Your Grace. The people know nothing of your true thoughts. Yet if they read this . . . and this . . .' He brandished another of the broadsheet papers, 'They will know only this and will take it as the truth and proof positive of your deceit. We must act instantly, sir. Even now, Your Grace, the people of that most Catholic of towns, Ghent, are said to be engaged in violent protests. Against –'

'Against me. They riot against me, Hawkins. Yes. I can see that now. No doubt as we speak they are burning me in effigy. The devil take whoever is behind this. I'll have him, Hawkins. We must find him. If I cannot have justice done me then I shall break this man's bones and those of his printer.'

'A noble sentiment, Your Grace. And one which I am sure would be approved by all honest Englishmen. But we have no clue as yet as to who might be the author. And already the sedition spreads. We have reports of peasantry attacking several English regiments. The farmers, you are aware, are no longer so keen as they were to sell us food. Our supplies are failing – from both this and from our lack of a port.'

'Is it that bad?'

'Bad, sir, worse than bad. In my opinion, this country is on the brink of a civil war. The Walloons and the Flemings no more wish to be subject to the Dutch than they do to the French, but set them at each other and God knows what will happen. Yes, they have proclaimed their allegiance to you and ultimately to Charles II and the Hapsburg dynasty. Given reason, they would have him their king and live independent of the French or Spanish. But, sir, believe me, if they suspect you of being partisan in any of this or of seeking to help the Dutch then they will divide again. And it is happening even now. Our spies in Ostend inform me that the people we have counted on within this very town are even now on the brink of abandoning our cause.'

Marlborough brought his hands up to his mouth, interlaced the fingers and cupped them to his lips, as if in prayer. He looked steadily towards the town, taking in every aspect of the defences. Then he turned and lowering his hands to his side gazed out to sea before turning back.

'We must act now. You can be sure that just as soon as King Louis and his marshals realize our true situation then we shall face another French army, fresher and stronger than the last. We have only one option, gentlemen. We must take this town now, by whatever means we possess.'

Cadogan stepped forward. 'If I may presume to suggest, Your Grace. Captain Forbes has a plan.'

'Captain Forbes?'

'Our naval attaché, Your Grace. He commands the bombships currently riding at sea. He has taken the opportunity to row ashore.' He turned towards the beach and beckoned. 'Captain Forbes, His Grace will see you now.'

From the beach a slight figure in the dark blue uniform of the English navy climbed up the dunes towards where they stood. At length he reached them. Captain George Forbes had a pleasant, moon-shaped face set in a permanent smile and even though he was only aged just twenty-one was developing the swarthy skin which marked out a mariner.

Cadogan motioned him towards Marlborough. 'Your Grace, allow me to present Captain George Forbes.' He looked at Forbes: 'Captain Forbes, you remember telling me that you have an idea of how we might take the port? Pray, inform His Grace of your plan.'

Forbes coughed and turned to Marlborough: 'It's really quite simple, Your Grace. I thought that we might send in a fire bomb.'

'A what?'

'A fire bomb, Your Grace. Sometimes known as an "infernal machine". We did something similar, you may recall, at St Malo in 1693.'

Cadogan interrupted: 'Against privateers there also, Your Grace.'

'I am aware of that, Cadogan. Go on.'

'Well, sir, at St Malo, we prepared a brig, eighty feet in length. A captured Frenchman. She sat high in the water, sir, high enough to sail close to the city wall. We filled her with powder, stacked her to the gunwales with incendiary bombs and piled her decks with whatever missiles we could find. And then we set a skeleton crew and sent her into the port. Sailed her close to the wall, abandoned ship and then let her go.'

Marlborough was suddenly captivated: 'And then?'

Forbes coughed again and coloured. 'Well, of course, at the time, Your Grace, it didn't actually work.'

Marlborough raised his eyes to the sky. Cadogan looked

both surprised and angry. Marlborough spoke: 'May one ask why?'

'Well, it would seem that as the jolly-boats left its side with the crew, the ship hit a rock. It listed and began to take in a quantity of water. Naturally, the powder became damp. In the end only one barrel went up and the French captured everything else. It was a little bit of a disaster actually. But we could correct it here, sir. I'm quite sure that it could work this time. The water is shallower here and there are no rocks. You must at least allow me to try, Your Grace. Think of the lives that it would save.'

Marlborough remained stony-faced: 'It didn't work?'

'No, Your Grace.'

'You killed exactly how many French? How many of their privateers?' Forbes stared at his feet and mumbled. Cadogan closed his eyes. Marlborough continued: 'Speak up, man. How many casualties did you cause?'

'A cat, Your Grace.'

Hawkins was unable to stifle a guffaw of laughter. Cadogan merely looked embarrassed.

'A cat? You killed a cat? Nothing more?'

'No, Your Grace. Only a cat.'

Marlborough spoke gently, containing his fury. 'Captain Forbes, might I suggest that you forget your anti-feline machinations in future and stick to finding means of killing Frenchmen. And while you are about it, of taking this town.'

Hawkins spoke up: 'There is but one way, sir.'

'Which is, James?'

'That we take it at once, both from land and by sea. Admiral Fairborne is ready to blockade the harbour and has with him two bombketches, the *Salamander* and the *Blast*. Their command falls to Captain Forbes. I suggest that you have them bombard the place. Then, immediately their barrage is lifted, send in the attack. You might place the attacking force under the command of the Duke of Argyll. You could do no better. And at their head I would further suggest a storming party of crack troops. Men who will fight on their own initiative, yet who are also trained to stand.'

'Grenadiers?'

'Grenadiers, Your Grace. We send in a storming force made up solely of Grenadiers, taken from several regiments – English and Scots – yet under the command of one man and instructed specifically to hurl their bombs and then engage the enemy man to man, by whatever means. That, Your Grace, I believe will be the only way in which to defeat the desperate men who hold this place.'

'And where would you have this attack take place? The directors of the trenches have reported to me that there is no weakness at all that they can discern in the fortifications.' Marlborough grimaced and shook his head. 'Vauban, again.'

Hawkins remained cool: 'Indeed. There is only one point of entry into the city, Your Grace. Through the West Gate. That alone is the route that we must take.'

'You would press an attack by way of the main entrance to the town? You must be mad, man.' He paused and gave the matter some thought: 'And who would you have lead this most hopeless of all forlorn hopes? What officer would be foolish enough or brave enough to offer his services? Young Johnny Mordaunt, perhaps. Though I dare say his father would never forgive me. But he triumphed against the odds at the storming of the Schellenberg.'

Hawkins shook his head.

'No, James. You're quite right. I cannot send him again. Who then?'

'I did remember a certain gentleman to you before, Your Grace.' Hawkins beckoned to a figure who for the last few minutes had been standing on the slope of the dune. Steel walked forward.

Marlborough nodded in greeting: 'Captain Steel. Of course, the very man. You will lead the assault, Steel. You and your Grenadiers.'

'I am honoured, Your Grace. Be assured that we will take the breach.'

'If anyone can do such a thing you can. I dare say that after so long a rest, your men may need a little sharpening up. You have four days, Steel.' Marlborough turned to Cadogan. 'William, find Argyll. Confer with him and take it upon yourselves to select the other regiments and to find the remaining Grenadiers for this thankless task.' He turned to Forbes, who throughout had been standing in embarrassed silence beside Cadogan. 'Captain Forbes. You are responsible for the two bombships, are you not? Well, we require a bombardment. No more, no less. No fireships or dead cats. Merely fire enough to bring down all hell upon that town and make a breach in its defences wide enough for my boys to pass through and do their work. Can you do that?'

Forbes nodded: 'I believe that I can, Your Grace.'

'Then, gentlemen, we have not a moment to lose. We press the attack in two days' time.'

Steel and Forbes saluted and as Marlborough turned away to confer with his generals, Steel intercepted Hawkins: 'Colonel. I wonder if I might have a word with you?'

'Of course, Jack. It concerns the assault?'

'No, sir. It is to do with quite another matter.'

He reached into his pocket, produced the sheaf of broadsheets and handed them to Hawkins. Hawkins smiled and nodded. 'Yes. We had just been discussing those. What do you know?'

'I know what they contain, sir. And how damaging it might

be. And I know that they are the work of a British officer. Perhaps two or more.'

'Yes. I thought as much.'

'But I do believe, sir, that I might be able to suppress them.'

Hawkins looked at him: 'You do? Who's the man?'

'You must know, sir, that I cannot name a brother officer to you, until he has confessed his part in this affair. But I intend to confront him, Colonel, with your permission.'

'Of course you must, Steel. And then report to me. This is good work, Steel. I shall make sure that the duke has word of it, should you succeed. For if we cannot stop these rags then your grand assault may surely be forlorn. For even if we take Ostend then we shall have to fight not only the French but the very people we have set free.'

SEVEN

There was no getting away from it. René Duglay-Trouin was stunningly handsome. Even his fellow pirates said so. And most of them without a threat. He, of course, was well aware of the fact and did his best to make the most of his already striking features. His nose was long and aquiline and his eyes of the darkest brown, which some said reflected the truth of the tale that his mother had been a mulatto. Tell him that to his face though and it would be the last thing you uttered. Certainly his skin was swarthy, but it was hard to tell whether this was the legacy of his birth or a product of his having served before the mast for almost a quarter of a century. His coat was a particular shade of royal blue, trimmed with real gold wire. It was cut in Paris, by King Louis' own tailor, and cinched in at the waist to accentuate his muscular figure. It lay permanently open to reveal a black leather waistcoat beneath, beneath which he wore a frilled shirt of pure white – clean every day and doused in lavender water. A pair of full-cut red breeches tucked into turned-down riding boots completed the dandified ensemble. Across his shoulder Trouin wore the yellow sash of a French naval commander.

His long fair hair was scraped back and tied with a ribbon of gold silk. Over it, he wore a black tricorne trimmed with gold lace and in his left ear a tiny ring of twenty-two-carat gold. The only flaw in Trouin's appearance was the puckered line of a scar which ran from just above his left eye down to his chin. But as a relic of his most infamous fight, this added more to his dashing appearance than it took away. At his side hung a sword. He had taken it from an English naval officer three years ago in a bloody engagement off Leghorn. It was of Italian manufacture and perfectly balanced. In his broad belt he had tucked a pair of pistols which he kept permanently loaded. Brass barrelled and mounted, they bore his name engraved on the trigger guard. It was a name to be reckoned with.

At thirty-three Trouin was enjoying a reputation as the scourge of the high seas and he wanted to look the part. And there could be no doubt, he did look every inch the gentleman pirate. At the moment though he preferred to affect the term 'privateer'. It had a ring of legality to it, and in the present climate, as he had recently discovered, the notion that war should be fought by legal means meant much to his friends in the French administration who were happy to retain him on their payroll.

The war had been good to Trouin, and he knew it. Perhaps it was not as instantly lucrative as pirating; but with all that he did sanctioned from Paris, everything had become so much the easier. For the last four years Ostend had been his home; if someone like Trouin could ever truly consider one place home. But there was no doubt that he felt at home here.

His ships, his flagship the *Bellone* and the smaller *Railleuse*, boasting sixty and forty guns apiece, lay at anchor in the safety of the harbour and he too was as safe as the royal signature on his commission from the navy. French by birth, born into a family shipping business in St Malo, Trouin had joined the French navy at sixteen. But with no notion of any real allegiance to any one other than himself, he had quickly taken to the more lucrative trade of piracy. Fortunately for Trouin, in 1689 war had broken out with England and within weeks he had found himself much in favour with his former comrades in the navy. Clearly, he had backed the right side. For King Louis' navy was now reckoned the most powerful in the world. The English, it was true, had taken measures to match its size. But as yet there was nothing to beat the French in a fair fight at sea. Or an unfair one – which was where he came in.

By the age of twenty he had his own command, a forty-gunner. Hadn't he single-handedly captured five English ships with her? His fame grew by the year. He could number ten men-of-war among his prizes to date and some two hundred merchant vessels. He made it his business to seek out English ships in particular. He nurtured a hatred of the English. He had been a prisoner in Plymouth ten years ago, three long months in a filthy hole of a prison where the brown rats had run free in the excrement and typhus had carried off more of his fellow inmates than the executioner. Of course he had escaped, Trouin always escaped. He had bribed a guard – the English were always open to bribery – and stolen a ketch. The English still had a warrant out for his arrest for piracy. But he had spent the last eighteen years cheating the hangman. Why change the habit of a lifetime?

Trouin pushed himself back in the stout wooden chair at the table which they were careful always to keep reserved for him in this tavern – *L'Etoile du Nord* – which passed for his headquarters and squeezed his broad hand a little harder around the waist of the pretty Belgian girl perched upon his knee. Not too hard. Just enough to hurt her a little and to remind her not to flirt with the crewman who was sitting over on his right and leering at her cleavage. She let out a little squeal and smiled at Trouin. What was her name? He had no idea. What did it matter anyway? All the women in the inn, tarts and whores, belonged to him one way or another, and he'd had most of them. Indeed all the women in the town could be his, he was sure, in whatever way he chose, if he had a mind to take them. He pulled the girl towards him and to her surprise, kissed her hard on the mouth, then squeezed her breast, grabbed her around the waist with both hands and placed her upon her feet on the floor.

'More wine, girl. Fetch more wine. Wine for everyone tonight. Wine for all my men. Beer if they want it. Keyt-beer. Understand? As much as they can drink. Get on.'

The girl hurried away and Trouin stood up. He was surprisingly tall, for his long legs were somewhat out of proportion to the length of his torso. In a swordfight though this could carry a distinct advantage, allowing him to outreach and outstep his bewildered opponent. He looked around the inn, peering through the fug of pipesmoke at the men who made up his command. They were a good enough company. Two crews, nigh on four hundred and fifty men all told and as typical a mix of nationalities as you could expect to find on any privateer. Mostly French and Belgians – no Dutch, of course. A few brace of Germans and a few more from Sweden and Denmark, surly, silent Vikings. By contrast there were the blackamoors. A round four score of them, mainly French Creoles who fought with him to maintain their liberty. And then there were the English. They were deserters mostly from the British navy or from the very army that was now outside these walls. He found that English soldiers made the best sailors and was always ready to welcome them in. Besides, it gave him a certain frisson to turn his old enemies and they were only too willing to do anything that would save them from return to a certain death on the gallows and only too thankful to have escaped service in an army which ran itself by the lash and made you stand in line when the shot came flying.

He saw some of them before him now, in various stages of drunkenness and debauchery. The room stank of their sweat, mingled with the discernible odours of wine, rum and cooking food. Tobacco smoke hung thick in the air and on one wall a small boy sat turning the handle of a spit on which, over an open fire, a sheep was cooking. The place sang with noise: laughing, shouting, cries for more wine and the giggling of the flirting, half-naked strumpets who constituted the female element of Trouin's nautical family. In one corner a blind Irish fiddler was playing what passed for a jig and several drunken sailors and their harlots were skipping and dancing to the music which was all but drowned out by the general hubbub.

Trouin looked at them all, filled with pride. This was his world, these people his own. Loyal to a man – well, almost. At least for as long as he kept them fed and watered and led them on to greater riches – or the promised dream of wealth. Slowly, he walked through to the other room of the inn, followed from the shadows by an immense figure of a man, his skin pitch-black, who was his ever-present bodyguard. Trouin had rescued him from slavery in the Bahamas eight years ago, though not before he had had his tongue cut out as a punishment for attempting to escape from his English master. He could neither read nor write and Trouin, proud of his classical education and a devotee of Homer, had christened him Ajax, after the Greek hero and strongman. He was the best protector that Trouin could wish for and his name was doubly appropriate, for if ever his master was in danger, he would, like his namesake, go mad with rage and fight with the strength of ten. Inseparable from his saviour and as loyal as an old dog, he carried in his right hand, tucked in close to his huge chest, an immense blackthorn stick and anyone foolish enough to appear to threaten Trouin would quickly know its wrath. At his side hung a razor-sharp scimitar of Arab design with a mother-of-pearl grip, plundered from a Turkish merchantman. In fact Ajax rarely drew the sword. For when he did he swung it with such assurance and faster than many slimmer blades that it never returned to its scabbard without first tasting blood. The two men, master and servant, made their way through the inn, and as they passed any in their path were quick to move aside.

While most of the inn was alive with conversation, at one table no one was speaking and the only sounds came from a bodhran and a penny whistle, played by two of the sailors which provided the music for the entertainment that currently held twenty pairs of eyes in its spell. Atop a round table that had been cleared of glasses and plates, a pretty, dark-skinned girl was spinning round above a broad glistening silver serving plate which was now transformed into a mirror, afforded titillating glimpses of her cleverly exposed sex. The pirates gawped and cheered and threw their coins – crowns bearing the head of the Sun King, English guineas and pieces of eight – onto the table. The girl kept a careful watch, and as the pile of silver and gold grew began to look to a man to her right, a huge fellow with massively muscled arms and a shining bald pate. Every so often he would nod his head and she would remove another garment. Her pimp knew just when to stop, just when she would have offered enough to titillate, to encourage just one of the men around the table to follow her up to one of the filthy bedchambers; he would leave lighter of purse and with the prospect of an unpleasant, agonizing dose of the pox and she would leave some few crowns the richer. Trouin knew too that there were other mirrors upstairs, cleverly placed so that those who had a mind to could observe the girls at their sport and gain as much pleasure in seeing as doing. At times he himself had enjoyed such harmless voyeurism.

This evening though, he was not in a mind to frolic. This was not an evening for sex or for killing, but for sport. He signalled to the girl's pimp who snapped his fingers. Instantly the dancer stopped her twirling and bent down to collect her clothes from the table. There was a collective sigh from the men gathered around her, for she was now clad only in the thinnest of gossamer scarves around her ample breasts and another tied across her thighs. But Trouin wanted to play and he was not to be deflected. As the girl and her pimp found their quarry for the evening, one of the younger sailors who had not encountered them before, Trouin fired a parting word at their customer.

'Be careful of her, Thomas. She's as common as a barber's chair, that one. No sooner is one customer out than another's in.' The other men laughed. He addressed the company: 'Cards, gentlemen. Let us play. Who will take me on?'

The men began to back away. Trouin's reputation went before him. Had he not killed a man in St Malo in a duel over a card game? And then there had been that incident in the Carolinas when he had lost 200 louis and over the next three days every member of the card school had been murdered – save for Trouin. No one was quite sure who had been cheating, but no one dared question the outcome.

Trouin addressed the room. 'Come now. What is it to be? Perhaps a game of basset? Or ombre? Come, Soucrouff? You there, Evans, Barty. What about you, Dick Hughes? Whose game for a hand? Bring the deck. Come, join me in the academy, gentlemen.'

Slowly, the men named moved across to the table. Their reluctance was easily explained. They knew that if things went badly one of them was sure to finish this night with a bullet through his heart.

Trouin slammed his cards, face up, on the tabletop. 'I win, gentlemen. Thank you for your company. And your sportsmanship. And now I think we shall call it a night.' He took one of the pistols from his belt and gently cocking the hammer with a soft click, laid it before him on the table. 'That is, if we are all agreed?'

As one, the four men around the table nodded their assent. Each of them laid down his cards, before standing and taking his leave with a short bow. They had played at lanterloo, with the knave of clubs high, and the others had taken care to ensure that Trouin had won every hand. As the last of his gaming partners left, he picked up the pistol, eased the hammer back down and, casting an eye over the pile of gold coins beside him on the table, took a puff from a pipe of sweet-scented Virginia tobacco which he followed with a short sip from a glass of cognac. All the while, his eye remained fixed on the curves of one of the serving-girls. A new girl. Thrilled by her novelty, he was wondering whether the evening might still hold other pleasures when a respectful cough made him turn his head.

The newcomer was the French governor of Ostend, the Comte de la Motte. 'Captain Trouin.'

'Governor. Please, join me. A glass of wine for the governor.' He beckoned to the girl. 'You, girl. Over here. Wine.' He turned to de la Motte, who was clearly out of breath.

'You are tired, Governor? You would prefer a glass of something cool instead. Beer perhaps?'

'No, no. Wine will be splendid, thank you. I have been hurrying to get here. I shall be fine in a moment.'

The girl arrived with the drinks and, as de la Motte recovered his composure and she bent far over the table to serve the wine, Trouin slid an unseen hand down the back of her skirt. For a moment her back went rigid with surprise and she spilt a little of the wine on the table. Then she relaxed. Trouin withdrew his hand as the governor took a drink. The girl turned, darted a playful smile at Trouin and left. He looked after her. Yes. Perhaps there would be time. Most definitely, tonight. Turning back, he realized that the governor had begun to speak in his customary, droning monotone. De la Motte was in a state of agitation.

'Captain, I really am most concerned. As the governor of the town I have a responsibility to the people. We are told that the British have bomb-throwing ships off the coast. What if they should use them?'

'I have no doubt about it. Why else should they have gone to the considerable effort of bringing them here, my dear Governor, unless they intend to use them?'

'Perhaps they merely intend to frighten us into surrender.'

Trouin laughed. 'If that is their intention then I am afraid, de la Motte, that they are mistaken. I do not intend to be coerced into abandoning this place. We shall sit here and wait for whatever foolish game the English care to play. But remember Governor, that while we are waiting our relief force is on its way.'

De la Motte smiled. 'Ah yes, the army. The king I believe has sent a column.'

'Damn the king and the army, man. I mean Jean du Casse. The admiral is a mere days away from here. You know he

132

sailed from Spain three weeks ago. It will be good to see him again.'

'Du Casse is coming here? I must prepare his quarters. What an honour! Du Casse!'

Trouin guffawed. 'An honour? Du Casse is no more a nobleman than I am. Good God, man. You're a Count. He only gained his honour by selling slaves in the Caribbean. The king made him an officer for looting a Dutch merchant fleet. He's a privateer, like me.' He bent his face close to the governor's: 'A pirate if you like, de la Motte. Eh? How d'you like that? Pirates – we eat children and boil our enemies alive. Haven't you heard?'

De la Motte was rattled by Trouin's sudden ferocity. The admiral's name was legendary, his rise to command had been meteoric. He was a hero of France. That at least was the popular version. But few knew him as well as Trouin, knew him for what he was: a ruthless buccaneer who had been created admiral by Louis for his services to the French after a terrible raid on Cartagena and his plundering of the English colonies at Port Royal, whose population of settlers he had sold into slavery, man, woman and child.

De la Motte seemed anxious. 'You really think he'll come?'

'Have no fear. Du Casse will lift the siege and I pity any man – or woman – who stands in his way. He'll be here within the week. You see if he isn't. Until then we sit and wait. Bombs or no bombs.' Trouin picked at his fingernails. 'So you see, my dear Governor I am not at all worried.'

Trouin poured himself and de la Motte another glass of wine and filled a third which had been standing empty on the table.

The governor looked puzzled. 'You are expecting someone to join us?'

'I am. And I can describe him to you. He is of medium

133

height and broad build. He has a pock-marked face and deep-set eyes. Green. He wears the uniform of an officer in the French army. And here he is.'

Their conversation was interrupted by the arrival of a man who, as Trouin had predicted, wore the uniform of a French field officer.

Trouin bowed briefly. 'Ah, Major Malbec. Welcome. A glass of wine? You know the governor?'

Naturally, Major Claude Malbec, commander of the garrison of Ostend, was well acquainted with the governor. Although, as he found de la Motte's conversation odious, he attempted to avoid his company as much as he could.

He smiled: 'Indeed. Comte de la Motte. A pleasure.' Noticing the glass of wine, Malbec sat down. 'You are kind, Captain. I cannot stay long. We have received intelligence that the English are assembling for a major assault. Their fleet too is likely to bombard the town within the next few days. Possibly tomorrow.' He took a long drink and turned to de La Motte. 'Governor. You are familiar with Marshal Vauban's drill for the safety of the garrison?'

De la Motte smiled and nodded his head. 'Yes indeed, Major. The routes to the safe blockhouses and casemates are well known by all the people of the town. We practise them once every week. You may rest assured that if the bombardment begins, which I sincerely hope it never does, then every man, woman and child in the town will reach them safely and remain within their shelter as long as it lasts.'

Malbec shook his head. 'No. I am afraid you are sadly mistaken in that assumption, Governor.'

'I'm not sure that I quite get your point, Major.'

'Really? It's very simple. You see, Governor, my men are more valuable than any of your civilians. Anyway, they are only Belgians, aren't they? Why should we bother if they get killed? I'm sure that half of them would murder us in our beds if they could. I'm afraid that they will simply have to suffer. I need every one of the blockhouses and casemates for my men. When the bombardment commences we shall strike the guns down from the ramparts into the casemates. Then, when it is over we will emerge and drive off the assault that is sure to follow. Otherwise – well, otherwise we will all be dead and the town will be lost.'

De la Motte spoke: 'Do you not think it a little unethical? To sacrifice women and children, even Belgian peasants?'

'It is my duty as a soldier. It is my duty to kill the enemies of France. And if that means sacrificing a handful of Belgian peasants, then so be it.'

Trouin had heard of Malbec's reputation, and of his conduct in the campaign in Bavaria, where, it was said, before the Battle of Blenheim he had ordered the massacre of an entire village. The women and children too. The man had no scruples and clearly no concept of any sort of honour. At least pirates operated within their own code of conduct. But this man was utterly without a soul.

'Yes, Malbec. I do see the governor's point. It hardly accords with the behaviour of a gentleman.'

Malbec grunted. 'Whoever said that I was a gentleman? I have never claimed that title.'

Trouin laughed.

De la Motte rose and bowed. 'Excuse me Captain, Major. I must return to my house. I grow neglectful of my prisoner.'

Trouin smiled. An English noblewoman, a countess by all accounts and strikingly pretty, had been captured aboard an errant English sloop in the Channel a week ago and, brought to the town in its capacity as a prison, hours before the arrival of the allied army, she was now installed as de la Motte's personal guest. It was presumed that she would remain in his care until she could be exchanged for a French prisoner of similar rank; that was, unless something else befell her. She was a valuable prize, but her political value did not deter the wilful Trouin from wanting to see whether he might not yet be able to number her among his conquests.

He winked at the governor: 'Remember our appointment, my dear Count. I intend to call upon you tomorrow, for the very specific purpose of meeting your fair prisoner. You know how the English fascinate me.'

'The countess will be enchanted Trouin, I am sure. But please ensure that you are not accompanied by any of your men. Do not forget that I am King Louis' ambassador here and it is my duty to safeguard the wellbeing of any member of the English nobility we take prisoner.'

'Do not worry, Governor. My intentions are wholly honourable. Do not forget that I myself hold the commission of an officer in the king's navy. I too, dear Count, have a reputation to defend.'

'Until tomorrow then.'

The governor left them and Trouin turned to Malbec. He was smiling. 'You really would do that? Save yourselves and allow the women and children to burn?'

'Most assuredly I would, Captain. Why on earth not? It is the logical solution.'

'Certainly, I grant you that your reasoning is most logical. You and your men, Major, along with my own of course, are without doubt the most valuable people in this town. It is simply that I am surprised that you should be quite so clinical, so divorced from any notions of humanity.'

'Humanity be damned, Trouin. I have nothing to thank my fellow humans for.'

'I know something of your history, Major. But, if you can, do tell me the cause of such bile.'

'You know something of me, I grant you, I grant you. But do you know why I have so little to thank the English for? You may recall an incident some thirteen years ago this very month. It was well reported. An English fleet opened fire upon Dieppe and Le Havre. Something about harbouring privateers. I am a Norman, Captain. Le Havre is my *home*.' Trouin could see the tears beginning to well in his eyes. Malbec went on: 'Two hundred civilians met their deaths that day. Among them were my wife and my two young sons. They were just nine and five years old. My wife's name was Marie.' He looked away, and after a short interval spoke again. 'And now, Captain Trouin, now I don't care who dies and that includes whomsoever's wives and sons may be caught up in whatever war I am fighting. I may wear the uniform of France and fight for the king. But believe me Captain, I live for nothing but death.' He stood and bowed.

Trouin gazed up at him: 'I am so very sorry, Major. Until we meet again.'

'Until we meet again, under the bombardment, Captain. When your men will seek shelter with mine in Marshal Vauban's blockhouses.'

Malbec turned smartly on his heel and clattered off across the stone floor, his sword clanking against his boot. Trouin poured himself another glass of wine and tossed it back in a single shot. He turned to the mute blackamoor, who stood motionless behind him.

'Come, Ajax. We'll take a walk. I think that we need some air. This room stinks too much of the military . . . and it reeks of sadness.'

Most of the dancing girls and harlots were gone now and those that were left were either slumped senseless over tables with their consorts or tangled in an amorous embrace. A dog was lapping at a pool of vomit close to where the Irish fiddler had sat and the boy turning the spit was snoring at his post. Trouin and Ajax walked out into the balmy night.

The *Etoile du Nord* lay on the south side of the town, within the defences but close to the Key, the landing place of the port and the centre of its maritime life. A covered gateway, protected by a fortified guard room, cut through the great walls leading on to the jetty from a labyrinth of narrow streets. High above them rose the great sixteenth-century church of St Peter and St Paul and it was here, in this meeting place of religion and trade, that Trouin had made his headquarters: at the sign of the North Star – the sailors' friend and guide. As sobriquets went it suited him well, he thought. The inn lay on the crossroads of two major streets: Paulus Straat and Sint Francis Straat. It functioned in effect as a citadel within a citadel. From its upper floors a sharp-eyed lookout would be able to see all traffic in this sector of the town and to give ample warning of the approach from any direction of anyone who might look threatening. But no one ever did, so full was the quarter of Trouin's men. Indeed so crammed was this part of the city with pirates that it now resembled some West Indian buccaneering town more than any Channel port. As they walked, Trouin thought over all that he had just heard and seen.

It was a pity that Malbec was a soldier; he would have made a good pirate. He presumed that what they said of him was true, that business in Bavaria. There was good reason for it. Yet still it sent a chill down even his spine. Women and children? Sell them as slaves by all means. Use them yourself. But to kill them in cold blood? He turned left, away from the inn and shadowed by Ajax, strode down the street, past the white-coated sentry at the guardroom and through the gate towards the Key. Beneath its arch a drunken French sailor was sleeping fitfully in a pool of urine. Trouin half-recognized him as one of his own crew. Perhaps he would put the man on reduced rations in the morning. He must have some discipline.

There was a commotion further along the street where some of his people had bought a pipe of wine and placed it in the middle of the carriageway and were forcing every passer-by to take a drink, at knife-point. A member of the clergy had protested and they were dealing with the man now, as Trouin passed, hoisting him harmlessly by his coat-tails to hang him up from the sign over a chandler's shop. The white-haired parson was bleating for his release.

Trouin laughed and nodded to the men. 'Let him down after five minutes, gentlemen. Remember, it doesn't do to mistreat a man of God. You never know when you might have need of him.'

Soon, he thought. All too soon this man of God would have his hands full. There would be corpses to bury and the last rites to give to those wounded in the bombardment. He paused on the Key and looked across to where his ships lay at anchor with their skeleton crews. A slight breeze was blowing in from the Channel, making him wish that he did not have to remain penned up in this hole for the immediate future; he longed to be riding the sea, bound for the Indies or the Carolinas, searching the horizon for a fresh prize. What he would have given to be there now. But he was here, in Ostend, waiting for the enemy's guns to open fire. He walked to the right, westwards along the quayside, caught the twinkling stars in an almost clear sky and noticed the answering movement of the darker, orange lights that came from the campfires which marked the English and allied lines across the marsh. An entire army lay there. A victorious army who believed they could take this place. But they were powerless without their navy. So many impotent soldiers, unable to even reach the town. He doubted whether they knew about du Casse. How would they react to his arrival?

If, of course, du Casse failed to sail into the harbour shortly, if he did not come to their aid and blow the English ships from the water, then he and his men, along with Malbec's soldiers would have to fight after all. Secretly Trouin longed to take on the British hand to hand, to see what they were really made of. But perhaps it would not come to that. The girl, the countess, might yet prove of use, somehow. He smiled as his mind began to investigate the possibilities. For now though they would have to wait and see. Wait for the onslaught and see just how determined these English soldiers and their Dutch friends and their navy were to take this place. See what damage they could do. Then, when he had gauged their strength and when they knew the true situation there would be time enough to resort to other means. Whatever they might be.

He turned to Ajax: 'We shall see what transpires, my friend, shall we not, once the bombs begin to fall and the townspeople begin to die. You see, Ajax, in many ways I am like Major Malbec. I do not care what might be the fate of these miserable wretches. But unlike him, I have other, less emotional, what you might call more rational reasons. Once the civilians begin to die here the governor will be desperate to find a way to make the British stop their shelling. And I think that I may know just the way.'

For there was one thing of which he was certain. The great René Duglay-Trouin had no intention of being taken by the English and tried as a pirate. He would not hang in chains at the harbour mouth like poor Kidd at Execution Dock, as a warning to sailors not to follow his example. He would *set* the example. He would win this battle against the great English general, their precious Lord Malbrook. Then he and his pirates would sail away from Ostend with as much of her treasure as they could carry and no doubt a few of her fine people to sell into slavery. And who knew, perhaps one of them might be the English countess. They would see.

EIGHT

Steel sat at the small wooden camp-table in front of his tent in the lines and dipped the quill pen into the pot of black ink. He glanced up at the morning sky and scanned the comings and goings along the 'street' – the wide, mud-churned alleyway that divided the officers' tents from those of the company's men. This was his least favourite aspect of soldiering; company accounts, bookkeeping. A clerk's work; but still a necessary part of any captain's job.

He gazed down at the paper before him, sighed and beginning to scribble, found his mind straying back to the brief, unhappy time in his youth that he had spent as a junior clerk in his uncle's lawyers' office in Edinburgh. Memories of apathy, boredom and the crushing despair of his mother's death came flooding into his mind, unbidden and unwanted. The army had taken him away from all that. The army and Arabella. Away from Scotland, from his roots, to a new life which was his alone to mould, as he wished.

Fifteen years of soldiering had taken him through the Guards and the King of Sweden's army, across Europe and had seen him grow from boy to man. He thanked God for

142

his good fortune and that he had survived when he had seen so many good men die around him. His mind turned again to the coming assault and he wondered if perhaps today would see the end. Every soldier knew that there was an allotted time for him to meet his death. You could not avoid fate. But sometimes, thought Steel, perhaps you could play the devil at his own game and stall him for just one more day. He wondered if there was any truth in what the men said – that the life of the man you killed would appease the gods of war and ensure that you would live another day.

The thought sickened him and he returned to the business in hand: requisition of stockings for a half-company. Requisition of shirts – five, coats – two. They'd be lucky to see any of those within a year. The men's coats, bright scarlet when they had left Dover four years ago, were now more a dirty brick-red. He continued scribbling. Requisition of shoes. Those at least he knew he might expect to have. It might not matter that their coats were running with dye, that their hats were holed and turned-down and their stockings stained with mud, but the duke was most particular that his men should be well shod. Well-armed too. Steel had already indented for extra ammunition for the assault – musketballs and grenades. He intended personally to inspect every man's gun. There must be no chance of a misfire at the most crucial moment. Steel rubbed at his temples and continued scratching on the ledger paper. It was hard to keep the mind focused on such mundanities when the prospect of death or glory in the assault loomed so large. And then there was the other matter to take care of for Colonel Hawkins. He would see to it immediately after drill parade.

Slaughter appeared before him and stood to attention: 'Men are all present sir and ready for you when you will.'

Steel smiled: 'Very good, Sarn't. Just as well to put them through their paces before we go.'

'You're right there, sir. We've been sitting in this camp that long, they'll have forgotten how to march.'

'Just as long as they haven't forgotten how to shoot, Jacob. That's all I ask of them now.'

'They're restless, Mister Steel. Need to see action.'

Steel closed the company ledger and rose from the table: 'They'll get it soon enough. Come on, Jacob. Let's see just how bad they've become.'

They walked across to where the company was drawn up in line, two ranks deep, a short distance beyond the tents. Steel could see that Slaughter had already done a good job with them. They were standing rigidly to attention and although their appearance would have probably had him cashiered at a St James's parade, here, in the field, they would do.

'Carry on Sarn't.'

Slaughter stepped to the right flank of the company, placing his spontoon firmly on the ground and his hand on his hip: 'Ready.'

The twenty-four muskets of the front rank were handled up to the angle between thigh and breastbone.

'Pree . . . *sent*.'

Two dozen guns smacked neatly into the crook of the right shoulder.

'Fire!'

The ragged volley shattered the air and the balls crashed harmlessly into the trees which Slaughter had chosen as their target. A few men, instead of ramming their charges home, had adopted the widespread practice of thumping the butts of their guns on the ground and the balls rattled harmlessly in the barrels and dropped out.

Steel grimaced and shook his head: 'Not good. Not good at all, Sarn't.'

He walked across to a man in the front rank whose ball lay on the ground before him. 'Come on, Tarling. You know the drill.'

'It's me ramrod, sir. Wood got wet last night, sir. It's all swelled up and won't fit down the barrel, sir.'

Next to him, Mulligan muttered, still staring straight ahead: 'Always was your problem, Tarling. Yer rod swelling up like that.'

The company sniggered.

Slaughter thumped his spontoon on the ground. 'Silence in the ranks there! Next man as speaks'll feel my bloody rod on their back.'

Steel shook his head again. 'Thank you, Sarn't. Get this man another ramrod. He's no bloody use to me without one.'

Slaughter looked at Steel with the doleful expression of a dog that, wishing to please its master, senses there is something very wrong.

Steel addressed the company: 'That was bloody awful.' He pointed across towards where Ostend lay in the pale morning sunlight. 'Do that when we get in there and you're all dead men. Now, we'll go again. On my command.'

Steel knew that this battle, like most of them, would be a close-quarter affair. More so here, for they would be confined within streets. Besides, their muskets were only accurate to a hundred yards. It would be a blasting match. And whoever could get in the greatest number of volleys would be the victor. They would fire at twenty paces or fewer within the town. It took twenty seconds for a trained soldier to load a musket, and at present he reckoned they must be taking thirty. That was two shots a minute. They needed to make it three.

He called across to Hansam: 'Henry, your timepiece, if you would be so kind as to oblige me.'

Hansam walked over and produced the pocket captured at Blenheim watch and handed it to Steel. 'Do be careful with it, Jack. Shan't find another of its kind.'

'I'll take care, Henry.' Steel took it and looked at the second hand. 'Right. I'm going to time you. Make ready . . . Present . . . Fire!'

Once again the fusils crashed out and smoke and flame belched from the barrels. Steel looked at the watch: Twenty-six seconds. You're still dead men. Cussiter, show them how it's done. Two paces forward. Right, make ready. Musket set firm in the hollow of the right shoulder. Body straight with elbows in an equal line. Make your butt breast high. Head up and take care to have your left knee a little bent. That's it. Well done, Cussiter. Now, present. Thumb away from the cock. Right foot back a little now. Forefinger before the trigger. Don't touch it, mind. Make your right knee stiff now. And keep your muzzle lower than the butt. That way you'll hit your man in the centre of his body. Right, Dan. Aim at that group of trees. Fire!'

Cussiter squeezed the trigger and the ball flew from the gun and hit one of a group of three trees at around the height of a man's stomach.

'Well done. Sarn't Slaughter, extra rum ration for Corporal Cussiter. And the same on my account for any man that can equal that. But within the time. Remember, twenty seconds only. Work 'em hard, Sarn't. Fire them off by ranks, rear and front. I'll be back within the hour.'

He walked down the length of the tent lines, row upon row of unbleached canvas. A miniature town made of sail-cloth within whose walls were played out all the tragedies and ecstasies of any community: births and deaths; family life, love and loneliness. The last few weeks had been a rare respite from the march. But Steel knew that with the coming assault, the illusion of domestic calm would be replaced again by a sea of pain.

Eventually he arrived at the lines of the larger, regimental officers' tents and in the centre found what he was looking for. He lifted the flap and entered the tent with its campaign furniture and cosy ambience.

Major Frampton turned to see his unexpected guest. 'Steel. I don't recollect our having an appointment. How can I help?'

Steel knew this was no time for niceties. 'I know what you're about, Frampton.'

The major frowned: 'I'm sure I don't know to what you are referring, Captain Steel. And kindly use my title when addressing a superior officer.'

'If I had my way you wouldn't be superior for any longer, nor have any title. The game's up.'

Frampton began to colour: 'I warn you, Mister Steel. Unless you desist from this abhorrent behaviour I shall have no alternative but to place you under arrest. Now kindly remove yourself from my tent.'

Steel could smell the fear. He strode towards the adjutant until their faces were barely two feet apart. 'Stop bluffing, Frampton. I know all about it.'

Steel cast his eyes about the tent and at last saw what he was looking for. A sheaf of printed papers protruding from the drawer of a wooden chest. He took a gamble. Pulling hard on the brass handle he tore open the drawer and reached inside for the papers. One glance was all it took. Frampton blanched.

Steel held the pamphlets before his face: 'These, Frampton. I know that you are behind these lies.'

For a second Frampton panicked, then recovered: 'Good heavens. How did those get in there? That is to say of course I know what they are. But what are you saying, Steel. Me? Behind them? Preposterous.'

'Don't try to deny it, Major. I heard you that night in Brussels. In the inn.'

Frampton stared at him: 'Heard me? Heard what?'

'You. In your cups. I heard you plotting.'

'You can't prove it was me.'

'So, you admit it.'

'Did I? No, I don't. It wasn't me, whoever you heard.'

'You and another officer.'

'Stapleton? You heard him?' Frampton stopped, realizing what he had said.

Steel smiled. 'You'd never make a spy, Major. Stick to soldiering and pray God that you get your head blown off before you pay your way to general and kill any more of your own men.'

'You didn't know. Did you?'

'I knew about you. And now I know enough.'

Frampton was sweating now: 'What do you intend to do? You'll inform Marlborough?'

'I think not.'

Frampton looked puzzled: 'Thank God. What then? What will you do?'

Steel laid the papers down on the chest and turned away from Frampton. 'I have a proposal for you. Firstly you will stop printing these sheets. You may well feel passionately about the sentiments they express, but I advise you to forget them. As far as you are now concerned Marlborough is the only man fit for the job of finishing King Louis and that were best done in Flanders. Should I hear that one word of sedition has passed your lips, one word in support of Peterborough

148

and the Spanish adventure, then our understanding will be at an end and I shall make your part in this affair known to the duke. I do intend to commit the truth to paper, Major, so do not consider having me disposed of – either in or out of the coming fight. Secondly, you will settle my mess bill and stop hounding me for credit until I give you the word. Don't worry, I shan't bankrupt you. Consider it merely an extended loan. I honour all my debts. And no, I'm not going to give you up, Frampton. It's too close to battle for that. And it would unsettle the men, the honour of the regiment is at stake. Whatever my personal feelings might be. But as for Major Stapleton, now that is a different story. He is not of our family. He can go to the devil. Well, to Colonel Hawkins at least. But he'll get the same treatment.'

He walked to the entrance and turned. Frampton was sitting at the small desk, his head in his hands. Steel smiled: 'Oh, and I would advise you to stay out of my way, Major. Should we meet have no fear that I shall not show you due deference, according to your rank. But bear in mind too what I know. And remember, don't try anything rash.'

Steel left the tent and retraced his steps through the regiment's lines to the training ground. Slaughter and the men were still hard at it. He stopped and watched, apparently unseen, and took Hansam's watch from his pocket.

Slaughter's voice rang out: 'Load. Ram down your charge. Remove rammers. Make ready. Present. Fire!' Steel watched the seconds tick away. Five. Ten, Fifteen. Twenty . . . one . . . two. With a crash the company opened fire. A good clean volley that rattled into the trees and ripped away the leaves and the smaller of the boughs.

With the watch still in his hand, Steel reached his men. 'Well done boys. Twenty seconds. That'll be three a minute. Keep that up and we'll give them a pasting they won't forget.'

There was a ragged cheer. Steel grinned: 'You've earned your rum, lads. Better get it while you can. Major Frampton's kindly offered to pick up the bill.'

An hour later, at the rear of the encampment, where the large, striped marquees of the general staff stood apart from the rest of the army's tents, Stapleton drew back a flap of pin-striped canvas and ducked his tall frame into the interior. It reeked of wine and lavender and stale sweat. In the waning light he was able to make out the figure of a man, who turned and addressed him.

'Ah, Major Stapleton. How good of you to come.' Colonel Hawkins walked forward from the shadow as Stapleton spoke.

'Do forgive me, Colonel Hawkins. A trifle late. Just back from huntin'. Damned hounds put up a hind and lost it. Shame. Have you been out yet? Poor country this.'

'Alas, rheumatics and corpulence no longer permit my indulgence in the thrill of the chase, Major. Not after deer, at any rate.' He smiled, but Stapleton watched as it quickly became a frown. 'Major Stapleton, I have asked you here on a matter of some delicacy. You will be aware that of late certain pamphlets have been circulating in the camp and more importantly, throughout the country, which are nothing less than slanderous against His Grace the Duke of Marlborough. It has been brought to my attention by a most reliable source – and to the attention of the Duke – that you are none other than the author of said pamphlets. What have you to say?'

Stapleton spluttered, his lisp becoming less well disguised. 'Of course I deny your accusation, Colonel. How could you possibly suppose . . . ?'

'By a most reliable source, Major, I mean a source in whose word I have the utmost faith.'

'You cannot be serious, Colonel. I have every confidence in the duke.'

'As I do in my source, Major Stapleton. Our intelligence is second to none.' On the last word, Hawkins leant forward and slammed his fist hard down on the oak table which stood between them with such ferocity that Stapleton started. 'Major Stapleton. I am in absolute earnest on this matter. Do you understand what I am saying to you?'

'You insinuate treason, sir. Why, why, I've a good mind to call you out.'

Hawkins laughed and shook his head. 'Ah, well, have you now, Major? You would do well to forget that you uttered that last statement. Just as I intend to. Major, take a look at me. I am an old man. I have had my last stag hunt and I very much hope that I have fought my last duel. Nevertheless, normally I would accept your challenge. But in this matter I am on commission from the duke himself. Specifically, he made me promise him not to defend his honour against you. Rather than our having you cashiered and tried for treason, a trial which you would most certainly lose, with . . . unutterable consequences, might I suggest that you instantly desist from printing this filth and pack your bags?'

Stapleton, dumbfounded, said nothing.

Hawkins continued: 'It is my intention to arrange for you to be posted to Spain, where your heart so evidently lies. I am sure that My Lord Peterborough will be able to find employment for you fighting General Berwick's army. I understand that the climate is somewhat challenging and that some supplies may be hard to come by in the Peninsula. The basic comforts of home, for instance. But then, you are a resourceful fellow. I'm sure you'll think of something to make your posting less arduous. And be thankful that I have not stripped you of rank.'

151

Hawkins poured himself a glass of madeira from a tall silver-mounted ewer and took a generous sip. 'Don't wait on my account, Major. You may go. I'm sure that you will have much to do before you leave us. And Major Stapleton, I would advise you to keep this as quiet as possible. You will also observe that you are under house arrest. Two gentlemen from the Foot Guards will attend you directly outside my tent. And Major, should I so much as catch you in conversation with any officer, my offer will be withdrawn and I will throw you to the wolves. Do you understand?'

Stapleton, who had gone quite white, answered in a barely audible voice, 'Sir. Yes, I quite understand. Thank you, Colonel. May I ask when I leave?'

'The sooner the better I think, Major. Don't you? Shall we say at dawn tomorrow for London, by way of Antwerp? Goodbye.'

NINE

Twisting a finger through her long fair hair, the little girl picked indifferently with her fork at the pallid, salted herring lying on her plate and turned to the thin, sallow-faced man who sat opposite her, gazing indulgently at her efforts.

'Daddy, the British won't really fire their guns at us, will they? We are safe here, aren't we?'

Marius Brouwer smiled at his daughter and nodded his head. At the age of five she was already able to understand much of what was said in the house. Sometimes, he thought, too much.

'Don't worry, Mathilde. The British would never do that to us. They know that in this town there may be many French and many people who support the French, but they also know that there are many people just like us. Good Belgian men and women and children who want the French to leave our country. They will not use their guns against us. If they do attack it will be by land and we must stay locked in our attics and cellars until they win. And don't worry, my darling, the British will win. You want the French to go home, don't you?'

Mathilde nodded her head and looked at her father. His smile told her that she had made the right response.

Marius leant across the table and tousled her hair. 'Good girl. Leave your plate now, if you don't want it. You've done well enough. Go off and play. Find your sister. She's in the yard. Go on.'

Skipping and singing to herself, Marius's daughter ran off into their tiny yard with its small vegetable patch to find her sister and her rag doll.

Marius's wife, Berthe, crossed the kitchen of the little house on Christian Straat and as she cleared away her daughter's plate and threw the scraps to their old dog, spoke quietly: 'D'you really think that they will not fire on the town? That's not what you told me last night.'

'What I tell you and what I tell Mathilde may be very different, dearest. As you know. The British are at war, they will do what they have to. In truth I don't know. I only have what I managed to get from the spy. He has spoken to the English and they speak about attacking after a bombardment. So we must expect the worse. He says that if we hear the bombs coming we must head for the shelters, like any other family. He does believe that they will attack by land. But he also said that he had heard that the ships were being made ready.'

Berthe's face turned deathly white and she stopped tidying the table: 'Marius, I'm frightened.'

He stood up, walked to her and placed a comforting hand around her slim waist. 'I know, my darling. But believe me, I trust the British. I don't believe the lies in those papers. Marlborough wants to help us. Anything he does will be in our interest.'

In truth he wished that he did believe what he said was true. That he did not really credit the news-sheets which had recently begun to circulate in the town with their stories that

154

the British general Marlborough, who had done so much in driving the French out of their country, really did have the interests of the Belgian people at heart. But if any of the new rumours were true then the man was just the same as any other general, any other conqueror, and they would be no better off under his rule, or Dutch rule, than they had been under the French. But that was not what Marius told his wife and his daughter. Those thoughts were only for him and his comrades in the people's movement. He pulled Berthe to him and gave her a long kiss on the lips, then forced himself to break quickly away.

'Now make sure that Mathilde and Anna stay in the house and if they do start to shell us get to the blockhouse as quickly as you can. The one at the Sluice Bastion. I'll join you there. I must go and see Louise and Hubert. We have to decide on a plan of action when the British enter the town.' He smiled. 'As they are sure to do. Take care. I won't be long.'

Marius opened the door and walked out into the still of the afternoon. It was a Saturday, the third day of July. Somewhere a small dog was yapping in an upper room and from the surrounding streets he could hear the sound of horses pulling their loaded carts across the cobbles. Overhead the shrill call of the seagulls provided its usual, incessant undertone, so constant that no one noticed it. Apart from that though the town was bathed in the quiet of the afternoon's peace. For it was after five and, apart from little Mathilde, everyone from the governor in his palace to the trades-people around the great town square had finished their dinner long ago and were enjoying what remained of their day of rest and sensibly taking a nap in the summer heat.

Marius crossed the Grote Place and looked up at the French royal standard of the fleur de lys that fluttered from the pole on the town hall. He was a gentle man at heart and abhorred the violence that so often swept his country. He had a kind, moonshaped face and soft brown eyes. A schoolteacher by calling, he was known for his oratory and outspokenness, although on Sundays he liked nothing better than to spend his day in the church, practising with the choir. Other than that his time was devoted to his family: Mathilde, her three-year-old sister Anna and of course, Berthe. Lately though, something new had stirred within Marius Brouwer. He had felt that he must make an effort to help his people. How, he wondered, could anyone, anyone of feeling, stand by and watch foreigners yet again despoil their land? And so he and a few friends had formed their little group – a movement of the people. Only he and a handful of others. They had christened it *schild ende vriend* – shield and friend – after the famous phrase used by the vengeful people of Bruges in 1302 to tell the French from the Flemish. Back then, at the height of the Flanders revolt, any man unable to pronounce the tongue-twisting phrase had been slaughtered on the spot. The French had been driven to reprisals and had finally been defeated at the Battle of the Golden Spurs, the flower of their nobility cut down. Of course, Marius did not intend to do the same to their current French oppressors. But the phrase made a fine name for their little group and upheld the correct principles. Most importantly, their right to political independence.

Marius would have told you that he hated no one, except in particular the French and the privateers in their employ who had lately transformed even his own godly enclave into such a den of vice. But he was prepared to fight anyone who threatened his principles and his family: French, Spanish, Austrian or British. Anyone who wanted to govern Belgium. For Marius there could only be one Belgium, that ruled by the

Belgian people. It was hard to know who to trust. Recently it had seemed to him that Marlborough had really meant what he had said. But now he was worried. Would the British really bomb the town as they seemed ready to do? By all that was holy, he hoped they would not, had prayed for it last night at the church of St Martin. Although he was sure in his heart that prayer was not necessary. The British were a civilized race – not barbarians. Weren't they?

Leaving Nieuw Straat he turned into the Capuchins quarter and reached the door of the schoolhouse where he taught. He knocked twice, and then three times and it opened. The room was empty save for two figures, a man and a woman. This was the Ostend underground, the people's forces of the Belgian republic. Or at least these were its officers. The other members were scattered about the town and in various farms around Ostend. But Marius and his two friends were the inspiration, the heart of the movement. They were not armed insurrectionists and they certainly could not have looked less like revolutionaries. And as far as they knew, to date, the authorities were unaware of their existence. But perhaps if the time demanded it they would have to fight.

Marius nodded to them. 'We haven't much time. We must make a plan for when the British take the town.' They said nothing and he noticed the expressions on their faces. Terror. Alarm. His own stomach felt hollow with fear. 'What's wrong? What is it? What have you heard? Tell me.'

The man looked anxiously at the girl and back at Marius before speaking. 'Marius, we have to act quickly. The British are without doubt going to open fire on the town. Perhaps tonight. Probably tonight.'

'How do you know this, Hubert? Who told you? You're certain?'

Hubert Fabritius nodded his head. A legal clerk by profession, he was not in the habit of saying anything unless he knew it to be absolutely the case, a fact of which Marius was only too aware.

'I have no doubt, Marius. The spy – de Groot – he told me. Only two hours ago. Said he had it direct from a redcoat officer. It's happening Marius. It's happening now.'

Marius looked at the girl, Louise Huber, an expert chocolatier whose divine creations were particularly in demand with the French garrison. He had known Louise from boyhood, and would have trusted her with his life – as she would him. She said nothing. Tears welled in her eyes. Then she nodded her head.

Marius looked away. Into nothingness: 'All right. That's it then. We need to get back to our homes and then get everyone into the shelters.' He paused, confused. 'But what plan do we have? The British could be in the town within hours.'

Louise spoke: 'Does it really matter, Marius? If that's the case then the French will be defeated. Then we can discuss plans.'

'You don't think that we need a plan of action? Terms of surrender and occupation? We must compose a petition to Marlborough at least. We need to appoint leaders.'

'You are our leader.'

'Fine then. But what of the rest?'

Louise, who had shoulder-length brown hair and was clad in a simple cotton smock dress and a shawl, placed a hand on his arm and flashed her pretty green eyes: 'Don't worry, Marius. It's more important now that you return to Berthe and the children. You know that we trust you. We believe that you'll know what to do, when the time comes.'

*   *   *

158

Steel stood on the highest of the dunes that flanked the road which led into the barred West Gate of Ostend and looked out to sea. He was becoming slightly irritated by the enthusiasm of the young man at his side who was pointing excitedly to the water.

'Look, sir. That's my ship, the *Triton*, and over there are the bombketches. You can just make them out, captain. See how they sit so low in the water. That's the *Salamander* and there is the *Blast*. What an honour to be allowed to direct their fire. Aren't they magnificent? Well, the *Salamander*'s a bit of an old lugger, I will grant you that. Commissioned in '87. But the other one's a beauty. You have to agree, sir. Look, she's ship-rigged. What d'you say to that, sir?'

Steel said nothing, but smiled and nodded, then looked across to Hansam, who had just joined them on the dune, and raised his eyebrows. Hansam caught his gaze and smiled. Clearly, Lieutenant the Honourable George Forbes of her Britannic Majesty's Royal Navy, was in his element. The admiral had placed him here on the shore to direct the fire of the bombships and Forbes considered it a great privilege to have been selected. Although had he known the admiral's real reason for wanting him off the ship – boy's got too much to say for himself. I can't fight alongside him . . . . – he might have thought otherwise. Beside Forbes stood two sailors, signallers from the bombships, equipped with the different coloured and hatched flags which they would raise to indicate the fall of the bombs inside the citadel. It was easier to see from here. Forbes had met Steel at the head of the storming party which now stood assembled on the road and had courteously invited him to watch the bombardment with his informed commentary. And now Steel was beginning to wish that he hadn't accepted.

Steel watched the enthusiastic young officer as he grew

more animated. He was slight of build and spoke in a pleasantly lilting Irish accent which reflected his origins in County Down, where his father the Earl of Granard was a prominent figure. Steel had learnt as much during his first three minutes in the young man's company. He was shorter than Steel and with strong features that spoke of his Celtic roots.

Steel looked away from him and out again into the Channel, following Forbes' outstretched, pointing hand and saw the bombketches bobbing on the water. Behind them they each towed a small tender.

'You see those smaller boats, tied to the ships. They're packed with spare shells. That's where the men sleep, too. The ships themselves you see are so filled with the mortars and *matériel*. You should see them close to, Captain. Really, you should. Funny thing is, it was the French that invented them, bombships. Of course, those early vessels of theirs were nothing compared to these. Do you know that to aim them one had to move the entire ship by means of a spring anchor. And they only carried two small mortars on their foredeck. Now these beauties have their mortars – sizeable pieces – mounted on a central revolving platform, like so –' He drew in the sand. '– in the centre of the ship. All the force of the blast is transmitted directly into the hull, which is reinforced to take it. And how many mortars d'you suppose they carry, sir? Guess, please. Well, I'll tell you. They carry no less than three mortars apiece. You ought to see the destruction they cause. You know the French used bombships first at Genoa in 1684? Terrible waste of ammunition – too many civilian dead.'

Steel let the boy gabble on. Of course he remembered the incident, even though at the time he had been only ten years old. The news had reached their household through an aged uncle with navy connections and it had appalled his family just as it had the rest of Europe. He remembered sitting in the little schoolroom at Carniston and hearing about the deaths of so many women and children. This wasn't the soldiering that he had been told about. There was no glory in this. From that moment it had been clear to him that the French were bad and looking back he could see how it spoke of Louis' future ambition, of his willingness to do anything it took to take over Europe. Perhaps that was what had first fired him to become a soldier himself; a simple desire to fight the French.

Since then of course the British had played at the game too. The names of Dieppe and Le Havre were written in the annals of infamy. Other attacks had followed, on Calais and Dunkirk. And now it seemed they were about to do it again.

Forbes was still speaking: 'At the moment, d'you see, Captain, what is happening is that the artillerymen, your fellows, on board the ships out there, are doing what we call "laying the ordnance". That is to say they are ensuring that each of the mortars is sitting properly in its bed. Very soon they will trim the fuses on each shell and then they will wait.'

Yes, thought Steel. Then we will all wait. His attack was not due to go in against the town until after the bombardment had lifted. But already he was feeling a little sick with apprehension. Clearly Forbes did not share his grasp of reality; had somehow, at the age of twenty-one, still not made the connection between his beautiful engines of war out there on the sea and the dreadful carnage which they were about to cause within the town. God, thought Steel. Was there no silencing the boy?

'Of course the only problem with the mortars is their accuracy. Or rather their lack of it. I suppose that's why I'm here. Of course it's inevitable that some civilians will be killed. But

161

it's the pirates we're really after. Must stop them taking our shipping. They're all in the pay of the French you know. Caught one four years ago, Jean Bart. Dreadful fellow. Escaped in a rowing boat. They say that the one they call Duglay Trouin is in there. King Louis' favourite. What a triumph it will be if we can take him, sir. Of course, that will be up to you and your men, that's the army's job, isn't it? Actually, I'm rather fond of the army. Wouldn't mind serving on land one day myself. See action on the field so to speak. Brother was a soldier. Perhaps you knew him, sir. Lord Forbes. Pleasant chap. Died at Blenheim.'

Steel had not known him, although he knew his name, knew him to have been respected by the staff and much loved by his men. Steel had heard that Forbes had fallen at Blenheim itself, in the last attack.

'I'm sorry to say Lieutenant that I never had the privilege of making your brother's acquaintance. Which is I am sure to my detriment. I heard that he died a hero, though. I sympathize with your family's loss.'

'Thank you, sir. Bound to happen though. Altogether too impetuous, poor James. Pays to be cautious in war, if you ask me. You have to know just where and when to go. Am I right, sir? Would you agree with that?'

Steel smiled: 'Oh yes, Lieutenant. Most certainly. It's all a question of caution. All about being in the right place at the right time. That's really all there is to it.'

Forbes beamed: 'I knew it. I'm awfully keen to meet your commander here, sir, General Argyll. Great admirer of the man. Splendid thing he carried off at Ramillies. Did you see it?'

Steel spoke quietly: 'Yes. I saw it.'

'How I envy you. Absolutely first-class feat of arms. Took a village single-handed. Fought off an entire regiment of damned Irishmen. Can't wait to meet him.'

162

I'm sure you can't, thought Steel. And I am sure that he will enjoy meeting you, an Irishman so inclined to praise the cold-blooded murder that Steel had witnessed of a fellow Irishman ten times his equal as a man. Religion, he presumed, lay behind Forbes' bigotry. Steel had no real love of it. It was religion, and the vices it brought in its wake, which kept him away for the most part from any house of God. Although on occasion, when circumstances demanded it, he had been known to pray.

Forbes was speaking again: 'I do hope that you are able to take this Trouin fellow. It would be a great service to the navy – and indeed to yourselves. He is the scourge of merchant shipping – all shipping. With him in command of the Channel the duke shall surely have no provisions.'

'Rest assured, Mr Forbes. We'll take him, or kill him in the attempt.'

Oh, they would take this French pirate, thought Steel. But he wondered how many innocent civilians would have to die to ensure that they did so?

One of Forbes' men was reading a message from the flagship. He turned to the lieutenant: 'Signal from the admiral, sir. Make ready.'

'I believe that we are about to fire, sir. I presume that you are well used to cannon fire, Captain. But I wonder whether even you will have ever seen anything quite like this. It ought to be quite a spectacle. Something I'll wager you'll never forget, sir.'

'Thank you, Lieutenant Forbes. I can assure you that you will have my full attention.' Of that there could be no denying.

Steel looked to his right, to where, ranged along the edge of the marsh, behind the Steene Trench, pointing eastwards, directly towards Ostend, the allied artillery stood waiting for the order to open fire. He could make out the gunners around their pieces; the dozens of portfire men poised over the touch-holes with their smouldering linstocks. Marlborough had ordered that the siege train – the huge twenty-four-pounders – should be brought up as close as possible before the marshes and even though it would be at long range, that the cannon should be set at their highest trajectory to attempt to lob their shot over the ramparts. To the east of the town, too, Dutch cannon had taken up position and were concealed behind basketwork gabions.

Out on the water, as Forbes had envisaged, the artillerymen on temporary transfer from the army to the bombships were putting the final touches to their charges. The mortars lay ready and the fuses had been cut to what the gunners reckoned was the correct length to allow them to land in the town before they burnt down through their cases to the explosive charge within.

The men-of-war, the forty- and sixty-gunners in Admiral Fairborne's squadron had drawn as close as they could to the shore and the gunners of ten vessels now stood ready by the open portholes. Twenty guns apiece were loaded: ten broadsides' worth and although their shot would not do anything like the damage of the bombships' weoponry, much of it falling out of range, their combined impact was sure to be terrifying.

And Steel knew that was what Marlborough must be hoping for at this moment. That the terror instilled by this tumultuous barrage would be enough to make the people of Ostend, or at least the garrison, open the gates without further struggle, without further bloodshed. And Steel too prayed to himself that it would happen and that their entry into the town would be clean and bloodless. But deep within he knew that his prayers would not be answered.

*   *   *

Marius hurried back through the quiet streets towards his house. He was barely thirty yards from his front door when he heard it. At first he thought that it must be a great clap of thunder, somewhere in the distance and instinctively he stopped. For this was the deepest thunder that he had ever heard and instantly, Marius Brouwer knew the terrible noise for what it truly was and ran, desperately, towards his door and his family.

The first six shells flew up from the bombketches and towards the town in an arc two hundred feet high and the townspeople gazed up at them in wonder. Within seconds though the more level-headed among them had realized fully what was happening. Mothers gathered their children into their arms and ran instinctively towards their homes rather than to the cellars, blockhouses, casemates and other shelters where they had been drilled to go in just such an eventuality. Vauban had planned for this very scenario many years ago and the drill had been practised diligently every month. But it did not prevent their panic. The great marshal himself had witnessed at first hand the effect of the bombardment of Le Havre by the British in 1694, had seen the people blown to pieces and the streets covered in blood and body parts. He had sworn that it would not happen again on French soil or in a French-held town.

But the shelters that he had so carefully designed were not now sufficient to embrace the growing population of a thriving sea port. Indeed they were barely large enough to contain the garrison and when that was swollen by two full crews of privateers, it was clear that Vauban's efforts to protect the population would be all in vain. And now the unthinkable was happening.

Realizing their initial mistake, the townspeople finally began to make for the protective casemates which lay under the bastions, beneath thirty feet of solid stone. But before anyone had reached shelter the great iron balls came crashing down into the town. The first to land fell to earth in the Grote Place, its fuse still sputtering. It rolled across the cobbles towards the town hall and lay motionless, smoking. Those people who had been unlucky enough to be in the square reacted in very different ways. Three men began to run towards side alleys. A peasant girl threw herself to the ground and four other men and a woman just stood and stared at the spinning, sputtering ten-inch-diameter iron globe. One of them began to move towards it, intent on picking it up and hurling it away.

Then the fuse burnt down and within the casing, as the flame made contact with the saltpetre and the powder, the charge caught and abruptly the man's world and that of the people about him came to an abrupt and violent end. The force of the explosion plucked cobbles from the street and hurled the girl high in the air. Of the three men nothing remained but shards of cloth and flesh. The woman alone remained. Blinded by the blast and with a bloody stump where her right arm had been severed by flying debris, she stumbled through the thick smoke and still descending stones and iron fragments. Mute. Shocked. Dying.

Then a fresh salvo of shells began to land and the great siege guns opened up from the fields and the cannon from on board the warships off the coast and Ostend recoiled in shock at the bite of modern war.

Standing on the strand, Steel gazed at the obscene, pyrotechnic beauty of the bombardment and the jarring, orangered explosions as the shells found their targets. It always amazed him how any human being was able to live through such a storm of fire. But live they did. Some were maimed, some blinded, others barely recognizable as human. But they lived. George Forbes too was watching, with a keen interest, diligently marking the fall of each of the shells, noting any that came down too short. From time to time he called across to the signallers and as the bombs began to fall with greater accuracy, Steel felt an uncharacteristic rising nausea at what he imagined must be taking place within the walls and knew that the time had come to take his leave. He half-walked, half-skidded back down the dune, where a few minutes earlier Hansam had preceded him.

Slaughter was standing beside the lieutenant, and both men were staring at the town from which thick plumes of dirty black smoke had now begun to rise.

The sergeant was the first to find words: 'Poor buggers. Doesn't seem right, sir. Women and children.'

'No, Jacob. It's not right. But we have no alternative. We are assured that the people have shelters. Let's hope that they have had time to find them.'

He thought again of Major van Cutzem's words. 'Please God that we never have to witness such things again . . . that we never again have to descend into that hell.'

Well, at least poor, dead van Cutzem had been spared the sight of the fresh hell that was unfolding this day in Ostend.

Seated at a stout oak table in casemate number four on the west side of the citadel, directly beneath the Florida Bastion, Major Claude Malbec of the feared Grenadiers Rouges, chewed on the stale tobacco in his mouth and spat. He drew a silk handkerchief out of the pocket of his waistcoat and dabbed gently at the corners of his mouth and the sweat on his forehead. The sweet scent of lavender pomade was curiously both comforting and disquieting. It reminded him instantly of easier times, in Paris. Of a girl he had kept as his

167

lover, in a house behind the Place Royale. Of the gaming tables at the Palais Royal and of the carnival atmosphere of those nights in the capital when you would wake up next morning with each of your arms around a naked girl and with dried blood on your sword blade and would not remember and not care how it, or they, or you, had got there. But with that evocative fragrance there came another memory. The haunting image of his dead wife. And as always when he thought of her, and their murdered children, he thought too of the British and his mind became lost in a red sea of hate.

With the heel of his ammunition boot Malbec ground the orange spit from the tobacco hard into the straw-covered floor and turned to his sergeant who stood by the door with his arm around a serving-girl, one of the *filles du regiment* who had marched in here with the garrison a year ago.

From outside their sealed shelter the scream of incoming shells crept into the room followed by the crash as they impacted. The walls shook regularly, with each fresh explosion, sending dust down from the eaves. The air though, save for the ubiquitous odours of sweat and tobacco, was surprisingly fresh. Marshal Vauban had thought of that, installing complex ventilation systems in each of Ostend's casemates, so that their inhabitants could last inside for days on end. There were latrines too, discreetly hidden behind a curtain wall, and storerooms for food and wine. A tamper-proof draw-well in the corner provided the all-important supply of fresh water.

Malbec called across to the sergeant: 'Müller. How long has it been now?'

'Half an hour, sir. Perhaps longer.'

'How long do you think they'll go on?'

'That's anyone's guess, sir. But I think they mean business.'

Malbec laughed. There was a hammering at the door.

Voices; first a man, then women. Pleading voices. The sergeant and his girl edged away from the door. The soldiers, who previously had been talking through the bombardment, became silent. Malbec sat motionless. At another table, across the room, his second-in-command, a captain who had joined the regiment before the recent defeat at Ramillies, looked anxiously towards the door.

'Major Malbec, sir, with respect, d'you suppose that we should let them in? They're being torn to pieces, sir.'

Malbec frowned and shook his head. 'My dear Captain Lejeune. How much you have to learn about war. And how much about life.'

The soldiers had begun to talk again now.

'I told you, Lejeune, when we locked the door. Let one of these damned peasants in here and you can be sure that the rest will follow. We cannot accommodate the whole town in this place. We must save ourselves to ensure that we can fight when the barrage lifts. That is the simple truth, Captain. Those are my orders. And you have yours. Besides, what's it to you? They're only Belgians.'

He laughed and spat on the floor. The captain stood up: 'With respect, sir. They are also human beings. It's . . . it's inhuman to do this. We must admit them, Major. You must allow it.'

The colour rose in Malbec's tanned face. 'We must do nothing of the sort, Captain. And if you oppose me again on this matter I shall have you court-martialled for insubordination. How long have you served with us, Lejeune? Four months?'

'Two months, sir.'

'Two months. And where were you before that?'

'I served in the Regiment du Roi.'

'And before that?'

'I was a cadet in the royal guard sir, at the court.'

'You were a courtier. And before that? A schoolboy. And now you presume to tell me how I should and how I should not conduct a war? Do you know how long I have served with the colours?'

'No, sir.'

'Too long, Lejeune. Too long to be taught my trade by a wet-nursed infant, like you. No, Captain Lejeune. I should caution you not to attempt to teach an old dog new tricks. You should have been with us in Bavaria. Shouldn't he, Sergeant Müller? Tell him about Bavaria, Sergeant.'

Müller, a big, bald-headed Alsatian, grinned: 'Oh, you should have seen it, sir. Terrible business it was. But we had to do it. Only way to turn those Germans against the English. Otherwise more would have died, see? Ain't that right Major Malbec, sir? Had to do it . . . That's what the major said.'

Then, remembering rather too vividly the dreadful screams as they had bayoneted the inhabitants of the little Bavarian village, the sergeant stopped and stared at the ground.

Malbec spoke: 'And that's why we have to do what we must do now, Captain.'

Malbec's men, who had remained silent and motionless during the exchange went back to their chores. One man began to sing.

> *Auprès de ma blonde*
> *Qu'il fait bon, fait bon, fait bon,*
> *Auprès de ma blonde qu'il fait bon . . .*

His song was cut short by a terrible, heart-piercing shriek from outside the doors and then . . . silence.

Malbec stared at the door, from beyond which there now came a low groaning. He tried to shut his ears and mind to it. Closed his eyes, and instantly saw the face of his wife.

170

They heard a shell come in overhead, the shrill whine as it descended. Close, closer, until it was almost on top of them. Instinctively, the men covered their heads and with an earth-shaking crash the bomb hit the ground only a few paces from the door of the casemate. More dust fell from the roof. Beyond the door they heard the screams begin again as people tried to run from the spinning black orb. Then the air outside the shelter was rent with a huge explosion. The door seemed to be pushed in and then sucked out by the blast. But still it held fast. Then, a dreadful stillness. And from outside the casemate there was not a sound. But then it came again. Worse this time, as the single groan was replaced with many more. Too many. Malbec opened his eyes and realized that he was pouring with sweat.

He cast a glance at Lejeune. The captain was staring at him. Malbec looked back to the door. And then, just for an instant, through the moans of misery without, he thought that he heard the particular, high pitch of a woman's voice.

'Save me. Save my boys. Save the children.'

And then something curious happened inside Claude Malbec's, seething, thumping, boiling brain. He rushed towards the door and, thrusting the big sergeant aside, slipped the bolts and pushed it open. Its base slithered across the cobbles slick with blood and gobbets of flesh. Malbec peered into the awful afternoon and was greeted by a scene from hell.

The street was smoking and strewn with people and things which he realized had recently been people. Great chunks of stone had been gouged from the buildings on either side of the street and lay on the cobbles with the scorched and splintered roof tiles that had been sent crashing to the ground in their scores. Wherever he looked, it seemed to Claude Malbec that something was burning: wooden rafters, carts, horses . . . human flesh. A noise from above made him look up and he saw yet more bombs coming in, flying across the sky like so many evil, black comets.

Suddenly he was aware of a press of people moving towards him. People with terrible wounds, missing limbs and parts of their faces. Women carrying limp children in their arms. Other children, some covered in blood, suddenly lost, orphaned and alone, wailing in their bewilderment. Their clothes had been shredded by the explosions and their exposed flesh was covered in burns and lacerations. In the crowd he could make out two or three men who appeared to be more or less unhurt, doing their best to help the wounded. Acting, it seemed to him, almost in slow-motion, Malbec reached out and grabbed one of the children – a girl of about eight – and gathered her to him. He could hear nothing over the noise of the explosions. Beside his feet, close to the doorcase, a woman was sitting on the bloody cobbles cradling one child in her arms, while another grabbed at her desperately. She turned her face to Malbec and mouthed what he took to be the word 'help', but made no sound. Still holding the girl, he leant down and helped the woman to her feet. By some miracle she did not appear to have been hit, merely in shock. One of her children though, the boy in her arms, was quite dead. There was not a mark upon him. The blast must have killed him, thought Malbec and suddenly his world spun back to normal speed.

He pushed the woman and her children back through the entrance behind him and, bringing the girl with him, ducked back into the casemate and slammed the door tight. And then Sergeant Müller was sliding in the bolts as a dozen bloody fists began again to beat against the outside.

Malbec turned and saw that a few other civilians had made it in. There were around a dozen townspeople in all. Malbec turned to the woman and gently wiped her face. He looked down into her eyes and a part of his mind begged a deity that he had long abandoned in his bitterness that in them he might see his wife's smile. But it was not Marie, could never be.

The woman stared back at him. 'Thank you. Oh thank you, sir.' She was shaking with shock and her hands gripped the dead child with claw-like, denying ferocity. 'Thank you. You have saved us. Thank you for saving my sons.'

Malbec stared at her.

'*Monsieur?*'

Her face was pretty, with blue eyes encased with red-rimmed skin. He looked at the boys. One, perhaps eight years old, had fair curls, the other, the one who lay dead in her arms, was around six and had straight dark hair. So like his own boys. But how old would they have been now? Eighteen and twenty. Men themselves. And if they had lived – if Marie had lived – he wondered what they would all be doing at this moment?

'Sir, are you all right?'

Captain Lejeune was standing beside him and it was only then that Malbec realized that his own eyes were filled with tears.

'I . . . Oh, yes, Captain. As you were. Damned dust.' Malbec took the handkerchief from his pocket and dabbed away the salt water. 'Can't see a bloody thing. This dust.' He staggered to a chair and sat down, heavily. 'I just . . . I just thought, I was wondering . . .'

He paused. Inside his head a beating drum was pounding, while somewhere a small voice was reaching up from his soul: Oh God, he thought. What have I done? Marie, forgive me.

He turned to the captain: 'Quick, open the door. Let in as many more of them as we can hold.'

Lejeune stared at him: 'But, sir –'

'An order, Captain. I order you to open that door and let

in as many as we can hold. Now, before I change my mind. Müller, help him. And you men.'

Malbec was thinking fast now. And then, before Lejeune and the sergeant had opened the door, he knew what had to be done, how he could make the guns stop. They had allowed in thirty of the townspeople now, in all conditions. Malbec watched as the room filled up.

'Right. That's enough. Close the door. That's enough of them.'

The room was full of wounded and dying people and the stench, even with the ventilation, was gut-wrenchingly rank. Sweat and blood mingled with saltpetre and powder smoke in a heavy, acrid fug. Instinctively, the French soldiers began to tend to the wounded civilians.

Malbec turned to his sergeant: 'Müller, I want you and the captain to go and find the governor. You should come across him in casemate number five. That's the one by the Lanthorn Bastion; directly across town from here, past the town hall. When you've found him, I want you to bring him here. As quickly as you can. Don't take no for an answer, use force if you must. We're under martial law now. And make sure that you get that English girl too – she's sure to be with him, he won't let her out of his sight. Bring them both here. Hurry man, quickly. And watch your step.'

The sergeant crossed to Lejeune and after a few words both men left the room. Malbec took a long draught from the goblet of dusty wine before him and stared again at the mother and her two sons. And as he savoured the bitter, gritty liquid he sat back in the chair and listened to the terrible music of Ostend's suffering.

How much longer could this go on, Steel wondered. How much more could the people of this town take? Three hours

174

of bombardment and still the mortars spat out their great iron balls and the cannon below him jumped back in recoil as their barrels grew to red-hot temperatures and had to be cooled down with freshly-dampened sponges. Behind its walls and tiered defences, the port seemed to spout fire from every quarter and a huge pall of black smoke had gathered above the houses and the great church spire of St Peter and Paul, blotting out the sun. Behind him, on the narrow road to the West Gate, his men grew restless. Naturally, Steel had rejoiced at the news that he was to lead the forlorn hope. You did not get anything in this army – advancement or booty – by holding back from danger. It was the only way. Besides, he had been specifically asked to lead the attack by Colonel Hawkins, and hadn't the order come directly from Marlborough? Behind his Grenadiers, the assault column snaked back through those plucked from other regiments. Finally at the rear came the bulk of the attacking force, under the Duke of Argyll: Mordaunt's regiment and de Lalo's Huguenots among them. Argyll himself was standing a little distance away, with Captain Forbes, on one of the sand dunes. And, as Steel had predicted, the two men were getting on famously.

Surely, he thought, the town would not stand much more of this firestorm? Surely soon they would either see the gates flung open and the garrison marched out under a white flag; or they would be given the signal to attack? But time passed. No men marched out, no signal came. And still the bombs rained down.

Governor de la Motte stumbled through the doorway of the Florida casemate and into the room. At any other time, the unusually swift entrance of the sweating, red-faced man would have been enough to make any of those who could

175

among the tortured inhabitants look round in curiosity. But it was the person who now followed the governor through the door who attracted the stares of the soldiers and the wounded townspeople of Ostend. The first thing that struck you was her beauty, which made a stark and poignant contrast to the broken and bloodied debris of humanity lying across the floor of the stinking casemate. Then there was her dress. Lady Henrietta Vaughan wore the same dress of yellow silk in which she had been captured in the Channel on the frigate that had been taking her from her father's estates in Ireland to Southampton. It was not that she did not have a change of clothes, nor that she had not been permitted to keep them by her captors; it was merely that this was her very favourite dress and she had thought that with the prospect of a successful British assault upon the town, she had better be looking her best.

Sadly however, in the course of their journey across town, the dress had become marked with soot smuts falling from the sky and at one stage had even been touched by a cinder, causing a small hole to appear in the skirt. Her face too was marked by black streaks, powder marks, but her coiffure had survived intact, which said much for the skill of her maid, who followed now in her wake. On the whole, however, Lady Henrietta was not in the best of humours. In fact she was quite out of sorts and if her ladyship's beauty was outmatched by one thing, it was her temper, as Major Malbec was about to discover.

She had made her way through the town with her face covered by a fan and flanked by servants and soldiers and had thus been mercifully unaware of the suffering unfolding around her. Brought up to remain phlegmatic, Henrietta came from a military family and was also thus not unused to the sound of cannon fire and musketry at parades. And she had a passion for fireworks. So of all the party that now sought refuge within Malbec's casemate, Lady Henrietta was the least shaken, although she was furious. Her eyes searched out the officer in command and without casting a glance anywhere else in the room, she headed directly for Malbec.

'Major. Please explain yourself. I am first ushered into a stinking godforsaken barrack room and confined there for the best part of three hours and then I am bidden to walk through streets, while we are under attack, merely because you desire my presence. Why, we might all have been killed. Were we not to remain within shelter on the other side of the town? It seems to me that you have brought me closer to danger here. You are aware that is expressly forbidden under the terms of my capture and parole. You will explain yourself, Major. I am aware that I have rights, as a prisoner of war.'

Malbec, who had recovered his composure, stared at her in disbelief. 'Rights? But you are no prisoner of war, madame. You are no officer. I grant you that you are an English noblewoman and thus you do have certain privileges as my prisoner. But these are not written in the articles of war. I am sorry if you have been unduly distressed, but it is hardly surprising when your own army and navy open fire on the town and murder hundreds of innocent civilians.'

Malbec gestured to indicate the wounded, who had been laid out in rows along the walls of the casemate. At the far end of the room a score of shapes covered with blankets marked out the dead.

For the first time Lady Henrietta looked around her. The sight that met her was one that would stay with her for the rest of her life. She gasped: 'Oh, dear God. No. Surely, this cannot be the work of our guns. Tell me this was not the work of British arms. No, I will not believe it.'

Then, at a loss for words, she appeared to stagger, as if

about to faint. Captain Lejeune hurried to her and helped her to a chair.

Malbec spoke again: 'I am afraid, madame, that is precisely the cause of this suffering. So now, what rights do you suppose these people here might believe that you should have?'

Lady Henrietta said nothing. She lowered her gaze and began to sob. At last, having been recovering his breath for the past few minutes, de la Motte spoke.

'Have you seen the city, Major? Those poor people. I . . . I cannot go on with this. We must open the gates to the British, before any more innocent blood is spilt.'

Malbec walked across to the corpulent governor who now noticed the presence of the wounded and the refugees.

'Major Malbec? What is this? Why have you let these people in? Your orders were to –'

'Yes, I am aware of my orders. I changed my mind. But now it is more important that we stop the bombardment. As you say, before more blood is spilt. But we shall not open the gates to the British. In fact we shall not lose. I have a plan, Governor.'

He signalled to Sergeant Müller and pointed to Lady Henrietta. Müller smiled and walking over to the chair where she sat, grasped her by the arm and pulled her upright.

'What the devil do you think you're doing, man? *Laissez moi, laissez!* Major! Tell your dog to unhand me!'

Malbec shook his head and beckoned Müller towards him. The sergeant came, grinning and dragging Lady Henrietta with him. Malbec turned back to de la Motte. 'You see, Governor, this English milady is our secret weapon. It's really very simple.'

He beckoned again and Müller pushed Lady Henrietta towards Malbec. She turned on him, taking the veteran completely by surprise. 'Let go of me, you ruffian.' Müller laughed and she turned back to Malbec: 'You, sir, are no gentleman.'

Her words were proud and fearless but her eyes betrayed her terror. Malbec addressed her, not looking at her but picking carefully at his fingernails with a small fruit knife. 'How amusing. You are the second person today to remind me of that fact. Of course, you're right. But you are most definitely a lady. And now, my dear lady, you are going to help the poor people of Ostend. You see, your friends out there seem determined to destroy this town and us with it. We can't let that happen can we? Can we?'

'What do you intend to do with me?'

He looked her straight in the eyes. 'I intend to do what any sane man would do in my position, gentleman or not. I intend to use you to stop this madness, in the only way I know how.'

An expression of puzzlement and alarm spread across Lady Henrietta's face. Malbec turned to Müller: 'Choose two men and take her ladyship for a walk. You will escort her up to the highest parapet that you can find. The Babylon Bastion will do, facing directly to the west, the one with the flagstaff. You will tie her to that staff. Securely, Müller, and make sure that she's in clear view of the British. We want to let them know who we have here. Oh, and Müller, try to make sure that she doesn't get killed. That is not in the plan. Then take cover and leave her up there but for no more than five minutes. Then we shall see what happens. Whatever you do, take care to avoid the pirate Trouin or any of his men. You should have no difficulty. As far as I know he was heading for the Pontoon Bastion, down by the Key. He believes that she's still his prize and he won't want her pretty head severed by a cannon shot before he can barter her with the British – or sell her on to some eager son of Mohammed.'

Lady Henrietta stared at Malbec: 'You can't be serious . . . By God you are. You're inhuman. This is murder, I shall be killed! It goes against all the laws of humanity.'

Malbec stared hard into her eyes. 'Don't talk to me about the laws of humanity. Your great duke broke those laws the minute he opened fire on this town.'

'I insist, Major. This is inhuman. It's barbaric. Let me go. I demand . . .'

She moved towards him, uncertain of what she intended, but as she did so Müller grasped both her arms tightly and bent them behind her back, making her wince. At the same time, her words were cut short as Malbec dealt her a stinging blow across the cheek with the flat of his hand. She screamed, then looked at him with blazing, pleading eyes and said nothing. And then Lady Henrietta Vaughan lowered her head and began to sob.

Malbec turned to Müller: 'Take her away. And remember – five minutes up there at the most. We don't want to tempt fate and make her into a martyr.'

De la Motte stared at Malbec: 'Surely you are not serious, Major. She's a woman, after all.'

'Yes, I know. And not bad, probably. Wouldn't you say?'

De la Motte looked even more aghast.

Malbec turned to Müller: 'Go. Now. Do it.'

The sergeant beckoned two men to him and together they frog-marched Lady Henrietta towards the doors. Two more soldiers opened them and before the desperate people outside had time to realize what was happening, had closed them hard behind the party and shot the bolts.

'And now, my dear Governor, we sit and wait. And if all goes according to plan, if her ladyship is not cut in two by a cannonball, then I do believe that by tomorrow morning we shall either have a visit from our British friends, under a flag

180

of truce, or, more simply and conveniently, they will have left. Either way, and whatever your scruples, you have to agree that our troubles do appear to be over.'

'Good God, James. What's that? There's a girl up there. There, on the highest part of that great gate. There's a Frenchman with her. No, now he's gone. She seems to be tied to that pole. What the devil are they playing at? Can you see any closer?'

'No. My Lord. Not without a glass. Merely that she is, as you aver, a girl. She must be terrified.'

'So would you be if you were forced to stand on top of that redoubt in this storm of shot. What's she doing up there, for God's sake?'

'Shall I tell the gunnery captains to cease firing at her, sir?'

'Oh yes, of course – well, no, not instantly that is. It might be a trick. Dammit! Who the devil is she?' Marlborough drew a glass from his saddlebag and opened it out.

Hawkins interjected: 'Might I suggest, Your Grace, that the French might want us to see her. Perhaps they think we should know who she is.'

'Are you inferring that she might be an Englishwoman? Surely not! Cadogan, send a runner. One of your aides; who's your most courtly man? Send him, whoever he is and get him to have a squint at her. See if he can put a name to her.'

Hawkins reached across to Marlborough: 'If I might trouble you for the glass a moment, Your Grace.'

Marlborough gave him the small brass telescope and Hawkins adjusted the focus. After a few moments he lowered the glass and closed it.

'There's no need to send for anyone, Your Grace. There is no doubt about it, I recognize her myself. That is Lady Henrietta Vaughan, the eldest daughter of the Duke of Romney.'

'Good God, man. Are you quite sure?'

'Sure as I've ever been. She was presumed dead. Her ship was taken by pirates these three weeks back. It is Lady Henrietta to be sure, Your Grace.'

Marlborough frowned. 'There is nothing else for it, James, we must stop the bombardment. Cadogan, ride down to the column. Pull back the assault. Have Argyll stand down. I am no man for parlay of hostages, but that is clearly what the French intend. Sound the retire. Make a signal to the admiral to cease fire, and you had better tell Lieutenant Forbes while you're about it.'

In Claude Malbec's casemate the misery continued. And then suddenly there was silence. Everyone strained to listen – the guns had ceased firing. Malbec sat back in his chair and closed his eyes. Again in the darkness of his mind he could see Marie's sweet, sad face. But this time she was smiling.

Colonel Hawkins was standing outside Marlborough's campaign tent when Steel found him the following morning. He held up his hand, smiling. 'I wouldn't go in quite yet, Jack. He's in the very devil of a mood.'

There was a commotion inside the tent and as they watched one of Marlborough's servants came running out, his cravat askew, bearing a plate of half-eaten beef.

Hawkins grinned: 'Haven't seen him like this for quite a while. That business with the girl really unsettled him.'

'Who was she, Colonel?'

'Name of Henrietta Vaughan. Daughter of the Duke of Romney.'

Steel stared: 'Good God.'

'You know her?'

'She is a first cousin to a lady of my acquaintance.'

'Is she, by God? Well if your lady is anything like her cousin, then you're a lucky man.'

Steel bristled: 'I did not say, sir, that the lady in question was anything more to me than an acquaintance.'

Hawkins understood: 'Do excuse me, Steel. None of my business. No business of mine at all. Merely a remark.'

Steel was wondering whether perhaps he should explain the current wholly chaste nature of his relationship with Lady Henrietta's cousin, Arabella Moore; sixteen years ago, as his lover, Arabella had purchased him his first commission. Before he had decided, a man in civilian dress, under escort, appeared behind Hawkins.

The colonel beckoned him forward with a friendly gesture: 'Captain Steel, this is Mister Brouwer. He has come from within the town, at considerable personal risk, to ask for an explanation as to why his people were bombarded. Naturally he is desirous of seeing the duke. But I thought that perhaps you might better be able to explain to him.'

Steel looked at Hawkins, searching for a clue as to what he meant. Leaving Brouwer with an apology, Hawkins moved across to him and said quietly, 'The pamphlets, Steel. Tell him about the pamphlets. Make sure he understands that they are libellous. Traitorous. Utterly unfounded. Make him believe in us again, in Marlborough. Lay it on about how the French must be driven out, how much we hate them. And tell him that once his town is free they can have their own government. And for God's sake don't forget to apologize for firing on his people.'

Steel nodded and with Hawkins walked across to Brouwer. 'This is Captain Steel, Mister Brouwer. A most trusted officer and confidant of the duke of Marlborough. Again I must apologize for His Grace being currently so indisposed. He suffers most severely from *mal de tête*, if you will excuse my use of the French. But I am sure that Captain Steel will explain everything quite clearly. You may use my tent, Steel – and give Mister Brouwer a glass of wine. You'll find it on the sideboard. You won't be disturbed.'

Steel nodded: 'Thank you, Colonel.'

He motioned Brouwer towards Hawkins' tent some yards away and as the colonel watched, began to attempt to explain their reasons for murdering women and children, and to rebuild the man's trust in Marlborough's army.

Almost an hour and very nearly two bottles of Hawkins' excellent hock later, Steel began to feel as if he might be succeeding. Quick to assess the man's modest social status, he had been careful to underplay his own position. He had spoken of his background with the emphasis on suffering, and told Brouwer how he had been compelled to leave the family home and forcibly indentured to a lawyer, and how he had run away to join the colours. Within minutes Brouwer had been made aware that Steel was no ordinary officer, no dandified fop who would throw his men to the guns to forge his own glorious reputation, but a natural gentleman. And Steel for his part, having set out to seduce Brouwer's soul with guile, quickly found his cynical veneer evaporating. He liked Marius Brouwer. The man had a rare honesty and a genuine sense of injustice which appealed to Steel's own instinct for fair play. In fact at one point in their conversation he had found himself beginning to question the moral integrity of his own generals. But he had quickly brought himself to order, remembering the vital purpose of his mission. And now, even as Brouwer remonstrated once again at the fact that Marlborough had only two years back ordered the burning of Bavaria, Steel could see the man was warming to him and exploited his advantage.

184

'Mister Brouwer, whatever you might have read, I can assure you His Grace did not authorize the killing of any civilians. That is not our way.'

Brouwer smiled: 'It was your way here.'

'Please. I beg you. You must believe me. We were under the impression that Vauban had constructed bunkers – casemates – in which your people would take cover. How were we to know that the French would seize them for themselves and shut you out?'

Brouwer nodded his head: 'Yes. You're right. I do see that now, Captain. It is the French and not yourselves who are the real monsters. As we always knew they were.'

The Belgian had said as much already, although clearly his mind had not really been made up. This time, though, Steel believed that he meant it.

'I'm so glad that you see that, Mister Brouwer. More wine?'

'Perhaps not, Captain. My head is not as strong as it was and if I am to get back into the town, then I must have all my senses.'

He paused and looked Steel directly in the eye, as if trying to tell whether or not the tall redcoat might be lying. How he hated this game, hated the war, hated the French. And how he wanted so very much not to hate the British. He and his followers needed a thread of hope and at present the only thread lay with Marlborough. He put down his wine glass:

'Very well. I will take you at your word, Captain. If we are to fight together, we must first be friends.'

He stretched out his broad-palmed hand in the newfangled sign of greeting and friendship and Steel, after hesitating a moment, took it firmly in his own. Fight together? Steel wondered what he meant. But it was of no consequence, for he had, it seemed, managed to bring Brouwer back to their cause.

He clasped Brouwer's hand between both of his own now: 'You have no idea how happy I am to hear you say that. You have my word that you will not regret it.'

Together the two men emerged from the tent. Colonel Hawkins, who had been waiting the whole time outside Marlborough's tent, looked across and scanned their faces anxiously for any sign of success. Steel met him with a smile which told him what he needed and had hoped to learn.

There was a shout from within the duke's tent. 'Are they not done yet, Hawkins?'

The colonel approached Brouwer: 'Good news, Mister Brouwer, His Grace is much recovered and is most anxious to meet you himself.' He turned to Steel: 'I think it might be politic if we went in now.'

They found the duke seated over a letter at his writing table. He was bald-headed and his long wig lay draped over a wig-stand on the campaign chest in the corner. A bottle of claret stood open on the table, with several glasses.

Marlborough looked up: 'Help yourselves if you wish, gentlemen. Mister Brouwer, my apologies. I trust that Captain Steel will have explained everything to your satisfaction. Be assured that we have found the root of the treason and have dealt with the man concerned. He will not make such a grave mistake again. As for the matter of your townspeople, I can only offer my sincere regret.'

Brouwer spoke: 'My Lord, your captain has given me his word. I believe that I can trust him, though I do admit it is hard. I came here a bitter man, My Lord, and I am still a bitter man. But I do understand. Sometimes we must all make sacrifices for the good of the country. And I do not believe that you are a bad man, sir. So I will trust you. We will help you with your plan in any way we can.'

Steel looked at Hawkins, who saw his puzzlement. Marlborough spoke: 'A plan, Captain Steel. Yes, a plan. It is Colonel Hawkins' idea. I'll come to the point. We need you to get into the town, Steel. Once there you will find Lady Henrietta and bring her out. Only then can we contemplate renewing our assault.' Brouwer looked concerned, but Marlborough went on, 'Do not worry Mister Brouwer. By that I do not mean that I intend to bombard your people again. We shall take your town by stealth and *force de main*. And of course, with your help.' Brouwer smiled; Steel frowned. Marlborough saw it: 'There's no need to be apprehensive, Captain Steel. The plan is really quite simple. Tell him, Hawkins.'

'It must be done under cover of darkness, of course. Mister Brouwer suggests no earlier than ten o'clock and with no moon . . .'

Marlborough took up the instructions: 'At that hour, you will embark upon a dinghy on the marsh, just in front of the lines. There's a small church, St Elizabeth's they call it, pretty little place. Unusually firm ground. Stands beside a stream which leads into the larger river. You may take only one man with you. I seem to remember a sergeant. What's his name?'

'Slaughter, sir. You have a fine memory.'

'I make it my business to know the men I command, Captain Hawkins?'

The colonel had rolled out a map of Ostend on the table and now indicated an area to the left. 'You will be rowed by night from here, with a local guide. Don't worry, he's on our side. Or at least he's been promised our gold if he gets you there. Now you won't go along the main creek, here,' he pointed, 'which passes too close to the south of the town. But along here, a secondary rivulet, leading off it and then parallel. This stream will take you to the marshes directly below the town. You leave them by a hidden waterway which gives on to the harbour close to the pontoon bridge, which as you know the French have blown up. Where the bridge was joined to the town there is a small water gate. The French think it to be blocked by debris, but it's open. We have friends inside the town, as you have already discovered. At the water gate you will be met by Herr Brouwer and members of his Flemish people's army. Excuse me Mister Brouwer, what's it called again, Hawkins?'

'The *schildendevriend*.' Steel looked at Brouwer, seeing him in this unexpected new role. Hawkins went on: 'It means "shield and friend" and that's exactly what they will be to you. Brouwer and his men are your lifeline, Steel. They will guide you in and get you out. They'll take you in through the water gate and hide you in a safe house. Then, when they're ready – it will be some time on the following day – they will take you out into the town and then it's really up to you. Peel off from them, find someone who looks as if he might be a privateer – shouldn't be too difficult – and pass yourself off as a deserter from the British army. Say that you're a Jacobite. Make up some story. They'll question you; pretty hard, I should imagine. Think you can take it?'

Steel nodded.

'I'm certain that in the end they're sure to believe your story. They know that no man in his right mind would think of going into that vipers' nest . . . Sorry, Steel. You'll be fine. Anyway, just lay on your best Scottish accent, sing the Pretender's praises and don't forget to curse the queen.' Marlborough coughed and frowned at Hawkins. 'So, Steel. Spin them a yarn. Make sure that you're taken either to the governor, de la Motte, or to Duglay-Trouin, the privateer. Don't bother with the garrison commander, he's the most likely to smell a rat. The pirate would be your best way in. If you can convince him then you've every chance of success. I'll wager that Lady Henrietta is his prisoner by now. They were regular infantry up there, tying her to the flagpole, not pirates. After Trouin realizes how the French stopped the guns, he's unlikely to let them take charge of her again. He won't want her harmed – his plan will either be to sell her back to us, or her father. Or, if I know a pirate, to take her off to the Indies or the Barbary Coast and sell her at a premium as a white slave. Very popular with the Turkmen, fair-skinned women, so I'm told. Doesn't bear thinking about.'

Marlborough, who had been signing a dispatch as Hawkins spoke, looked up at Steel: 'There is one more thing, Captain Steel. Before you rescue Lady Henrietta, you and Mister Brouwer must ensure that there is a sally-port open to the west of the town. Any of the bastions will do, although the best would be to the north, beneath the glacis. Colonel Blood and his ordnance officers have made plans of the position and it appears that that is the only area of the defences not raked by more than two fields of fire. Opening such a port is the only way now that we will be able to take the city without greater delay.' Marlborough folded the letter and placed it on the table. 'It is not exactly what we had planned, Steel, but necessity drives us. We had expected this bombardment to flush the garrison out. Now all that we have probably succeeded in doing is killing innocent people.' He looked at Brouwer: 'Lady Henrietta's presence too puts everything in a very different light.'

Steel nodded: 'I understand, Your Grace. And thank you for the honour of choosing me for this task. I won't let you down.' He looked at Hawkins. 'When do I go, sir?'

'We haven't a moment to lose, and it must be a moonless night – you go tomorrow.'

TEN

Steel wrapped the thick woollen boat cloak more tightly around his shoulders, pulled down the brim of his tricorne and pushed his chin deep down into his chest, partly to find some warmth in the chill of the night and partly, instinctively, to hide himself from the gaze of the French sentries who, he knew, were watching every inch of the river and as far into the surrounding marshes as they could see. The muffled oars, pulled with expert care by two sailors from Fairborne's squadron, cut into the black waters of the creek, pushing the tiny boat ever further away from the dwindling shape of the chapel of St Elizabeth-of-the-Marsh, where they had cast off, along the shallow waterway and ever closer to the enemy.

The night-time marsh was alive with creatures. Unidentifiable shapes scurried across its surface close to the boat and curious, guttural cries came from all sides. Most noticeable though were the mosquitoes. Steel felt one boring into the flesh of his forearm. He cursed and slapped at it.

'Damned biting flies. I swear, Jacob, we'll all die of marsh fever before this siege is ended.'

'D'you really think so, sir? I prefer to think that the Almighty might have a more interesting fate mapped out for you and me, Mister Steel.' Slaughter swatted a large mosquito which had alighted on his face.

'Jacob, it's Captain Steel, if you will. And when we're in the town for heaven's sake don't call me that; or "sir". Better still, nothing at all.'

'Sorry Mister . . . sorry, sir. I'll try to remember.'

From aft, in the darkness came a whispered warning: 'Please. You must be quiet, *messieurs*. The French will hear us.'

Their companion was a Belgian, by the name of van Koecke. A small, hook-nosed man who before the war had been a dishonest grocer and now found that his skills in selling his customers short could be used in a similar fashion to supply the army of liberation. He also had a useful local knowledge and always with an eye to lining his pockets still further, offered his services – for even the most dangerous of trips, if the price was right. He had declared his ardent wish to rid his country of the French when they had met him at the church. He would do anything to make it happen. But he had still been happy to take their gold. Half of it was payable as they left the lines, the remainder on safe delivery of his two 'deserters' to the town's water gate rendezvous.

Steel nodded towards their guide and was silent. The little boat continued slowly on its way, rocking gently on the shallow water. He could see the southern ramparts of the town now, silhouetted against the sky, despite the lack of any moon. Then they veered towards the south and the silhouette began to diminish. Steel knew that they must be reaching the end of their journey, taking another tributary into the farthest creek before turning back northeast. This would be the most dangerous moment, as they passed directly beneath the walls of the small star fort of St Philip, which was still held by the

191

French. Sure enough, as he watched, before them the water opened out into a broader estuary and they debouched into the creek. Cautiously raising his face, Steel gazed up at the walls of the fort and saw figures – light-coated sentries in tricorne hats with shouldered muskets – silhouetted on the ramparts, walking slowly towards and then away from each other, in routine guard patrol. The oarsmen slackened their strokes now, their experience telling as they eased the boat up the creek with hardly a sound, save the occasional creaking as the oars worked in the gunwhales and the gentle lapping of the water against the hull.

Within a few minutes, which to Steel seemed an eternity, they were clear of the fort and dead ahead he was able to make out the ponderous mass of what he presumed to be the remains of the pontoon bridge which had linked the town with the coastal plain to the east. Somewhere in the darkness a curlew trilled its distinctive call. Steel gazed at the smashed bridge. To its left he could see the glimmering lights of the houses on the Key and beyond it the tall masts of two ships which lay at anchor in the harbour. Now the boat hugged the eastern shore, the oarsmen making what use they could of the shadows by the bank. Ostend lay in plain view before them. A huge, squat monolith of menacing fortifications and church spires. As they drew level with the shattered pontoons the oarsmen turned the boat directly towards the town and rowed along the path of the bridge. Now ahead of them Steel could see a small landing jetty and beyond that what looked like a ragged hole in the sea wall. The water gate.

Within seconds it seemed that they were inside the opening. A few more strokes on the oars and the boat's keel was grating against the wood of a jetty, jolting Steel into reality.

Van Koecke spoke in a whisper: 'Now, gentlemen, you may stand up. Please, go ashore now. Take care. Your journey by boat is over. Your hosts await you. Please.' He turned to Steel: 'And, sir. The money, if you please.'

Steel produced a bag of coins and handed it to van Koecke, who flashed him an unctuous smile. 'Good luck, gentlemen. May God preserve you. And goodnight.'

Gingerly, Steel and Slaughter clambered from the boat with the help of the oarsmen and stepped on to a low, slippery stone staircase and slowly climbed on to the jetty. As they found their feet, already they could hear the sound of the boat pulling away into the darkness, the muffled oars slipping through the water. And then it was gone and they were alone. They said nothing, unsure of who might be listening.

There was no lamp in the gate tunnel, although it was lit by two shafts of yellow light, borrowed from the windows of houses above. Into one of them now, from the shadows at the end of the jetty, stepped two figures, also wrapped in cloaks. Steel moved a hand on to the hilt of his sword and motioned to Slaughter to stay back. Both he and the sergeant had left their fusils with the company and were armed instead with swords, Steel with his own great Italian blade, Slaughter with a smaller weapon, lent to him by Tom Williams. In addition Steel had slipped a pair of loaded pistols into his belt. The two figures ahead of them stepped forward, further into the light. One of them, who now appeared as a genial-looking man in his late twenties, removed his hat.

'Good evening, sirs. Captain Steel, this is my friend Hubert Fabritius.'

'Good to see you again, Mister Brouwer. This is Sergeant Slaughter.'

'We are here to help you, Captain, as you know. But with so many dead, killed by your guns, you must also know there is little love for the British in the people of Ostend right now. Now, we must go, before the sentry hears us.'

Steel said nothing, but obeyed Brouwer as he beckoned them to follow him further into the vaulted passage which led away from the gate. It continued into the darkness, boring into the very heart of the fortifications, but barely wide enough for a man to pass through. At length they came to a wooden door. Brouwer turned the handle and opened it no more than a crack. He peered through into the street beyond and when he was satisfied that they would not be observed, pushed it further open and signalled them to follow him. They emerged on to a narrow, cobbled street and walked quickly down its length until they arrived at a junction. This street was wider and with larger, more prosperous-looking houses; the light from their windows bathed the passers-by with a warm yellow glow. They paused in the shadows and at last Steel had a moment to think. He had known that his presence in a town which had been so recently shelled by British guns would be problematic, but he had not expected the dreadful sense of guilt which now descended upon him. He surveyed the scene.

The town was filled with activity, unusually for such a place at this time of the night, and he knew the reason. It was only too evident. A cart passed them on the street, pulled by two men, running. Its contents had been covered with a tarpaulin but there was no mistaking them. As it pulled away Steel caught sight of a limp hand hanging out of the back. Bodies. They were disposing of the corpses of the civilians before they grew noxious and disease became yet another threat to the surviving population of the besieged town. Walking past an alleyway he happened to look down it and glimpsed the sight of a woman crouched down over what looked like a pile of washing. She had her hands upon it and appeared to be shouting. Steel paused, intrigued. But his curiosity turned to bitterness as he quickly realized that the washing was not what it seemed but a lifeless human form and that the woman was in the act of grieving over it. He turned back and caught up with Slaughter and the others.

The sergeant looked grim: 'It's terrible, sir, what we've done, ain't it? I mean, when you see it up close. Poor beggars.'

'Yes, Jacob. It is terrible. But what choice did we have? Thank God we stopped it when we did. Thank God for whatever ungentlemanly scoundrel put Lady Henrietta up on the ramparts. He may have given us the devil's own task, but he's saved the lives of half this town.'

Brouwer turned and hissed a warning to be silent. Looking down, Steel noticed that Slaughter's feet had automatically fallen into step with his own and felt suddenly self-conscious. Quickly he double-stepped and managed to lose the rhythm.

'Must be careful of that, Jacob. Looks like we're marching. Mustn't be seen to be doing that, even if we are deserters.'

Again Brouwer looked back at them and glared. Steel realized how their English voices would mark them out and thought too how obviously soldierly they must appear to anyone with an eye for the military. What typical, unmistakable soldiers they were. And how important it was to conceal that fact – until the moment arrived. One more word to Slaughter.

'And Jacob. Stay with me. And remember, if anyone talks to you, forget trying to be French. Be a bloody Irishman. You're meant to be a deserter. You're off to join the bloody pirates. And do try to walk like someone who has finished with the army. Not as if you're swanking through Horse Guards in your dress uniform.'

Slaughter made a poor attempt at a slouch. 'Yes sir.'

Steel grimaced. 'And for God's sake don't call me sir. I'm Jack, remember?'

Slaughter smiled. 'Right you are then, Jack.'

'As you were, Sarn't. There's no need to do it more often than needs be.'

Brouwer had given up attempting to silence the Englismen and he sighed with relief as their conversation was interrupted by music. It floated gently above them and seemed to come from somewhere over to the left. It was the sound of an organ rising in a crescendo and as Steel listened it was joined by voices; the unmistakable words of the *Dies Irae*.

Marius Brouwer saw his puzzled look: 'They sing for the dead. The people are holding a service of Requiem. In the Petrus and Paulus Church. For the dead people killed by your guns.'

Steel shook his head. 'I'm truly sorry. Believe me. If we could have prevented it . . .'

Brouwer looked away and continued walking in slence. He led them to the right, towards the south of the town, but then he quickly darted into a left turning and brought them back around towards the west.

Pausing, he offered an explanation: 'We will go to my house tonight. You need to rest before meeting Trouin and it's too late now. Besides, the city is a shambles and there has been too much misery for one day. Come.'

With Fabritius bringing up the rear, they followed him through the streets where the grisly evidence of their bombardment lay across cobbles. Their feet crunched over shattered glass blown from the windows and pantiles from the roofs. The smell of gunpowder hung heavy in the air and at every turning it seemed to Steel that from one place or another, from the open windows of so many family homes, he heard the sound of sobbing. A clock chimed the quarter-hour and he noticed that the music had stopped, some time ago perhaps.

* * *

The streets were filled with people of all races and colours. Alongside the pale-skinned Dutch and Belgians, mulattos rubbed shoulders with latinos and huge, bearded men from the Russian steppes that reminded him of the northern wars of his youth. There were Africans, as black as jet and even Cathars walked here with confident familiarity. Nevertheless, thought Steel, two tall men of military bearing would stand out horribly. Sensing that Brouwer was still bristling with bitterness, he attempted to make conversation, whispering as they walked in the shadows.

'I had not expected your town to be so cosmopolitan, Mister Brouwer. It must be a fascinating place in which to live.'

Brouwer did not look at him. 'It is my home. We like to keep ourselves to ourselves. We do not live in this part of the town. Only foreigners settle here. Besides, most of them are rogues, Trouin's men or those who have followed them here. They've taken over the town and the French do nothing about them. They don't make life easy for us. Our children are no longer safe. It was bad enough with the French garrison, but these men, they are no better than animals. That is why we need you, to help us get rid of this scum. We need to build a new town, and after that a new country. A place that we can be proud of and which looks to no other nation for its government.'

Steel was surprised by the candid passion with which he spoke, more evident than at their last meeting. He could see for himself the men that Brouwer was talking about. To live here would be intolerable for any man attempting to safeguard a young family. Suddenly he understood Brouwer's motives and with them much of the general malaise that troubled this downtrodden little country. As they walked deeper into the town, further to the north, the streets seemed

197

to become less strewn with filth and were certainly lacking the parade of potential villains that Steel had noticed in the southern part of the place. They stopped outside a neat little house with blue blinds at the windows whose wooden shutters lay open. Inside he could see a candle burning. Steel wondered what time it was now. Approaching six in the morning, he thought. As if in answer the clock in the tower of the town hall chimed the hour. Six.

Brouwer knocked gently on the door and after a short while it was opened by a woman of roughly his own age. She was small and pretty, in a homely sort of way, and was simply dressed in a brown skirt and cotton shirt. Brouwer planted a kiss on her cheek and muttered some words of Flemish.

He turned to the party: 'This is my wife, Berthe. She will look after us with some breakfast.'

He ushered the two soldiers and Fabritius into the house and with a quick glance into the street to make sure that they had not been followed, closed the door behind them. The house smelt of fresh baking. To Steel it seemed as if someone had transported him back twenty years to his mother's kitchen at Carniston, their house in the Scottish lowlands. He was standing close to the cook, beside the range, a small boy again, asking, in as pitiable a voice as he could manage whether there might be any extra dough left over from the sweet biscuits she was making. He had always been rewarded for his perseverance. And now the sensation came back to him of the taste of those biscuits on his tongue and he felt instantly warm and safe.

Slaughter leaned over and whispered to him: 'Oh, can you smell that, sir. Real home baking. That's a rare treat that is. And real coffee too.'

Steel, jolted back to the present by his sergeant's reeking

breath, was conscious too that another, still more tempting smell had joined that of the cakes – the unmistakable aroma of freshly brewed coffee, a rarity in camp in recent weeks when so-called 'coffee' had been concocted from all manner of roots and herbs – and had tasted precisely as if it was nothing more than that.

Brouwer saw the anticipation on their faces and for the first time since they had met him, he smiled. 'You would like some coffee, I think. Please sit down.'

He pulled out two chairs from beneath the small, plain table that dominated the room, whose only other furnishings were a few engravings of street scenes hung on the walls and a pile of books, and a third for Fabritius who up till now had been utterly silent. Steel glanced at him and noticed how serious he appeared.

He tried a direct approach: 'So, Mister Fabritius, are you of the same persuasion as Mister Brouwer, here? You believe that Belgium can really be free?'

Fabritius stared at him with empty, red-rimmed eyes.

Steel looked away. 'I'm sorry.'

Brouwer spoke: 'My friend will not speak to you, Captain. But please do not be offended. I think he is too sad to talk to anyone. It is simply that your bombardment killed his father and destroyed his house. No more.' He turned to his wife. 'Now, where is that coffee?'

Steel looked again at Fabritius, who he now noticed was digging the nails of his right hand as deep as he could into the flesh of the left without drawing blood, in an obvious effort to control his rage. Rage against the British and rage, thought Steel, against me.

Berthe poured the coffee into four bowls and they drank it, gratefully. Eventually Brouwer spoke: 'You will stay here until tonight. Rest while you can. We have beds. The children are with their grandmother in the Upper Town. So, you will rest here and then I shall show you where Captain Trouin can be found. Then Captain Steel, I will say that it is up to you.'

Steel nodded: 'You are more than generous Mister Brouwer, particularly after what has happened.'

Brouwer shook his head: 'To tell you the truth, I no longer know what to believe, Captain. I can only praise God that my own wife and children were not among the dead or wounded. But like Fabritius, we had friends who were killed. My children had such friends. Children, killed, injured horribly.' He paused and cradled the still-warm bowl of coffee in his hands. 'Tell me, Captain, would you have stopped it if they had not put that woman up on the ramparts?'

Steel looked away. 'I . . . I don't know. Perhaps. Probably. Yes, if it had been up to me, I would.'

'But you told me that you did burn people out of their homes in Bavaria?'

'Yes, that much is true. Although, actually it was the Dutch that did it.'

'Of course. Our friends and neighbours the Dutch. But on Marlborough's orders, no?'

Steel looked anxiously at Brouwer.

'Don't worry, Captain. Of course I will help you, as agreed. But I will not fight for you. I will take you where you want to go, but then I will go back to my family. They are what matters most to me now. You will take the girl – if you can prise her away from under Trouin's nose. Then you must leave quickly by the same gate that we will leave open for your attack. It is coming soon?'

'Within two days.' He prayed that he was right.

Brouwer grasped his forearm: 'Then we will welcome your army into the town and the French and their friends will leave for ever. But now you should rest. And your sergeant.'

Steel put down the bowl of coffee. 'Thank you for your hospitality. We realize the danger in which you are putting yourself and your family.'

Brouwer darted his wife a nervous glance. But she had not heard or was not listening. Besides, her English was not as good as his.

Steel went on: 'Before we rest, can you tell me about the English lady? You know where she is? You're sure that this pirate, Trouin, has her?'

'Quite certain. One of my friends gave me the news shortly before your arrival. It seems that when he found out about what the garrison commander had done with his prize Trouin went himself to the governor and demanded that he take personal care of the girl. Apparently the garrison commander protested and there was a scrap. Mostly verbal – full of threats. Trouin won, needless to say. As far as we know she's being held at his headquarters. He occupies an inn on the south side of the town. We passed near there on the way to this house. His men patrol the entire quarter. It's not a place I like to go, but I'll take you there tonight. But no further; after that you're on your own.'

This was bad news, thought Steel. Judging by the way that Brouwer spoke about this French privateer, Lady Henrietta would doubtless be more difficult to find and snatch than she might have been had she been held by the French garrison. And he was sure now that he could not count on any physical assistance from Brouwer or any members of his patriotic movement which seemed to be something less than the dynamic people's army that Hawkins had implied. So much, he thought, for the high command's confidence in an armed uprising. These people might have been passionate about their belief in their country, but given a pasting by Lieutenant Forbes' precious mortars, the fight had gone out of them.

Marlborough's plan had backfired with serious conse-quences. It was clear that if Lady Henrietta was going to be freed then he and Slaughter would have to bring it about without help.

They spent the rest of the day at Brouwer's house, in a small, damp bedroom in the attic that stank of mildew and once, he presumed, when the house might have belonged to a shipping clerk or customs officer, perhaps, would have housed the maid-of-all-work. Barely large enough to take the two Grena-diers, it was lit only by a single window in a gable end which looked across the adjoining house and the neighbouring roof-tops, out to sea. Steel rubbed the dusty glass and peered through the mottled pane. At first he could see nothing for the sea haar. But gradually, as the day drew on shapes began to emerge and by midday the entire British flotilla was evident in all its splendour. And next to the frigates and men-o'-war bobbed the hated bombships. Steel sat on one of the two stools that were the room's only furnishings and looked down at a tray on the floor which bore plates, two glasses and an empty beer-bottle, evidence of the food that had been pre-pared for them by Brouwer's wife. He wondered that there was as yet apparently no lack of provisions in the town. Surely a siege must eventually entail deprivation if not star-vation. Yet here they were enjoying fresh meat and beer. It occurred to him that one of Vauban's key maxims was to lay in enough for a two-week siege and that the pirates must also have brought in supplies which they had doubtless sold at a hefty premium. And surely the surrounding farms would have driven in much of their livestock before the gate was closed? Whatever the reasons, to Steel it was clear that, how-ever Ostend was eventually taken, there was no way that they were going to starve either the garrison or the pirates out of the town. Slaughter had fallen asleep and was snoring heavily in a corner of the room, his head resting on his folded coat.

Steel pondered their situation, wondering at the sheer unpredictability of war that one moment would have you standing in line under fire and the next task you with rescuing a woman, who in this case happened to be the cousin of your former lover.

The day wore on and afternoon turned to evening. Slaughter awoke and went back to sleep, then woke again. Despite their close relationship, unique in the army between an officer and a non-commissioned man, they had spoken little to each other in the last few hours. Both knew what the other must be thinking, the worries that always passed through your mind before going into action. Slaughter's remedy was always sleep and Steel wondered how he managed it. He had merely to close his eyes and his mind became a maze of different thoughts, none of them particularly comforting. There were the concerns which dogged him from day to day: an unpaid mess bill, the growing hole in one of his boots and the lice he couldn't shift from his coat collar, the welfare of his men. And then there were the other thoughts. The fear of death and maiming. The disquieting notion that he might die without ever fathering a child. The longing for a woman with whom to share his life and regret at losing those he had known before. And all the while his mind was haunted by the dark presence of the fear that might take hold of him when the moment came to go into action. It had never happened yet and he prayed it never would. He had seen other men taken by it, almost unawares. Some froze and were cut down where they stood. Others turned and ran only to be dishonoured or executed for cowardice. For any soldier and particularly for someone like Steel whose

203

life was devoted to soldiering, this was a fear worse than any other. And so he sat and thought too much and did not sleep.

At length, as the light was almost gone, there was a knock on the door and Marius Brouwer entered, his face yellow-tinged and other-worldly in the light of a flickering candle: 'We should go now, gentlemen. I will take you to where Trouin is.'

Slaughter stirred. Steel turned to him: 'Sarn't, you stay here with Mister Fabritius. If I'm not back within two hours, take yourself back to the lines somehow, if you can by the sally port beneath the glacis. Brouwer assures me that it will be open. If you can do so, on your way out of the town make certain that it remains that way. When you get back find Colonel James Hawkins on the duke's staff. Do it personally, Jacob. I'm not sure who to trust any more. Tell him that I have been discovered and that Lady Henrietta is a lost cause. Most important of all is that we must storm the town. We must absolutely not bombard it. We must take it by assault, as we had planned.'

'But sir –'

'Don't argue Jacob. Those are my orders.'

Slaughter knew better than to protest again. 'Yes, sir. But mind and be careful, Mister Steel.'

Steel smiled at him and shook his head. Brouwer looked at the two men, uncertain as to what had passed between them.

Steel turned to him: 'Right, Mister Brouwer. I'm ready. Sergeant Slaughter will stay here. He'll keep out of sight. If I do not return he has orders to regain our lines and advise that we should attack the town, but that we must not again fire on it. We'll need you to open the sally-port.'

Brouwer smiled: 'Thank you. I understand what you have

done. You think that you can manage it on your own? To rescue the girl from Trouin?'

'I think that I must. It is the only way.'

Out in the street, Brouwer went ahead of him, at a little distance. He had thought it less conspicuous to travel separately. They gradually worked their way back into the less respectable quarter of town. Steel was jostled by a huge mulatto and narrowly avoided tripping over the recumbent form of a Chinese sailor asleep in a doorway.

Walking by way of the narrower streets, they eventually emerged on to an expansive cobbled area, filled with all the apparatus of the sea. Winches, pulleys and crates had been hauled in here, through the Keygate to safety within the defensive walls, although, as if to mock them, a hole some three feet wide and several feet in depth, surrounded by splintered cobbles and a brown bloodstain marked where one of the allied mortars had scored a hit.

It was well after midnight, but the street was still alive with activity. Steel stepped out of the path of a group of three sailors, each supporting the other in their efforts to negotiate the cobbles. To his left a man was throwing up in the gutter, while over to the right a tart was negotiating prices and positions with a prospective client. From up ahead, he heard the unmistakable noise of a tavern. Raised voices, fiddle music, laughter and someone singing a shanty. They rounded a corner and the place came into view, a large, half-timbered structure that had seen better days but was evidently doing a brisk trade. Above the door a sign flapped in the breeze: a single gold star against a blue ground – *L'Etoile du Nord*.

Trouin's headquarters was just as Brouwer had described it. On either side of the doorway stood a large armed guard. As Steel watched a man staggered out of the door and stumbled up the street towards him, clearly quite drunk. As he approached Steel he doffed his hat and then veered off towards where Brouwer was standing, twenty yards away. Tripping over a loose cobblestone the man cannoned into Brouwer, knocking him to the ground. Brouwer stood up and cursed and then, unnerved by the tension of the situation, uncharacteristically muttered an insult. Steel looked round but, determined to keep up the appearance of being alone, made no attempt to go to his aid. But then, to Steel's amazement for one in such a condition, the drunk drew his sword and began to hurl insults back at Brouwer, who, weapon less, put up his arm to cover his face.

There was only one course of action. Steel ran to Brouwer and placing one hand firmly on the drunken man's shoulder, turned him and with the other landed a punch to his face which sent him back against the nearest building. The man slammed into the wall, slid down and slumped into unconsciousness. Instinctively, Brouwer went to thank Steel and then quickly stopped himself and dropped back into the shadows.

Rubbing at his bruised knuckles, Steel turned back towards the inn and walked cautiously, but without wanting to appear nervous, towards the two guards at the door. He was wondering how much of the encounter they had seen when from behind them another, taller man appeared. Like them, he did not wear any recognizable military uniform, but a red sash wrapped around his waist and an elaborate, gold-trimmed hat betrayed his rank as some sort of officer.

He looked at Steel: 'You have business in here, friend?'

Steel bowed and said in passable French with deliberate flattery, '*Monsieur le Colonel*, I seek an audience with your captain – Commander Duglay-Trouin. I have come to offer my services to him, in the name of France, and in those of King Louis and King James.'

The man looked at him hard, then laughed: 'You want to see Trouin? Are you quite sure, *monsieur*?'

Steel held open his cloak so that the officer could see his coat beneath, which, to signify his treason, he had turned inside out to show its white lining. Thus reversed, he could easily now have passed for a white-coated French infantryman.

The man stared at him, taking in his appearance. The curious semi-civilian dress, the unusual sword which hung at his side, his lack of a full-wig and his unkempt look. He rested his hand on his sword. Steel felt his heart pounding. Clearly, the man was suspicious.

This was time for something more. Steel played a wild card: 'You must let me see Captain Trouin. I have come here in great personal danger expressly to fight at his side. I swear it to you. Death to the bloody English and their queen. Long live France and all true Jacobites. Long life to the pope, God save him and the devil send death to Marlborough and all his whoreson army.'

It was a virtuoso performance. He spat on the cobbles, and waited to gauge the man's reaction. There was a silence and then the pirate began to laugh. The two others joined in and eventually he spoke.

'I am sorry, sir. We cannot be too careful. There are English spies everywhere. You'll find Commander Trouin in here, unless he has already repaired to his bed. Will your friend be joining you?'

Damn, Steel thought, they had seen Brouwer. Doubtless they had seen the two of them together, seeing off the drunk. He crused silently and noticed that the officer was still watching him closely. There was nothing for it but to include the Belgian. He turned and caught Brouwer's eye, then used the first Scots name that came into his head.

'Come on, Lieutenant Macleod. We're in luck. They'll take

us both for soldiers.' He winked and beckoned. Brouwer, totally nonplussed, could do nothing but go along with Steel.

The officer nodded: 'Well then, in that case I will bid you goodnight, gentlemen. And good luck with Commander Trouin.'

Steel bowed and as the officer ducked back into the inn, he turned to Brouwer, whispering as they passed the guards, 'Christ. I thought the game was up. I'm afraid that you'll have to come in with me. But leave as quickly as you can – don't hang around. And try to look a little more, um, military. I'll see you later. I have an appointment with a lady.'

And with that, he was gone. Brouwer nodded and as Steel disappeared into the crowded inn, wondered how to manage a 'military' bearing. He had never been interested in being a soldier. He had spent his life preaching peace, and sworn never to take up arms. Until recently of course, but then only as a last resort, to defend his country and his family. Nervously, Brouwer looked about him and wished that he had never met the tall Scottish officer. Yet his sense of duty told him that he must do this for his town and for his family. So pushing back his coat, he thrust a thumb in his belt and set his face into what he took to be a military attitude. Then, with a thirst brought on by fear, he walked across to a small vacant table and sitting down, tried to puzzle out how an officer in the British army might ask a serving-girl in a tavern full of pirates to sell him a mug of ale.

ELEVEN

Steel found what he was looking for without much difficulty. René Duglay-Trouin was unmissable. He sat at the head of a table of men against the furthest wall of the inn, distinguished from the others not only by his clothes but by his very presence which marked him out to Steel as a leader. It did not take Trouin more than a few seconds to come to the same conclusion about Jack Steel.

Steel pushed through the throng of drunks and whores towards the pirate's table. Trouin waved away the girl who had been sitting on his knee and gazed at Steel and as he did so one of his men whispered in his ear.

He spoke and the room around him fell silent. 'So, you have come to offer your services to me, Mr . . . ?'

'Thomson. Jack Thomson.'

'I am flattered Mister Thomson. You do me an honour.'

Thomson. It was hardly convincing. Steel had settled on it, his mother's maiden name, the previous evening. He had also tried to modulate his voice but was acutely conscious that even to a Frenchman, his gentle lowland Scottish accent might shine through, in particular marking him out as a

209

cut above the normal rank-and-file deserter. He knew that eventually he would have to admit that he was an officer and that would beg new questions. Clearly, that time was now. He smiled at Duglay-Trouin yet maintained his essential air of sang-froid. Never before, not on any battlefield, had he felt so desperately exposed. He sensed the pirate's eyes boring into his skull, attempting to seek out the truth.

Trouin frowned: 'Mister . . . Thomson. You do not, forgive me for saying so, but you do not strike me as the normal sort of deserter that we see.' He paused and Steel knew what was coming next. 'You are an officer I think? Yes?'

Steel swallowed. Unsure as to whether Trouin had already penetrated his subterfuge, he could only play along. 'Yes. I must admit that I am, sir. At least I was. I was until lately an officer in Queen Anne's army. But I cannot fight for those colours any longer. In truth, Captain, I was fighting for a lie.'

'You interest me. How was that so?'

'I was not fighting for our true monarch, sir, King James. In truth, my conscience has long troubled me and now at last it has driven me to this. I saw such things at the late battle, sir. Our own, I'm sorry, Marlborough's own troops killing in cold blood men whose only fault I knew to be that they followed the Jacobite cause. It has turned me, sir. I now count myself among them. I desire to fight against the queen, sir. For King James III, the true King of Britain.'

Trouin clapped him on the back. 'So. You are a Jacobite. Good. We have other men of your persuasion in our ranks. Perhaps you will know some of them. But tell me, why join us? Why not join one of the Jacobite regiments of the French army?'

Steel had prepared his answer. 'Because, Captain, in so doing I would almost certainly come up against my old comrades in battle, on the battlefield that is. And in such a situ-

210

ation I would be torn in two directions. With you I might serve the French and yet it would seem be less certain of meeting my old regiment.'

Trouin paused, considering the validity of the argument. Steel sensed himself sweating with fear of discovery.

At last, Trouin spoke: 'That is very true, Mister Thomson. It does not do to kill old friends, whatever side you are on. What was your rank?'

'I was a captain, sir.'

'Well Captain Thomson, then perhaps you should retain your rank . . . when you join us.' A sense of relief swept over Steel. But Trouin had not finished. 'There is but one problem. Whereas in your world an officer is naturally considered a gentleman, indeed is that before he becomes an officer and is valued as such above the ordinary man, here, in the world I inhabit, I tend to prefer the company of the commoner. Officers, I have found as a rule, tend not to be as trustworthy as they would have us believe. You understand me?'

This rankled with Steel, but he knew that to disagree would be suicide. 'Perfectly, sir.'

'So tell me, Captain Thomson, why I should trust you?'

'Because I speak the truth, sir, not merely because I count myself a gentleman. Because I fight like ten men and because, as a British officer I can be of great use to you. I am also no mere posturing gentleman-soldier, but a veteran. I fought with the Swedes at Narva, with Marlborough at Blenheim. I did not purchase my captaincy; I earned it with the colours. Are those reasons enough for you?'

Trouin nodded and smiled. 'If what you say is true, and increasingly I am inclined to believe you, Captain, then, yes. That is enough for me – almost. You are right about the last thing, certainly. We could use a man like yourself, to pass as the enemy and afford us surprise. Yes, that would be good.

And I tend to believe your motive too. As to your fighting abilities, I think perhaps that we should make up our own minds.' He called across the room: 'Which one of you men has the guts to take on this Scottish gentleman? He wishes to join us and I believe that we need to test his skill at arms.'

Steel looked on as three of Trouin's men rose to their feet at one of the tables. As if by tacit agreement, only one, a tall, muscular man with a single continuous eyebrow, and wearing a filthy leather jerkin, walked across to Trouin.

'So, Alexis. You feel like a bit of sport. Think you can beat him? He's a professional soldier you know.'

The man laughed. He spoke slowly and with contempt. 'You know me, Captain. Do *you* think I can beat him?'

'I believe that you will. And if you do, ten gold pieces. But Alex, my friend; if he should beat you . . .' Alexis grinned. 'Well, who knows? Fair?'

The man grinned again: 'Fair, Captain.'

Trouin turned to Steel: 'Your choice of weapons, *monsieur*. Swords, pistols, hatchets, pikes? What do you favour?'

Steel drew back his cloak to reveal the sword which hung at his side and slowly eased the great blade from its scabbard. He watched it flash in the lantern light.

'Swords, sir.'

Trouin looked closely and covetously at the sword, with its fine damascening and delicately darkened markings. 'That is a fine weapon, Captain.'

'A family heirloom, Captain. It was made in Italy by Ferrara.'

'I thought as much. I have rarely seen its like. It would take a true swordsman to handle such a weapon.'

'I get by.'

'Well now, let's see how you get by with Alexis.'

Steel's opponent drew his own sword, a heavy-bladed

scimitar of Turkish design with a flat blade. It was shorter than Steel's weapon, but he knew that, if wielded properly, it would have sufficient power to sever a man's arm as soon as touch it. It reminded him of the swords used by three Ukrainian Cossacks, the Zaporozhne, that he had encountered in the army of Tzar Peter in the northern wars and it occurred to him that with his angular face and long moustache the man's roots might lie in that distant place. He also wondered how skilled he might be in the use of his blade.

Trouin pushed at the crowd of his men and tavern girls that had gathered around the two contestants. 'Clear the floor. Give them room.' He turned to Steel: 'Gentlemen. You may begin . . . To the death.'

Steel looked at him: 'We did not agree on that, sir.'

'But that is ever the way in my world, Captain Thomson. There is no other way. Now, begin.'

He clapped his hands and Steel's adversary assumed a crude version of the *en garde* position. Steel, who had thrown off his cloak and coat, did the same and extended his sword-arm. The pirate circled him, throwing the scimitar from hand to hand with worrying dexterity.

Steel drew back his own blade and held it upright in the *en garde*. The pirate looked confused. For an instant he left the scimitar in his right hand. Steel struck, lunging with lightning speed for the man's left side and finding flesh. The point of his sword cut into the man's side, drawing a gout of blood. The pirate hardly flinched. He was angry now and keen to attack. Steel lunged again. A feint this time to the right and the man fell for it. He swore in an unintelligible tongue and attempted to parry but Steel's blade was gone and once again was slicing into the Russian's right side. This time the pirate felt the pain. Steel could see the colour rising in his face as he lost control. Now, he thought, this will turn

213

into a very different sort of fight, for his opponent had cast away reason, had abandoned the desire or the need to construct his attacks. Now, Steel knew, this would be a fight to the death. He was up against a madman. He recovered and attempted to guess what his opponent would try next. It was harder to anticipate the tactics of a maniac. The man leapt at him, catching Steel completely off-guard. He brought back his sword-arm but not before the Russian had made contact with it and then the rest of his body.

The two men fell to the ground in a sprawling heap and the man pinned Steel down with his sheer weight. Winded, Steel realized with horror that his sword had been knocked from his hand. He glanced to the right and saw it lying close by. Stretching out he tried to reach it.

The Russian drew back his head and brought it crashing hard down on to Steel's cranium. The pain was incredible. Steel thought he was going to pass out. He shook his head, and saw blood flash before him. The big Russian was standing above him now, laughing. Steel, careful not to let him know how aware he was, moaned and stretched again for the sword. The Russian moved his foot forward to crush Steel's hand – and that was his undoing. Steel brought his left foot up hard, directly into the Russian's groin, and felt it connect with gristle and bone. The man keeled over on to his back and lay there grasping his genitals.

Slowly, Steel sat up, leaning on his hand for support. Now he managed to reach the sword. He pulled himself up and sword in hand walked across to the Russian. But he was not finished. The man spun over and with more speed than Steel could believe for one his size, moved to his own weapon. Then he turned. Steel was ready for him. He cut towards the head, cavalry-style this time and instinctively the man ducked. But that was exactly what Steel had planned. The

214

sabre cut was merely a feint, stopped in mid-air. Instead Steel twisted his sword-hand forward and brought his blade up directly beneath the Russian's chin. It missed, just, but connected with the man's left ear, severing a sizeable chunk. The Russian screamed and grabbed at his bloody head. Then Steel was on him again. He recovered the sword with a flourish and swept it across the Russian's belly. Not deep enough to kill. Just to draw blood. The man sank to his knees. Steel moved closer and kicked him hard in the chest making him fall backwards.

Sensing that the Russian had no fight left in him, Steel stood over him. The man looked up at him with pleading eyes. Steel held the great blade poised at his throat.

Trouin spoke: 'Excellent. Superb swordsmanship. And not a little street-fighting too. You surprise me, Captain, I had not known that the English could fight so dirty; particularly an English officer. I'm sorry – a Scottish officer. And now, he is yours, sir. You must decide. Kill him or spare him. The choice is yours, Captain Thomson.'

Steel looked down at the Russian and wondered again whether their paths had crossed before somewhere in the Swedish wars. He felt sorry for the brute, but he knew that only two minutes ago the man had been ready to kill him. He knew what he had to do. It went against every grain of integrity as an honourable man and an officer. But if he were to succeed here in his subterfuge, if he were to save the lives of hundreds of innocent people, not to mention Lady Henrietta, there was no other way. He looked one last time into the man's eyes and leaned hard down on the blade which slipped easily into the pirate's throat.

Trouin applauded: 'Bravo. Well done, sir. He deserved to pay with his life. He knew what had to be done. That is our way. And now I have no doubt of your loyalty. Come, you need a drink.' He nodded to two of his men who went to remove the bloody corpse and clapping Steel on the back, offered him a goblet of wine. 'Let us drink to your joining my crew. Welcome. You are a natural fighter, sir.'

Steel took a long draught of wine and savoured its bitterness. 'I need to fight, Captain. It's the only way I know. Over there I fought for Queen Anne. In here . . .'

'You fight for me.'

Steel shook his head and laughed. 'No, sir. I fight for money and easy women. Most of all I fight for myself. I swear allegiance to the one true king, King James III. But, if you'll have me, I will do your work.'

'I will have you, Captain. What I could do with ten of you! Once we've finished here, and taken what we can, money, vittles and good, white slaves, then we'll sail for the Caribbean. Have you ever seen the Caribbean, Thomson? No? Then you've a rare treat in store. Sunshine every day; ships laden with treasure, ripe for the taking. And women the same. Women of all sorts.' He took a long swig of wine and wiped his lips on a delicate silk handkerchief that he extracted from his pocket. It smelt of oranges. He belched and went on: 'I've done with this place, Captain. What the British started here we shall finish. We'll let them stew outside there for another few days, knowing that we have the girl. And then, when they're least expecting it, we'll burn this godforsaken town, butcher those we don't take and sail out of the harbour free men. And will the British navy give chase? Well, what do you think, as long as we have something that I know they want. For we have something here, something belonging to our English friends. Something to which no harm must ever come. And they know we have her. Such a plan, eh Thomson? Such a plan.'

Steel had to admit that it was sound, though hardly what

216

he had in mind. It was clear that he would have to act quickly to effect Lady Henrietta's escape. He thought fast: 'Did I hear you mention women, Captain? By God, there's nothing like a fight to put me in want of a woman.'

Trouin leered at him: '*Monsieur*, you are full of surprises. I swear, I shall never underestimate the English, or the Scots again. So, women you say. What is your taste? We have many here to choose from. But first we have business.'

Steel blanched and wondered whether all along Trouin had seen through his disguise. He scanned the room for Brouwer and saw him sitting alone in a dark corner, nursing a tankard of ale. Brouwer caught Steel's gaze and quickly looked away.

Trouin laughed: 'Come. It's nothing serious. I believe that you may enjoy our little entertainment. And it will give you time to get your breath back before meeting the ladies. A prizefight – you like such fighting?'

'It can be most entertaining, Captain. Between evenly matched fighters, of course, and with the proper conditions.'

Trouin smiled wryly: 'Oh, We have evenly matched fighters. And as to the rules, well, we have those too.'

He ushered Steel through a door and into a dimly lit barn in which straw bales had been laid around the walls to act as seats. The place was full already with French sailors, a few regular soldiers from the garrison and Trouin's crewmen. All were eager for the contest. Most were drunk. Several appeared to be taking wagers and money was changing hands fast.

Trouin ushered Steel towards a hay bale across which had been laid a thick red velvet cloak. 'Plase join me here, on my own seat.'

'You honour me, Captain.'

Steel sat down a short distance from the captain and was aware of the huge black bulk of Ajax taking position behind them. Across the back of the barn sheets of material had been draped upon a cord to provide a makeshift dressing room for the contestants. No sooner had they sat down than a man in a green coat – Steel recognized him from the inn as one of Trouin's senior officers – walked to the centre of the room and clapped his hands to silence the crowd.

'Gentlemen. Gentlemen, please. A contest of four rounds . . . or as many as it takes for a kill, between in the left corner The Pride of the Amazon and in the right The Fury.'

The combatants were led out and Steel gasped. For these were not the great hulking prizefighters he had been expecting, but two girls in their late teens or early twenties. They looked, from their glazed expressions, as if they had been drugged or at least made tipsy and both were dressed in a short shirt and a thin skirt of chiffon or cambric. The most extraordinary thing about them, he thought, was that both were uncommonly pretty.

Trouin saw his bewilderment: 'You see Mister Thomson, how we like to do things here. We like a little spice with our meat, eh? Both of these women were caught stealing from the company's funds. This is their punishment. They will go at each other until first blood is drawn and then we will decide – I shall decide – if the contest will continue. The winner has the privilege of further entertaining me in my bed. Although perhaps tonight I shall take them both.' He turned to the master of ceremonies and waved his hand. 'Let the fight begin.'

The two women squared up to each other and the plumper one lunged. But the other girl was quick on her feet and sidestepped so that her opponent fell sprawling to the floor. The room erupted in catcalls and cheers as the girl staggered to her feet, only to be hit with a smart uppercut by the other. Reeling, she put her hand to her jaw and eyes blazing now with genuine anger raced towards her opponent and drove her fist directly into her chest before twisting her arm behind her in a lock. It was almost too much for Steel to watch, although around the room the atmosphere was electric. The second girl, the Amazon, twisted in her grip and managed to turn just enough to grab hold of her shirt, which she tore away, forcing her opponent to let go. Half-naked now, the one they called The Fury ran at the other who was twirling the shirt in the air, in triumph.

The room was filled with whistles now and lewd suggestions. Making contact with her opponent's back, the Amazon shoved her forward face down on the floor and began to stamp on her. The girl screamed and Steel tensed at the sound. Surely, he thought, Trouin will stop it now? The Amazon was kneeling now, grinding her knee into the small of the blonde's back. She grabbed her left arm and twisted it behind her. The blonde was crying now, begging for mercy. But still her opponent twisted and pulled at her arm. Suddenly the victim gave a terrible scream.

At last Trouin intervened: 'Enough. I think that will do.'

Instantly the Amazon stopped her torture and stood up, making no attempt to hide her nakedness. The other girl remained on the floor, whimpering.

Trouin ignored them both and turned to Steel. 'So, it is settled. A pity, I preferred the blonde. But you can't have everything in life, can you, Captain?'

Steel tried to ignore the drama being acted out behind him where the blonde girl, her arm dislocated, was being helped up and carried off. He smiled: 'I don't know. Can't you?'

Trouin laughed. 'Now, Captain, women – take your pick. We have many. What is to your taste? Mulatto? A northern Valkyrie perhaps with blonde hair? Perhaps you like that? Margareta.' He beckoned a blond girl and pushed her towards Steel so that she careered into him and he felt her soft warmth. She smiled at Steel, who returned her gaze.

'No, Captain. My tastes are . . .'

'More exotic, I'll wager. You prefer a black girl. Well, we can accommodate you there too.' He looked about the room and made to signal to one of the women.

Steel stopped him. 'No, no, Captain. On the contrary, I favour an English girl. Or Scots. Or Irish perhaps. That is to my taste. But always a girl with spirit.'

Trouin thought for a moment. 'Then I must tell you of someone. Someone very important and exquisitely beautiful – an English milady.'

Steel feigned ignorance, and gave Trouin a puzzled look. The pirate rose to his curiosity: 'No, really. I have an English lady. And I intend to use her, in every way imaginable.'

Steel shuddered but smiled at Trouin: 'Who is she? What's she doing here? Can I see her?' He paused: 'I don't believe you. You're full of hot air, there's no lady.'

The pirate to Trouin's left went for his sword but the captain stayed his hand: 'No, no. Captain Thomson doubts my word. If he is to serve with me then he must trust me completely.' He thought for a moment: 'Come, we will go to my house.'

He clicked his fingers and Ajax followed them towards the door. Steel glanced again at Brouwer whose face now wore an expression of undisguised terror. Trying not to be noticed he mouthed to Brouwer: *Get out. Go.* But the man seemed rooted to the spot – and then Steel and the others were out in the street.

They walked a few paces before turning sharp left. Ahead of them stood a house, rather grander than the others in the street with a pair of Doric columns and what passed as a portico. Trouin made an extravagant gesture with his arm.

'Behold, Captain. My humble dwelling. It's not much, but it is the finest house in this quarter. Belonged to the harbour master before he went missing. Please come in.'

Trouin pushed the door open and they entered a soaring hall with a black and white marble floor and a painted roof supported on six columns. From the centre was suspended a massive crystal chandelier of Venetian design containing perhaps five dozen white candles. Clearly, thought Steel, the harbour master had been able to command a healthy living. Or, more likely he had been creaming off a personal levy on imports and exports. Either way, the man had evidently met his maker. Steel gawped at the opulence. Trouin watched him.

'Yes, I too was surprised at this place. Of course I have brought a few things here. I'm very fond of works of art. I am something of a dilettante, you know, a collector.'

Steel looked about the hall. At intervals around the walls plinths held marble busts of Roman emperors, presumably, thought Steel, the product of Trouin's global lootings. On the walls hung the sort of paintings he might have expected to find in a grand country house. The furniture was heavy, much of it French. Trouin caught him eyeing up an ormolu and boule-mounted secretaire.

'A gift from the king. His Highness King Louis, that is, Captain. I am one of his favourites, you understand. He values my loyalty. Do come through. This is my favourite room, the salon.'

He opened a door and led the way into a room even grander than the hall. Another chandelier hung from the ceiling, holding, Steel thought, perhaps a hundred candles. More pictures lined the walls. One in particular, a huge canvas depicting a flayed ox, struck him as extraordinary in its detail. Trouin motioned him towards it.

'Please, Captain. Take a closer look. It is my supreme possession. A masterpiece, do you not think? It was painted by the great Rembrandt van Rijn. A Dutchman, unfortunately, but what a painter. Are you familiar with his work? I believe the late King of England was a collector. It is a favourite of mine. See how the blood glistens on the flesh. So realistic, so intricate. As if I had flayed the beast with my own hands. One could almost touch the living article, don't you think? Quite delicious.'

Trouin held his hand a few inches away from the painting, almost compelled, it seemed, to touch the paint.

Steel watched him and wondered how such a man, who only a short while ago had sanctioned the killing of one of his own men and had presided over a barbaric spectacle in which two girls had fought until one of them had been crippled, could possibly appreciate such a glorious work of art. He stared at Trouin, with his pomaded wig, his gold-trimmed coat and flamboyant hat and tried, without success, to get the measure of him. And Trouin continued to stare at the ox. At length, unable to resist any longer, the pirate touched the painting, running his fingers along the furrows of the impasto and seeming lost in an almost sexual ecstasy. After a few exquisite moments, he stepped back, yet continued to stare at the painting.

'Ah, Captain, what it must be to be a painter. What a talent. We mere mortals must content ourselves with our lesser abilities. Well, you can't have everything, can you?'

Steel shrugged: 'I don't suppose that Mijnheer van Rijn would have been much good as a soldier.'

Trouin laughed. 'I dare say that you're right. But he certainly knew the look of dead meat and blood.'

Steel felt a chill pass through him. Perhaps this man, for all his cultivated airs, was no more than he had first appeared: a simple, cruel, petty dictator.

Walking slowly around the room, Trouin came to a halt before a full-length portrait of an aristocrat. It had been painted, Steel guessed, around fifty years before and depicted the subject standing before a castle which an army, presumably his own, was busy attacking. They appeared to be winning.

Trouin sighed: 'I should wish to be remembered like that. To have my image painted in such a pose, before the scene of one of my many victories. D'you suppose I could find someone to do it?'

'I dare say you might, in Bruges or Brussels. I hear the Belgians have a fine tradition of painting.'

'But there, you see, Thomson, you have the measure of me. For I cannot wander freely in those places. I am an outlaw now. Doubly so, for I am employed by the French and now Marlborough has pushed them from Flanders. Soon we shall leave here. I think perhaps that we'll drop anchor at Port Royal again. These people are no more than boors, they have no manners, no finesse. Do you not agree?'

Steel nodded.

'Well, that is by the way. But tell me this, Thomson. Do you suppose that I will be remembered as a monster or a rich and kind man? A philanthropist? A friend of the people? No, do not concern yourself with an answer. I know what you are thinking. I will be recorded in history as a monster, I think.'

Steel bit his lip: 'I do wonder, Captain. With such taste as this.'

Trouin laughed: 'You surely should have been a courtier, Captain. You are something of an enigma to me. You have fine

223

manners, yet you fight as hard as any child of the gutter. I must admit, I am puzzled. I expect to learn a great deal more about you in the coming days, Captain. A great deal more.'

Steel picked up a piece of fine Chinese porcelain that sat on an ornate gold-mounted cabinet beneath a huge, gilded overmantel mirror. But his mind was not on the craftsmanship. He would have to be careful from now on, he realized. Clearly, Trouin picked up on the slightest of things, and was liable to find him out if he made the smallest slip. Already he had allowed his experience at court to show through the pretence. But he was unable to resist one more comment.

'You live like a king, Captain.'

'I am a king, Captain Thomson. Here, in my own world. The French with their stupid fat governor and that brutish major, think that they control this town. But the fact is that this is my world, Captain. For the present at least.' He paused and considered Steel's remark again. 'You know how a king lives, then? What do you know of kings?'

Steel said nothing, regretting the rash comment.

'How much I have to learn about you, Captain. You shall be my hobby. Come.'

Passing through the salon, they entered a panelled corridor. Trouin turned right and then left. After a few paces he stopped outside a doorway on either side of which one of his men stood guard. Steel noticed that each was armed with a cutlass hanging at his side and a brace of pistols tucked into his belt. Steel wondered what he might expect to find inside. More paintings perhaps? A horde of golden coins? A king's ransom in crown jewels? Trouin reached down to turn the key which sat in the lock.

'And here we are.'

Steel looked above the high doorcase to where the panelling held a small inset painting depicting Leda being ravished by Zeus in the guise of a swan. Trouin nodded to the guards, turned the brass door handle and opened the door.

He entered and called to Steel: 'Come in, come in. Come and see the most precious treasure of all.'

Followed by the two guards, they entered a boudoir, hung with printed cottons. In the centre of the room stood a large four-poster bed with floral-printed hangings and by the tall window at a simple, painted dressing table, sat a girl. She had her back to them. But even from this angle, Steel knew her. He jumped as Trouin clasped his shoulder, and recoiled from the man, who was tense with lust.

Trouin whispered: 'Well, what do you think of her. She's a rare beauty, eh?'

Steel had to agree. Henrietta Vaughan was something quite rare. He had met her on several occasions in London with her cousin, his mistress Arabella Moore. Mainly these had been social gatherings, but on one memorable occasion Lady Henrietta had stumbled into her cousin's bedroom when Steel and Arabella had been making love. It had been a sight that she was not likely to forget and as she turned Steel saw in her eyes that she recognized him instantly. She was more beautiful than he remembered. But even in that first glance he detected the haughtiness that had unsettled him on their first meeting.

Trouin noticed the look that passed between them. 'So, it is as I thought. She is exactly to your taste. Am I right?'

Steel smiled: 'Of course, Captain. How could any man not be smitten with such beauty. She is my ideal.'

Steel had not thought that Lady Henrietta would be able to hear him across the room. He was mistaken.

'How very kind you are, sir. I do not believe that I have had the pleasure of an introduction. Captain Trouin, perhaps you would be so kind.'

'Of course. Lady Henrietta Vaughan. Captain James

225

Thomson, late of the British army. Captain Thomson has elected to join me. A most wise decision, don't you think, madame?'

'I deplore deserters. In particular, I deplore deserters from the ranks of my own countrymen. You have ceased to be a gentleman, sir. You are no more than a traitor.'

Steel smiled. How like her cousin in spirit she was. 'My Lady, I am sorry to have offended you. I but follow my conscience.'

'Then it is a strange conscience that would have you join a band of cut-throats and pirates, Captain.'

'I would rather fight beside such men than for a government which murders innocent people on account of their religion and which serves a usurper to the thrones of England and Scotland.'

'You are a Jacobite?'

'And proud of it. I know no king but King James.'

Lady Henrietta smiled. He had been certain that she had recognized him. If so then she was playing this game with him and must have realized the true reason for his being here.

'You are foolish, sir, to follow a king with no throne. Queen Anne is our rightful monarch and her dynasty must prosper. You would do best to recant.'

Steel was enjoying the game now, warming to his role and the thrill of subterfuge. 'I am a man of honour, My Lady and would never betray my true loyalties.'

'That's not what I heard, sir.'

Steel froze and felt a sudden terror in the pit of his stomach. For the words had not come from Lady Henrietta but from somewhere behind him. Steel knew the voice instantly; he did not need to turn to see its owner, but did so all the same. He gazed hard and incredulous into the pair of close-set, grey weasel eyes that smiled at him with a ghastly familiarity and knew that, failing a small miracle, he was deep in trouble. Sergeant Stringer.

The man spoke: 'Mister Steel, sir? Can it really be you? I had thought you must have been killed long before now. You're very reckless, you know. You should be more careful. Saw you in the inn. Couldn't believe it was you, sir, had to come and see for myself. Brought your little Belgian friend too. Saw you signalling to him in the inn. Silly bugger should 'ave cut and run while he had the chance. Takes some men that way, fear does.'

Steel saw that behind Stringer two of the pirates were holding Marius Brouwer in a tight grip. He was as white as a sheet and a fleck of blood at the corner of his mouth showed that he had already taken a beating.

Stringer leered at Steel. Trouin spoke, slowly: 'You know this man?'

'Know him, sir? Why I'd know him anywhere. This man is a British officer.'

'But of course he is, Sergeant. He has told me all about himself and his reasons for wanting to join our crew.'

He looked at Steel and smiled, unwilling to believe that this newcomer might be justified in his evident suspicions of Steel or that his own judgement of the man might be at fault. 'And now, God forgive me, I trust him. He's a good fighter too, Sergeant. As good as they come. He killed Alexis.'

The man shook his head. 'Oh my good God, Captain. What a loss. And at what a price. You've been 'ad, sir. No disrespect meant, Captain. But you've been good and 'ad. And he's killed one of your best men an' all. I tell you, this man is no deserter. He's a liar.'

Steel attempted to look indignant. Trouin looked at him, searching for any self-doubt. 'Is this true, Captain Thomson? Have you lied to me?'

227

'On my word, Captain Trouin, I am no liar. I serve only you and the true king.'

Stringer laughed and spoke again: 'What did you say his name was, sir? Is that what he told you? Thomson? Oh no. No, no. This man's name is Steel. Mister Jack Steel. Captain now in Queen Anne's army. Why he's a friend of the duke 'isself they say.'

Trouin looked at Steel again and back to the man: 'You're mistaken, Stringer. Or perhaps you're just drunk. I trust this man.'

'More than you trust me, sir? Who was it as saved your life at Dunkirk, sir? Surely you trust me before you believe a stranger? And smell my breath, sir. Am I drunk?'

Trouin considered the situation and turned to Steel. 'He's right. He did save my life and risk his own.'

Steel decided to bluff it out. 'I have never seen this man before in my life, Captain. I –'

The words were lost as Stringer spat a wad of tobacco into Steel's face and struck him in the solar plexus with a blow so unexpected and of such ferocity that it bent him over double. He held his stomach and feigned the severity of the pain, then straightening up, with all his force struck Stringer on the side of the head with a wicked left hook that sent him crashing into a gilded escritoire. And then Steel was upon him, fists pounding into stomach and face. Stringer straightened his leg and connected with Steel's groin, sending him backwards, broken over in agony.

Getting up from the floor, Stringer spat teeth and blood and yelled at Trouin, 'He's a bloody spy, sir. Don't listen to him.'

Again, fighting through the pain, Steel launched another attack and threw himself on Stringer as the words left his mouth. He drew back his own head and with a swift move-

228

ment smashed it hard against the other man's forehead sending Stringer to his knees with a groan. Steel too tasted blood. Steadying himself, his hand went to his sword hilt. Stringer looked up and stared at Trouin with pleading eyes and in that instant Steel knew he had lost. Trouin signalled to the two guards and Steel found his arms pinned behind his back.

'Enough. I know when Sergeant Stringer is telling the truth. He's lied to me often enough, and paid for it often enough to know not to do it again. Besides, why should he lie to me about a spy? And why didn't you mention this man before, Captain?' He motioned across to the terrified Brouwer.

Stringer rose shakily. He wiped away the blood from his mouth with the back of his hand and walked unsteadily across to Steel, pushing his face unpleasantly close until Steel could smell his breath.

'This, sir, is Captain Jack Steel of her Britannic Majesty's army.' The words came slowly, through Stringer's haze of pain. 'He's an officer in Farquharson's Regiment of Foot. My old regiment, before I saw the light. He commands the Grenadier company. Or he did when I knew him in Spain last year. Nasty bit of work, he is Captain Troo-in. Did for my old major. Remember me telling you about him? Poor bugger – that business in Bavaria. Tried to trick me an' all. Tried to 'ave me hung he did an' then he caught me again, in Spain. They were going to do for me there as well. Course, he couldn't hold me, sir. None of them could, not Nathaniel Stringer. Too slippery I am, see. Ain't I, Mister Steel, sir? And I bet you thought you'd seen the last of me, sir. Didn't you, now, sir?' Stringer paused, looked at Steel and smiled. He allowed the captured officer to wait for a few moments in a silence which became excruciating with tension.

Trouin looked from one man to the other. 'Clearly, you've no love for this man, Sergeant.'

Stringer spat again, this time taking care to ensure that the phlegm struck home on Steel's foot and slithered from his boot to the carpet. 'To tell you the truth, sir, I'll not be happy till he's in the grave. My soul shall not rest easy as I live and breathe. And nor will that of my dear old major. Man's a traitor, sir. Worst sort.'

Steel sensed that one of the pirates holding him, the one to his right, either because of the drink or the fact that he was leering at Lady Henrietta, had momentarily slackened his grip. He had to move quickly. Pushing the guard away with his left hand and all the force he could muster, he brought his right across to his belt and, drawing one of the two pistols, cocked it and took aim at the pirate to his left. He had thought to shoot Stringer, but the man had moved across and it was to cost him his life. Steel's gun went off with a deafening crack in the little room and the pirate crumpled to the floor, a bullet through his forehead. Steel drew the other pistol and pulled on the hammer. It would not move. He applied more pressure and gradually felt it ease back until the gun was cocked. It was too late. He felt the point of a sword at his throat. Steel stiffened and looked up at Trouin.

'I think that will be enough, Captain Thomson. Or should I say, Captain Steel. Bind him.'

While the remaining guard held Steel's arms painfully behind his back, Stringer wound his own belt tightly around his wrists. When it was done, Trouin lowered his sword and returned it to its scabbard. He looked at Steel and shook his head.

'My dear Captain. I cannot tell you how much you have disappointed me. As Sergeant Stringer says, I was completely taken in. And I do not enjoy being made to look a fool.' His words were aggressive, filled with venom.

Steel attempted to regain what composure he could.

230

'Sergeant Stringer, what an unexpected pleasure. Though I have to say it is all yours.'

Trouin ignored his bravado: 'And now, Captain. You present me with a problem. What are we to do with you and your friend?'

He crossed the room and picked up a small box from the bureau. He opened the lid and a tune filled the room. A simple, childish air, a nursery rhyme whose innocent associations seemed to be mocked by the tense horror of Steel's situation.

'I have decided. Yes, I think that we shall take a short walk. I have a diverting little room below the tavern, down just a few stairs. Come, Captain Steel. Let me take you there – and your unfortunate friend. I'm sure that you will find it most entertaining. We'll take the girl too. She most certainly must not be allowed to miss out on the evening's entertainment.'

The words, so lightly said, burned their potential meaning into Steel's mind and he fought to conceal his terror. He could not imagine what sort of evening Trouin had in store. But he knew that the captain must be furious at having been taken in by his disguise. And he knew too that when such a man's pride was hurt and in such a manner there would be no way for honour to be regained other than by pain and almost certainly death.

TWELVE

The room was square and windowless, a cold stone cellar, lit only by the light of the flaming, pitch-soaked torches which stood in iron brackets around the walls. It smelt of blood and human ordure. Steel noticed with apprehension that around the walls at intervals, chains with manacles had been fastened into the stones. It looked for all the world like the sort of medieval torture chamber he had heard about in boyhood history lessons. He shuddered. In one corner there even stood a brazier and in another a wooden table covered with what looked suspiciously like bloodstains. In another area lay a filthy divan on which four of the pirates, all of them drunk to various degrees, were taking turns with two half-naked serving-girls. They did not stop as Trouin entered, nor did he attempt to make them. There were other pirates in the room, most of them sitting in chairs or on stools. All these too seemed to Steel to be the worse for liquor. Those that could do so and remain steady, which was only a few, got to their feet and went to greet their captain. Trouin acknowledged them with a wave and was rewarded with a cheer; he turned to Steel.

'You see. I do believe in rewarding my men when we have the opportunity. I know how to treat them well. Don't I, boys?'

Another faint cheer went up.

'Now lads. Here's a little sport for you. We've captured some spies.' He signalled to Stringer who pushed Steel before him, further into the room. Another of the men entered with Marius Brouwer. The Belgian looked terrified. Behind them a third pirate followed with Lady Henrietta. Trouin turned to another of his men. 'Strip this English gentleman to the waist and put him in those manacles. Do the same with the other one. You can leave the woman for me.'

Steel spat: 'You bastard. Leave her alone. And let this gentleman go, you have no quarrel with him. It's me you want.'

Trouin turned on him, smiling: 'Oh, you're quite wrong there, Mister Steel. I have very much a quarrel with this gentleman, for without his help you would not have been admitted into this town or have infiltrated our little band. He has much to answer for, more than you even. He is a traitor, Steel and for that I assure you he will pay. As for milady, she has done me no great wrong. But by the rules of piracy she belongs to me, to do with as I please. So, I would advise you, Mister Steel, to keep a civil tongue in your head. You will find that it makes for a much easier time with us. And there will be a moment as the evening wears on when you do wish that things were easier. I can assure you of that.'

Trouin grabbed Lady Henrietta around the waist with a grip so tight that she felt almost suffocated and dragged her across the room.

She tried to struggle. 'Let me go! Get away from me!'

'And you too, My Lady. You would do better not to resist. It will go so much easier for you. Who knows? You might even end up enjoying whatever lies in store.'

233

'I order you to let me go. At once!'

Trouin slapped her hard across the face. Just once, and she was silent. Then, pushing her roughly against the far wall, he thrust first one slim fair hand and then the other through the pair of manacles which hung from the wall and snapped them shut. He stepped back. 'Yes. Very pretty, madame. Perhaps if . . .'

Reaching forward he grabbed the material at the décolletage of her dress and pulled hard. It ripped and the bodice of the dress fell away, fully exposing her ample white breasts. Lady Henrietta, unable to cover her shame, gasped and stared hard at her assailant.

Trouin laughed. 'Yes. That is so much better. Don't you all agree?'

Stringer was beside him now. 'Oh yes, Captain. I must say that's very nice, sir. Lovely, ain't she. Quite lovely, if I may say so.'

Trouin moved across to Steel, whose waistcoat and shirt had now been removed. The pirate stared at his hard muscular torso and caught sight of two long scars, one which ran down his side, from shoulder to stomach, the other down his arm. The pirate moved a finger along each of them, feeling the puckered skin.

'You look as if you may have seen some action, Captain? Am I right?'

'More than you I dare say and in better company, Trouin. And in the service of my country.'

Trouin tut-tutted and shook his head: 'No, *monsieur*, there you do me an injustice. You see, I too fight in the service of my country. Of course, there is a little self-interest involved. And I am sure the same is true of you. But I am engaged by King Louis. I fact, as I think I have already mentioned, I am rather a favourite of His Majesty.'

Steel smirked. 'I find that hard to believe, *monsieur*. I had heard that you were an officer of France. But now I see that you are no better than a common thief.'

Trouin bristled. 'You will regret that comment, Mister Steel. And you are quite wrong. A thief I may be, as you say, but I am far from common. I have the most refined tastes, as you have already seen for yourself.'

He crossed the room again to where Stringer was still ogling the half-naked form of Lady Henrietta. Trouin stood back and looked carefully at her as if she were a work of art. 'Yes, I covet only the most beautiful objects.'

Pushing the Englishman aside, Trouin extended his hand and, flexing the long fingers, ran it slowly down her exposed breast, lingering and teasing her form just as he had done with the thick gobbets of dried oil paint in the Rembrandt of the flayed ox. 'I covet and enjoy only the very finest things, Mister Steel. D'you see?'

Her face contorted with revulsion, Lady Henrietta tried in vain to pull away from him.

Steel strained against the manacles which cut painfully into his wrists. 'You bastard. Take your hands off her.'

'Oh dear, Captain, another mistake. You have to learn that you must never, ever give me orders. But you are right; it would be a shame to spoil such perfect beauty, wouldn't it? Particularly as I have not yet decided what to do with so fine a prize. Who d'you suppose will pay the most for her? Your people or some fat sultan? Or perhaps I shall keep her for myself. Or should I just give her to my men, for their pleasure? I am a generous man, you know.' He reached out towards Lady Henrietta and again took hold of one of her breasts. With a firmer grip this time, making her gasp. She looked away. 'So very irresistible. Yes. Later perhaps.'

Trouin let her go and walked over to Steel who stared at

him hard in the face. 'Call yourself a man, Trouin? You're no more than an animal.'

Trouin froze. He shook his head. 'And again. Will you never learn? I think that Mister Steel needs a lesson in good manners. Let's teach him how to be a gentleman, shall we? Sergeant Stringer – perhaps you would take a particular pleasure?'

Stringer snapped out of his titillated trance before the half-naked woman and gave Steel a smile. Then he clicked his fingers at two of the pirates and walked across to a hook on the wall where a cat-o'-nine-tails hung. Taking it down he walked over to where Steel was hanging, his arms straining uncomfortably against the chains which were high, even for a man of his height. Stringer brought the cat up level with Steel's face and flicked it gently through the air, letting him see it. Gradually he began to whip it back and forth with more force until the knotted ends of the leather thongs began to make an obscene crack. The two pirates took hold of Steel and turned him round so that the manacles crossed over above his head, stretching his arms still more painfully in their sockets and he was staring at the stone wall with his bare back exposed to the room. Then each of the men grabbed hold of one of his legs and held it firm, pushing down on to the floor. Steel, unable to see behind him, guessed at what was coming.

Stringer's first stroke hit him like a hammer blow, smashing into his shoulderblade like a blunt object. The second, laid upon the same place with unerring precision, did likewise. Steel remembered that it had been Stringer who had schooled the drummer boys of the regiment in their task of administering punishment floggings. He gritted his teeth and took care not to bite or swallow his tongue. For unlike any official military flogging, he had not been supplied by Trouin with

236

the customary piece of leather on which to bite. He had seen this punishment meted out many times in the British army – to the rank and file – and part of him had always been curious to discover how it felt. But this was not the time or the way in which he had thought he might make that discovery. The third stroke brought a different sensation of pain, more acute, as if someone had stuck a hot needle into his back. And that was how it continued. Within minutes Steel was lost in a rolling sea of pain. No one was bothering to count the strokes as they would have on a punishment parade, but in his mind he registered every one to a total of twenty. Then, to his surprise, it stopped.

Somewhere from within his mist of pain Steel heard Stringer's voice: 'But Captain, sir. I was just getting into a rhythm.'

Trouin was being merciful. The two men turned Steel round to face the captain. Stringer, downcast, was standing at Trouin's side, cradling the whip on which Steel could see what he took for gobbets of his own flesh. He gagged with rising nausea.

Trouin addressed him: 'So, Mister Steel, how does it feel to be on the receiving end of that most barbaric of punishments, which nevertheless I am sure you have ordered for your men so many times. And for the most trivial of offences? Perhaps now you will have better manners. Not that you will ever have the chance, I think.'

Steel said nothing. He could feel the blood and sweat mingling as they ran in rivulets down his back which throbbed with rhythmic pain. Looking down he saw that pools of blood had also collected around his feet. Trouin looked across to where Marius Brouwer was hanging from a similar set of manacles. He too had been stripped to the waist and his scrawny white form made a contrast to that of Steel. Trouin went over to him.

'But you now. What about you? You are most certainly not a man of action. What on earth were you thinking of getting yourself involved in this business? You are an idiot. This is not the thing for schoolteachers to get mixed up in – not at all. They might get hurt.'

On the last word, Trouin pushed against Brouwer and swiftly brought his knee hard up into contact with the man's groin. Brouwer gave an agonized shriek and then a moan.

'Silly little man.' He turned back to Steel: 'But Captain, do you not agree that he must learn that you cannot be a traitor and be allowed to get away with it. Spies and traitors must be punished. Isn't that right, Captain? Boys?' There was a cheer and yells of approval from the company around the room. 'But we are not savages. We shall hold a proper trial. Every man is allowed a fair hearing. Now, who will defend this wretch?'

Stringer stepped forward: 'Begging the captain's pardon, but may I be allowed that privilege, sir?'

Trouin nodded: 'So. We begin. The charge is that the accused, this man, did allow an enemy of the town and the people to enter Ostend with the express purpose of laying it to waste, murdering every one of its inhabitants, including the company of Captain René Duglay-Trouin and, most importantly, abducting that lady you see over there. How do you plead?' He looked at Brouwer, who had gone ashen white and was trembling with fear.

Stringer spoke for him: 'He pleads guilty, m'lud. There is no other plea and in effect, Your Honour, we have no defence.'

'In that case I find the defendant guilty as charged of treason.' The pirates cheered. Trouin stood at the head of the mock court and held up his hand. 'Justice will be done. I have decided. This is a man who would betray France.

Sentence will be passed. Justice must be seen to be done. There is only one sentence for such a crime – death.'

Brouwer began to shake. Trouin continued: 'And first, we must teach him not to betray us, not to talk of us ever again. Ajax, I think you know what to do.'

Steel looked on as the huge negro advanced upon Brouwer. The Dutchman screamed. Ajax smiled at him and, while one great black hand held open Brouwer's mouth, dislocating the jaw, the other reached deep inside and grasped hold of his tongue. And then pulled. Marius let out an unearthly shriek and it was done. Mercifully, Steel saw, Lady Henrietta had fainted.

Ajax threw the bloody tongue on the stone floor. Trouin snapped his fingers and one of the pirates loosed his dogs who fell upon the organ, fighting over who should have the larger share. Marius was still screaming. But the noise was so weird and otherworldly that it seemed not to come from his mouth, but from somewhere deep down within. It felt to Steel, even in his own agony, as if the entire room was shouting.

Trouin spoke: 'So, then. You all know the punishment for spies. And now boys, I hand the wretch over to you, what there is left of him. You may exact our own justice, in our customary way. You need some target practice, do you not?'

Steel had heard tales of pirate torture, but thankfully till now had never witnessed it. As he watched, some twenty of the crew who were not too drunk to stand gathered around Brouwer. One of them, a grinning Moor, took a few paces back and drew a small dagger from his belt. Taking care to aim, yet swaying on his feet, he drew back his arm and hurled the knife at Brouwer. It struck him on the arm, lodging deep in the flesh. The pirate cheered and punched his fist into the air. Immediately another, a dark-haired Spaniard, took his place, this time hurling a short tomahawk at Brouwer, which struck him on the left hand, severing two of his fingers. The Belgian screamed and stiffened with pain. Steel watched as Stringer stepped forward and drawing his pistol, cocked it. Steel looked away, heard the report and the scream and gazing back saw that the ball had passed through Brouwer's right kneecap. Stringer grinned, looked Steel directly in the eyes and winked.

'It'll be your turn soon, Mister Steel, sir. Don't you worry.'

Steel did his best to smile and wondered how long that would be. He needn't have worried. A full half-hour later, they had still not done with Marius Brouwer.

Steel could not bear to look. The pirates were taking their time now, making every cut, every shot, every blow hurt as much as possible, prolonging the poor man's agony as far as they could. Brouwer's body was a mass of cuts and he was covered in blood. His legs too were bleeding heavily. It seemed there was hardly a part of his body that had not been ripped or gouged by some weapon. And still they came on. Surely to God, thought Steel, this vile butchery could not last much longer. He knew that there was no point in protesting. That would only make his own suffering worse. He knew too that in part this spectacle was being enacted for his benefit. That Trouin, who had stood throughout in a darkened corner of the room, looking on, was revelling in what he knew would be Steel's increasing terror. And Steel knew too that Brouwer was a lost cause. He prayed silently that the man would expire soon. He was thankful at least that Lady Henrietta was still in a faint and that Trouin had not thought to force her awake. It occurred to him though that, when his own turn came, the pirate captain would ensure that she was fully conscious of what was happening to him and that she saw every ghastly, degrading stage in his own slow execution.

Brouwer was crying now. Or rather he was trying to cry. He had lost an eye to one of the daggers and the bloody hole gaped sightlessly out at the room. And, of course, he was unable to speak. But still a ghastly sound emanated from the gaping, gory ruin of his mouth. Through his miserable mewings Steel thought he could detect that the man was now begging for death. He thought about Marius's family, the children soon to be orphaned and poor Berthe. They would know nothing of this, of the way their father had died like a butchered animal. When Steel returned to them and broke the news – as he kept reassuring himself that he would – he would tell them that their father had died a hero, fighting to the end. When he got out of here. He looked around and suddenly began to doubt that certainty. If he got out of here. The pirates were flagging slightly in their perverse exertions now and it seemed to Steel that Brouwer must be on the brink of death.

Trouin too noticed both and advanced from his dark corner. 'Gentlemen, I believe that this miserable miscreant has at last paid for his crime.'

He nodded to Ajax. The pirates stepped back as the giant walked up to Brouwer who did not seem aware of anything beyond his own suffering and who had stopped even the small, animal noise which until now had signalled that he still retained a breath of life. The blackamoor snatched up Brouwer's head by the hair and at the same time drew the huge pearl-handled sword from its scabbard at his side. Then, with one quick and terrible move, he flicked up the blade with such power that it completely severed the Belgian's head, which flew from the body in a horrid, spouting arc, before falling to the floor.

Trouin applauded: 'Oh, well done. Bravo. Ah well, that's the end of any idiotic notions of freedom for these peasants.

Better to embrace the only true code of life, the code of the corsair. Eh boys? Let's have a song.'

Steel looked on as, even with the mutilated, headless corpse of Brouwer still hanging on the wall, one of the pirates took up a fiddle and began to play and a few others, less inebriated than the rest, managed a passable jig. With the music, Lady Henrietta stirred and awoke. Looking across the room she focused instantly on Brouwer's decapitated body and screamed. The fiddler played on and Trouin walked towards her.

'Oh no, dear madame. Don't worry. We still have his head.' From behind him Ajax pushed the bloody severed head, now impaled upon a pike, towards her face and she fainted back into unconsciousness. Trouin stroked her breast. 'Such a sensitive beauty. So very soft. So . . . ready.' He stopped himself and turned back to Steel. 'But now, Captain. We come to you.'

Steel felt his throat grow dry with fear as Trouin approached with the huge black man as always close behind.

'What I wonder will be your fate? What should we do, do you think, to one who so blatantly disregards the code of honour by which we live? Who sullies my own house and the very earth with his presence. What shall it be?' He turned to the pirates. 'You will decide, men.'

The fiddler stopped playing and those who were able, through the alcoholic haze, looked towards Steel.

'We shall take a vote on it. That is the way of the pirate. We are fully democratic, are we not? A band of brothers.' There was a cheer from the company. 'So what shall we say first? What exquisite end shall we devise for this traitorous scum?'

There was a groan from Lady Henrietta in the corner, who was coming round.

Trouin heard it. 'Ah. I believe that our other guest is waking up. And just in time for our little entertainment.'

She was staring at him, wide-eyed. Slowly her head turned and she surveyed the room, saw the shambles that remained of Brouwer hanging from the wall by chains. But she did not scream this time, merely gawped. She looked across to Steel and he could see the pure terror in her eyes.

Trouin saw it too: 'Do not be afraid, madame. Your fate will be as nothing compared to your friend here. We were just deciding what to do with him. Have you any imaginative ideas?' She said nothing. 'No? Well then, I shall put it to the ship's company. What is it to be? Shall we pull out his tongue too, like that fool? Or shall we blind him first?' A cheer went up around the room. 'Yes, good. Or perhaps, yes, perhaps we should simply geld him and prevent him from siring any more of his breed to sully this earth with their dishonour.'

Another cheer, louder this time. Stringer huzza-ed. Steel grimaced.

'Yes. Perhaps that would be the way. What do you say, Mister Steel. Would you rather be without sight, or without your manhood? Speak up.' Trouin smiled and cupped his ear in mock deafness. 'I can't hear you.' He bent his face closer to Steel's: 'Come on, tell me, Captain. What's it to be?'

No words came to Steel, but in a last defiant gesture he managed to summon up sufficient phlegm in his mouth to spit directly into Trouin's face. It was too much. The pirate lashed out and dealt Steel a stinging blow across the face. His head spun. He felt as if his jaw had been broken. Then Trouin's fist connected with Steel's abdomen and knocked the breath from him. He closed his eyes. Another blow came in fast, then another and another, with unexpected strength, until Steel felt as though the pirate must be splitting his organs beneath the taut skin, smashing the bruised bones. Then, as suddenly as it had begun, the frenzied assault stopped. Steel blinked and watched as Trouin wiped his spit from his face with a bloody, gloved hand and spat words back in his face.

'You disgusting piece of filth. When we've finished with you your own mother won't know you and no other woman will ever want to know you again. Oh yes. We're going to let you live. You will be a worthless piece of shit, a blind, castrated beggar.' He turned to his servant. 'Ajax, you may begin. And then we shall all enjoy whatever pleasures may be had from this English milady. I think I have decided not to sell her after all. I think that I will keep her for my own amusement, and for whoever else in my crew I deem worthy to sample her.'

He moved across to Lady Henrietta and with a deft gesture ripped off the remaining portion of her yellow dress, leaving her yet more exposed, half-naked in only her short petticoat. 'Yes. Well Ajax, don't stare, she's not for you. You would kill her. What are you waiting for? Get on with it.'

Steel stared wild-eyed as the negro bore down on him, a short knife gleaming in his hand. He struggled against the chains but only succeeded in gouging further into the cuts around his wrists. But he knew that the agony was nothing to that which he was about to experience. Reaching Steel, Ajax grasped his left arm and with a swift motion flicked the tip of the blade towards it. It made contact and left a faint, thin line along the flesh. Steel felt nothing and gazed at it and as he did so blood began to trickle from the cut and the pain kicked in.

Trouin laughed: 'What's wrong? He's only playing with you, Steel. He just wanted to make sure that the blade was keen enough before he got on with the real business. Continue.'

Again the blade flickered forward, cutting another thin line into Steel's arm and then again and again. The black giant stepped back and surveyed Steel, who had forgotten in his terror and pain what it was they intended to do to him first. Blind him or castrate him. It didn't seem to matter. Again Ajax advanced towards him and Steel closed his eyes, waiting for the awful impact of the razor-sharp metal on his skin.

But before it could happen the room burst into thunderous noise as a volley of musket shots raked the door and shattered the wood around the lock. Steel opened his eyes. In front of him, thankfully, Ajax had stopped in his tracks, distracted by the cacophony and Steel watched with the others as through the white smoke around the door uniformed men began to pour into the room. For a moment Steel thought that it must be a dream, that he must have passed out under the pain or be having hallucinations. He was uncertain whether he wanted to will himself back to reality, knowing what it would bring. And then it gradually began to seem real. There were voices – dimly, he saw two ranks of men form up and level their muskets at the pirates. He was conscious of a movement to his right. One of Trouin's men hurled a knife at the soldiers, missed and paid with his life as another shot rang out. Steel's mind was spinning. Surely the British assault had not yet begun? And how would his men know to find him here?

He peered into the smoke, looking for a familiar face; Williams, Hansam. Instead though he saw only anonymous soldiers. And the coats they wore – white. These were Frenchmen, regular army. Steel shut his eyes again, unable to take it in. He opened them and across the room he could see Lady Henrietta, still shackled as he was. And then a voice was talking to him. In English. He turned his bloody head towards it.

'Jacob?'

Jacob Slaughter pressed his face close to Steel's ravaged features. 'Don't worry, sir. You're safe now. Christ almighty, but what they've done to you. This place is a butcher's shop. Looks like we came just in time, sir.'

Steel mouthed words. None came. He wanted answers.

'Don't try and talk, sir. You're safe now. And the lady.'

He looked across to Lady Henrietta still half-naked as she was, and looked quickly away, finding only Brouwer's headless corpse, still hanging in chains from the wall.

'Poor bugger.'

Another voice rang out from the doorway and Steel strained to see from whom it came. A tall young French officer was standing framed in the arch.

'Captain Trouin, I am placing you under house arrest for gross misconduct. This is not the behaviour of a French officer.'

Trouin grinned at him: 'But I am not a French officer, merely an officer in French pay, *monsieur*. Unlike you I did not lick the king's arse to get my commission. I earned it in blood.'

The officer prickled: 'You will desist from such conversation, sir. And hand me your sword.'

Trouin considered his options. There were none, for the present at least. Reluctantly, he unbuckled the wide leather belt that encompassed his hips and let the sword clatter to the stone floor.

'Come and take it for yourself. If you have the stomach for it.'

The officer signalled to his sergeant who moved swiftly across to Trouin, picked up the sword and handed it to the lieutenant who spoke again: 'And now, you will release your prisoners into my care.' He saw Brouwer. 'What is left of them. The keys, if you please, Captain.'

Trouin reached into his waistcoat and produced a ring on

246

which were hung several large keys. He threw it across the floor. The officer gestured to two of his men, one of whom stooped to pick up the keys. Then, together they went across to Lady Henrietta. While one of them covered her nakedness with a cloak, the other worked the key in the locks of the shackles before helping her down.

Trouin spoke: 'You wil regret this, Lieutenant. What is your name?'

'Lejeune, sir. And I would advise you to choose your words most carefully, Captain. For what I have witnessed here is evidence of an act of gross indecency and will surely result in your court-martial.'

Trouin laughed: 'D'you suppose for one minute, young man, that I am afraid? That I am at all intimidated by your justice? I am not subject to your military laws, nor to any others. Do you know who I am? What I have done?'

'That, sir, is only too evident.'

It occurred to Steel that he recognized the voice. He peered through the still smoky room which now reeked of powder, mingled with the stench of sweat and blood. Did he know his saviour? A French officer? He tried to place the man, but his head was still filled with images of blood and he was trying to grasp the reality of the fact that he had been saved by some miracle from a fate so agonizing as to be unimaginable.

The two soldiers, having escorted Lady Henrietta to the safety of their comrades, now turned to Steel. Carefully, they unlocked his chains and eased his bloody arms out of the manacles and down from the wall. One of them folded him in a cloak. Somehow Steel managed to mutter a grateful word of thanks before Slaughter came to his aid and helped him slowly across the room, towards the French. He looked up into the eyes of the officer, who spoke first.

'Monsieur, I cannot express my sorrow. This is monstrous. Thank God we were in time.'

Steel just gazed at him and said nothing. Then he had it. He recognized the face from what seemed now like years ago. A village, an angry peasant mob. This was the terrified junior officer that he had saved from a lynching, D'Alembord's lieutenant. And now it seemed the man had found a chance to repay that debt. Steel thanked God. He smiled through the blood that had crusted around his face, and tried again to speak.

Lejeune saw it: 'Do not thank me, Captain. I see that you know me and yes, this is a debt of honour. But it is no more than I would do for any man. This is not war, it is cold-blooded murder. Worse than that. This is not the war that I fight, Captain. I hope that you will believe that, that we in France do uphold a code of honour.'

He turned to his men, uttered a command in French and the rear rank filed around and to the side of the front and slowly and deliberately began to take Trouin's men prisoner, binding them together in pairs.

Again the pirate commander laughed: 'D'you think that these few drunkards are all of my men, Lieutenant? Don't you know that I have many more above in the tavern and others on the two ships lying in the harbour? Don't you suppose that they will rescue me?'

Lejeune shrugged. 'Your men in the tavern are already under my guard, *monsieur*, on their way to the cells. As for those in the harbour, we shall see. Soon though, I surmise that we will have more pressing problems. We have received information that the British are about to attack – most probably in the morning. Even now my major is making plans to defend the town.'

Trouin spat: 'Malbec? What does he know? Does he

know of this? I can't believe that he ordered you to arrest me.'

'He didn't. I came here on my own initiative. And thank God I did.'

Leaving behind a small party to take care of the mess that had been Marius Brouwer, they left the cellar, Lejeune first with Lady Henrietta, followed by Steel and Slaughter. Then came Trouin and behind him in small groups, contained with stout ropes and prodded on by bayonets, his men. For Steel every one of the stone steps they took back up into the real world, away from the charnel house of the cellar, was agony. He made no sound. But with every pace the pain in his entire body seemed to grow, cutting through him like a red-hot knife. They reached the main room of the tavern, which had been cleared of Trouin's men, and went out into the street. It was early morning now and the bells of the great church had begun to chime for matins. Steel turned to Slaughter and smiled and finally found the words.

'Christ Jacob, you took your bloody time.' And as he spoke he felt his knees suddenly give way and then there was no choice but to let himself go, thankfully into the peaceful velvety blackness.

THIRTEEN

Steel awoke with a start. The nightmare had been horribly real, the pain palpable. Exhausted and drenched in sweat, he lay flat on his back. Opening his eyes he blinked at the cool light streaming in through a small mullioned window and stared up, hypnotized momentarily by the lacework of patterns the shadow cast upon the ceiling. He had no idea where he was, and could not recall how he had come to be here. Outside he could hear seagulls calling and concluded that he must be in a port, or at least close to the sea. His fuzzy mind began to make sense of it all, bringing a feeling of dark foreboding and the beginnings of memory. Ostend. A mission for Hawkins. A girl. And blood. Too much blood. He thought that perhaps he should sit up. Tentatively, he flexed his right arm, and instantly a pain shot along it from fingertip to armpit. Putting his weight on his left elbow, he tried with some difficulty to raise himself up. And as he did so the pain in his back, his arms and his stomach hit him with nauseating clarity.

Closing his eyes, Steel fell back on to the bed. And only now did he begin more fully to remember, and in that one ghastly moment it occurred to him that it had not been a dream.

Now Steel relived the full horror of what had happened. The thought brought an unaccustomed feeling of panic. Then he recalled the rescue and it dawned upon him that he must be in the house of a friend. He relaxed and let his arms move across his torso – he was naked. He reached for his legs and found to his relief that both were still there. Moving upwards he felt for any terrible wounds that he might not have remembered. All seemed as it should be. He opened his eyes and saw that he was lying on a wooden bed, a simple affair, covered with a clean sheet and a blanket. Turning his head to the left brought a pain in the muscles. On a table beside him stood a flask of water and a glass. Lying across a white porcelain bowl was a small, clean towel. He saw that his coat, breeches and waistcoat had been carefully draped across the wooden chair opposite the table along with his sword and belt. They looked as if someone must have brushed them. A clean shirt hung on a hook at the door, and in the corner of the room were his prized boots, which too it seemed had been polished. It was only then that Steel realized that someone else was in the room. For a second he panicked again, then managed to raise his head and saw Jacob Slaughter. The sergeant was sitting on a wicker-seated chair, across from the bed, close to the door.

He smiled at Steel: 'Good morning, sir. Cup of coffee for you?'

Steel forced a painful smile and felt the scars on his face contract. 'Thank you, Jacob. Yes, that would be nice. Have you any notion where we are?'

Slaughter rose and crossed to the table where Steel saw now there was a tall jug of coffee. He watched as the tall sergeant poured out the thick, almost black liquid into a small blue and white china bowl.

251

'Private house, sir. Belongs to a woman by the name of Huber; friend of poor Mister Brewer, if you remember, sir.'

Steel remembered. And Slaughter's grim expression told him that his memory did not fail him.

'Terrible business that, sir.'

Steel blanched at the thought. In his mind he saw the indelible image of Marius Brouwer's ghastly, shrieking, maimed head. Gratefully, he grasped the steaming bowl of coffee and took a long draught, before speaking, slowly and trying not to show his latent fear.

'Where's Trouin now?'

'Still under arrest, sir. But it can only be a matter of time till the French commander finds out and lets him go. Then that lieutenant of his'll be in for it. We'll need to move as soon as it gets dark, sir. Get back to the lines.'

Steel sipped from the bowl. 'What time is it?'

'Coming on for five in the evening. You've been asleep all day. Like a baby.'

'Lady Henrietta?'

'She's next door here, sir. Asleep an' all, I should guess, after what they done to her.'

'How is she?'

'She was in a pretty bad way, kept crying and shaking. Shock, sir. Like one of the new lads when the balls start flying – battle shakes. You know, trembling and can't stop gabbling. Some as wet themselves. Not that she'd done that, sir, if you pardon me.' Slaughter blushed and continued, 'It's seeing so much blood on a battlefield that gets 'em. Reckon that was what done for her too, all that blood. Seeing poor Mister Brewer an' all that. You too, sir. You weren't a very pretty sight, if you don't mind my saying so.'

From the extent of his pain, Steel did not find that hard to believe. Only now did he take in the fact that somehow he had been carefully cleaned up and his wounds dressed. He ran an experienced hand over the dressings. Whoever had done this had been no novice.

'Did you do this, Jacob? Patch me up? Made a pretty good job of it.'

Slaughter laughed and shook his head. 'Not me, sir. It was that Miss Huber. Seems she was a nurse with the Frenchies for a while.'

'Then I am in her debt as well as yours. But you still have not told me how you came to our rescue.'

'We heard that your disguise had been turned. A serving-girl in the tavern heard it from one of Trouin's men, boasting how they was going to kill you good and slow. All sorts of things. One of Brewer's people came to tell Miss Huber, who found me and Mister Fabritius at his house. So I says, "Jacob, you can't let them do that to Mister Steel". And I was on my way to find you and that's when I spotted the French lieutenant. Or at least, he found me. Recognized me from the village, see and took me for a spy. Well, of course I told him what I was up to and the rest you know, sir.'

Steel smiled and shook his head, gently: 'I gave you an order, Jacob. I told you that if anything happened to me you were to return to the lines. You deliberately disobeyed a direct order, Sarn't.'

Slaughter looked down at the floor: 'Yes, sir.'

'Bloody well done. You have my permission to do the same again if the occasion ever demands it. Thank you, Jacob, truly. I am for ever in your debt. You saved my life, and Lady Henrietta's.'

'Weren't nothing really, sir. Couldn't ha' done it without the lootenant. God help him.'

'Yes, I dare say he'll need more than God to help him when Trouin gets hold of him. I only pray that he can remain alive long enough for us to return. Then, perhaps I can repay the favour and take him prisoner. Now, let's see how much of a cripple that bastard's made of me.'

Putting all his effort into raising himself up, Steel pushed away from the bed and managed to sit. Christ, but he hurt. Slaughter noticed the pallor come over his officer's face.

'You all right, sir? Shouldn't be too hasty.'

Steel smiled at him: 'Thank you, Jacob. She's done well, our Miss Huber. I'm as good as new.'

Slaughter nodded his head and raised his eyebrows. 'And I must say you do look it, sir. Fit as a flea you are . . . I don't think. You look right buggered up, if you want my opinion, Mister Steel.'

Steel stood and crossed the room to where a shirt hung on the door. Painfully, he pulled on the loosely-cut white garment and laced it up before wrapping the stock around his neck.

'You may have your opinion, Sergeant. It's of no consequence to me. And it's Captain Steel, do remember, Jacob. Now, it's time we were going I think. Lady Henrietta is . . . ?'

'Next door, sir.'

Steel, having pulled on his breeches, was now buttoning his waistcoat. His boots followed quickly and he suppressed a groan of pain.

'Thank you, Jacob. See and get our kit ready if you would. I'll wake Her Ladyship.'

As the sergeant rattled down the narrow staircase, taking Steel's sword and belt with him, Steel approached the neighbouring bedroom. He knocked lightly on the door. There was no reply. Unable to resist, he turned the handle and entered. Lady Henrietta Vaughan was lying asleep on a bed similar to the one he had recently vacated, in a similarly neat little room, beneath a crisp white sheet. Steel wondered whether she too were naked. He stared at her for a moment and then turned to go. But as he did so she slowly opened her eyes.

'Who's that? Captain Steel, is that you?'

Steel turned back towards the bed: 'My Lady?'

'Do not go, Captain. Please, stay a while. I wish to thank you.'

'Thank me, ma'am? It's not me you need to thank but my sergeant and that French officer. They're the ones that saved both of us.'

'No, no. You mistake me, Captain. You are the one who in the first instance came into this accursed town to save me, and for that I must thank you not least. And for the terrible pain you endured on my account. How are your wounds?'

'They can be borne, ma'am. I heal quickly as a rule. But what of yourself, My Lady? You have slept? You should have more rest. Let me leave you now.'

She smiled at him and in her face Steel saw something of the look of his first love, her cousin Arabella Moore. It was mostly, he thought, in her eyes. The resemblance shook him and took him back again to his first meeting with the woman back in London whose intrigues had sent him into this town to rescue Lady Henrietta. Here, he thought, was the young and gentle Arabella, the Arabella who had taken him under her wing and into her heart and taught him about love. The fearless, shameless young woman who had bought him a commission in the Guards and had then done her best to keep him away from Horse Guards, locking them both into her boudoir for days on end so that on more than one occasion he had had to take his leave by way of the window to be present at the morning parade. Lady Henrietta noticed his gaze and blushed. Steel became aware that he had been staring at her for some time:

'I'm sorry, ma'am. It was just that . . .'

She smiled and nodded her head: 'It was just that you saw in me something of my cousin, Mister Steel. Am I right?'

She grinned with an inward satisfaction and yet, he thought, no hint of jealousy. 'May I call you Jack?'

'If you wish to, ma'am. And you are quite right in your supposition, of course. And I apologize. It was unforgivably discourteous.'

'On the contrary, I take it as profound flattery, Captain. My cousin is reckoned a most beautiful woman and even if she is ten years my senior, she has retained her looks most remarkably.' She looked away. 'Is it very long since you last saw her, Mister Steel?'

Steel had heard her, but did not reply. He found himself gazing at her again. The resemblance was uncanny; those eyes, the nose and that divine mouth with the little upward twist at the corners of the lips. There too were the same high cheekbones and most of all the hair, fine and fair, like so much silken thread. Lady Henrietta's hair was tousled now after her sleep and lay fanned out across the pillow.

She smiled warmly at Steel. 'Why, I do believe you are doing it again, sir.'

Steel shut his eyes and looked away. He shook his head. 'I am most terribly sorry, My Lady. I shall leave you now. You really must rest. And once you are ready we need to get away from this place. That devil Trouin may be under lock and key, but even now his men will be primed to find us, and as soon as the garrison commander realizes what has happened, he too will come looking for you. For us. We have to leave within the hour at most, My Lady.'

She tutted and pushed the sheet a little away from her face, revealing the perfection of her collarbones. 'Do call me Henrietta, please, if I am to call you Jack and if we are to go

256

on the run together. And I am not tired. Please come and sit with me; tell me how we shall make our escape.'

He walked over to the bed and sat beside her. Looking down now, he saw the gentle undulations of her body beneath the sheets and chided himself, for the image that entered his mind was that of her as she had appeared in the cellar. Closer, she was even more like Arabella. Steel felt a strange yearning. Not for Arabella as she was now, as he knew her to be at court: jealous, sly, conniving. But for Arabella as she once had been. His Arabella, then, but now an unattainable, vanished, imaginary presence. Yet suddenly she was here again, lying in front of him, in an all too tangibly fleshly form.

'Dear Captain Steel, I do swear that, flattering as it might be, if you should ogle me once again in such a manner, I really shall protest most loudly.'

She giggled and as she smiled at him he saw in her eyes more than a hint of attraction. Steel tried to caution himself, to tell himself that he was not in love with this woman; that it was her cousin's youthful ghost that had so intoxicated him. But try as he might, the curve of her body and the flash of her eyes would not let logic prevail. A sharp twinge from his torn and flayed back brought Steel back to the very real danger of their circumstances. 'We should go soon. As soon as possible.'

'How do we escape?' she said, helplessly.

'We must wait until nightfall. We can go by way of a small door in the west wall. Brouwer told me about it. It's what they call a sally-port, built by the defenders so that they could attack any besiegers and take them by surprise. Seems the Frenchies have forgotten about it. Marius hadn't. He told me that he and his friends had played in it when they were boys, pretending to be smugglers or pirates or Spanish invaders in

257

the great siege. Funny, that. Well, we'll make sure that Marius has the last laugh. Brouwer's men will have it open for us. You, me and Sergeant Slaughter. It's the same door we're going to use when we make the assault. Probably tomorrow.'

'You intend to be in that assault, don't you?'

'Be in it? I intend to lead it.'

'Is that not very dangerous?'

'Yes.'

'Will you die?'

'Perhaps.'

'I should not want you to die, Jack. I don't think I could bear it.'

He looked into her eyes: 'I am a soldier. It is my profession. I know of nothing else.'

'You know of me.' He did not answer, but looked away. She spoke again: 'And I know that you are a good man. And that you must not get killed. Is it really worth it?'

He looked up at her: 'It must be worth it. It's what I believe in, what we fight for. We fight the French, we fight King Louis to stop him from taking all of Europe. That surely must be worth it. If not then my life is no more than a worthless lie.'

For a few minutes she said nothing. Then: 'When you have taken this place, what then?'

'Then we shall go on to take another town. And another and another, as Marlborough directs. Dunkirk, Lille. Who knows, even Paris perhaps. And on the way, God willing, we may find another French army to fight and to defeat.'

'You will not return to England until you have finished?'

'I am a soldier, Henrietta, an officer in Marlborough's army. I have a position, I have responsibilities, men who depend upon me. How can I return home and leave them wanting?'

'Perhaps you might contrive to engineer such a posting to St James's if you knew that someone was waiting there for you. Perhaps that might make a difference. If someone truly cared.'

The thought was beyond hope. Could she really mean it?

'You barely know me,' he said, softly, hardly daring to speak the words. And how *can* you know me? he thought.

She took his hand between both of her own: 'When two people have been through what we two have endured together, they truly know each other. You must trust me, Jack. Do you trust me?'

He looked at her again, took in the full beauty of her face and then, propping himself up painfully on one elbow he bent towards her and kissed her again and again, savouring her taste and the musky scent that sent his head reeling.

There was a knock on the door.

Steel broke away from Henrietta and stood up, before adjusting his dress and brushing down his clothes. Another knock. He looked down at her, smiled and was rewarded with the prettiest of glances. Yet now behind her smile he detected a note of seriousness. He turned towards the door.

'Who is it?'

'Sergeant Slaughter, sir.'

'Come in, Sarn't.'

The door opened and Slaughter stepped into the room. He looked first at Steel then at Lady Henrietta. 'I'm very sorry, sir, but you've a guest downstairs. It's the French lootenant, sir.'

Lady Henrietta, who had drawn the sheet close up to her chin, made to get up. 'Should I . . . ?'

Steel motioned her back down: 'No, please don't. Better that you stay and rest. We'll be going soon.'

With Slaughter before him, Steel left the room and closed the door.

Downstairs he found the lieutenant who had come to his rescue, waiting with two white-uniformed French infantry-men. Steel froze, on instinct, clutched for where his sword should have hung and saw it held in Slaughter's arms. Lejeune saw his reaction, smiled and guessed correctly at his thoughts.

'Do not worry, Captain Steel. I am not about to take you prisoner. I have come merely to check on the state of your health. Lieutenant Dominique Lejeune at your service.'

Lejeune bowed and Steel returned the gesture. 'Lieutenant, how can I ever thank you?'

'There is no need. I consider a great personal debt to have been repaid. What sort of men would we call ourselves if we were not able to fight without paying heed to at least the most rudimentary rules of war? For, surely, war must have some rules, must it not? Certain terms of engagement? After all, while we may be on opposing sides are we not at least all human beings? I have rescued not only you Captain Steel, but also the honour of my country. I cannot tell you how very pleased I am that you seem so much improved. Are you aware that you have been in a fever for more than a day? You are fortunate to have such a man as your sergeant, here. Take good care of him, sir. He would be an asset to any army.' Slaughter smiled and shrugged. Lejeune went on: 'And don't worry, Captain. I am sure that I was not followed. My men are quite loyal to me. To no one else. You understand . . .'

Steel began to speak: 'But –'

Lejeune cut him off. 'No, Captain. As I say, I have no intention of arresting you, or asking for your parole. Why should I? There is simply no point. What good would it serve? You would only be merely a trial to us here. And if you do not return to your lines then I am sure that will be the signal for My Lord Marlbrook to unleash more violence upon us from the skies. The bombs will fall and more innocent people will die. But if you return then perhaps you can tell them that at least one French officer intends to conduct this battle with a degree of honour.

'I am well aware that you wish to get back to your own men. I would feel exactly the same in your position. It is simply our duty as officers, no? And so, you may return to your own lines. If, that is, you can find a way to do so. Perhaps your new Belgian friends can help. Perhaps they already have. They seem more intelligent and less . . . shall we say less of the rustic savage than their country cousins. And they are quite safe from me. I am a realist, Captain. I know that we must eventually succumb to your General Marlbrook, that Ostend is lost already. I intend to see that the town is surrendered with as little bloodshed as possible. Be assured that I shall keep my major occupied until you have gone. And you must take your milady. She has suffered quite enough. Do not on any account leave her for Trouin and his savages.'

'And what about you, Lieutenant? Won't you be arrested for helping us?'

Lejeune smiled at him: 'Yes, that is possible. Already I believe that my commanding officer, Major Malbec, is looking for me. And his accursed sergeant, that Alsatian halfbreed. I have managed to avoid them so far, but it's inevitable. Actually I suspect that Trouin has got to him already. I only hope that you can end the siege before Trouin has a chance to take his revenge upon me.'

Steel thought for a moment. 'You could come with us. I would vouch for you. You could pass the war in safety in England or Scotland. Not in prison, of course. I'm sure that we could find you a suite of rooms in a comfortable country house. I could arrange surety. You would be merely on parole.'

Lejeune laughed: 'Thank you, Captain, but no. To do that would be to desert my post and my men. And you know that I could never do that. I think that you and I are very alike, Captain Steel. We may fight in different armies and for different causes, but in our hearts we are both soldiers. We try to do the best we can in a trade that is, at its worst, no more than murder. It is up to you and I, Steel, to lift it above that. To cloak our deeds in glory. To find honour in the basest of circumstances. But you must go now. Your friends will know the way and I will make sure that you have no trouble, as far as I can. Goodbye, Captain Steel. It has been a real pleasure to have known you. I only wish that we might have met under rather better conditions.'

Steel bowed, lower than before, in an attempt to emphasize the fact that he truly was in Lejeune's debt. 'It has been my pleasure, Lieutenant. Farewell, until we meet again. Which I am certain will be in a better situation. And thank you once again, from the very bottom of my heart.'

As the door closed after Lejeune, Steel turned to Slaughter and shook his head. 'By God, Jacob. There's a man I'd be proud to meet on any field of battle. He makes you think that all's not lost, that war is about more than blood and death.'

Slaughter nodded: 'Reminded me of Lieutenant Hansam, sir. A good, honest gentleman. Which is something that I don't often find myself saying about any Frenchie.'

Steel took his sword, which Slaughter had offered to him, and buckled it around his waist. 'Yes. I do know what you mean. He did remind me of the lieutenant. I wonder how Henry's getting on without us. I think it might be time that we returned to the company. Heaven knows what they've been up to without us to look out for them.'

*   *   *

Night was beginning to come in faster now. Across the town and in many of the windows near Louise Huber's house in a street off Christianstraat, the candles were being lit behind lace curtains as prayers were said before food. Louise entered the small sitting room and lit the wick in a stub of tallow, startling Steel and Henrietta from the gentle twilit reverie in which they had been luxuriating for fully half an hour. Slaughter followed close behind her. He looked agitated.

'Begging your pardon, Captain Steel, sir. But we should be going now. Don't you think, sir?'

Steel nodded: 'You're right, Sarn't. It's time.'

As Slaughter and Louise left the room, Steel turned to Henrietta and spoke softly. 'The chance to gaze upon your beauty, ma'am, shall be my reward for guiding us safely back to the lines.'

Louise opened the door of her house and looked out into the street. Two small children were playing hopscotch on the shattered cobbles and a man was loading a dray with debris from a half-demolished house that had been hit during the bombardment. Apart from that the street seemed to be empty. She turned and beckoned to Fabritius, who stood before the others. He signalled to them in turn and together, the small party moved to the door. Steel did not say goodbye to Louise, but made only a short bow. Slaughter, copying his officer, did the same and Henrietta gave a short bob and flashed a grateful smile. Then they were in the street and the door shut behind them. In the half-light, they moved as fast as they could over the irregular cobblestones, being careful to make as little commotion as possible. Fabritius led the way, sliding swiftly and almost silently through the familiar streets while the others followed, quite lost although attempting as best they could to behave as if they were native to the confusing network of alleyways that led through the town to the western defences and the promise of freedom.

They came to a crossroads and Fabritius made to turn left, then stopped in his tracks. Two white-coated soldiers were deep in conversation in the centre of the junction, one puffing at a pipe. They did not look as if they were about to move. Fabritius froze and turned to look at Steel. His face was a mask of terror. It was a sight Steel had seen many times before on the field of battle, the horror that seized men on their first view of the carnage caused by a cannonball, the look that told him that the veneer of invincibility by which every soldier lived his life had been torn down or punctured, by which he knew that its wearer had suddenly realized how easily he might die. In Fabritius' case Steel knew that it had been triggered by the thought of Brouwer dying so horribly. For an instant he thought that their guide might run and leave them here.

Before Fabritius could move, Steel grabbed him by the arm and met his gaze: 'Stay with us, man. Think of Marius. What would he have wanted? Think of your people.'

Fabritius stared at him blankly. And then, just as quickly as it had come, the look vanished. 'I'm sorry, Captain. I . . .'

Steel smiled and let go of the man's arm. 'Say nothing. Just get us out of here.'

Fabritius ducked into the shadow offered by the overhanging eaves of one of the few half-timbered buildings to have survived the bombardment intact and they followed his lead. Looking back, their guide made a gesture with his hand that they should turn and go back the way they had come. And so they continued, dealing with each potential threat as they encountered it and seeming to take three paces backwards for every one they advanced, for what seemed to all of them far longer than the hour that it was in reality. At length however, as the lapping of the sea grew ever more audible, Steel realized, with rising hope, that they must be nearing the western walls. If Fabritius and his yet unseen comrades in the *schildendevriend* had done their job, then somewhere up ahead of them there lay the small hidden door in Vauban's otherwise impregnable walls which would take them out on to the dunes and back to safety.

Steel shuddered, his soul still shaken by memories of Trouin's cellar. He thought of Brouwer, of his loyalty and his suffering and wondered what might have happened had he not persuaded him to ignore the pamphlets and have faith in Marlborough. Who, he wondered had betrayed whom? He longed to escape this place of darkness. If only for a few hours, until the moment at which he would have a chance to return with the assault party and avenge the poor man's death. If only they might hasten a little, get as far as the sally-port. Surely, he reasoned against himself, they might run a little of the way. Then he froze.

Above them a voice called out words of challenge: '*Halte. Qui passe? Annoncez vous.*'

They had been seen. Slaughter darted Steel a worried glance as all four members of the party stopped in mid-step. Steel brought his foot down on the stones with silent care and listened. Again the French voice rang out.

'*Annoncez vous.*'

Realizing that they had no other option, Steel was about to reveal their position and hope to fight his way out when to his astonishment another voice answered the first.

'*Claude. C'est moi, Marcel. Ne tirez pas.*'

Steel closed his eyes with relief. Up on the parapet walkway, the counterguard that ran directly over their heads, the two sentries were now talking and laughing. Steel caught something about a girl in Dunkirk–Suzanne. The men laughed again. Now was their chance. He poked Fabritius in the shoulder. The Belgian turned and nodded and slowly the little party began to move north along the parapet wall. Each step was torture. Every footfall a carefully measured decision. Twice Slaughter slipped on the cobbles and let out an involuntary curse under his breath. They paused. But the guards appeared not to have heard and the sound of their ribald laughter covered the fugitives' painful progress. So hard was he concentrating on the process that the opening in the wall took Steel by surprise. This was not, he realized, the door in the outer defences, but merely through the inner wall. And it was unguarded. Fabritius had done his work well. God knew what had happened to the guards. Perhaps, with the death of Brouwer, his Belgian comrades had decided to become less passive in their resistance.

Quickly now, they slipped into the passageway through the parapet, directly beneath the feet of the patrolling sentries, and emerged in the ditch between the inner and outer defences. This, Steel was only too well aware, would be their most vulnerable moment. Instinctively they pressed themselves flat against the wall and began to edge gingerly around, still further to the north. They had not gone more than thirty yards when Fabritius turned left and broke into a run, glancing behind to make sure the others were still with him. Steel followed with Henrietta while Slaughter brought up the rear. Their footfalls made scarcely a sound. There were no cobbles here, for the ditch between the two walls was sown with short-mown grass to allow the crossfire from defending cannon to cut down any attacking force that made it thus far. This night though, thought Steel, for once, Vauban's cunning had turned in favour of King Louis' enemies. They were quickly across the ditch and up against the far wall. Now was the moment at which any sentry, glancing casually in the moonlight across towards the allied camp, would without doubt catch sight of them. Steel imagined the sudden shout, the levelled muskets and the shots. But none came. Instead he heard Fabritius' soft voice, hissing a whispered direction.

'Sir. Here, Captain.'

Steel peered towards the Belgian and saw that he was motioning them to join him in a wide tunnel built through the rock. It was a sturdy brick and stone structure, beautifully made to Vauban's precise instructions and lit from above by slits cut into the roof. Together, they advanced into its semi-darkness and as they reached the end Steel strained his eyes to see anything other than the flat brick wall of a dead end. He turned to Fabritius and was about to say something when the man advanced towards the wall and swept away a tangle of rushes and foliage. Steel saw that beneath was a small wooden door, set into the outer rampart and framed with brickwork. Confident that his countrymen had done their work, Fabritius grasped the black iron handle and turned it. Slowly the door opened and they found themselves peering into a darker blackness than that which surrounded them. They were inside in an instant and Slaughter, being careful not to make a sound, closed the door behind them. Then, darkness. Steel could see nothing. Neither was this the sort of darkness of a house at night when one's eyes gradually become accustomed to the shadow until a room can emerge quite clearly. This was darkness beyond imagining. And it was hot.

The tunnel had been designed as a sally-port, a route out of the fortress along which defenders might pass to make a surprise attack upon any besieging force. There had been no thought given to ventilation beyond the first twenty or so yards and those shafts were long since blocked by foliage and masonry. Steel heard Henrietta gasp.

'Jack? Captain Steel? Are you there? I can't see a thing.'

'Here, My Lady. We're all here. All right, Sarn't? Mister Fabritius?'

'Sir.'

'Good, Captain. I think we should move. There is not much air in here, I think.'

'Yes, you're right. Let's get on. Careful, My Lady. Here, take my hand.' Steel extended his arm in the direction he judged Henrietta to be and made contact with her waist. He passed his arm around it and squeezed. 'You'll be all right now, My Lady. Stay with me, ma'am.'

Each of them using one hand to feel the wall of the tunnel, they all began to walk as fast as they could given the conditions, towards where they presumed they must eventually find the door that would lead them out of the fortress. From time to time Steel gave a gentle squeeze to Henrietta's waist. Up ahead he could hear Fabritius' boots against the hard earth of the tunnel floor. They seemed to be descending very gradually now, down a shallow slope. It was taking them, he presumed, directly on to the dunes. They had gone some two hundred yards when Steel became aware that he could no longer hear Slaughter behind him.

He turned sharply in the pitch-black and looked without success back down the way they had come. 'Jacob? Are you with me?'

Nothing. Then, from ten, perhaps twenty yards to their rear he heard a quiet voice.

Letting go of Henrietta, Steel retraced his steps. He could hear Slaughter now.

'No. No, I tell you. I'll never go down into that place. Never. You can't force me to. I won't go down.'

'Jacob? Are you all right? What's wrong?'

The voice fell silent and Steel approached until he was standing almost immediately over the figure of the sergeant, who was evidently sitting with his knees drawn up and his back against one of the tunnel walls. Even in the blackness, Steel recognized the smell of fear. He crouched down and found the man's arm.

'Jacob, don't worry. We're going to get out of here soon. We're almost at the door and then there'll be as much air as you can breathe and we'll be out in the open and among friends. Come on, man. This isn't like you.'

But he knew that it was. For all his bravery on the battlefield, his calmness and control and his huge physical presence, the sergeant had one secret fear. He could not abide enclosed spaces. He had discovered it as a lad when they had forced him to go down one of the newly opened coal mines in his native County Durham. It was the reason that he had run away to join the colours. To be here now, thought Steel, must be pure hell for him.

Slaughter mumbled, 'Sorry, sir. It's just the dark and the walls. And the heat, sir. I can't go on.'

'You must go on, Jacob. People are depending on you. What would your lads say if they saw you like this, eh? Think of that. Come on. I'll keep hold of your arm. Come with me.'

Taking care not to move too fast, Steel gently brought Slaughter to his feet and began to walk with him down towards the others.

Fabritius heard them: 'All right, Captain?'

'It's fine. My sergeant just caught his head on the roof. Fellow's just too tall. Fine for a Grenadier, rotten in a tunnel. Let's get on.'

They began moving. Steel had found Henrietta again and with his left hand in hers and his right keeping a firm grip on Slaughter's trembling forearm, they moved slightly faster than before. After a few yards, Steel became aware that the air had turned foul with the unmistakable smell of human excrement. The stench came from a neighbouring sewer whose thin lining had long worn away and was leeching its contents into the soil.

Slaughter pulled up: 'That's it, Mister Steel. That's it. I've had enough. I ain't going on any further into this hot, stinkin' hellhole. Let me out. I'm going back.'

Steel increased his hold on Slaughter's arm and spoke in a whisper. 'Stay with me, Jacob. We're going to be fine. I'm sure it's not far now. Come on man, ten yards. I'm sure.'

Fabritius had gone on ahead and Henrietta, desperate to be clear of the stench, went after him, pulling Steel on. He hoped that he was right and the end would come soon. And then he saw it, the merest glimmer of light – no more than a pinprick. They had all seen it now and the smell of the sea was overwhelming. There was no door, but what had originally been an open hole, cleverly concealed by a fold in the ground, had become covered over the decades with foliage and tree roots to create a natural barrier. Steel moved ahead and with care drew his sword.

'Stand back, all of you.'

With a great stroke he cut at the roots and was surprised at how easily his blade sliced through them. Two, three, four more cuts and they could see the sky. A few more and he had cleared a hole wide enough for a man's arm. Slaughter stepped forward and took hold of the sword hilt.

'If you don't mind, sir, I'll give you a hand.'

Within minutes the two of them had cleared a hole sufficient to pass through and then they were free. Together they half-ran, half-tumbled down the dunes at the foot of the outer ramparts of the fortifications which towered forty feet above their heads, a sheer wall of stone, shining in the moonlight. Steel bent over and caught his breath. Henrietta was lying on a dune, her body rising and falling with the rhythm of her gasps. Beyond her he could see both Fabritius and the huge frame of Slaughter gratefully taking in lungfuls of the salty air. Never, he thought, had any air ever tasted quite so sweet.

Over the dunes and along the far shore, the sun was cresting the eastern horizon and through the camp, as the women roused themselves and hands fell to milking cows and kneading bread, a pack of officers' hunting hounds had already begun to give tongue to the new day as Steel got to his feet and pulled the muslin shirt over his head. His muscles were still horribly stiff, his bruised bones ached and the scars on his back were only just starting to heal. He thought that one of his ribs might have been broken during the ordeal with Trouin and had decided to keep Louise Huber's bandages on for the time being, just in case. He pulled on the brocaded blue waistcoat somewhat gingerly, waiting for the impact against any still-open wounds and knew he had been right to be cautious. For there were some, and the sharp pain began to bite into him as he fastened the buttons. He looked down at Henrietta, asleep under the blanket and pulled on first his trousers and then his boots before reaching for the heavy red coat which hung on the hook above him.

She stirred: 'Jack, is that you?'

He bent down to kiss her forehead: 'Hush, my darling. Sleep now. I won't be long, I promise. I've been called for by Duke. I'll see you in the morning.'

Eyes still closed, she smiled and turned deeper into the blankets. Steel straightened up and, being careful not to rattle the blade in the scabbard, picked up his sword with care and moved towards the door. He turned one more time, took in the pure beauty of the sleeping form in his bed and then, snatching up his hat from the table, stepped outside into the pale dawn and went to rid the world of René Duglay-Trouin.

FOURTEEN

Using the small, sharp knife that he kept for just such a purpose, Marlborough sliced through the soft flesh of a ripe pomegranate and popped a sliver into his mouth before wiping his lips upon a white napkin. He ate thoughtfully, then spoke as he cut again into the fruit: 'You say that you have discovered a way into the town, Captain Steel? You're certain it is viable?'

'Quite certain, Your Grace. It is a small sally-port on the northwestern side of the defences, so small as to be hardly detectable. It was by way of that gate that we effected our escape.'

Marlborough, swallowing another piece of fruit, smiled at him: 'Yes. That was well done, your rescue of Lady Henrietta. Her Majesty will be most grateful for that. Very good, Steel. So, to the sally-port. You're sure it is disused?'

'Quite so, My Lord. We had to cut our way out. But it is quite as serviceable as when first built by Vauban.'

The duke laughed. 'I do declare, you are a constant joy to me, Captain Steel. Not only do you find us a secret means by which to enter the citadel, but you do so by way of employing one of Marshal Vauban's own defensive stratagems, just the sort of feature which so often frustrates our conduct of a siege.' He chuckled and turned to Hawkins, who was standing close by in the commanding officer's ornate campaign tent, eating a peach. 'Don't you love the irony, Hawkins? The great master's genius is going to prove his countrymen's own undoing.'

The colonel, with juice dripping down his chin and his mouth full of fruit, was unable to answer and merely nodded his head and narrowed his eyes in approval.

Marlborough became abruptly serious and looked hard at Steel: 'In earnest though, you have done well, Captain. I gather from Colonel Hawkins that Lady Henrietta is safe and no worse for her dreadful experiences.'

'Yes, sir. She is quite safe now. I have undertaken to safeguard her personally.'

Marlborough raised an eyebrow and wiped his sticky hands on the napkin. 'Oh have you, Steel? How very noble of you.' His tone and the pause that followed unnerved Steel a little. Marlborough's laugh broke the tension. 'No matter. I trust that you know what you are about, Captain Steel. But you might take a care to remember who it was that recommended you at court for this duty. Eh, Hawkins? D'you hear that? Captain Steel is taking personal care of Lady Henrietta. He might have a care, d'you not think?'

Hawkins, who, after finishing the peach had just helped himself to a little more of the excellent ham on which he had breakfasted, grinned. 'Oh, he might have a care, Your Grace. Indeed. But then I am sure that Captain Steel is always careful in such matters. Are you not, Jack?'

Steel shook his head: 'I mean, sir, merely that I intend no harm to come to her.'

'Very good, Steel. As you will. But be careful whom you

274

make your enemies. In particular at court. Our gracious sovereign is a woman – remember that. For women have more influence in the conduct of this war than you may know, Steel.' He paused: 'There was some talk of torture, was there not? Her Ladyship was not at all harmed? You are sure of that?'

'Not at all, Your Grace. Merely gravely insulted.'

'I guessed as much. And yourself? We were quite beside ourselves with worry. Poor Colonel Hawkins was most distressed.'

'I suffered a little, sir.'

'But you are quite fit now, I trust. Fit enough to lead the assault?'

'As fit as I'll ever be, Your Grace. Am I to take it then that I shall have the honour of leading the initial party, sir? To open the way? I have a personal score to settle, and a debt to repay.'

Marlborough looked at him: 'You really are a most extra-ordinary man, Steel. Most of my officers, as brave as ever they might be, would be thankful to have escaped with their lives from such a place as you have lately quit. Yet you insist on returning. More than that, on leading the attack. You say you have a score to settle. May I enquire as to what, exactly?'

'Your Grace, I intend to deal personally with the pirate, Trouin. He murdered a friend of mine and insulted another.'

'You know, Steel, you must never allow vengeance to rob you of your senses. It is an intoxicating demon. Are you certain that you wish to do this?'

'I have never been more resolved on any matter, Your Grace.'

'Nevertheless, be careful not to place yourself in any unnecessary danger, Steel. I should not like to lose you. Least of all to an act of revenge. It would however, be most propitious should you find yourself in such a position to dispose of Mister Trouin. From what Colonel Hawkins tells me, we cannot allow him to escape.'

He looked down at the map spread before him on the table and traced with his finger a route along the sand north of the dunes which then cut across and entered the town at the place Steel had told him they would find the sally-port. Then he pointed in turn to the small oblong blocks, each of them signifying the position of a battalion that had been drawn up in line to the west of the marshes and muttered each of their names silently as if to remind himself just how strong his army was. The army that would follow Steel into the town.

He looked up at Steel: 'Very well, Captain. You shall lead the assault. Take fifty men – no more. Grenadiers, your own fellows. Choose them well. Take them along the beach and across the dunes and into the town by way of your secret gate. Once inside, you must find a means of opening one of the main gates. After that whatever you do is your decision. You may have a battalion of Dutch to your rear as support should anything go amiss. Aside from that you are on your own. Do I make myself clear?'

'Quite clear, Your Grace. And thank you.'

'Don't thank me, Steel. I'm sending you back into hell.'

Major Claude Malbec stood in the private office of Ostend's troubled governor and looked down through the iron cross-bars of the window on to the morning bustle. In the square of the Grote Markt, beneath the bomb-damaged bulk of the town hall, the traders had set up their stalls, despite the events of the previous few days and people had come to buy as they always did. But there was something not right about the scene, he thought. The townsfolk seemed to have an air of apprehension. They walked not with their usual confidence

276

but with their shoulders hunched and their heads downcast. And from time to time through their midst a cart would pass, its covered contents denoting that another body had been found in the rubble.

For the last fifteen minutes Governor de la Motte had endured Malbec's bitter tirade against him, his administration and the man's own junior officer, who, it appeared, had helped some precious prisoners to escape. He wondered when the major would finish and allow him to get on with his breakfast of the precious salted ham and black bread which lay untouched on his sideboard. But as Malbec turned from the window his expression told de la Motte that his stomach would have to wait a while longer.

'What was the boy thinking? Damn him for an insubordinate pup. I'll have him hanged for treachery.'

'Isn't that a little excessive, Major? After all, he is an officer. And in any case, his mother is a favourite of the king. We can only guess at who his father might be. I hardly think you'd get away with it. Look on the bright side, Major. As I understand it, the lieutenant prevented further acts of atrocity by Captain Trouin.'

'That's all very well, Governor, but the man is merely a junior officer. He had no right to take such a decision, nor to make such an attack. He might as you say have prevented Trouin from further acts of apparent indecency. But what's that compared to letting British spies escape and handing over our hostage? It's madness. Worse than that, it goes against all the principles of war.'

'It does?'

'Governor, I am a soldier. I have always been a soldier. I am not a diplomat, I am not a politician. I am a simple soldier. Allow me my modicum of expertise in that domain. It is unmilitary. It goes against all the rules. Whatever Trouin was up to there is simply no excuse for delivering spies back to the enemy. They should have been shot. And now that honour devolves upon Lieutenant Lejeune.'

'Major, take care. You cannot have him executed. It would benefit no one. Haven't we got enough to worry about?' He paused and eyed the ham. 'Have you had breakfast?'

Malbec did not hear him: 'When I find him I've a good mind to string him up myself, by God. No court-martial – just give me the rope.'

De la Motte sighed: 'Major, please. I am sure that Lieutenant Lejeune had his reasons. It was surely a courageous thing that he did, you must agree with that. You and I are well aware that for some weeks now Captain Trouin has been abusing his position of power. He may be the king's own appointee, but this time surely he has overstepped the mark once too often.'

Malbec threw up his hands in despair. 'And so now he is held here in the king's prison. And what will you do now, Governor? Keep him there until Paris sends a wagon for him and he is taken back to be tried for his crimes by the king himself? But . . . Oh, no. Wait a minute, I quite forgot. Trouin is the king's man, his favourite. D'you suppose that Louis will take your word for it? You may be destined for the block over this matter, but personally I intend to disentangle myself from this mess. I grant you that to kill Lejeune would be foolish. He has too many friends at court. But have you thought of us? How does it look for me? For you? I am Lejeune's superior and you command the entire town. The responsibility for the Englishmen's escape is ours. What will our fate be now? If we survive this siege, once Trouin reports to the king, what is our destiny? And who's to say in any case that we will survive the fight? With the girl gone, there's nothing to stop their precious Marlbrook from telling his men to open fire again – nothing whatsoever. These English have no scruples, I tell you, and I should know. They don't care about women and children, about how many of them will die as long as they get their precious town. I tell you, we'll all be blown to atoms. And all because of Lejeune.'

Suddenly the governor found that he had lost his appetite. He frowned: 'The girl may still be in the town for all we know.'

'Don't delude yourself, de la Motte. She's back in their lines all right. Our one precious lifeline, gone. I hope the lieutenant's satisfied. In fact, de la Motte, I'm glad that I can't hang him. He'll be able now to hear the screams of the women and children when the English open fire again. And he'll know that he caused that suffering.'

De la Motte had turned pale. 'Do you really think the English will bombard us again?'

'It's beyond a doubt. Why shouldn't they? They've nothing to lose. And they've no conscience. As a people, you know, they're morally bankrupt.'

'Then surely we must surrender, declare the town an open city. Trouin can't stop us doing that.'

Malbec stared at him, wide-eyed: 'Surrender to the English? Are you mad? I have never surrendered a command and I do not intend to start now on the provocation of a junior officer. No, Governor. We will not surrender. We shall sit this one out. We'll watch the people die. And when the English come, as they are sure to come at some point, after their guns have run out of ammunition, then what's left of us will be ready for them behind our own cannon. They'll still have to storm the defences. And then we'll have them. We'll take more than a few to hell with us, de la Motte. I assure you of that.' He crossed to the window and looked out beyond the square, over the defences. 'Marshal Vauban knew exactly what he was doing here. Every one of those bastions gives covering fire to another. There's no single place in the ramparts that doesn't have at least four cannon raking it. We've more than enough food, you know that well enough, and fresh water. Sooner or later they're bound to run out of bombs. Perhaps we should send Trouin out to frighten off their fleet. Yes, that might really be a plan.'

Malbec's talk of 'taking a few to hell' had made de la Motte feel decidedly queasy. Breakfast was now a forgotten thought. He pushed his waiting plate to one side.

'You really want me to release him? Captain Trouin? You know that he's bound to go after Lejeune?'

'Well, that would be an end to one problem. One king's man ridding us of another. What a nice touch! Though I would be sorry for the lieutenant to miss the women's screams. Still, it would be justice. Yes, we must release Trouin. Can there be any question about it? Besides, we need his band of cut-throats. You know, de la Motte, we're going to need every man we can get. There's a whole army out there, sixty thousand men, and the only way we're going to stop them taking this place is to blast them off the face of the earth.' He smiled: 'And that, with Captain Trouin's help, is exactly what I intend to do.'

Steel watched with amusement as Henry Hansam stood with one stockinged foot on a patch of grass and emptied out his right boot, cursing as he did so.

'Damned sand, gets in everywhere. I'll be pleased when we take our leave of this place, Jack, sea breeze or no blessed sea breeze.'

Steel finished adjusting his sword belt and slung his fusil across his shoulder, having ensured that it was loaded.

'You'll get your wish soon enough, Henry. What time d'you have?'

280

Hansam finished pulling on his boot and delved into his waistcoat pocket for his watch. 'Eight minutes before two o'clock, Jack. Not long to go now.'

'Just long enough for a few words, perhaps. D'you think?'

Hansam nodded. Steel turned to Slaughter: 'Sarn't, have the men gather round me. And have them stand easy.'

The company was positioned at its jumping-off point, in a low clump of sand dunes some half a mile from the town's ramparts, out of view of the sentries and sheltered from the wind. Steel stepped up on to a large stone from one of a trio of long-ruined houses and looked down at the assembled company. Fifty men, Marlborough had told him and that was precisely the number he would take. He had ordered Slaughter to ensure that all the veterans were with his party. Men like Dan Cussiter, a corporal now, and Matt Taylor, the self-appointed company apothecary. Dependable fighters like Mackay, Tarling and Milligan. Henderson, the Borders lad, Jock Miller from Dumfries and the lanky athlete Jeremiah Thorogood, the best cricketer the regiment could field. And the rest of them. Against his better judgement too, Steel had agreed at their insistence to take both Hansam and Williams. The remaining few men he had left in the care of number four company's commanding officer, Robert Melville, with the instruction that should the company return in insufficient numbers to form, they were to be taken into his command. For this was as dangerous a task as Steel and his men had ever been charged to perform and he knew that their chances of coming through must be less than fifty per cent. He knew too though that of all the men in Marlborough's army there were none better suited to the challenge. He took off his tricorne hat and placed it under his arm and began: 'Men. Today, we have been given the great honour of leading the assault and ending this siege.' A quiet hurrah came from the left. Steel smiled and nodded his head towards it. 'Thank you, McLaurence. You all know as well as I do what that means. Some of you fought with me at the Schellenberg and at Blenheim. Others went into the attack with us at Ramillies. You all of you know what it is to assault a fortified position. What it means to be the "forlorn hope". But this is an assault unlike any you will have attempted before. We must be secret, we must be silent and we must be swift. Every man must look out for himself, and for his comrades too. I've been in this town and I've met this enemy, and I can tell you now from that acquaintance, this day will not be easy. But we have been chosen by the duke himself and we must honour that choice. The fate of the war rests now in our hands, lads. Remember that and go to it with a will. And remember above all else, you are Grenadiers.'

Despite the fact that Slaughter had ordered the men to be silent, a muted cheer went up. Steel smiled at them and replaced his hat.

'Officers, take posts. Sarn't, with me.'

With whispered words of command, they assembled into the unaccustomed formation of a double file and moved left, through a gap in the dunes.

To avoid being seen by the sentries on the forward walls, the only way that they were going to be able to reach the foot of the ramparts and the open gate was on the outside of the dunes, close to the sea. Happily the tide was out; nevertheless the sand was still soft and liquid in parts. Fine-grained, as Hansam had said. So the strand was soft and the Grenadiers sank easily into the sand to just above their ankles. Soon their white stockings were wringing wet. Two of the men cursed. Slaughter whispered harshly into the darkness: 'Quiet there.'

Steel looked round at the noise, and wondered whether the guards had heard it as clearly as he had. There was not a breath of wind now and it seemed that every sound carried over the flat sands with deafening clarity. It was an approach march like no other he had ever known and he wished to God it were over. The town remained some five hundred yards ahead of them. They were strung out in their files, hugging the dunes as closely as they could, making use, as he had taught them to, with all the guile learnt as a boy from a poacher's son, of every hillock and each tuft of the coarse, tall grass. Unusually, they had also removed their tall mitre caps and tucked them into their waistcoats. Their fusils were ready loaded and primed, Steel's own gun included, even though it was slung across his shoulder. His sword he held in his hand, anxious that it should not clank inside the metal scabbard and he had instructed Williams to do the same. The young ensign was walking close behind him, like Steel doubled up, so as to present the smallest possible profile to any inquisitive enemy eyes.

They were immediately under the walls now. Steel looked up at the endless, towering expanse of smooth stone, and tried to remember exactly where the narrow tunnel was that led to the gate – the gate which he hoped, prayed, would still be open. He looked along the length of the wall to the right. To where, according to his memory, it ought to have been. Christ almighty! There was no opening.

Williams, close behind him, spoke in a whisper: 'Can you not recall where the gate was, sir?'

'If I knew that, Tom would we still be here?'

He looked to his left and again saw nothing that even looked vaguely like the entrance to a tunnel. For one awful moment Steel wondered whether he had not arrived at the wrong section of wall entirely, whether the area he wanted was not round the next jutting bastion of the walls. He hoped that it was not the case, for the sentries patrolled just inside the ravelin on a covered way and if the Grenadiers were forced to detour along the wall then they would surely be heard. He looked right again. He had been so sure it was here. The men would be getting restless now, wondering why they had stalled. Soon they would start to be afraid.

He smelt Slaughter's breath close behind him. 'Beggin' your pardon, sir, but I don't suppose you're lost, are you?' Steel turned and stared at him, unamused and said nothing. 'Only, sir, I was wondering as to why you hadn't taken us down to that hole over there.'

He stretched out his arm and pointed to the left, to where, in a section of the wall more mottled and moss-covered than the rest, Steel was now able to make out the merest hint of an indentation.

'Jacob. You're a bloody marvel.'

Slaughter shrugged: 'Dunno why I did actually show you where it was, sir. Last thing I want to do now is get back into that filthy hole. Worse than any bloody battlefield it was. All that blackness.'

'Don't worry Jacob. Safety in numbers, eh?'

The sergeant shook his head and, turning away from his officer, cursed softly. Turning left, Steel indicated with his hand for the leading men to follow him and the company fell in. Sixty men in single file now, with Hansam bringing up the rear. After fifty yards he stopped. Slaughter was right. Barely noticeable from the side, the wall dipped inwards and there in the centre lay a black hole, barely wide enough for a single man to pass through it at a time.

He turned to Williams: 'In here.'

Pushing into the blackness, Steel was surprised to find this time, coming from the beach, how quickly his eyes grew accustomed to the lack of light. Still, as they pushed on, the darkness grew more intense. After perhaps three hundred yards in the pitch-black and stifling, airless heat, the Grenadiers began to see chinks of light up ahead. No one spoke. What air there was tasted rank, tainted by the stench from the leaking sewer and men and officers alike had tied their cotton stocks around their faces. In the thin glimmer before them, Steel saw a door. It appeared to be shut, although there was light clear to see around its edges. He prayed that it would be open. And then he was against it. The column came to a clanking, shuddering halt. Men swore and sweated and prayed.

Steel leant against the wooden frame and pushed. Nothing happened. He pushed again. It was solid. Christ, he thought, the French had found it and blocked it up and he and his men were trapped. A terrible possibility occurred to him. It must now be close on three o'clock in the afternoon – there would be no time to get out of the tunnel before the tide began to come in. He wondered how high it rose in the tunnel. Certainly the ground had seemed dry enough. But how long would they be baulked like this? And if the French decided to open the door of their stinking prison, they would be shot like rats in a barrel. There was always the probability too that if they stayed where they were they would gradually die of asphyxiation or, when the allied cannon on the shore above the trenches began the bombardment which would precede the main attack they would be trapped by explosions within the town, or blown to pieces as their own guns raked the walls with fire. He wondered how long they had until any or all of that happened. He pushed and pushed again at the door. They had lost valuable time already; he tried to imagine how much. Ten minutes? The sweat was pouring off him now. He turned back into the darkness.

'Two men. Help me here.'

Squeezing themselves into a space that had only ever been designed to take one small man, Steel and the two Grenadiers put all their weight against the wood and shoved. Slowly, to Steel's intense relief, the door at last began to move. Within seconds it was fully open. Light poured into the entrance. They were standing in the outer tunnel now and the light cascaded down upon them from the slits in the rock. Steel saw the reason for their difficulties. Someone, presumably Fabritius and his friends, had placed three stout wooden barrels filled to capacity against the door to disguise it from anyone who happened to poke their nose down the main tunnel. The deception had worked, but Steel wondered whether the Belgian would have realized how heavy the weight of those barrels would have seemed to those opening the door and what terror his ruse had caused in their ranks. No matter, they were in.

Steel waved Slaughter on ahead and turned to Williams: 'Tom, follow me.'

His plan when they emerged into the town was to leave Hansam in command of the leading platoon and take Williams, Slaughter and a handful of men in search of Trouin and Lieutenant Lejeune. Two by two now, the Grenadiers filed through the narrow doorway and into the wider passageway, which led directly into the base of the citadel. Now, thought Steel, the fun will begin. They might be inside, but how did you hide a company of redcoats in a fortified town teeming with the enemy? As if in answer from twenty yards ahead of him, on top of the inner rampart, there came a terrific explosion and he watched as the packed earth erupted and bricks, shards of stone and clods of clay were flung ten, twenty feet into the air.

He turned to Slaughter: 'Bugger me, Jacob. Those are our

guns firing. They've begun the bombardment early. Now we're for it.'

The sergeant, relieved to be free of the tunnel and keen to be at the French, grinned at him. 'Well at least we don't need to hide any more, sir.'

Up above they could hear the sound of men scurrying to man the embrasures, officers shouting shrill commands in French. Steel snapped back to his senses and turned to Slaughter.

'Sarn't, I think that we might dispense with any pretence of secrecy now, don't you? Have the men make ready their grenades. And have them replace their headgear. If we're going to die, we're damn well going to do so with dignity.'

Slaughter smiled again and barked the order: 'Replace caps.'

Above their heads a French captain heard the words and instantly grasped the situation – redcoats in mitre caps – the English were within the walls. Steel heard the order.

'Tirez!'

No sooner had he heard it than a half-dozen musketballs were whistling past his face. A man went down, hit in the arm and groaning.

Steel moved fast: 'Take cover. Tom, Sarn't Slaughter, with me. You men there, to me, now!'

There was a flight of stone steps a short distance away and Steel knew that if they were not to be pinned down here by French musketry, they had to get up on to the counterscarp, and those steps. They were their only hope. Without waiting for support he sprinted across the ditch towards the steps and realized to his relief that the others were right behind him. Another French shot struck home, puncturing the throat of one of the Grenadiers. He could not tell who. But Steel had made it to the steps and began to climb.

He called back to Hansam: 'Henry. You have the company.'

Hansam nodded in acknowledgement and began to give commands. Steel glanced back down to the wider tunnel up which they had come. He had accomplished the first part of his task. The gate lay open now and he knew that soon the men of the Dutch battalion in support would be pouring up the tunnel in their wake. Now, he thought, to find Trouin. And his mission was no longer for Marlborough and Hawkins alone. For only in taking revenge, Steel realized, would he ease his conscience and assuage the growing guilt at Brouwer's death.

A noise made him look up as he climbed and he saw before him an officer of French infantry with his sword outstretched. Behind him, rattling down the steps, came four of his men. Steel knew the only way to meet him was to attempt the unexpected. Rather than stand and wait for the officer's attack, he lunged forward himself so that the Frenchman's own impetus carried his body hard on to the point of Steel's blade. The officer's eyes spread wide with terror as he felt the weapon penetrate his torso. He looked down, tried to clutch at it and then Steel withdrew the weapon and still advancing, pushed the dying man off the steps. The men behind were thrown into confusion. Steel could see that these were not the French infantry he was accustomed to meeting on the battlefield, but Walloon troops, French-speaking Belgians. For an instant they stood and faced him. Then one of the Grenadiers, Cussiter, he thought, discharged his fusil at one of the Frenchmen and the ball caught him on the cheek, spinning him round. That was enough. The other three, one of them dragging their wounded comrade, turned and fled back up the steps.

Steel raised his sword in the air: 'Grenadiers, with me!'

With a great shout the redcoats came rushing up the steps

behind him and as he reached the top of the flight he saw that the remainder of the section of Walloons had taken flight along the ramparts. He caught his breath and, standing on the parapet for a moment, glanced towards the allied lines and saw laid out before him the bulk of the force that had been selected to consolidate the attack. And seeing it he knew that, whatever might befall him now, surely the French must surrender the town. There were ten battalions in all, advancing steadily along the dunes towards the western gate. He knew that the balance of his own regiment, twelve companies of musketeers, were among them, with Colonel Farquharson at their head. And with them came their old friends from Ramillies: Meredith's, Temple's, Macartney's, Farington's and the Guards. He knew too that Argyll's men were down there and wondered what sport the duke would enjoy today, how many Papists he might butcher in the name of humanity.

All that Hansam had to do now was hold the breach for the Dutch and then together the combined force would open the West Gate. If the resistance they met was as slight as that which Steel had just sent into a rout then the assault would be swift.

For his own part however, Steel knew that the day's events had only just begun. Now, as he heard the firefight intensify at the mouth of the tunnel, he led his party away from Hansam and the core of the company and along the course of the wall, trying to remember the route Fabritius had taken and transpose it into reverse order. At length, to the left he saw an opening and motioning to the others to follow him, ducked into it. To his intense relief there was not a single Frenchman in sight. The end of the short tunnel through the second wall gave out on to a familiar street. Above his head the sound of running feet told him that, as planned, Hansam was drawing the garrison towards the gate.

He looked round to check his men. There were ten of them all told, including Williams. He had a feeling that Trouin would not be in his headquarters. That was too obvious and also too vulnerable a place. No, Steel knew that a man like Trouin needed to be at the hub of things. To exercise control he must be seen to be in the cockpit of command. His men might be fighting in the streets, but Trouin would be in the governor's office. That was where they would take him.

Operating on instinct, Steel headed southeast and soon found the straight thoroughfare of St Sebastian Straat. He turned to Williams: 'Tom, this street leads directly to the town hall. That's where we'll find Trouin. It's too dangerous to march straight down it, we'd better use the sidestreets. But if we get separated try to keep on this course. Understood?'

'Sir.'

Still in single file, Steel led the party right and left down a series of narrow streets. They saw no one and even amid the intermittent cannon fire as Marlborough's shore batteries sent the cannonballs against the ramparts, their steps rang out on the cobbles with alarming clarity. There was noise, certainly, but it was the familiar clamour of men going into battle, commands being given to lay cannon and for companies to stand-to. Of the townspeople though, there was no sign, not just in the backstreets but along the wider avenues. The inhabitants, Steel guessed, must have gathered in the shelters, desperate to avoid the bloody fray that they knew must soon envelop their homes. They turned to the right and the area seemed strangely familiar. Steel realized that he had been here before. Although part of Christian Straat had been disfigured by the allied bombardment and several houses lay in ruins, this was clearly the street to which poor Marius Brouwer had brought them on his first visit. In fact his house was only a few doors away from where they now stood.

Suddenly, Slaughter caught Steel's arm and whispered softly, 'D'you see, sir? By the door over there.'

Steel had seen it. There, in the doorway of Marius Brouwer's little house, was a shadowy form. It stood, motionless and barely visible in the deserted town under the dim light from the horned moon. From its stature and the silhouette though Steel could tell that it was a man, and that he was armed with a sword. He was about to approach when there was a sudden commotion ahead of them. Steel pressed himself flat against the wall and the others followed. Looking down the street they saw a party of men, perhaps twenty or thirty of them, fully armed with muskets and an assortment of blades. They were running fast and the two in the lead and another pair to the rear each carried a flaming pitch-covered wooden torch. While several wore the white coats of regular French infantry, others were in civilian dress or the faded coats of other armies. And in the torchlight, even at a distance, Steel recognized several of them as Trouin's men. They were coming hard down the street now, straight towards the Grenadiers it seemed. Surely now, he thought, they must be seen. He prepared to fight, looked at Slaughter and nodded. And then, without letting up in their pace, the men turned sharply to the right down a smaller alleyway, in what Steel reckoned to be the direction of the West Gate. And as they did so the orange light from the torches carried by the last two in the group momentarily illuminated the figure in Brouwer's doorway. Then the street was returned to shadow and silence. But it had been enough and Steel was in no doubt. He would have known that profile anywhere.

FIFTEEN

As Steel tightened the grip on his sword, he heard Slaughter ease back the hammer on his gun. Steel spoke: 'Not a word.'

The figure moved into the light. 'Captain Steel? Is that you? Oh, thank God, sir. Thank God I've found you.'

Steel was relieved to see Fabritius, but noticed that his face wore the same mask of terror that he had seen on it as they had fled the town.

'Mister Fabritius. Are you quite all right? This is no place for you. You should take cover. Where is your family?'

'That's just it, Captain. I need to talk to you. I need your help. You must come with me.'

'Calm down, man. What the devil's the matter?'

'We need your help, Captain. My family. The French know who we are, what I have done. They know that I helped you. Please, you must save us.'

Steel weighed up the situation. If he were to help Fabritius then he might lose the chance of taking Trouin by surprise. Yet to abandon the Belgian would merely add to the weight on his own conscience over Brouwer's death. There was no contest.

'Of course we'll come. Where are your family now? Shall I fetch more men?'

Fabritius looked at the handful of redcoats and seemed troubled. 'No, no, Captain. I am sure you will be enough. Come with me, please.'

It took them perhaps twenty minutes to cross the town. Despite Marlborough's assurance that he would not bombard the defences, the night still crackled with the sound of gunfire, musketry mostly. Parties of French infantry could be seen running through neighbouring streets, yet still Fabritius managed to keep clear of them. He had taken Steel and his men directly across the town to the southeast, as far as they could go. At length they crossed the road which led to the monastery of the Capucins and passed a windmill which had taken several hits during the bombardment and now stood looking like some grotesque giant skeleton, its remaining two sails sticking out like paralysed, crucified arms, its windows and warehouse door acting as the empty sockets of the eyes and mouth.

At length Fabritius stopped, found Steel and spoke in a whisper: 'Over there, Captain, sir. We are here.'

Steel looked ahead and instead of Fabritius' house as he had expected, saw the vast bulk of one of Vauban's casemates, set beneath the furthermost bastion of the fort, the Lanthorn Bastion, the last before the port and strongest of them all. They advanced towards the stout oak doors of the casemate which were firmly shut and, he presumed, locked. To his surprise, Fabritius pushed them and they swung wide. At Slaughter's command the handful of Grenadiers poured through the opening – into emptiness. The inner yard of the casemate was deserted, save for four horses tethered in the far corner. Steel froze. Something was not right.

He turned to Fabritius: 'Where are they? Your wife and

children?' Fabritius stared back at him. Steel tried again: 'Well, man. Where are they?'

Fabritius said nothing but pointed towards the large wooden door at the rear of the yard.

With their guns held at the ready, loaded and cocked, the redcoats, led by Steel, his sword drawn, moved gingerly across the yard towards the inner door. Steel pushed and like the outer doors it too swung open.

The interior stank of human ordure and stale wine. Broken wine bottles and opened packing cases lay strewn across the floor and in a far corner two dogs were chewing on something which might have been a rat. The room was lit by candles and in the half-light Steel saw in the centre of the room a woman and two small children huddled together. Beside them, tied to a chair, sat Lieutenant Lejeune, who was stripped to the waist. Yet it was not on Fabritius' family nor the lieutenant that Steel's gaze now fell, but on the man at the end of the room.

Duglay-Trouin was seated close to the rear wall, behind a heavy oak garrison table. Beside him sat Stringer. For a moment Steel thought that he might be too late, but then Lejeune turned his head and Steel could see that he had not yet been mutilated, but merely badly beaten. The French subaltern managed a feeble smile. Steel saw that the far end of the room was filled with Trouin's men. There were more than a score of them, heavily armed and aiming their muskets directly towards the Grenadiers. Trouin spoke, his voice echoing against the walls.

'Captain Steel.' The privateer smiled with satisfaction, then looked down at his hands and picked at his fingernails with a pocket knife. 'As you can see, we had not yet begun to enjoy ourselves with the lieutenant or Madame Fabritius. You have quite spoilt Ajax's fun.'

Steel looked him in the eye. 'You're finished, Trouin. In minutes this place will be full of redcoats. We're in the walls. The town is ours, or soon enough will be.'

'Are you quite certain of that, Captain? My sources tell me that the bulk of your force is still to enter. Even now they are fighting for their lives on the ramparts. And how many men do you have with you here? Six that I can see. Do you really propose to arrest me with six men. Captain Steel?'

'No, Trouin. I'm going to kill you.'

Trouin laughed again, his bellow echoed by the higher snigger of Stringer. 'I see that you have brought your sergeant with you. Your heroic rescuer.' He paused: 'Now, drop your weapons.'

Steel glanced at Slaughter and nodded, but gave him what might have been half a wink. Reluctantly the sergeant and three of the men placed their guns on the floor.

Trouin went on: 'You see, Captain Steel, I have the upper hand. Always. You cannot win this game. Such a clever plan, don't you think, to use Mister Fabritius to play on your sentiment. Stringer here said that you were "soft". And do you know, Steel? I didn't believe him. But I see he was right. And soon you will die.'

Steel could see that the pirate was becoming drawn into his own rhetoric. Stringer looked uneasily at the Grenadiers, particularly those who had not yet grounded their weapons.

But Trouin continued: 'You think that your great army, your General Malbrook, is going to win this battle. But you're wrong. Why do you suppose I was released? Major Malbec authorized it because I have two ships in the harbour, Captain Steel. Two fine ships, both armed and rigged and crewed and ready to sail. And those two ships are faster and more powerful than any vessel your precious navy can muster. I intend to sail them out of this harbour and to board your bombketches before your sailors are even aware that I am there. Then I shall turn your own bombships on your flotilla and blow it from the water. And when that is done I shall turn them inland, on your army, whether it's in or out of this miserable town. Not that it will matter to you, because by then of course you'll be dead. You and I and Ajax have an appointment. We are going to resume where we left off when we killed that Belgian scum. Who knows, we might let you live. It would be amusing to see how long you lasted on the streets of Port Royal as a blind, impotent beggar.' He noticed the two Grenadiers who had not dropped their weapons. 'You men there. I said drop your guns. I'll give you a chance. I'll count to five. One . . .'

Steel had no reason to doubt Trouin. He had seen the two ships in the harbour as they had rowed in three nights ago and although he was no sailor, they made a fine sight. One at least had looked low enough in the water to be a sloop. As to the threat, Steel had seen what Trouin was capable of. He realized that he was sweating hard beneath the thick red coat. Knowing that at all costs he must not show his fear he spoke through it.

'You're a fool, Trouin, if you think that you'll get away with it.'

Trouin smiled and continued to count: 'Three.'

The pirates prepared to fire. And again Steel caught Slaughter's eye, for as he had been talking he had gradually been working his right hand further behind his back, seeking a small pocket which lay just at the peak of the two tails of his coat. He had got it now and with infinite patience inched his index finger deeper inside until it rested on a hard, cold object – the small knife he always kept in the hidden pocket. Carefully, Steel closed his thumb on the knife and slowly began to draw it out. It slipped neatly into the fold of his hand and using a fingernail he opened the blade and felt his hand close around cold steel. In a split second the knife was out and flying through the air towards the pirate closest to Trouin whose musket was pointing directly towards him. It hit the man in the centre of the forehead and he sank to his knees, stone dead. There was an instant in which time froze and Trouin gazed in disbelief at the dead man and the protruding knife.

Then all hell broke loose. Trouin shouted and six of the pirates managed to get off a shot, their balls flying for the most part over the heads of the Grenadiers, although one grazed Lejeune's right shoulder and another hit one of the redcoats. The two Grenadiers who still had their weapons fired and three of Trouin's men went down. Tom Williams dashed at another and with a swift backhanded cut, flensed away the flesh from his cheek. Steel yelled, 'Down' and his men ducked low and reached to retrieve their grounded weapons. Fabritius pushed his wife and children, screaming now, to the floor and as two of Trouin's men knelt to fire their fusils, Steel rushed at Trouin, headlong through the smoke. And connected with . . . nothing. Looking around he searched in vain for the Frenchman.

And at that moment the noise of the struggle was lost in another, louder sound which rocked the room. A huge explosion and not far away, he thought. A musketball sang through the air past his cheek and thinking quickly he ran, bent double, towards where the shot had come from and found to his satisfaction that his head connected with a man's lower abdomen, winding him and knocking him over.

Steel straightened up and quickly grabbed a musket lying across the body of a dead pirate. Praying that it was loaded, he cocked it fully, before pointing it point-blank at the winded man and pulling the trigger. The man's head exploded in a welter of blood and brains. Steel hurled the gun to the ground and looked around. To his left he saw Slaughter bayoneting another of Trouin's men, while elsewhere the Grenadiers were fighting their own battles. Six of the pirates lay dead on the floor with one of his own men. Apart from the few of Trouin's men left fighting, he could see no others in the room and of their leader too there was no trace. Fabritius' family were huddled, cowering, in a corner, and the Belgian lay spread-eagled on the stone floor. His eyes were wide open. Steel ran across and dropped down on to one knee. The man had been killed by a single shot to the head. Steel cradled his head for an instant and looked across into the accusing eyes of his wife. The room was suddenly quiet and standing, Steel saw that the remaining pirates had given up the fight. He walked over to the table and bent to retrieve his knife from the pirate's body. He wiped the blade clean on the man's coat.

'Sarn't Slaughter, we'll need to move fast if we're to catch Trouin. It sounds as if they've a battle on their hands out there, but that won't stop him from taking the bombships. What d'you suppose that explosion was?'

'Dunno, sir. Ammunition magazine going up most likely.'

Steel found Williams: 'Tom, take Mackay and Mister Fabritius' family and head for the west walls. Find Lieutenant Hansam, if you can. If not, then any British officer will do. Tell him to send word to Marlborough to warn the fleet – Trouin intends to capture the bombketches and turn them on us. And tell him that I'm going to try and stop him. Oh and Tom, you might ask him to send some men if he can spare them, to the harbour.'

Steel turned to Lejeune who had found his shirt and coat and did not look too much the worse for his ordeal. 'Lieutenant, do you suppose that you might be up to handling a sword?'

The Frenchman smiled: 'Captain Steel, if you do not allow me to carry one then I shall take one for myself. For the moment at least it seems that your enemy is mine also.'

Cussiter approached them and handed Lejeune his thin, standard French pattern infantry sword, which he had found among the pirate's weapons. Steel drew his own heavier blade and moving towards the door, turned to address the remaining redcoats.

'The rest of you load and prime your weapons and fix your bayonets. Keep your heads down and your senses keen. I intend to finish that heartless bastard and I'm taking you with me.'

Marlborough sat astride his grey mare in a gaggle of staff officers on the single road which led directly into the city and watched closely through his spyglass as the afternoon's events unfolded before him. He had seen the assault force go in, and had watched the struggle on the western rampart as Hansam's Grenadiers had fought hard with the reinforced Walloons before being relieved by the Dutch. His carefully aimed barrage had taken out battery after battery of enemy cannon and minutes before one of the few guns he had ordered to fire in support had scored a hit on a powder magazine, sending men and debris high into the air. Now as he looked on, the West Gate stood wide open. The Grenadiers and the Dutch had done their work and now the task of securing the place fell to the lead battalions of Argyll's brigade.

He turned to Hawkins: 'This was a masterful plan, James. Quite masterful. Why, barely half an hour ago I could not have stood here for fear of being hit by one of the garrison's guns. There is still resistance to be sure. D'you see? There, to the south. Blue coats and white fighting along one of the ravelins. But tell me that I am wrong when I say that the place is as good as ours.'

Hawkins shook his head sagely: 'Take care, Your Grace. Argyll's men may be fierce enough but they're not used to the sort of fighting they'll encounter in there. Remember, the town is filled with pirates.'

'Privateers, James. Something quite different. But do you not share my faith in Captain Steel? He is your man, after all, and he has served us well this day. I am confident that he will already have subdued the privateers.'

'Steel has but one company of men, Your Grace, and we do not know how many Trouin may command.'

'Steel has but one company, James, and he is but one man. But they are Grenadiers and I'd rather have that one man with me than all the officers in King Louis' army.'

SIXTEEN

The narrow streets were choked with soldiers. Some wore the red coat of English or Scots regiments, others the white of France or Dutch blue. Many of them were wounded, some of them were dying. Most though were just struggling to stay alive. In fifteen years of soldiering Steel had seen little to match the chaos and savagery of this glorified street brawl. Not even the mayhem of Blenheim village could compare for sheer animal violence as men fought with anything that came to hand and even their bare fists to gain a few yards. He passed one street and saw Argyll's redcoats driving back the French. But on entering an adjoining alley he found himself caught up in the headlong rout of a half-company of English infantry. He had thought that the hottest fighting would be in the west, where the attack had come in. But it seemed now to be everywhere, and the further they moved into the south of the town, the more complex the combat seemed to become. He had thought that by now the battle might be won. The explosion of a main powder magazine might, in any other siege, have prompted the defenders to lay down their arms. But here it seemed, in this den of thieves, it had not stunned the enemy into submission, but strengthened their resolve.

Steel turned to Slaughter: 'What d'you make of this farrago, Jacob? Who's winning, do you reckon?'

'Hard to say, sir. I thought once we were in the town we'd have had 'em. But something's got their dander up, Mister Steel. They don't seem that inclined to yield.'

Steel ducked as they crossed a junction where a firefight was taking place between two companies of opposing infantry. 'Yes, I suspect that the duke's intelligence may be at fault. It seems to me there's more here than Walloons. Most of these men are regulars, Frenchmen. There's ten, fifteen different regiments. Probably came in after Ramillies. And then there's Trouin's lot.'

Steel began moving faster, dodging as best he could between the individual mêlées taking place it seemed at every turn. Vaguely recognizing a system of streets close to the church of Peter and Paul, he found himself standing at the foot of its great stone bulk and paused in the shadows for breath. They were almost there now; two, perhaps three streets away from the gate that led down to the Key and to Trouin's ships.

He half-turned to the men: 'To me.'

But when he looked round, Steel found himself to be completely alone. He had outpaced the others and they had lost him in the warren of narrow, clogged and smoke-filled streets. He listened for their footsteps but could hear none distinct from the cacophony of the battle that seemed now to rage on all sides. Then he did hear something, and it froze his blood. The noise came from directly behind him. The unmistakeable, heart-stopping sound of the hammer of a musket being pulled back to half-cock, prior to being fired. He presumed that it must be a Frenchman, or one of Trouin's men. Or perhaps it was Trouin himself.

Without turning he spoke: 'I am aware that you are there, whoever you are. I am a British officer and I am empowered to offer you quarter – if you drop your weapon. We have taken this town, or soon will and I guarantee that you will receive fair treatment. You have my word on it.'

There was a short, mocking laugh. 'Your word, have I? I'm not sure that will be good enough for me, Mister Steel. You see, I have orders.'

Steel recognized the rasping voice of Sergeant McKellar, Argyll's butcher. 'It's Captain Steel to you, McKellar. And I've no time to come with you to Argyll, if that's what you mean. I have urgent business.'

'Well that would make two of us then sir, wouldn't it?'

'I'm sorry?'

'I'm sure you are sir, but not as sorry as you're going to be when I put this bullet in your brain.'

Steel paused: 'You have orders to kill me? From Argyll, I presume.'

'You might like to think that sir, if you will. I'm not at liberty to say.'

Steel played for time: 'Would you oblige me then by telling me precisely why you have been asked to kill me?'

'Treason, sir. Fraternizing with the enemy, in particular with Jacobites of which sympathy you are yourself suspected.'

'By whom?'

'Couldn't say, sir.'

'By your master and by no one else. Don't be foolish, Sergeant. You and I have no quarrel. And you know that I'm no Jacobite. I have the ear of Marlborough himself.'

McKellar laughed again: 'Lord Argyll says that the duke hisself might be a Jacobite. And wasn't he shut up in the Tower for it?'

It was true. Marlborough had been imprisoned for

suspected Jacobitism, fourteen years ago, though nothing had been proved.

Steel tried another tack: 'How did you find me?'

'Well, seeing as you ask, it was a stroke of luck. His Lordship had just said to me, "McKellar, I want that traitor Steel. Dead or alive, now. Head for wherever the fighting's fiercest. Steel's sure to be there." So there I was, about to set off when up runs a young officer. Smart-looking lad, recognized him at once as one of yours.'

'Williams,' said Steel.

'That's it, sir. Mister Williams. He finds Lord Argyll and he asks him to send reinforcements to you. Tells him that you're to be found by the Key gate. Asks him to send word too to Marlborough. Something about a pirate going to capture a bombship and guns being turned and to be sure to warn the fleet.'

For a moment Steel's thoughts wandered from his own plight to a grander scale of horror. 'And did he? Did he warn the fleet?'

'Did he my arse! No sooner has Williams left us than His Lordship says to me he'll be damned if he's going to save a few sods of wet bobs. Now off you go and find that traitor Steel. So here I came. And here you are, just as he said.'

Steel heard the hammer being cocked back to its full tension and, still unable to fathom a way out, played a final delaying tactic. 'I presume you'll call this accidental.'

'Or enemy action, sir. All the same in a battle, ain't it?'

Steel was well aware of the uses of 'accidents' in the fog of war. How many unpopular officers were there whose families slept soundly believing them to have died with honour bravely in the field, but had later been found to have received a bullet wound to the back of the head? It was understood that someone must have discharged their piece half-cock. An accident. But Steel knew better. They all did. It was how the army cleansed itself of bad blood and rotten officers. So the commanders turned a blind eye and the sergeants said among themselves that it was the most honourable way for any such useless an article to meet his maker.

But Steel was damned if he was going to join their ranks. Yet at this moment there seemed little choice. He winced as he heard McKellar move, easing the gun into his shoulder, preparing to squeeze the trigger.

'I'm sorry, sir. Just following orders.'

Steel closed his eyes and braced himself.

The shot rang out. Then – nothing. He opened his eyes and turned to the rear, expecting at any moment to feel the agony of a ball entering his brain. Instead, he saw Sergeant McKellar lying face down in a pool of his own blood. Standing over him was the welcome sight of Dan Cussiter, his gun smoking as he bit the top off another cartridge.

Cussiter spat out the paper and spoke: 'Lucky I came along, sir. Saw what he was trying to do, sir.'

'Thank you, Dan. I am in your debt.'

'Why was he going to kill you, sir? One of our own men.'

'It's a long story, Dan. Someone in the high command, someone very powerful indeed would like to have me killed it seems. Apparently I am an enemy of the state.'

Cussiter laughed as he rammed home the bullet: 'You're the best officer we have.'

Steel pushed at McKellar's corpse with his foot. 'Not according to his master.'

There was a clatter of running feet and round the corner appeared Slaughter, Lejeune and the missing Grenadiers. The sergeant spoke: 'Sir, we thought we'd lost you.'

'You almost did, had it not been for Cussiter here and his keen eye. Any sign of Trouin?'

'None. And there's fewer of his men now too. The Walloons are surrendering in droves. Some of the French too.'

'The Key Gate is around the next bend. It's my betting Trouin will have left men to guard it. If we can take it quickly enough we've got a chance of getting across the bridge over the ditch and on to the Key. God knows what we'll find there. Stick close to me. You too, Lejeune.' The lieutenant nodded. 'And, Jacob. I know you're old, but keep up. Don't lose me again. Right. Now.'

Running as fast as he could manage, Steel led the party round the back of the great church and on to the wide street which ran just inside the walls of the town. Directly opposite them stood a tall bastion at the top of which men in red and white coats were in the throes of a life-and-death fight. He remembered the place from when he and Slaughter had first come ashore from the little rowing boat. Sure enough, as he looked along the wall to the left he saw a gate – the Key Gate – and as he had predicted two of Trouin's men stood guard. He turned and to his relief saw that his party were all still with him. Then waving two fingers in the air to beckon them on, he darted from the shadow and across the boulevard into the darkness at the foot of the bastion. Within seconds the others too were safely across. Slowly, Steel edged round the curtain wall and looked towards the gate. Trouin's guards were talking to each other now. Both held muskets which he knew would be loaded. Ducking back, Steel unslung his gun before moving forward again and dropping to one knee. He pulled back the hammer to full cock and whispered to the rear.

'Dan. The one on the right's yours. Make it count.'

Cussiter, the keenest shot in the company, moved forward to join Steel and easing back the hammer of his own gun, took careful aim. The two shots rang out almost simultaneously and as the smoke cleared they saw the effect. Both guards lay on the cobbles. Steel patted Cussiter on the back as the Grenadier was reloading then, pausing only to sling the still-smoking fusil over his shoulder, he loped along the wall and dashed through the gate. He had been half-expecting to see more of Trouin's men on the narrow bridge but it was quite deserted. Lejeune was up with him now, with Slaughter and rest close behind.

'Well, Lieutenant. It looks like we're in luck.'

They moved fast across the bridge and reached the open space of the Key on to which he and Slaughter had first stepped when they had come here three days ago. It seemed an eternity. Little had changed; there was the same air of abandonment, the same broken packing crates and empty fishing nets. There was though, one important difference and as he saw it, Steel's heart sank. The two ships which had been moored here had gone – Trouin's ships. They were too late. Steel sat down on a packing case, ground his boot hard into the cobbles and spat.

'Damn the man.' He looked towards the sea and walked over to the edge of the quay. There at the foot of some stone stairs a small dinghy bobbed at anchor. Steel turned and called to Lejeune and Slaughter, 'How are your sea-legs, Lieutenant?'

'I'm afraid that my only experience of rowing has been on the lake at Versailles.'

'Sergeant?'

'I'm no sailor, sir. But I'll have a go.'

Steel turned to the Grenadiers: 'Come on lads. You've just volunteered for the marines.'

Claude Malbec, as he had told de la Motte, was a simple soldier, had been no more or less these past twenty years. He had a soldier's eye, a soldier's brain and above all a soldier's instinct for knowing which way a battle was going. And at this moment, standing on the highest rampart of the western defences, Malbec knew that things were not going well for the French. Of course he had known all along that, barring a miracle, Ostend was already lost. That miracle, he had thought, might have been Duglay-Trouin and his ships. But as yet nothing had been seen of either and Malbec wondered whether the pirate had not simply cut and run with his men. After all, what was Ostend to him? He supposed that he should have known better than to have trusted the man. But he had seemed genuinely taken with the idea of sinking the English navy. And, naturally, Malbec had told him where to find Lejeune. He presumed the lieutenant must be dead by now. The young fool had it coming, though he hoped that Trouin had not been too savage. The boy had just not been cut out for the army, had never really understood it, or the way it worked. As far as Malbec was concerned if you didn't understand the system and play it to your best advantage; if you were too damn fair, then you would end up like Lejeune. Dead meat.

Malbec gazed along the fortifications and out to where the early evening sun glistened on the sea and the English ships bobbed at anchor. Turning back to the town he beheld a less serene scene. Far below him, both in the grass-covered ditch on one side and in the street on the other, the ground was covered with dead and dying men. Directly below him a company of Dutchmen were engaged in a close range firefight with a mixed bag of French infantry and Walloons. Malbec watched as the Dutch gave fire, dropping half a dozen men from the French ranks and then as they reloaded, saw the French do the same, with similar effect. And so, he thought, you will continue, until one side or the other has had enough and turns tail. That was how it happened, how it always happened. How it had happened before his eyes for two decades. He surprised himself by wondering whether men might not one day find a better way of settling their differences. In this case it looked as if the Dutch would win. Perhaps he thought, he could do better. Malbec turned to the matter in hand, to his own men, the half-company of veteran French infantry drawn up at right angles to the walls, facing directly along the parapet behind half a dozen stout, earth-filled wicker gabions. Malbec knew that, if the enemy were to take this vital area of the town then they would first have to secure this spot. And he intended to refuse it to them. He doubted whether he would survive, but the past few days had served to remind him that he had little left to live for. Just as well to die here, in Ostend as anywhere else. He tightened his sash and brushed his coat where smuts from the cinders and ashes floating on the air had settled and wondered again whether Trouin would attack the flotilla. Well, it was probably too late now, certainly to save him and his men. A cacophony from the staircase told him that soon, once again, he would be plunged into the deadly lottery of firefight and mêlée. He saw his sergeant, the big man from Alsace, Müller, the bald-headed barrel-maker.

Malbec called out to him: 'Müller, have the men hold their fire until the enemy are within twenty paces. Twenty. No more than that. I want every shot to find a target.'

And then the first of red-coated attackers burst round the corner of the parapet wall and above the noise Malbec screamed the command: 'Make ready. Present. Fire!'

Forty muskets spat flame and lead and once again, as he knew they would, the men began to fall.

The little boat moved remarkably smoothly through the dark waters of the inlet. Steel weighed up the odds. Of the original ten, only five remained with him. He scanned their weary, powder-caked faces: Slaughter, Cussiter, Miller, Taylor, Thorogood. He would have trusted any with his life. They had lost Milligan in the mayhem of the streets. Williams he had sent fruitlessly to Argyll and with him Mackay. Five men, plus himself and Lejeune. Seven against how many of Trouin's men? Of an initial strength of over four hundred the pirate must have lost perhaps half. That still left two hundred men split between the two vessels. Six against two hundred. For an instant he thought that this was madness. They were going to their deaths. And then he thought of the bombships and of Marlborough and Hawkins and Henrietta. And he knew that he had no choice. He peered ahead, trying all the time to get a better picture of their adversaries.

Trouin's two ships were quite different from one another. The larger one, evidently his flagship, was a converted man-o'-war, a square-rigged three-master of around 300 tons and perhaps a hundred feet in length. Even at this distance Steel could see that she bristled with cannon. He counted twenty-five gunports a side. And they were open. Clearly she had been made ready for battle and he presumed that it was on her that Trouin must have based himself and most of his crew, using the other, smaller, faster vessel as the raider with which to take the bombketches. The brigantine was half her size with only two masts and half the guns and even to Steel's untrained eye, it was clear that she was built for speed rather than combat. So it was for the warship they would head. For Steel knew that, even if the raider had her orders, with their commander taken or killed, the pirates would lose hope and abandon the attack.

They had muffled their oars with the men's neck stocks and they made hardly a sound as they cut through the water. To their left Ostend was a smoking ruin. Flames leapt skywards from the blown magazine and three more now that had been fired by Argyll's infantry and the town was bathed in an evil orange glow. Steel prayed that it would not light the night sufficiently to mark them out to any sentries on Trouin's flagship. She was leaving the mouth of the harbour now, but they were drawing ever closer and he knew that he would have to judge their final approach with care, coming in hard under the lee of the stern gallery yet taking care not to create too great a wake. He was no sailor, and did not have a clue as to how to achieve such a manoeuvre. Acting on instinct, he signalled to the oarsmen, three Grenadiers and Lieutenant Lejeune, to feather their oars for a moment. Then, as the boat lay calm, he waved them back down into the water and urged them to pull as fast as possible. It did not have quite the desired effect – the oars seemed to make more noise than ever. For a few breathless moments they were immediately beneath the light of the stern lantern, exposed to full view. Steel saw the ship's name carved in gilded letters above the gallery: *Bellone* – 'War goddess'. It seemed a good omen.

Then they dropped under the overhanging bulk of the stern. Steel pointed along the ship, towards the bow, indicating that they should move in that direction. Each of them using one hand against the side of the ship, they coaxed the little boat the length of the hull until she lay directly beneath the raised anchor.

Steel beckoned to Slaughter and whispered: 'Sarn't, you follow me up on deck. Leave two men down here to secure the boat. Bring Cussiter and Miller with you. I take it the lieutenant will want to come with us.' Lejeune nodded. Steel grinned: 'Give me two minutes before you follow.'

Steel unslung his gun and removed his cumbersome red coat and then, settling the sling back on to his shoulder and with his sword firmly in its scabbard, he reached up and grasped the anchor cable with both hands. With a supreme effort he pulled himself up so that his legs were crossed around the chain and shinned up its length until he was on top of the anchor. Two smaller ropes stretched out before him, secured to the rigging. He grabbed at one and hauled himself up until his head was level with the rail, beside a small swivel gun. He scanned the deck and pulled himself aboard. Placing his boot on the slippery wooden planks with as little noise as he could manage, he sank to his knees and ducked behind the capstan.

The deck seemed surprisingly sparsely occupied. Steel could count only six men. He could make out Stringer, the blackamoor Ajax and four others. All appeared to be occupied tending to the sails and the wheel. The odds were suddenly balanced. But why a skeleton crew? But before Steel had time to contemplate what that might imply, he was aware that someone was at his side.

Lejeune spoke in a whisper: 'Where is Trouin? Can you see him?'

Steel shook his head, held up six fingers to the lieutenant and shrugged. Lejeune looked puzzled. There was a noise from their left, a clatter followed by a splash.

'Bugger.'

Slaughter's voice, though barely audible, was enough to make two of the crew turn their heads, and Steel knew that the game was up. He drew his sword. Lejeune stood and pulled from his belt one of two pistols he had taken from the dead pirates. All the men had turned towards them now and Steel watched as one of them bore down upon him, lunging wildly with the tip of a captured cavalry sabre. A crash from his left told him that Lejeune had fired and from the corner of his eye Steel saw one of the pirates fall. Then

Lejeune too drew his sword as another of the crew closed with him.

Steel parried the cavalry blade with ease and cast it off to his left before riposting to the man's right side. He struck home and the pirate jumped back instinctively but not before Steel's razor-sharp weapon had taken a slice clean through his ribs. The man reeled, clutched at his side with his free hand and looked back at Steel then attacked again with a strength born of desperation. Steel stepped back and let him come on then parried again and drove the blade deep into the man's chest, withdrawing it as he fell to the deck.

A crash of musketry drew Steel's attention and he saw Miller fall back, shot in the chest at close range by a tall pirate armed with a pistol and an axe. Slaughter was up with them now, clutching his sword. He came *en garde* against Miller's killer with a clumsy elegance and took the full force from the downward cut of the axe against his blade. Steel moved round the capstan and looked across the deck as a small heavily mustachioed man in a ragged red coat with officer's facings bore down on him with a cutlass. Steel parried again but the man pushed against his blade with unexpected strength and it flew from his hand to the deck. Steel backed off and the man smiled through his whiskers then came at Steel again, slowly now, relishing the ease of killing another English redcoat, as he had so many before. It was so simple. They fought with such care and honesty, did not realize that brute force will always win at close combat. They never learned.

He stood back for a second, smiled at Steel and pointed his blade at his chest. To the man's bemusement, Steel did not panic, but smiled back and then he gave the pirate another surprise. Before the man knew what was happening, with all the strength he could muster, Steel had brought his boot hard up into his groin. The pirate dropped his cutlass and fell to his knees, howling with pain. Steel stooped to pick up his sword.

'Weren't expecting that, were you? That's not what British officers do, is it? We're gentlemen, we don't fight dirty. Well I'm a bloody gentleman and I bloody well do.'

Steel raised his sword and brought it down upon the man's head, slicing through skull and flesh. He turned and saw that Lejeune had accounted for one of the pirates and was advancing towards a second. On the starboard side Slaughter hurled another over the side and Steel noticed Stringer who was advancing up the deck towards the sergeant, a sword in each hand.

Steel called across, 'Jacob! On your right!'

Slaughter turned and as he did Stringer rushed him, raising the sword in his right hand. Slaughter parried the blow and tried to riposte, but he was too slow and Stringer's second weapon cut into his thigh. Slaughter groaned and pushed the blade away with his own, knocking it from Stringer's sweaty palm.

Sensing the smaller man's panic, Slaughter lunged and his blade sank into Stringer's left side, but at the last moment the deserter sidestepped and it missed vital organs. It was though deep enough to stop him in his tracks. Stringer dropped the remaining sword and held the wound, the blood seeping through his fingers. He staggered backwards and collapsed beside the stairs to the quarter-deck, knocking his head against the lower step. Slaughter followed, but before he could finish Stringer off, from behind the ship's wheel another of Trouin's men came tumbling down the stairs and fell upon the Grenadier with a war cry the likes of which Slaughter had never heard. For an instant he looked at his new attacker and saw dark skin, almost red in hue, short black hair and a face covered with white and black and blue markings.

In his hand the man held a small axe, a tomahawk. He cut down with it towards Slaughter's head, but the sergeant managed to fend it off with the edge of his sword. Instantly the Indian attacked again, with greater ferocity, swinging the axe blade from the opposite direction. Slaughter ducked and felt it cut through the collar of his coat. He moved back and attempted to raise his sword-arm against a third attack. But it didn't come. The Indian froze in mid-gesture as Lieutenant Lejeune's sword pierced him clean through the heart. The Frenchman withdrew the blade and smiled at Slaughter whose senses were reeling.

'Bloody hell, sir. What devil was that?'

'Iroquois. An American devil, a native from their woodlands. They prey on the settlers. A few are in the pay of my king.'

'Must be daft. I wouldn't bloody pay them. Bloody savages.' He nodded to Lejeune: 'Thank you, sir. Consider yourself an honorary Englishman. Even if you are a French gentleman.'

Lejeune laughed and turned away and found himself looking directly into eyes that spoke pure evil.

Ajax had hung back from the fight, but now he knew his time had come. That was what Trouin had told him. If you are attacked, wait for the others to tire themselves out. Then you can take them all. The blackamoor looked deep into Lejeune's eyes and doing so he brought his right hand up so quickly the motion was all but invisible.

The French lieutenant felt the cold, curved scimitar penetrate his chest. Steel looked on in horror as slowly and deliberately, the huge man slid the full length of the blade deeper and deeper into Lejeune's body. For an instant, the young

315

lieutenant looked at Steel with pleading eyes. And then he dropped his sword to the deck and he was gone.

His reason lost in a haze of fury and revenge, Steel rushed at Ajax, his sword flailing and felt his blade penetrate flesh and stop on bone. He looked and saw that he had gouged a hole in the man's upper arm. But Ajax merely turned and, grasping Steel's sword by the wide blade, wrenched it from the redcoat's hand and apparently oblivious to any pain, pulled it free and threw it across the deck. Then he turned to Steel. His hand went up and with it the huge, jewelled scimitar and as he began to bring it down Steel watched in horror. For an instant he dropped his gaze and saw Lejeune's narrow weapon lying where he had let it fall. Steel stretched for it and found the hilt a moment before Ajax's blade descended.

Rolling away, he felt the scimitar cut down and hit the flesh of his calf and then, pushing with all his might he drove Lejeune's blade deep up and into the blackamoor's heart. The huge man fell hard on to Steel's body and for an instant their faces were level. Steel thought he saw the barely perceptible trace of a smile cross the man's face and then, as he watched, the cruel eyes glazed over in the blank stare of death.

With difficulty, Steel heaved the limp form away. He dragged himself across the bloody deck and sat up against the starboard rail. Looking down he could see the wound in his leg. He had been lucky. The scimitar had taken a chunk of flesh and muscle and left it flapping. He had seen such wounds often enough to know that it was serious, but if properly handled would not leave him crippled. He looked about. Slaughter crossed the deck and helped him to his feet.

'That's it, sir. That's all of them. We've looked below decks and there's not a soul down there.'

A skeleton crew, thought Steel. Trouin had tricked his pursuers and taken the smaller ship.

'All dead, Jacob?'

'All save one, sir.'

Stringer, though unconscious, was still breathing. Holding his bleeding leg, Steel bent down towards him. Slaughter slapped his face to bring him round. Stringer groaned and opened his eyes. Steel spoke close to his face: 'Where's Trouin? Tell me and you'll live. Don't and I'll kill you now.'

Stringer struggled to speak, finally he found words: 'You're too late, Steel. He's not here. Just left me to guard 'is flagship. Trusts me, see. On the other ship. He's going to take the bombships and blow up your fleet. Seen her flag, have you? Same as yours. Nothing you can do about it.'

He grinned at Steel who straightened and looked up at the main mast where a cross of St George fluttered in the evening breeze. Trouin was sailing under friendly colours. He found Cussiter and nodded across towards Stringer.

'Dan, get that bastard down into the boat and try and keep him alive till we get back. I want to see him hang.'

Stringer was right. He was too late. Steel looked out from the quarter-deck and saw Trouin's fast-rigged brigantine pulling hard away from them. She was two hundred yards distant now, and making speed through the calm waters, heading directly for the first of the bombketches. There was no light aboard the squat English vessels and Steel knew that the crew would be resting in the dinghy tied up to the rear. At most they would have only three men on each ship. Trouin's plan was simple and perfect. His men would board each one silently and kill the crew and and perhaps even take on a man-o'-war. Maybe more. Then he would be at liberty to open up with their mortars and all the cannon he could find and destroy first what he could of the flotilla and then turn on the army. And there was nothing Steel or anyone could do to stop him. The flotilla was as good as lost, and with it, Ostend.

Malbec had not thought that it would end like this. But like many old soldiers he had always believed that there was an allotted time for him to die and he felt that this was not that moment.

He would not die here, but be taken prisoner. He could not help admiring the tall redcoat officer who had fought so hard and accounted for so many of his men. Now he knew that the hour had come. He presumed he would be taken to England and if he was lucky, within a few months exchanged for some unfortunate English officer. Then he would rejoin his regiment and the war. That was how things worked. It was not the same for the rank and file, of course. If they were taken prisoner rather than killed out of hand then their lot might be a great deal less certain. Perhaps they might rot for years in the prison hulks at Dartmouth or even be pressed into the service of the enemy. For the officers there were different rules. For the lucky ones, who lived to fight again. England, he thought, might not be so bad after all. He was inquisitive too to know the true character of a people for whom, for so long, he had nursed so intense a hatred. The people who had killed his wife and children, the people who had taken his life.

And so Malbec held out his sword to the redcoat officer: 'Sir, I would be honoured if you would accept my surrender. I could continue the fight. But I regret that today, I do not have it in me to do any more killing.'

Argyll smiled at him. He had originally thought to kill this man, along with all his Frenchmen. 'No quarter' had been the orders he had given to his battalion before the assault.

318

But there was something about this particular French officer that told the duke that to kill him in such a way would not be right. Perhaps it was the way he held himself. Or the look in his eyes and the scarred, care-worn face that told Argyll that in a curious way that he and this Frenchman had too much in common. A shared history of battle. A brotherhood. So he accepted Malbec's sword, and watched as his men piled the enemy muskets and dragged away the dead, and then settled down to await the return of Sergeant McKellar.

There was one chance, thought Steel. One slim chance left for them to stop Trouin and he meant to take it. As they stood staring down at Lejeune's body, he turned to Slaughter.

'There must be a magazine on board. Trouin didn't take the guns. He must have left powder. Jacob, have you got a tinderbox and a slow match?'

'Sir. But what . . .'

'Come with me.' He called to Cussiter: 'You too, Dan. Here, give me a hand.'

They found what he was searching for on the lower deck. Although most of the powder had gone with Trouin and of what was left much was damp, Steel reckoned there would still be enough for his purpose. They were well past the mouth of the harbour now, drifting under canvas and yet just barely visible to the flotilla, although still a good half-mile away. As they moved the barrels of powder close together, Steel explained.

'We need to warn the fleet. This is the only way. We've got to blow up this ship.' With a rope rubbed in more powder leading from the barrels up to the deck, Steel trimmed the length of slow match that Slaughter had produced and waited as it burned down.

Cussiter had climbed down into the dinghy. Watching Trouin's brigantine as it grew closer in the twilight to the first of the ketches, Steel was increasingly conscious that there was not a moment to lose.

'You'd better go, Jacob. I'll jump after I've lit the fuse.'

The sergeant shook his head: 'I'm not leaving without you, Mister Steel.'

'You bloody are. Get off the ship now, Sergeant. That's a bloody order. Jump man.'

With Slaughter still protesting, Steel pushed at the Grenadier's chest and toppled him over the side of the ship. He tumbled, arms sprawling, into the dinghy, his fall broken by Cussiter. Steel looked down and saw that neither of them was seriously hurt. Then he turned back towards the stairs. It was the only way. The explosion would alert the fleet and then perhaps they would have a chance before Trouin and his men reached the bombships.

Kneeling down, and with the pain from his bleeding leg growing ever more intense, Steel lit the fuse with care and prayed that he might still have time to jump clear. He watched it burn down the staircase and run along the lower deck towards the powder hold. Then he hobbled as fast as he could across the deck.

He had not quite reached the rail when the flame entered the first of the barrels. The explosion ripped through the heart of the old warship and Steel, his arms and legs flailing, half-jumped, and was half-blown high above the deck and out towards the sea. Around him all the air seemed to have been suddenly sucked out of the world and as he tried to stay conscious, he felt the pressure squeezing the eyes from his head and then he was falling in slow motion into an endless, weightless, suffocating void.

* * *

All afternoon he had stood on the deck of the small escort ship and watched what he could of the action on shore. Leaving the bombketches further out in the sea, he had come closer into the shore with the majority of the other ships, to have a better view of the assault. Now though it seemed to Lieutenant Forbes that it was over. Cheering seemed to be coming from the strand and the explosions had stopped. He turned from the rail and was about to descend to his cabin when without warning the sky was split in two by the biggest single explosion he had ever heard. To his left, just to the north of the town, the lowering greyness of the dusk was transformed into brilliant orange and the silhouette of a three-master was clearly visible. A man-o'-war, sailing out of Ostend. Forbes gasped.

But it was not so much the dying ship that alarmed him as the other vessel, a brigantine which was also illuminated by the flash. Running English colours, she was heading directly for one of his bombketches. But he was quite certain that this was no ship of theirs. She looked more like a pirate vessel. Forbes caught hold of one of the gawping sailors.

'Make a signal to the admiral. Assume enemy in sight under false flag. Respectively suggest, sir, you engage enemy immediately to stop taking away bombships.'

He need not have bothered. For Admiral Fairborne was well aware of what was happening and as Forbes peered through his telescope towards the brigantine, the *Triton*, the only ship left in the vicinity of the ketches, began to veer sharply and to come alongside Trouin's vessel. The lieutenant watched in admiration as the great warship prepared to show her full might to the privateer. This was how Britons made war, he thought. This, surely was the very measure of glory.

*   *   *

321

And as Forbes looked on and waited for victory, another pair of eyes were held in rapt attention by the unfolding action. Clinging to the stern of the upturned dinghy, Steel supposed that he should count himself the most fortunate man alive. The explosion had blown him clear of the flagship and into the water. His only visible injuries were a few cuts from flying debris, although a sharp pain in his side told him that one if not more of his ribs had taken some of the force of the blast and might well be broken. Slaughter and Cussiter had also managed to climb upon the dinghy and Matt Taylor was clinging to an oar. A short distance away Thorogood, the cricketer, was sitting on a piece of the ship's gallery that had been blasted away by the explosion. Of Sergeant Stringer though there was no sign. Steel could only presume that, wounded as he was, he must have sunk to the bottom. What was left of the *Bellone* was sinking now though Steel wondered how deep the bottom was so close to the harbour and prayed that the wreck would not block the port to allied supply ships. He could hear nothing but a buzzing in his ears and hoped that his deafness would not be permanent. His arms weak, his body aching and bloody, his wounded leg throbbing, he wondered how they might make it back to the shore. But his problems were dispelled as he saw the *Triton* come alongside Trouin's ship and run out her guns to give the brigantine a pounding and blow the devil back to hell.

And then a strange thing happened. Before the *Triton* could fire, with a thunderous volley the brigantine opened up with every gun on her port side against the great English warship. For an instant the two vessels were lost to sight in a welter of smoke and splintered wood. But as it blew away it became clear that Trouin's ship had turned away after firing and was already making sail under the fresh wind, heading fast out into the open sea. Now at last the *Triton*'s guns blazed, but already Steel knew, the brigantine would be out of effective range. He looked on, incredulous, as Trouin and his men drew ever further away from the flotilla. Away from Ostend. And away from him. And this time, for once Steel realized that there was nothing he could do but watch.

EPILOGUE

The stench of death hung about Ostend for weeks. But Steel did not care. He was going home. Not to Scotland, but at least across the Channel to London. For once the prospect of leave was filled with possibilities. Filled with Henrietta. A clap on the shoulder-blade surprised him from his reverie and re-awakened pain in his raw back. He tried not to wince.

Lord Orkney raised his glass towards Steel. Clapped him again on the shoulder: 'You're a credit to the army, Sir. A credit. Isn't that so, your Grace? A credit.'

Steel smiled, mumbled his thanks and looked first at Marlborough and then towards the door. The Duke was well aware that Steel wanted to leave; to find Lady Henrietta, set off for the port and the journey home. But he was damned if he was going to waste one iota of the glory that Steel's action had brought to his command. He extended his arm to move Steel further into the tented room, where a group of officers stood in conversation.

'Argyll. You've met Captain Steel?'

'Indeed your Grace. We are well acquainted.'

The familiar face caught Steel with its cold grey eyes and

he felt a chill pass through his body. Then he thought of Sergeant McKellar, lying dead on the cobbles and smiled back. And Argyll knew and looked away.

Other officers smiled at Steel. Muttered words of congratulation. Colonel Hawkins tapped him on the shoulder: 'You look tired, Jack. You've earned your leave. That was well done.'

'But we lost Trouin. And his crew.'

'But we took the garrison, Jack. And the town.'

Cadogan spoke: 'We have the port, Colonel, and that is what matters. That, after all was the prime objective. It was a great success and at such little cost'.

Steel could have punched him. At little cost perhaps for the army as a whole. Five hundred men. But how many of those had been from his company? He had lost too many good men in the assault and up there on the ramparts with Hansam. Thankfully the lieutenant himself and young Williams had both come through unhurt. But too many Grenadiers would stay in Ostend forever. He thought too of Brouwer and of Lejeune, of a widow and two fatherless children in a ruined city and of a mourning mother at the court of King Louis. He realized, not for the first time, how war brought all sorts together in grief.

But this was a time for joy. He was going home – that was, if he ever got away from this damn tent and the incessant hubbub of the general staff.

Thankfully, his hearing had returned within a day. Taylor had dressed his wounds, the scratches from the explosion and the deeper hurts inflicted by Trouin's men. He had bound up Steel's broken rib – a simple fracture – and applied an ointment to his bruises that Henrietta said smelt of saffron and turmeric.

He wondered what Arabella would make of his relationship with her cousin, knew that she might exact some subtle form of revenge and was strangely excited by that danger. Again Steel realized that his mind had wandered and that he had missed entirely what Marlborough had just said.

'I'm very sorry, Sir. I . . .'

'Sorry? Don't be sorry, Steel. You have nothing for which to apologise. You have earned your leave. Earned it well. But don't stay long, Steel. We need you back here with the army. Isn't that right, Hawkins?'

The Colonel nodded: 'Indeed, your Grace. Even now I have a mind to put the Captain to good use.'

Marlborough laughed and walked across the room to be welcomed into another group of officers.

Steel stared at the Colonel, who said nothing and took another long draught from the glass of wine which one of the Duke's servants had just replenished: 'You knew. You engineered the whole affair so that I should get her out.'

'Now Jack, don't jump to conclusions. That may well be so, but what does it do to conjecture now? She's out. You're safe and Ostend is ours.'

Steel thought for a moment: 'Did the Duke know anything of your plan?'

Hawkins ignored the question.

'We needed to get to Trouin. To stop him from taking complete control of the channel coast. We had to have some means of luring him into the town, of persuading him to stay until we could take the port. Her ladyship seemed to be the obvious answer. He likes a pretty girl.'

'But he got away. You risked her life and he got away.'

'But we did take the town, Jack. And you heard Lord Cadogan. That's what we came here for. Isn't it?'

Steel shook his head. Such intrigue was lost upon him. He was merely a soldier.

*   *   *

And so Steel sailed for England with Henrietta. The bells of St Margarets rang out in his honour and at last the Queen put her name to the letter of commission for his Captaincy. And later that month the same ship that had taken him to Dover docked there again to offload its cargo of French prisoners, officers on parole. And Claude Malbec did what he had sworn he never would and set foot on English soil. And at the same moment an ocean away, on another ship – a fine brigantine bobbing at anchor in a shallow, palm-fringed bay – another man also counted himself lucky to be out of Ostend. And he swatted away the flies and drank down another glass of madiera and cursed at the heat and the dearth of pretty girls. But the worst of his curses he reserved for a tall Captain of Grenadiers.

HISTORICAL NOTE

Unlike Blenheim, the battle of Ramillies was Marlborough's victory alone. As his biographer Winston Churchill rightly opines, even his detractors cannot ascribe it to Eugene or another of his generals. It was a brilliant display of generalship and arguably the highpoint of his career. Indeed the weeks succeeding it saw him at the very pinnacle of his achievement, lauded by a nation and praised at home. He was though, as in this book, reluctant to accept the proffered position of governor of the Netherlands, rightly foreseeing the problems it would bring.

Ostend, along with Dunkirk and St Malo was, as Cadogan points out, a nest of privateers and thus a thorn in the side of any British force on the continent. It was chiefly for this reason that it was taken and to provide a necessary port of supply for the army. While the rescue of Lady Henrietta Vaughan is as fictional as her character, the pirates are not, although we do not know for certain whether the very real figure of René Duglay-Trouin was present among them at Ostend. In 1706 he appears to have taken part in an action off the coast of Brazil. Trouin was indeed a favourite of

Louis XIV who considered him a loyal Frenchman and he often tended to deceive the enemy by fighting under an English flag. He was certainly ruthless although his penchant for torture as depicted here has no personal basis but is founded on the habits and code of conduct of his fellow pirates of this particularly savage era. The year after Ostend he beat an English flotilla in the Battle of the Lizard and in 1711 captured Rio de Janiero. In 1709 Trouin was ennobled and took the motto *Dedit haec insignia virtus*, 'Bravery gave him nobility'. By that stage his kill total was 16 warships and more than 300 merchant vessels from the Englsih and Dutch fleets. In later life he commanded the French fleet at St Malo. He died in 1736. Ten ships of the French navy have been named in his honour and his statue stands today in St Malo.

I may also seem a little heavy-handed with my depiction of the callousness of John, 2nd Duke of Argyll (1678–1743) and it is not my intention to offend that illustrious family. However, it is well documented that he had a sincere loathing of Jacobitism and was utterly ruthless as a soldier, as well as unquestionably brave. He was also noted for his fiery temper and tendency to be vindictive. In the heat of battle he was always at the front and while he had the capacity to be merciful, on occasion his passions would surely have overcome his reason. Notably he fought a duel in 1710 with a Colonel who accused him of having changed political parties and won, wounding the Colonel. He was a Whig fundamentalist, believing in a modern world based on logic rather than sentiment and superstition: the world that Steel sees emerging around him. It was Argyll too who was one of the instrumental figures in the Act of Union of 1707, only a year after his actions at Ramillies and Ostend. He was among those responsible for the eventual fall of Marlborough and himself rose to be Commander-in-Chief of the British Army. He lies in Westminster Abbey in an elaborate tomb designed by a Frenchman. This is not his first fictional outing. Argyll also appears in Scott's *Heart of Midlothian* as an old man with a softer, more merciful heart.

The siege of Ostend was in fact broken by a storming party of fifty British Grenadiers at the head of a Dutch force who took the port after a heavy bombardment lasting three days principally by two bombketches, rather than my single afternoon, which reduced much of the town to rubble or as one contemporary put it: 'a heap of rubbish'. While the British lost only five hundred men, the loss of life among the civilian population of Ostend surely ranks with the similar treatment meted out to Copenhagen a century later as one of the more ignominious episodes in the history of the Royal navy.

I have taken some licence with the pamphleteering activities of Frampton and Stapleton. Although not without reason. I have merely condensed the events of the following year, in which Marlborough's popularity was gradually eroded by the fact that the Dutch government imposed by the allies upon the Brabant estates gradually incurred the enmity of the people, who detested the Calvinism of their heavy-handed neighbours even more than they hated the despotism of the French, who at least were Catholic. There was also a Belgian underground movement and I have reason to believe that it used the old medieval title, although perhaps it was not quite as nationalistic as I have painted it.

Marlborough, despite his general popularity, particularly among the rank and file, was constantly subject to attack in the press and officers in the army continued to intrigue against him. The author of numerous scurrilous attacks on Marlborough, one John Tutchin, was arrested for libel, flogged and died of his wounds in the Queen's Bench prison in September 1707. Although Marlborough was privately accused of being responsible for his death, no charges were ever brought.

Ostend today is a changed place. Not only was it reduced to rubble by the British in 1706, but also suffered severely during the two world wars. It is possible though to still trace the course of some of Vauban's impressive fortifications. Many of the street names are also new and I apologize for any inconsistencies.

For those with a mind to see more of Vauban's works there is no better starting place than with the superb models now kept in the Musee de l'Armee in Paris. For surviving examples the pas de Calais offers Gravelines, Fort d'Ambleteuse, and at Calais itself Fort Nieulay, while nearby the citadel of Lille retains much of the original atmosphere. Standing on a ravelin, climbing a counterscarp or walking through a gate into a defensive ditch one can, with a little imagination, manage to conjure up something of Steel's Ostend.

With Ostend secure, Marlborough now had a permanent base for the entry of supplies and reinforcements into Flanders. This in turn strengthened his continuing pressure on the government and the Queen that the war must be won in the northern theatre rather than in Spain as was contended by Peterborough. Compared to the big four victories of Blenheim, Ramillies, Oudenarde and Malplaquet, Ostend is now largely forgotten. In this it is characteristic of the many bitterly-contested smaller actions which Marlborough fought henceforth until the end of the war over the next six years, actions in which the British Grenadiers as they came to be known would distinguish themselves particularly in their bravery and daring. As Trevelyan put it: 'losing more men in a hundred forgotten assaults and sallies . . . than they ever lost in the four famous battles of the war.' And, although they do not know it yet, it is through these forgotten victories that Steel and his company must now march on the road to a final peace.

Keep reading for the first pages of

BROTHERS IN ARMS

the next Jack Steel adventure.

Brothers in Arms is available now in hardback.

ONE

The familiar, acrid stench of smoke and powder drifted with the staccato rattle of musket fire up towards them across the river. Captain Jack Steel, standing on one of the wooden pontoon bridges laid earlier that morning over the river Scheldt, was drawn away for a moment from the spectacle of battle unfolding before him by the sound of laughter.

Looking to the left and down towards the water, he saw three of his men pissing into the river, the pale streams of urine arcing against water and landscape as they competed to be the highest. Steel listened to their laughter and boastful claims and decided to allow them one more moment of innocent fun. For who knew if this day would be their last – or indeed his own? The remainder of Steel's company of Grenadiers, fifty-one men all told, stood and sat at their ease directly to his rear, as they had been told they might. They talked among themselves, not of the battle going on below them, nor of anything to do with the war, but of other things: of women and booty and glory and the various virtues of English porter and Scottish ale. But gradually their diverting conversations were turning thin and more men became silent by the minute.

It was hardly surprising, thought Steel. They had been here for near on two hours now and it was not hard to see the telltale signs of impatience and growing unease that came when death was near. The long march to the guns had taken them sixty miles in fifty hours, some of it cross-country, and now those who chose to stand, drawn to the music of the battle, found themselves reluctant yet compelled spectators looking down on a bloody struggle. There was nothing worse than this for a soldier, thought Steel, save of course death itself, and maiming. Nothing worse than this waiting. For with it came the rising fear that clawed away at your guts and lurked like some evil spirit or canker inside your brain. The knowledge that soon, very soon he reckoned now, they too would be part of that maelstrom of hot lead, cold steel and all too yielding flesh down there in the little valley. And if that moment was to come, then he damned well wished it would come soon.

Steel turned to the men behind him and found at only a few paces distant the company's young, rosy-cheeked ensign, Tom Williams, now aged twenty and no longer the gauche boy he had been when he had purchased into the battalion – Sir James Farquharson's Regiment of Foot – four years ago this summer. Williams had joined the colours shortly before the great victory at Blenheim, Marlborough's first great triumph in which the regiment and in particular Steel's Grenadiers had won renown. Steel had grown to feel an almost fatherly obligation to Williams in that campaign and he felt no less close now, imparting when he could sage advice and reasoned reprimand where necessary.

'Tom, I think that we might fall the men in again now. It shouldn't be too long before we go, by the look of things. But we'd best keep them on their mettle, eh? You might inspect their weapons again. That sort of thing. I want every musket checked and re-checked. And make sure that their bayonets are all well greased. Oh, and before you do that get those three idiots back from the river. Their tackle might just prove too tempting a target for the French, and we don't want to draw enemy fire without good cause.'

Williams laughed. He loved Steel's wry wit and envied him his way with the men. It was the pinnacle to which he aspired. And what better model to have? The ability of this man to combine all the qualities of a gentleman with a genuine empathy with his troops picked him out as a natural leader. Yet at the same time it seemed that Steel always kept an implicit awareness of his own station and their place. In short, Jack Steel was everything that a soldier should be, thought Williams: cool in battle, ruthless and implacable in combat, level-headed, intuitive and pragmatic. Throw into the equation the fact that he was also enviably handsome, and at six foot tall a giant among men, and you had a worthy hero for any young subaltern. This was precisely how Williams hoped the men might see him when he too rose to the rank of captain in command of his own company – if he should manage to survive that long.

He knew that he mustn't think that way. Hadn't the sergeants told him so in his first battle? And Steel for that matter, more times than he could remember. But still he could not banish the dark thoughts from his mind. Like Steel, he knew that if there was any obvious target for the enemy it was sure to be an officer. And, like Steel, Tom Williams was tall for his time. Both men were remarkable in an age when the average height was a good ten inches less. But then these were grenadiers – a company of giants, hand-picked from the regiment and the army as much for their stature as their skill at arms. They were the storm troops of the army, the first into any fight and more than likely the last men out.

Williams turned to the company's senior sergeant, a similarly tall, bluff Geordie with an infectious grin named Jacob Slaughter, whose hard-bitten face told of countless actions and larger engagements. 'Sar'nt Slaughter. Those men there – discourage them from that, if you will.'

He had learnt his style of command direct from Steel, and the coolly laconic order still did not sit quite as easily as he would have liked on his lips. The sergeant smiled at the boy's attempt, confident in the knowledge that Williams could do no better than model himself on Captain Steel, and in turn barked a command towards the clowns on the river bank.

The three men suddenly went quiet and hurriedly buttoned their Greeches. Then, turning back towards the company, they scrambled up the muddy slope and returned to the grinning ranks. As they passed their captain, Steel nodded and ensured that they could see his gaze, half disapproving, half amused. As they hurried into rank Slaughter shouted further commands, which were echoed by the other sergeants and corporals of the company. Then, careful to be firm but not too forceful, he began to use the wooden staff of the long sergeant's half-pike to urge the files back into line and dress the ranks, ready for the long-awaited march attack.

Steel knew of course that all their muskets were clean and had been checked. In fact they had been cleaned and checked these past two hours, and at all the halts on the long march that had brought them to this place. He knew too that every man's razor-sharp socket bayonet, newly issued to replace the old plug variety, was slick to perfection with grease so that it would slide smoothly from the scabbard when the time came and slot with ease on the steel nipples at the end of their muskets before slipping just as easily between the ribs of the French when eventually they met them on the field below. But he knew too that in their present condition anything must be done to keep the men's minds off the carnage now so evidently taking place to their front.

Steel stared back into the smoke of the battle. He heard the crash of musketry again and the distant cries of anguish caught on the wind that he knew would also be only too audible to the men. Behind him, as if to affirm his fears, one of the younger recruits to his largely veteran company vomited onto the white-gaitered legs of the man to his front, who, naturally, turned and swore at the youngster and, even though he carried his musket at the high porte, still attempted to swing a punch. Sergeant Slaughter shouted to both of them and, mouthing oaths, went to help the terrified and now mortified recruit to regain his composure and wipe the dribbles of vomit from his scarlet coat. Steel turned back towards the enemy. He would give almost anything now to propel his men into a state of readiness, bursting to be at the enemy. Yet at the same time he wanted to make them feel at ease. It was a hard trick, this balancing act. But, he told himself, hadn't he done it many times before? And didn't he know most of these men like his own family? Better, now he thought of it. He turned to Williams.

'A song, I think, Tom. Let's have a song. Who's the best voice in the company, would you say? Taylor? Dan Cussiter?'

'It must be Corporal Taylor, sir, to be sure.'

'Then Matt Taylor it shall be.'

Steel scoured the ranks for the man.

'Taylor. Where are you? Come on, Matt. Give us all a tune. Sing up above the guns. And be sure to make it a good 'un. "The Rochester Recruit" or something similar.'

Corporal Matthew Taylor, a gangly, bankrupted clerk from Hounsditch and for the last six years, since the start of this war, the company's invaluable and learned apothecary and medical expert on account of his knowledge of herbals, cleared his throat and began to sing in a hearty tenor:

'Oh a bold fusilier came marching down through
    Rochester,
Bound for the wars in the Low Countries.
And he sang as he marched
Through the crowded streets of Rochester,
"Who'll be a soldier for Marlborough and me?"'

As one the company joined in, with the familiar chorus:

'Who'll be a soldier, who'll be a soldier,
Who'll be a soldier for Marlborough and me?'

Steel smiled to see how, as ever, the magic worked so quickly on the terrified men. That was the answer, for now at least: the way to kill a few more idle moments. Set them thinking about their beloved 'Corporal John' – John Churchill, Duke of Marlborough, ennobled by the Queen after Blenheim – about how he had won so many great victories for them and how today was sure to be another. Blenheim, Ramillies and . . . What, he wondered was the name of that little hamlet to their front?

'Tom. What's the name of that village?'

'Place called Eename, sir.'

No, thought Steel, that would not do. It hardly had a martial ring to it. Better of course the larger place to their left. Oudenarde. That would look better in the history books and on the broadsheets in the London coffee houses. Blenheim, Ramillies and Oudenarde. Not forgetting Ostend, the lines of Brabant . . .